THE AGE OF INNOCENCE

THE AGE OF INNOCENCE

Edith Wharton

edited by Michael Nowlin

broadview literary texts

National Library of Canada Cataloguing in Publication Data

Wharton, Edith, 1862-1937
    The age of innocence

(Broadview literary texts)
Includes bibliographical references.
ISBN 1-55111-336-8

I. Nowlin, Michael Everett, 1962-   II. Title.   III. Series.

PS3545.H16A62 2002   813'.52   C2002-900671-6

Broadview Press Ltd. is an independent, international publishing house, incorporated in 1985.

North America:
P.O. Box 1243, Peterborough, Ontario, Canada K9J 7H5
3576 California Road, Orchard Park, NY 14127
TEL: (705) 743-8990; FAX: (705) 743-8353;
E-MAIL: customerservice@broadviewpress.com

United Kingdom:
Thomas Lyster Ltd
Unit 9, Ormskirk Industrial Park
Old Boundary Way, Burscough Road
Ormskirk, Lancashire L39 2YW
TEL: (01695) 575112; FAX: (01695) 570120; E-mail: books@tlyster.co.uk

Australia:
St. Clair Press, P.O. Box 287, Rozelle, NSW 2039
TEL: (02) 818-1942; FAX: (02) 418-1923

www.broadviewpress.com

Broadview Press gratefully acknowledges the financial support of the Book Publishing Industry Development Program, Ministry of Canadian Heritage, Government of Canada.

Broadview Press is grateful to Professor Eugene Benson and Professor L. W. Conolly for advice on editorial matters for the Broadview Literary Texts series.

PRINTED IN CANADA

The interior of this book is printed on 100% recycled paper.

Contents

Acknowledgements

I am very grateful to the Social Sciences and Humanities Research Council of Canada for a Standard Research Grant that enabled me to hire a research assistant for this project, and to the University of Victoria for granting me some internal SSHRC funds for travel expenses connected to this project.

I owe many thanks to Julie Brennan, who proved herself a first-rate research assistant, and did most of the work for the notes. Her intelligence, energy, and interest in Edith Wharton have been indispensable in putting this book together. I also want to thank Diana Rutherford, who helped set the copy text and prepare the manuscript. Finally, I have been helped in small but significant ways by several scholars and librarians I have met while working on this project: I would like to thank Patricia Willis and Ruth Carruth at the Beinecke Rare Book and Manuscript Library at Yale University, M. Joan Youngken of the Newport Historical Society, Donna Campbell of Gonzaga University, and Julia Ehrhardt of the University of Oklahoma.

I would like to thank the following individuals and organizations for permission to re-print passages from copyrighted materials:

The Letters of Edith Wharton, eds. R.W.B. Lewis and Nancy Lewis. Reprinted by permission of the Estate of Edith Wharton and the Watkins/Loomis Agency. Copyright © 1988 by R.W.B. Lewis, Nancy Lewis, and William R. Tyler.

Archival material from the Edith Wharton Collection at the Beinecke Rare Book and Manuscript Library at Yale University. Reprinted by permission of the Estate of Edith Wharton and the Watkins/Loomis Agency.

Photo of Edith Wharton with the Newport Archery Club. Reproduced by permission of The Newport Historical Society (P27).

Publisher's newspaper advertisement, 1920.

Introduction

In 1921, the recently established Pulitzer Prize was initially to be awarded to Sinclair Lewis, the title of whose best-selling novel *Main Street* would become a by-word for the narrow-minded, repressive, small-town America the book ruthlessly satirized. The vote was overturned, the prize granted instead to Edith Wharton's *The Age of Innocence*, on the grounds of its being, according to one newspaper notice, "the American novel published during the year which shall best present the wholesome atmosphere of American life and the highest standard of American manners and manhood." That Wharton's novel might also be a cosmopolitan's satirical portrait of provincial America appears to have escaped the notice of those responsible for overturning the original decision.[1] The Pulitzer decision appears to have rested on a "genteel" or anti-modernist reading of the novel, one that Edith Wharton's background and class affiliation would seem to have invited. As Rutger B. Jewett, her conservative editor at Appleton, remarked to her after reading the manuscript: "Personally I am delighted with the story. It is a valuable contribution—a picture of old New York which has been thrown into the discard. I do not know of anyone else who could have created the picture. How you would detest New York life to-day! If it seemed petty and narrow before, it would now seem blatant and chaotic, without rhyme or reason."[2] However critical of the pettiness and narrowness of old New York life *The Age of Innocence* might be, readers like Jewett read it more surely as a critique of an even more senseless, socially and morally incoherent "modern" present, and in this they were abetted by Wharton's ambiguous ending to the novel.

Wharton's autobiography *A Backward Glance,* written more than a decade after *The Age of Innocence,* seems further to encourage a nostalgic, anti-modernist interpretation of her novel. "When

---

[1]   See W.J. Stuckey, *The Pulitzer Prize Novels: A Critical Backward Look* (Norman: University of Oklahoma Press, 1966), pp. 39–42.

[2]   Letter from Jewett to Edith Wharton, 20 August 1920 (Edith Wharton Collection, Yale Collection of American Literature, Beinecke Rare Book and Manuscript Library).

I was young," she writes, "it used to seem to me that the group in which I grew up was like an empty vessel into which no new wine would ever again be poured. Now I see that one of its uses lay in preserving a few drops of an old vintage too rare to be savoured by a youthful palate; and I should like to atone for my unappreciativeness by trying to revive that faint fragrance."[1] It may be that the "unappreciativeness" she felt compelled to atone for never manifested itself so brazenly as in the satirical thrust of her greatest novel. For if the modernist "age" had lost its innocence, so had Edith Wharton, who by 1919 had lived a life far more adventurous and intellectually rich than could have been expected of a woman of her class and background. If Wharton is paying homage to the New York of her girlhood in *The Age of Innocence*, it is the homage of a misfit who knew she couldn't go home again. Drawing on her extensive readings in anthropology, she likens that New York to a "tribal," pre-historic world; and she continues in this vein in *A Backward Glance*, where the value of old New York, "for the generality of readers, lies in the fact of its sudden and total extinction, and for the imaginative few in the recognition of the moral treasures that went with it."[2] The language of anthropology pervades *The Age of Innocence*: its most "advanced" characters are reading about primitive peoples or are becoming archaeologists, and a museum full of now meaningless ancient "objects" figures prominently in a crucial scene.

But *The Age of Innocence* is most obviously an historical novel, and remarkably acute and specific about the nature of historical change, particularly the processes by which profoundly disruptive forces—technological, economic, demographic, or moral—become absorbed into the fabric of daily life and, as it were, normalized. Written in 1919, but set in the mid-1870s and, in its epilogue, at the turn of the century, Wharton's novel both exaggerates the gulf separating past and present, and more subtly represents the sources of continuity between them, with an eye to an uncertain but necessary future. It looks backward to look forward, in effect, doing the same cultural work as such nine-

---

[1] Edith Wharton, *A Backward Glance* (New York: D. Appleton & Co., 1934), p. 5.
[2] *Ibid.*, p. 7.

teenth-century historical novels as Nathaniel Hawthorne's *The Scarlet Letter* and George Eliot's *Middlemarch*, even to the point of having the state of a nation as its subtextual preoccupation. Wharton's title, "The Age of Innocence," which she eventually chose over "Old New York," invokes a comparison that weighs favorably on the side of "experience," the vantage point of modernity, even as it invokes a process that is as much evolutionary as catastrophic. Her title alludes to Sir Joshua Reynolds's portrait of a young girl,[1] and if we are willing to equate this figure with the "lost" girlhood of Edith Wharton, we must recognize that a girlhood world that can be so minutely reconstructed cannot really be said to be lost (or "extinct") at all; rather, it is a safe but limited state one *grows out of* and yet *grows from*, just as great imperial nations grow out of small, homogeneous "tribes," and civilizations evolve from states of savagery.

Wharton would make such equations in a collection of essays called *French Ways and Their Meaning*, published in 1919 and explicitly addressed to Americans. From her vantage point in France, she celebrated the fact that Americans as a people were "growing up," and preparing to play an important role in world affairs, despite tendencies suggesting impending cultural chaos. The most significant of these tendencies seemed to be the growing heterogeneity of American life due to decades of massive immigration from Southern and Eastern Europe, and increasing uncertainty about the proper relations between the sexes wrought by a liberalization of sexual mores and the imminent success of the suffragette movement. Wharton's response to these tendencies was complex, as became her ambiguous situation: she was a cultural conservative proud of her "Anglo-Saxon" and Dutch pedigree and seemingly indifferent to the matter of women's suffrage; she was also an independent woman who had adopted France as her "home." *The Age of Innocence* seems to mock old New York's obsessive fear of "foreigners," to represent the collapse of tribalism and the triumph of cosmopolitanism as inevitable, and to undermine Newland Archer's despairing sense that "the stupid law of change" tends only deathward. But it also makes the memory of cultural cohesion an

---

[1] See Chapter V, p. 82, note 2.

essential ingredient of meaningful progress. It makes the memory of "the tribe" a governing fiction that, like the social and intellectual elite it sustains, supplies a standard or an authoritative point of reference against which the vicissitudes of American history can be measured and found either decadent or promising.

Edith Wharton: Life, Works and Critical Reputation

As for so many others who lived through it, the apocalyptic moment in Wharton's life and in the "civilization" she identified with was World War I, and if *A Backward Glance* clarifies anything it is the extent to which *The Age of Innocence* is, as much as if not more so than F. Scott Fitzgerald's *The Great Gatsby* or Ernest Hemingway's *The Sun Also Rises*, a post-war novel. "Not until the successive upheavals which culminated in the catastrophe of 1914 had 'cut all likeness from the name' of my old New York, did I begin to see its pathetic picturesqueness."[1] For Wharton, those "successive upheavals" were largely technological, demographic, and economic—that is, public, historical changes. But Wharton also went through successive upheavals in her private life, the most striking of which she chose—as became her old New York sense of propriety—to keep private.

Wharton was born Edith Newbold Jones, on January 24, 1862, on East 21st street in New York City. She was the youngest and last child of George Frederic Jones and Lucretia Rhinelander, both from established and socially prominent families. Her father had made a small fortune in New York real estate investments. She had two older brothers, Frederic, almost sixteen years her senior, and Henry, almost thirteen. She speaks most fondly in memoirs of her father, whom she associated with stifled poetic aspirations, and with a wonderful library, every volume of which she claimed to have explored. She speaks far more ambivalently of her mother, a reserved woman and a model of the society hostess that Edith would have assumed herself destined to become. She would in later years become estranged from her family, particularly her two brothers, but would remain on lifelong terms

---

[1]   *Ibid.*, p. 6.

of closest friendship with her sister-in-law "Minnie" Cadwallader Jones and her daughter Beatrix Jones, even after Frederic and Minnie had divorced.

A post-Civil War economic depression forced the family abroad, and between the formative years of 1866 and 1872, Edith would live in Rome, Paris and Florence, and travel through Spain and Germany as well. At a very young age she became familiar with great European art and architecture and with several modern languages. (She would become fluent in French, Italian and German.) The Jones family returned to the United States in 1872, and like the denizens of old New York in her novel, would divide their year between a brownstone house on West 23rd street in New York, and a summer home called Pencraig in Newport, Rhode Island. Edith herself would grow up dividing her time between numerous social obligations and the private world of what she would later describe as "omnivorous" reading. In her teens, she read widely in poetry (from Homer and Dante through to the English Romantic poets), in the great Victorian essayists, in classics, and in French and English art and literary criticism. She read what "classic" novels she could get her hands on, but by her own account her mother eventually forbade her to read contemporary novels. Her mother, it appears, typified the old New York attitude towards "people who wrote," an attitude she mocks at various points in *The Age of Innocence*.[1]

Nonetheless, and despite her gender, Edith Jones set out to defy this attitude, it seems, from an early age. At fifteen she produced in secret a novella called *Fast and Loose* to which she even appended mock reviews. This juvenalia testifies to a nascent sense of vocation that would emerge forcefully two decades later, and an alertness to the institutions of the literary marketplace that would never wane. With the uncharacteristic aid of her mother, she had a volume of poems called *Verses* privately printed in 1878. Genteel in character, these attracted the notice of Henry Wadsworth Longfellow and William Dean Howells, who published one of her poems in *The Atlantic Monthly*. In 1880, she published two more poems in the New York *World*.

---

[1]   See *ibid.*, p. 68.

Coincidentally, Edith Jones made her social debut in the same year that she made her debut in the arena of commercial literature. From the standpoint of old New York, of course, the former event was of far more consequence. She was initially courted by Harry Stevens, who went so far as to join Edith and her family in southern France in the late summer of 1881. She became engaged to him after her father died in 1882 (and after she had inherited $20,000 in a trust fund).[1] The engagement was shortlived: announced in August, it was broken off in October, probably due to Mrs. Stevens's sense that Edith made a less than ideal match for her son. A year later, Edith met Edward Robbins ("Teddy") Wharton; she would marry him in April 1885, at the age of twenty-three, at Trinity Chapel in New York City. Despite Teddy's upper-class Boston background, Harvard degree, and generally amiable temper, they had fundamentally different interests that would later take their toll on their marriage. Teddy shared none of Edith's passion for books and ideas and intellectual company, preferring a sportsman's life. Though they would travel adventurously together (including a cruise of the Aegean Islands in 1888), they would come to live relatively separate lives as Edith became a professional writer and spent more of her time in Europe. The couple remained childless, which has fostered considerable speculation about the extent to which the Wharton marriage was a celibate one.

Though Wharton was an adept hostess and exceptionally knowledgeable about such domestic arts as interior decorating and gardening, she also worked hard to develop her interest in what she thought of as the masculine terrain of serious ideas, and in this she was abetted by a number of lifelong, Platonic friendships with older men, who fostered her creativity and helped fill an obvious void in her marriage. Among these was the New York art collector Egerton Winthrop, whom she credits in *A Backward Glance* with "fill[ing] some of the worst gaps in my education." Winthrop introduced her to the great French novelists, historians, and critics, and more significantly, to her mind, "to the wonder-world of nineteenth century science."[2]

---

[1] Purchasing power today of approximately $345,000.

[2] *Ibid.*, p. 94.

More precisely, he introduced her to Darwinism and the evolutionary paradigm, as this impacted not only the biological sciences but the nascent human sciences of sociology and anthropology as well. By Wharton's own account in a letter of 1908, Charles Darwin and Herbert Spencer were among "the formative influences of [her] youth."[1]

Winthrop was but one of several distinguished male friends. The most emotionally significant of these was probably Walter Van Rensselaer Berry, whom she met in the summer of 1883 while at Bar Harbor, Maine. Berry became a prominent Washington lawyer interested in international affairs, and would eventually serve as a judge on the International Tribunal in Cairo and become President of the American Chamber of Commerce in Paris. On Wharton's own testimony, he was the most constructive critic of her writing—stern and fastidious, but with her artistic interests ever in mind. Starting in 1893, she also became friends with the French novelist and man of letters Paul Bourget, a member of the French Academy who would later facilitate her access into prominent Parisian intellectual and social circles. Her lifelong love for and extensive knowledge of Italian Renaissance art helped solidify her friendship from 1909 onwards with one of the foremost authorities in the field, Bernard Berenson, whose home outside Florence, Villa I Tatti, would be the site of many visits. She was also a supporter, friend, and distant relation of that American icon, the roughrider, trust-buster and imperial adventurer, Theodore Roosevelt. Though theirs was not as intimate a friendship as those described above, she occasionally met with and corresponded with him during and after his presidency. They shared common roots in old New York, and they both transformed themselves and adapted to a changing world in which America was destined to play a more powerful and prominent role on the geo-political stage than had once been imaginable. As governor of New York, Roosevelt makes a cameo appearance in the epilogue to *The Age of*

---

[1] *The Letters of Edith Wharton*, ed. R. W.B. Lewis and Nancy Lewis (New York: Macmillan, 1988), p. 136. On *Herbert Spencer* (1820–1903), the English philosopher and sociologist identified with the doctrines of "social Darwinism," see Chapter XV, p. 166, note 1.

Innocence, in a scene which testifies to his importance in facilitating the transition from an older America to a newer one. Though Wharton wrote a poem for *The Saturday Evening Post* on the occasion of his death in January 1919, *The Age of Innocence* may contain a more subtle elegy for the man she considered a "great leader," and of whom she wrote, "No one will ever know what his example & his influence were to me."[1]

Wharton's connections to powerful, intellectual men should not obscure the importance of the female friends she cultivated and maintained throughout her life: Minnie Jones, Sara Norton (daughter of Charles Eliot Norton[2]), Margaret "Daisy" Chanler, and her closest ally during the war years, Elisina Tyler. Wharton's correspondence implies a great respect for the intelligence and experience of all these women. And early in her career Wharton, who paid tribute to such exemplary women novelists as George Eliot and George Sand, found a contemporary model in Vernon Lee, the pen-name of Violet Paget, an English writer on Italian subjects settled outside of Florence. Still, as the identification with women novelists writing under male pseudonyms partly suggests, Wharton assumed the world of great art, serious ideas, and social and political power to be a predominantly masculine one, and enjoyed being privy to it and holding her own intellectually.

The most important friendship for Wharton's sense of herself as a first-rate writer was with the novelist Henry James, who also facilitated her relationship with another man who undoubtedly influenced her sense of herself as a sexual being: William Morton Fullerton. Her friendships blossomed with both men after she had become a commercially successful and critically acclaimed novelist, committed firmly to an artistic career.

Wharton was thirty-five years old when she published her first book for a commercial publisher, *The Decoration of Houses*, a didactic essay on interior decorating which she co-authored with her architect Ogden Codman. The project suggests modest

---

[1]   *Ibid.*, p. 422.
[2]   *Charles Eliot Norton* (1827–1908), American author, co-editor and founder of *The Nation*, and Harvard Professor of Fine Arts from 1875–98.

literary aspirations, appropriate for a woman of the leisure class who presided over a Park Avenue house in New York City and her Newport estate, Land's End (large by most people's standards, though dwarfed by the mansions of the Gilded Age's nouveaux riches), and spent a good part of each year of her early married life travelling in Europe. But by the late 1890s, Wharton was regularly publishing stories in the nation's most prominent periodicals; by 1901, she had published two volumes of stories and a novella. She published her first novel at age forty, an epic historical novel set in eighteenth-century Italy called *The Valley of Decision*. This novel, which owes something to Wharton's friendship with Vernon Lee and Wharton's lifelong interest in Italian history and culture, has not stood the test of time well, though it anticipates her more subtle engagement with historical transition in *The Age of Innocence*. It is most readily remembered for having brought her novelistic ambitions to the attention of James, whose equivocal, verbose response after reading it seems to have had an impact on her:

> ... my desire earnestly, tenderly, intelligently [is] to admonish you, while you are young, free, expert, exposed (to illumination)—by which I mean while you're in full command of the situation—admonish you, I say, in favour of the *American Subject*. There it is round you. Don't pass it by—the immediate, the real, the ours, the yours, the novelist's that it waits for. Take hold of it and keep hold, and let it pull you where it will.... All the same *Do New York!* The first-hand account is precious.[1]

For her next novel, Wharton did indeed *do* New York, producing in 1905 the phenomenally successful *The House of Mirth*, a satirical study of the leisure class focused on the tragic heroine, Lily Bart, a penniless socialite who struggles to keep a place among the idle rich without marrying for it. After *The House of Mirth*, Wharton was a household name among readers, and until

---

[1] Henry James, *Letters*, Vol. IV, ed. Leon Edel (Cambridge, Mass.: Harvard University Press, 1984), pp. 235–36.

her death thirty-two years later, she would publish, on average, over a book a year.

The process by which Wharton became an ex-patriate is somewhat more complicated. In 1901, she bought and restored a mansion on a vast property in Lenox, Massachusetts, which she would name The Mount. The decision would seem to have signalled her desire to reside permanently in the United States. But annual sojourns in Europe as well as a deteriorating marriage helped precipitate her eventual decision to stay in Europe. By 1908 she was regularly dividing her year between the Mount and Paris, as well as enjoying visits to England where she was entertained by Henry James and the circle of friends that included Howard Sturgis, Gaillard Lapsley and Percy Lubbock. She spent much of her time apart from Teddy, though he did on more than one occasion accompany her and James on long automobile excursions.

In 1908, she met Morton Fullerton, an American who had long been Paris correspondent for the London *Times*. Greatly admired by James, Fullerton seems by most accounts—and as his various erotic entanglements, both heterosexual and homosexual, suggest—to have been preternaturally charming, though even to an enchanted Wharton he seemed a brilliant man unable to realize his potential. Wharton makes no mention of Fullerton in any of her published and unpublished memoirs, but her letters to him (letters she had repeatedly asked him to return) came to light years after her death. They attest to a passionate sexual affair that occurred when opportunity allowed over the next few years, and they show Wharton at once infatuated, vulnerable, and ultimately humiliated (though like others who fell prey to Fullerton's charms, she remained on good terms with him after the affair). In the meantime her relationship with Teddy, who seems to have suffered from depression and paranoia, became increasingly unbearable. In 1909, she discovered that he had been embezzling money from her trust fund to keep a mistress. There is no evidence that Teddy ever found out about Fullerton, and ultimately Wharton was able to sue successfully for divorce, after selling The Mount in 1912.

It may be that too much has been made in recent years of the Fullerton affair. But with the exception of her wonderful satire

The Custom of the Country (1913), Wharton's best work of the teens—*Ethan Frome* (1911), *The Reef* (1912), "The Long Run" (1912), *Summer* (1917) and finally *The Age of Innocence*—is preoccupied with stifling marriages and illicit sexuality, and with the irrational power and anti-social nature of erotic desire. These works are pervaded by the experience of intense sexual pleasure, an experience that Wharton may not have enjoyed before Fullerton. In one of her outlines for *The Age of Innocence*, she has her protaganist running off with his mistress and consummating their love, parenthetically emphasizing the "contrast between bridal night with May & *this* one."[1] In the finished version Newland Archer can only yearn enviously after the "exquisite pleasures" he imagines Ellen Olenska to have paid for through acculturation in European decadence. However variously Wharton might be registering her private mid-life crisis in this period of her greatest fiction, the works all seem decidedly pessimistic about heterosexual relations and romantic love.

After her divorce from Teddy was granted by the French courts in 1913, Wharton considered buying property in England. She was in England when the war broke out in August 1914, and she returned to Paris to embark on one of the most heroic enterprises of her career. She began establishing charities with the help of her good friend Elisina Tyler: first, a workroom for seamstresses and unemployed women, then, as refugees came pouring into France, the American Hostels for Refugees and later the Children of Flanders Rescue Committee. She worked indefatigably to raise money, putting together *The Book of the Homeless* in 1916, a remarkable anthology of original contributions by some of Europe and America's leading writers, statesmen, and artists. She also became a staunch propagandist for the Allied cause, touring the devastated French countryside and the trenches and writing articles for popular American periodicals that she later collected into *Fighting France: From Dunkerque to Belfort* (1915) and *French Ways and Their Meaning* (1919). Wharton's war work earned her the admiration of the French government: in 1916 she was made a Chevalier of the Legion of Honor.

---

[1]   See Appendix A2.

As it did for a younger generation inspired by Hemingway, the war marked for Wharton the irrevocable end of an older nineteenth-century order. It was accompanied by more immediate, personal losses as well, the death of Henry James in 1916 being perhaps the saddest for her. While writing fiction about the war, she also produced her finest work about the old order in a manner clearly evoking the example of James, the great American novelist fondly known as "the Master." She did so after establishing permanent residency in France by buying two homes, Pavillon Colombe, outside Paris, where she would reside in summers, and Ste. Claire du Vieux Château in Hyères, where she would spend her winters for the last seventeen years of her life.

Though it is tempting to see *The Age of Innocence* as the culmination of her career, Wharton in fact remained prolific, publishing seven more novels (including an ambitious two-part portrait of the artist, *Hudson River Bracketed* [1929] and *The Gods Arrive* [1932]), the four novellas collected as *Old New York* (1924), a memoir, a critical study of the art of fiction, and numerous stories and essays. Wharton's critical reputation waned, however, especially among young readers and writers drawn to the modernist experimentation of James Joyce and T.S. Eliot, to the Bloomsbury writers, or to the new American luminaries Fitzgerald and Hemingway. Wharton certainly did not help her case much by denouncing and trivializing the narrative experimentation of Joyce and Virginia Woolf, and cultivating a *grande dame* demeanor that her autobiography *A Backward Glance,* and later Percy Lubbock's *Portrait of Edith Wharton* (1947), helped solidify. Her novels also struck many as reactionary, and increasingly out of touch with the post-war American scene she pretended to write about with authority. But despite some of the obvious shortcomings of her later fiction, Wharton remained vitally interested in contemporary political, cultural and literary developments, and from today's perspective seems much more attuned to the general movement known as modernism than many younger writers and critics once suspected. Familiar with and loving the works of Walt Whitman, Friedrich Nietzsche, and Igor Stravinsky before the war, she admired the work of and became friends during and after the war with André Gide, Jean Cocteau, Sinclair Lewis, Aldous

Huxley, and Bronislaw Malinowski.[1] (She even famously praised *The Great Gatsby* in a personal note to the author, who unfortunately was drunk and told her an off-color joke during his one and only visit.)

In her lifetime, Wharton published over forty books—novels, short story collections, poetry, travel writing, criticism, journalism—while conducting a vibrant social life. She left at least four indisputable American classics—*The House of Mirth*, *Ethan Frome*, *The Custom of the Country*, and *The Age of Innocence*—and has enjoyed a place in the American Academy of Arts and Letters since 1930. She died in 1937, and was buried in Versailles near her beloved friend Walter Berry.

Wharton's major works have always been in print, and her writing career received important critical and scholarly attention in the decades following her death. Blake Nevius's *Edith Wharton: A Study of Her Fiction* (1953), Louis Auchincloss's *Edith Wharton* (1961) and Millicent Bell's *Edith Wharton and Henry James: The Story of Their Friendship* (1965) kept her works canonical, so to speak, though they stood on the periphery of the narrow masculinist, modernist canon that informed the study of literature during the 1950s and 1960s. Wharton's precarious status as a female (and thus implicitly second-rate) Henry James was fundamentally re-assessed when her private papers became available for study; a "Wharton revival" can be traced back to the publication of R.W.B. Lewis's 1975 biography, *Edith Wharton*, and Cynthia Griffin Wolff's psychobiographical study of the fiction, *A Feast of Words* (1977). The Fullerton letters came to light a few years later and, coupled with an earlier sexually explicit document unearthed by Lewis and Wolff, helped generate highly speculative interest in a much darker

---

[1] *André Gide* (1869–1951), French novelist and essayist, author of *L'Immoraliste* (1902); *Jean Cocteau* (1889–1963), avant-gardist French novelist, poet, and film-maker, author of *Les Enfants Terribles* (1929) and director of the film *Le Sang D'Un Poet* (1930); *Sinclair Lewis* (1885–1951), American novelist best known for *Main Street* (1920) and *Babbitt* (1922), the latter of which was dedicated to Wharton; *Aldous Huxley* (1894–1963), British novelist, who credited Wharton's *Twilight Sleep* (1927) as an important influence on his most famous work, *Brave New World* (1932); *Bronislaw Malinowski* (1884–1942), Polish-born anthropologist who worked in England and the United States and did innovative field work among tribes in Melanesia; author of *Argonauts of the Western Pacific* (1922) and *The Sexual Life of Savages in North-Western Melanesia* (1929).

Wharton. But the greatest impetus for the numerous studies of Wharton's works generated over the past two and a half decades has come from feminist criticism, with its agenda of reclaiming a specifically female canon and elucidating overt or covert feminist themes in writing by women. Elizabeth Ammons's *Edith Wharton's Argument with America* (1980) remains crucial in this regard. So does the essay on Wharton by Sandra Gilbert and Susan Gubar in *Sexchanges* (1989), volume two of their three-volume study, *No Man's Land: The Place of the Woman Writer in the Twentieth-Century*, and so does Shari Benstock's more recent biography *No Gifts from Chance* (1994). Some critics, such as James Tuttleton, have denounced what he takes to be a "feminist takeover" of Wharton and distortion of her work.[1] From a less conservative angle, the feminist case for Wharton is being refined and shaken somewhat by questions about the nationalist, imperialist, racist, and most understandably, class implications of her work (with Ammons herself taking a far more critical look at Wharton). More attention has recently been paid to Wharton's ghost stories, her war writing, and her later novels, as seems inevitable given the mountains of commentary that Wharton's major novels—and especially *The House of Mirth*—have generated over the past decades. Today, with her major novels routinely taught in literature courses, her minor works being re-issued for the first time in decades, and movie and television adaptations becoming commonplace, Edith Wharton's reputation as one of the giants of American literature seems as secure as it will ever be.

The Age of Innocence: Production and Critical Reception

When Wharton began writing the novel she initially called "Old New York," she was in the midst of several other projects, none of which have fared remotely as well, either commercially or critically, as *The Age of Innocence*. Despite the offense she took at having her "work treated as if it were prose by the yard,"[2] commercial consid-

---

[1] See James W. Tuttleton, "The Feminist Takeover of Edith Wharton," *New Criterion* 7 (March 1989), pp. 6–14.

[2] See Appendix B2.

erations always played a part in Wharton's artistic deliberations, and particularly in 1919 when she was facing what for her was financial strain. Her income was adversely effected by the income tax and a depressed real-estate market in the United States, and she was renovating and refurbishing her recently acquired French homes, supporting her sister-in-law Minnie Jones, and had just established trust funds for three of the Belgian refugee children connected to her Children of Flanders charity. She thus accepted an offer of $18,000 from the *Pictorial Review* for the serial rights to her next novel. She had two novels in progress that she might submit, but "The Glimpses of the Moon" was at a standstill and *A Son at the Front*, her second attempt at a war novel, was rejected as commercially unviable by both Arthur Vance, editor of the *Pictorial Review*, and by Appleton, who promised her a $15,000 advance for her next novel. After drafting at least three outlines,[1] she began *The Age of Innocence* late in the summer of 1919 and submitted the first fifteen chapters to Rutger B. Jewett of Appleton early in November. Jewett was delighted with what he received, regarding it precisely as "a novel of 'The House of Mirth' type" that presumably the public expected from Edith Wharton. She finished the novel in March of 1920, making it among the most rapidly composed of her major works, a feat seemingly belied by its formal intricacy and carefully researched detail. She knew, as she wrote Jewett in January 1920, that she had done "a super-human piece of work in writing, within a year, the best part of two long novels, entirely different in subject and treatment, simply to suit the convenience of the Editor of the Pictorial ..."[2] *The Age of Innocence* was serialized in four parts in the *Pictorial Review* from July through September, and was published by Appleton in October. While *A Son at the Front* would not be published until 1923 and would meet with predominantly negative reviews, Wharton's "super-human piece of work" clearly paid off in the case of *The Age of Innocence*. The novel sold over 100,000 copies in North America and Great Britain, and earned her over $50,000 within two years.[3]

---

[1] See Appendix A.
[2] See Appendix B2.
[3] Purchasing power today of approximately $440,000.

The novel was also blessed with good reviews from diverse quarters. William Lyon Phelps in *The New York Times Book Review* went so far as to exclaim that "Edith Wharton is a writer who brings glory on the name of America, and this is her best book."[1] His favorable opinion, if not his hyperbole, was generally echoed by the other leading newspapers both in the United States and in England. Wharton's novel was acclaimed, notably, by the young Edmund Wilson, whose review amounts to a corrective (and provocative) assessment, for the benefit of the modish readers of *Vanity Fair*, of the woman he thought "the only one of our novelists whose work, for intensity and finish, stands comparison with the best fiction of England and France."[2] And Gilbert Seldes, who would pioneer the study of American popular culture and play an instrumental role in publishing that modernist landmark, *The Waste Land*, praised Wharton in *The Dial* for keeping "the novel as written by Henry James" fresh and valid. Seldes was hardly alone in noting the Jamesian qualities of *The Age of Innocence*. Perhaps the most noteworthy negative assessment of the novel came from the progressivist critic Vernon Parrington, who objected to the woman he called "our literary aristocrat" for much the same reasons he objected to James in his monumental and influential *Main Currents in American Thought* (1927–1930): that is, the precious art of Wharton dealt with too rarified a segment of the American scene and thus had little to offer her democratic compatriots in the way of a "realistic" reflection of their own world. "There is more hope for our literature in the honest crudities of the younger naturalists," he wrote, "than in her classic irony; they at least are trying to understand America as it is."[3] Contemporary reviewers did not generally entertain this simplistic distinction between a supposedly democratic realism and an aristocratic formalism (a distinction famously attacked years later by Lionel Trilling in *The Liberal Imagination*). Most thought the subject matter of *The Age of Innocence* fundamentally "American" and its satire contemporary in its relevance.

---

[1] See Appendix C6.
[2] See Appendix C1.
[3] See Appendix C2.

Wharton was irritated by what struck her as undue emphasis on the text's anachronisms. Here is a particularly high-toned example of such criticism from the anonymous reviewer for the *Literary Digest*:

> The book is full of anachronisms which are so sure to be noticed by old New-Yorkers that we shall only mention one or two. It is claimed that there was no club box in the old Academy of Music; it was considered a distinct innovation when it was introduced, much later, in the new opera-house. Newland and the Countess could not have met at the Metropolitan Museum in the Park, for it was not until the '80's that it was moved from Fourteenth Street. De Maupassant was unknown in the early '70's and Rossetti's "House of Life" was not published until 1881. Joachim never visited America as a violinist.[1]

Though Wharton had a formidable memory and was also relying on her sister-in-law Minnie Jones's research at Yale and careful reading of Ward McAllister's study of the New York "Four Hundred," *Society as I Have Found It*, errors were made that first troubled Wharton, but which she came to deem irrelevant to her artistic aim. The most glaring mistake was the use at Newland and May's wedding of the opening to the funeral service from *The Book of Common Prayer*, a mistake which even Jewett saw in the light of what we would today call a Freudian slip. This was corrected in subsequent imprints, as well as the reference to Guy de Maupassant pointed out by Phelps in his *New York Times* review (it was changed to Alphonse Daudet). Frustration with nitpicking drove Wharton to propose to Jewett that she append a preface to subsequent editions defending her sense that what historical novels do is "evoke the intellectual, moral, and artistic atmosphere not of one year but of ten years.... Any narrower field of evocation must necessarily reduce the novel to a piece of archeological pedantry instead of a living image of the times."[2]

---

[1] "Mrs. Wharton's Novel of Old New York," *Literary Digest* 68 (5 February 1921), p. 52.
[2] See Appendix B9.

Even before the revival of interest in Edith Wharton began in the 1970s, *The Age of Innocence* was destined to endure as an American classic. The novel has remained in print throughout the century. It was successfully produced as a play in 1928, and has been filmed three times: in 1923, in 1934, and most memorably in Martin Scorsese's opulent treatment of 1993, starring Daniel Day-Lewis and Michelle Pfeiffer. Though the novel would continue to be underrated by makers of a modernist canon after World War II who put Ernest Hemingway, F. Scott Fitzgerald, and William Faulkner at the apex of American fiction, Fitzgerald biographer Arthur Mizener included *The Age of Innocence* as the only novel penned by a woman in his 1967 book, *Twelve Great American Novels*. R. W. B. Lewis and Cynthia Griffin Wolff offered prominent, nuanced, and relatively conservative readings of the novel in their landmark works of the 1970s; both tended to read the novel biographically, as Wharton projecting herself onto the figures of Newland and Ellen. Although it has generally been more partial to *The House of Mirth*, feminist criticism has still managed to find much of interest in *The Age of Innocence*, especially in its images of female entrapment and its pervasive irony, which invite subversive readings of its polished, novel-of-manners surface. Elizabeth Ammons, for example, insisted in 1980 that the novel be read as a feminist critique of the "child-woman." Recent criticism has concerned itself more with Wharton's interest in ethnography, in American destiny, in matters of race, and most generally in her representation of how social subjects are constituted and how they perform their identities.

Reading *The Age of Innocence*

Though Wharton was generally impatient with criticism comparing her work to that of James, a comparison seems entirely justified in the case of *The Age of Innocence*. Some readers have gone so far as to see in the work an homage to James, the close friend who had passed away during the war years, and whose letters Wharton had so recently been instrumental in publishing. Newland Archer's name recalls both Christopher Newman of *The American* and Isabel Archer of *The Portrait of a Lady*, and at one point in the novel

Newland's friend Ned Winsett describes him as an apt subject for a painting entitled "The Portrait of a Gentleman." The novel freshly deploys James's international theme of "innocent" Americans colliding with more sophisticated European mores. And it seems architecturally arranged, with its exquisite symmetry, its scenic progression, and its selection of dramatic details for their meaningful relation to the work of art as a whole. But where the comparison most obviously applies is in Wharton's virtually perfect handling of James's principle that the action should be filtered through the consciousness of a central character. Reflecting upon problems of technique in his preface to the New York edition of *The Portrait of a Lady*, James discovered that placing "the centre of the subject in the young woman's own consciousness" would give him "as interesting and as beautiful a difficulty as [he] could wish. Stick to *that*—for the centre," he added emphatically; "put the heaviest weight into *that* scale, which will be so largely the scale of her relation to herself."[1] Encompassing Newland Archer's sensitive but limited viewpoint is that of the very witty, omniscient narrator who not only knows Newland better than he knows himself, but also knows that Newland's little world is doomed to pass away. For our narrator enjoys a proleptic perspective, that is, the perspective of one writing in 1919 and informed by the experience of the future.

Wharton's remarkable control of what is sometimes called the limited omniscient point-of-view is most in evidence in the fact that nothing is revealed of the inner lives of either Ellen Olenska or May Welland, the two women Newland is profoundly affected by throughout the novel. We are positioned with Newland to make inferences about the nature and meaning of those lives from what Ellen and May say and do; but in a world where women are well versed in what Newland recognizes as "the arts of the enslaved," what women say or do reveals nothing certain about who they might "really" be. Ellen remains an enigmatic figure for Newland throughout the novel. Enchanted by her from the outset, he constantly endeavors to interpret her actions and words in a favorable light, but is just as constantly afraid that he is being

---

[1]   Henry James, *The Portrait of a Lady*, vol. 1 (New York: Scribners, 1908), p. xv.

taken in. Of May's character he remains far more certain, and at one point in a fit of despair concludes that "never, in all the years to come, would she surprise him by an unexpected mood, by a new idea, a weakness, a cruelty or an emotion." As events transpire, he could not be more wrong. Wharton is not only demonstrating her mastery of Jamesian technique in this novel, but using it to render the dilemma of a specifically male point-of-view, the dilemma of a man whose very patriarchal privileges and the egotism founded upon them make it impossible for him to know the women he is supposed to be in love with.

Wharton brilliantly establishes the central conflict and the novel's key themes in the opening scene at the opera. On the surface, she prepares us for what can certainly be read as a very fine love story, the story of a man torn between two women, one of whom embodies duty and the other desire. The opera the New Yorkers are attending is Charles Gounod's *Faust* (1859), and Newland, arriving fashionably late, enters during the scene in which the innocent Marguerite wonders to herself whether the man she has just become smitten by "loves her" or "loves her not" (*"M'ama ... non m'ama"*). Wharton alludes to the threshold dividing "innocence" and faith from "experience" and disillusionment: those familiar with the opera know that by the next act Marguerite finds herself seduced and, as far as she knows, abandoned by Faust, acting with the aid of Mephistopheles. Looking not at the opera but across the theater at his future fiancée, Newland naively identifies the virginal May with Marguerite, anticipating the day when he shall read Goethe's *Faust*[1] with her on their honeymoon (thus metonymically associating literary education with sexual initiation). The limits of his own worldliness, however, will be exposed through the relationship that will develop between him and May's cousin, the Countess Ellen Olenska, whose appearance at the opera shocks old New York sensibilities. If May harbors an "abysmal purity," Ellen harbors something quite different. Having returned home to seek refuge—and as it turns out, a divorce—from her vicious European husband, provocatively dressed and with a "Josephine look" that associates her with revolutionary France, Ellen embodies an "expe-

---

[1]   *Faust*: See Chapter I, p. 60, note 2.

rience" that Newland finds from the outset sexually and romantically alluring. As though to disavow this, he pushes May to announce their engagement that evening and assumes the chivalric role of protecting her cousin from malicious gossip. And as the novel progresses, Wharton will continue to render his growing obsession with Ellen (and its sexual dimension) through his overt attempts to deny it—such as hastening his marriage to May—and his tendency to idealize their relationship through the outmoded paradigm of courtly love.

But the opening scene also suggests that *The Age of Innocence* will be more than a story of passion in conflict with duty; rather, it will be a love story whose implications extend to fundamental questions about the meaning of human "culture," about the effects of modernity on individual desire, and about the effects of a double standard on male and female sexuality.

The novel opens with a ritual, the first of several to be depicted and one that will be repeated. As ritual, the annual production of *Faust* and the intricate social details attendant upon it provide the basis for Wharton's sustained depiction of old New York society as akin to a primitive society. The repetitive nature of rituals evokes a cyclical conception of time meant to counter the relentlessness of modern linear time that haunts this novel from the outset. Gounod's *Faust* is also about a bargain to regain youth, and this resonates in the New Yorkers' fear of change, which is associated with contamination from outside forces leading to tribal decay and even death. Wharton compresses such themes in her description of the old Academy of Music in the second paragraph:

> Though there was already talk of the erection, in remote metropolitan distances "above the Forties," of a new Opera House which should compete in costliness and splendour with those of the great European capitals, the world of fashion was still content to reassemble every winter in the shabby red and gold boxes of the sociable old Academy. Conservatives cherished it for being small and inconvenient, and thus keeping out the "new people" whom New York was beginning to dread and yet be drawn to; and the

sentimental clung to it for its historic associations, and the musical for its excellent acoustics, always so problematic a quality in halls built for the hearing of music.

Knowing proleptically that the new Opera House will indeed be built, the narrator presents change in the form of expansion and greater opulence as virtually inevitable. Furthermore, as if to underline the fact that her New Yorkers are paradoxically capable of surviving only by embracing change, which entails "new people" who threaten their identity as a coherent, exclusive "tribe," she describes them as always already in the process of doing so, however strenuously they may deny this. A careful reading of the novel will reveal the adaption to change and the absorption of strangers and differences to have always been in operation.

For example, though Wharton's New Yorkers live like an aristocratic clan, their wealth is as commercial in origin as the new money of the mysterious Julius Beaufort who has married his way in, or the new money of Mrs. Lemuel Struthers, the tawdry sources of which are conveniently forgotten when the entertainment she has to offer becomes indispensable. Old Mrs. Manson Mingott, whose "immense accretion of flesh" seems to embody the monumental force of tradition, once suffered a more precarious status, but has somehow survived the disgrace of her father to become the clan matriarch and Ellen's chief defender. Shrewdly anticipating the northward development of Manhattan, she has moved up near Central Park and boldly declaims that "We need new money and new blood." (And yet for all Mrs. Mingott's playful irreverence, she mercilessly upholds the letter of clan law when Regina Beaufort seeks forgiveness after her husband's transgression—a transgression that uncannily repeats that of Mrs. Mingott's father Bob Spicer.) Even Newland's cloistered mother, Mrs. Archer, must acknowledge what is irresistible by annually (and ritualistically) "enumerat[ing] the minute signs of disintegration" spelled by changes. She is bolstered in this by the Reverend Ashmore's annual Thanksgiving Jeremiad against a chosen people whose Biblical prototype answers, "It is hopeless, for I have loved strangers and after them I will go." For Mrs. Archer, listening to the Reverend fulminate against dangerous social trends, "it was terrifying and yet fascinating to feel herself part of a community that was trending."

Despite Wharton's ironic depiction of historical change as a disavowed but integral fact of social life, her narrator also knows from the standpoint of 1919 that the changes which old New Yorkers were facing were occurring at an unprecedented pace and on an unprecedented scale from what they had previously accustomed themselves to. The technological changes on the horizon alone promise to transform daily interaction so radically as to warrant the depiction of Wharton's New Yorkers as a prehistoric tribe. Consider the scene in which Julius Beaufort laments having had to make the trip to Skuytercliff that interrupts Newland and Ellen's meeting:

> "If only this new dodge for talking along a wire had been a little bit nearer perfection I might have told you all this from town, and been toasting my toes before the club fire this minute, instead of tramping after you through the snow," he grumbled ... and at this opening Madame Olenska twisted the talk away to the fantastic possibility that they might one day actually converse with each other from street to street, or even—incredible dream!—from one town to another. This struck from all three allusions to Edgar Poe and Jules Verne, and such platitudes as naturally rise to the lips of the most intelligent when they are talking against time, and dealing with a new invention in which it would seem ingenuous to believe too soon ....

Imminent technological inventions are destined to make science fiction seem realistic. By the turn of the century, as Wharton's epilogue reveals, the telephone and five-day transatlantic voyages were commonplace. When Wharton was composing the novel, airplanes and skyscrapers were soon to become commonplace as well. Such technological transformation was undergirded by the post-bellum economic expansion that would make many fortunes and shape the materialistic ethos of what has come to be called "the Gilded Age." Railroad, steel, and manufacturing money would displace from prominence the pseudo-aristocratic wealth of Wharton's old New Yorkers. Wharton satirized the vulgarity, ostentatiousness and unscrupulousness of the nouveaux riches in *The House of Mirth* and *The Custom of the Country*; in *The Age of Innocence*, she only foreshadows their emergence through the ambiguous character of Julius Beaufort.

Demographically, New York City's population would swell to such an extent as to reduce to mere traces the seemingly homogeneous, provincial "society" of Wharton's old New York. One obvious source of this growth was immigration, which had been crucial for New York's economic, political, and social development for decades. A French observer in 1864 (two years after Wharton's birth) wrote his father that New York presented him with "a confusion of tongues, and one wondered where in this cosmopolitan Babel were the authentic Americans."[1] To his friend Ned Winsett's suggestion that he go into politics, Newland recoils, taking it for granted that "the country was in the possession of the bosses and the emigrant ...." As early as 1855, over half of New York City's residents had been born outside the United States; between the end of the Civil War and 1873 (when *The Age of Innocence* roughly begins), two hundred thousand immigrants a year were arriving.[2] From the 1840s to the 1870s, the immigrants were predominantly Irish and German. In Wharton's adult lifetime she would see the city demographically transformed further by large scale immigration from Southern and Eastern Europe: between 1880 and 1919, of the more than twenty-three million immigrants who entered the United States, seventeen million entered through New York City, and many of these made the city their home. The largest proportion of these were Russian Jews and Italians.[3] By 1920, the year in which *The Age of Innocence* was published, white native-born Protestants were outnumbered five to one.[4] Arguably

---

[1] Ernest Duvergier de Hauranne, "Eight Months in America," in *Writing New York: A Literary Anthology*, ed. Phillip Lopate (New York: Library of America, 1998), p. 252.

[2] Edwin G. Burrows and Mike Wallace, *Gotham: A History of New York City to 1898* (New York: Oxford University Press, 1999), pp. 737, 1111–12.

[3] See Kenneth T. Jackson, ed., *The Encyclopedia of New York* (New Haven: Yale University Press, 1995), p. 583.

[4] See Ann Douglas, *Terrible Honesty: Mongrel Manhattan in the 1920s* (New York: Farrar, Straus & Giroux, 1995), p. 304.

the novel's theme of native New Yorkers besieged by "foreigners" conflates past and present immigration patterns and experiences. Julius Beaufort has all the coded characteristics of a Jew who is successfully "passing" (unlike Simon Rosedale of *The House of Mirth*), and Ellen's "Bohemian" characteristics extend to having an Italian maid. Widespread concern among Anglo-Saxon elitists and other nativists about either the necessity of Americanizing immigrants or their unassimilability led to the passing of restrictive immigration laws in the early 1920s.

Wharton certainly shared these concerns, as is glaringly apparent in a passage from *French Ways and Their Meaning* about what the rich English language "has shrunk to on the lips, and in the literature, of the heterogeneous hundred millions of American citizens who, without uniformity of tradition or recognised guidance, are being suffered to work their many wills upon it."[1] A debased language for Wharton augurs a defunct culture, even a lost civilization, a possibility that seems to stare back at Newland and Ellen in their climactic visit to the old Metropolitan Museum near the end of the novel. Looking at "the recovered fragments of Ilium" brought from Cyprus by Luigi de Cesnola (a successfully Americanized Italian immigrant), Ellen muses: "It seems cruel … that after awhile nothing matters … any more than these little things, that used to be necessary and important to forgotten people, and now have to be guessed at under a magnifying glass and labelled: 'Use unknown'." Scenes like this one express the catastrophic view of historical change Wharton articulates at the outset of *A Backward Glance*. But this is countered by her more consistent representation of change, including radical change that needs only a generation to establish itself, as gradual or immanent in earlier conditions. Newland's son may later jocularly think of his father as "prehistoric," but father and son are also described as "born comrades," and they seem to communicate admirably well across generational lines.

Of course, Newland Archer's own change from model tribesman to a peculiarly modern subject who comes to question

---

1   Edith Wharton, *French Ways and Their Meaning* (New York: Appleton, 1919), p. 50.

the most fundamental laws of his culture is the crux of the novel, and it takes the mysterious, darkly-coded "foreign" woman, Ellen Olenska, to work the transformation that divides him, as it were, from himself. The Newland Archer we meet in the opening scene may feel himself the intellectual superior to his fellow tribesmen, but, like any of them, "he was content to hold his view without analysing it, since he knew it was that of all the carefully-brushed, white-waistcoated, buttonhole-flowered gentlemen who succeeded each other in the club-box, exchanged friendly greetings with him, and turned their opera-glasses critically on the circle of ladies who were the product of the system." At the ritual that opens Book Two—Newland and May's wedding—we find a man so alienated from his own cultural "system" that he has become a helpless spectator of what is supposed to be the happiest event of his life:

> Archer wondered how many flaws Lefferts's keen eyes would discover in the ritual of his divinity ["Good Form"]; then he suddenly recalled that he too had once thought such questions important. The things that had filled his days seemed now like a nursery parody of life, or like the wrangles of mediaeval schoolmen over metaphysical terms that nobody had ever understood. A stormy discussion as to whether the wedding presents should be "shown" had darkened the last hours before the wedding; and it seemed inconceivable to Archer that grown-up people should work themselves into a state of agitation over such trifles, and that the matter should have been decided (in the negative) by Mrs. Welland's saying, with indignant tears: "I should as soon turn the reporters loose in my house." Yet there was a time when Archer had had definite and rather aggressive opinions on all such problems, and when everything concerning the manners and customs of his little tribe had seemed to him fraught with world-wide significance.
>
> "And all the while, I suppose," he thought, "real people were living somewhere, and real things happening to them ..."

Priding himself on being intellectually advanced, Newland, we learn early in the novel, has familiarized himself with "the books on Primitive Man that people of advanced culture were beginning to read …." Halfway through the novel, he has "grown" to see his own social order to be as quaint, arbitrarily ruled, and child-like as evolutionary anthropologists thought primitive societies to be. Sexual politics are inseparable from the crisis of cultural orientation Newland experiences. His meditations on the arbitrary nature of old New York's cultural "system" follow from his impulsive defense of a radical principle that cuts to the heart of patriarchal privilege. "Women ought to be free—as free as we are," he exclaims in a fit of impatience at Sillerton Jackson's judgmental insinuations about Ellen. We find him thinking out the implications of this outburst in the opening pages of Chapter VI, in a lengthy passage that recalls Isabel Archer's night meditation in *The Portrait of a Lady*. "The case of the Countess Olenska had stirred up old settled convictions and set them drifting dangerously through his mind." The unsettling of convictions about the absence of sexual desire in "nice" women or the legitimacy of the institution of marriage leads Newland to one of the most famous realizations in the novel, one virtually axiomatic to readers trained in the tenets of cultural studies: "In reality they all lived in a kind of hieroglyphic world, where the real thing was never said or done or even thought, but only represented by a set of arbitrary signs…." What we would call "femininity," he intuitively recognizes, is a socially constructed and performed attribute. Unfortunately, recognizing this never helps him get any closer to either Ellen or May.

Written in the same year that the suffragette cause would be won in the United States (though decades before it would triumph in France), *The Age of Innocence* seems clearly to engage feminist issues, and yet it is very difficult to pin Wharton down to any kind of programmatic perspective (a point I will elaborate on below). Her conservative sensibility and her anthropological readings would have affirmed her sense that custom was always more determinant than abstract legal claims in such matters. Abstract "right" (a word Ellen Olenska learns to see as "ugly") is not directly at issue in the novel; Newland's struggle with his own custom-bound perspective and the mystery of female sexuality are. For the "freedom" that Newland would rashly extend to women is precisely a sexual freedom—the freedom to leave a husband or unsatisfactory marriage; perhaps the freedom from the constraints of marriage altogether; perhaps, most wildly, the freedom to define and take charge of their own sexuality. What might this entail? Newland at first takes solace in the reality that his speculations are idle, since "'nice' women ... would never claim the kind of freedom that he meant ...." But this self-abnegation, even self-enslavement, on the part of the tribal women ironically makes the prospect of his sexual conquest of the virgin May so fatal, so foreordained and predictable as to threaten to quench all desire in the act of fulfillment. His right to ravish the bride will only bind him to the tribe further, and make him a dreaded "copy" of all the other tribesmen—like his prospective father-in-law—who have symbolically conquered before him. In his musings, Newland gropes after "natural" female sexual energies that "culture" represses. His framework for resisting the "factitious purity, so cunningly manufactured by a conspiracy of mothers and aunts and grandmothers and long-dead ancestresses," is Darwinian: "Untrained human nature was not frank and innocent; it was full of the twists and defences of an instinctive guile." But Newland's reasoning here seems tautological; for culture's conspiracy of matriarchs and nature's endowment of "instinctive guile" seem to work to the same end—namely, reproduction of the species or the tribe. May is associated with fertility through her name and through the similes identifying her with Diana the huntress. But so harnessed is her "natural" sexual power to the service of cultural reproduction and sameness that she comes to embody for Newland the antithesis of desire and self-determination.

Ellen, by contrast, seems to harbor a sexuality unregulated by tribal mores and unmoored from reproduction, and thus produces in Newland nothing but desire and dreams of self-determination. She embodies, that is, a sexuality that is ever different, that is fundamentally disorienting rather than culturally binding, that renews rather than sacrifices itself. "*Each time you happen to me all over again,*" Newland exclaims to her, after struggling to find words adequate for the feelings she incites in him. His struggle with words and the emphasis on his own passivity here—and indeed the silences that accompany his and Ellen's encounters—are indicative of the difficulty he has in finding a meaning for her outside the terms of his own cultural categories. His romance with her is mediated from beginning to end by "literary" texts and the fantasies that might accompany them: Gounod's *Faust*, Dion Boucicault's play *The Shaughraun*, Dante Gabriel Rossetti's sonnet sequence, *The House of Life*. Newland and Ellen's relationship always borders on a comedy of miscommunication. More than once she insists that they do not speak the same language, a statement that tauntingly leaves Newland guessing about what language she does speak. Beaufort's instant interest in Ellen leads him to conclude the worst (though Beaufort's shadowy presence might have forced him to confront the darker implications of his own instant interest). But it also reaffirms Newland's sense of her as a victimized damsel in need of chivalric defense from predatorial men.

Ellen, finally, shows herself to be much more realistic than her romantic champion. When she boldly asks him whether it is his idea that she should be his mistress, since she cannot be his wife, he flailingly retorts: "I want—I want somehow to get away with you into a world where words like that—categories like that—won't exist. Where we shall be simply two human beings who love each other, who are the whole of life to each other; and nothing else on earth will matter." To which Ellen rhetorically responds: "Oh, my dear—where is that country?" Such a place presupposes the anarchic dream of doing away with the institution of marriage, and thus the categories of "wife" and "mistress" that are predicated upon it. Experience has taught Ellen that such dreams lead only to "smaller and dingier and more promiscuous" societies. And if her own experience were not enough to confirm this, she has the example before her of the scattered Medora Manson, whose experimental life has landed her in the company of the sinister free love advocate Dr. Agathon Carver. Social "reality" in this novel finally dictates Newland's choices: to be a faithful husband, to be a hypocritical husband with a mistress on the side, or to be a faithful husband who finds consolation in fantasies about an ideal woman whom he will never know in the flesh. In each case, Newland hardly escapes being a "copy" of other men, just as America—the "New land"—has in Ellen's estimation failed to make any revolutionary break from its old world origins.

Wharton's novel from beginning to end seems to support the commonplace "sex-radical's" claim (voiced, for example, in Emma Goldman's 1911 essay "Marriage and Love") that men and women have been acculturated to remain strangers to one another. At the same time it seems to balk at, or at least refuse to offer, revolutionary solutions to this problem. Its tenor is finally tragic-ironic; it concludes on a note of Jamesian renunciation. And yet the epilogue to the novel—set a quarter century after the novel's main events—introduces ambiguities that de-stabilize even as they permit both conservative and progressive/feminist readings of the novel. Newland's life, we learn, has been fruitful if uninspiring, and he has adapted gracefully to a radically transformed world: bridging past and present orders, he believes deeply that "there was good in the old ways," while acknowledging that "there was good in the new order too." Despite technological marvels that have shrunk distances and contracted time, Newland seems as "distant" from the women in his life—especially Ellen—as he has ever been, even when he finds himself outside her apartment in Paris. But his son Dallas Archer's engagement to "Beaufort's bastard" Fanny Ring suggests not only that tribal barriers to outsiders have collapsed completely, but that the sins of the fathers have lost their power to determine the fate of the children. Is this a good thing? His perspective seems to merge with the wise omniscient narrator's here: "Nothing could more clearly give the measure of the distance that the world had travelled. People nowadays were too busy—busy with reforms and 'movements,' with fads and fetishes and frivolities—to bother much about their neighbours. And of what account was anybody's past, in the huge kaleidoscope where all the social atoms spun around on the same plane?" The absorption of old New York, with its hierarchy, exclusivity and even cruelty, into a burgeoning American empire (represented by the bigger Metropolitan Museum "crowded with the spoils of the ages") makes what he once thought of as a society hostile to differences into the very safeguard of difference, an older order resistant to a vast, powerful levelling and standardizing process that dehumanizes people into inter-changeable "social atoms." This vision—consciously or uncon-sciously informed, we might surmise, by proleptic awareness of the horror of modern warfare—disturbs the epilogue's apparent affir-mation of progress and the liberalized sexual mores that enable Ellen Olenska to live alone in Paris and Dallas and Fanny to enjoy the kind of "companiate marriage" that would soon become a mainstay of bourgeois society. Wharton's notebooks show that she entertained the idea of a sequel to the novel, alternately called "Homo Sapiens" or "The Age of Wisdom." This was to be the "History of Dallas Archer & Fanny." She left us instead with a bril-liant, enigmatic conclusion to an already nearly perfect novel.

The Age of Innocence in Cultural Context: A Note on the Appendices

Appendices A to D of this volume give readers useful informa-tion pertaining to the genesis, production, and initial critical reception of the novel, as well as a selection from Wharton's late memoir, "A Little Girl's New York." Appendices E to G help provide a cultural and discursive context (by no means exhaus-tive) for Wharton's novel.

"Appendix E: Wharton and Others on the Status of Women" provides an overview of some prominent American perspectives from the 1910s on women's social position, on the value of the vote, and on marriage and sexual freedom. It includes the views of the very popular former president, Theodore Roosevelt; of the president of the National American Woman Suffrage Association, Carrie Chapman Catt; of the "Bohemian" anarchist and free love advocate, Emma Goldman; and of Wharton herself as she compares the social worlds of French and American women, and describes her visit to a Moroccan harem.

As a well-read, well-traveled, independent-minded woman, Wharton could not but have been alert to the feminist issues that were part of the intellectual life of her times, and her novels clearly concern themselves with women's roles, women's social condi-tioning and the choices made by women condemned to restricted lives. Still, Wharton's statements outside of her fiction on the status of women are ambiguous at best and often overtly anti-feminist. A noteworthy exception to these occurs in her 1915 tribute, written in French, to her friend Jean du Breuil de Saint-Germain, a feminist sympathizer killed in the war. "It is Jean du Breuil," she writes there, "who opened my eyes to a question of which—I admit it to my shame—I had not until then understood the immense implications." Du Breuil opened her eyes primarily, however, to the plight of working-class women. She clarifies her position as follows: "In short, one would be tempted to say that women who argue for the right to vote could very well do without it, but it is necessary for those women, so much more numerous, who do not even know what it is, or why others are demanding it in their name."[1] A more unpalatable statement can be found in *A Backward Glance*, where she decries "the 'monstrous regiment of the emancipated': young women taught by their elders to despise the kitchen and the linen room, and to substitute the acquiring of University degrees for the more complex art of civilized living."[2]

In relation to the prominent voices represented here, Wharton's views in some respects accord with Roosevelt's, though it is hard to imagine her sympathizing with his bombastic over-valuation of women's child-bearing capacity. There is no evidence I am aware of that she read Goldman, though she must surely have heard of one of "new" New York's most famous radicals, who was deported in December 1919. Nonetheless, the representation of marriage we find in *The Age of Innocence*, as well as some of the views of marriage entertained by an awakening Newland Archer, accord in uncanny ways with the tenor of Goldman's pamphlet.

"Appendix F: Ethnographic Discourse, Victorian to Modern" provides students with brief readings selected to clarify the emergence of a more relativistic and self-reflexive ethnography out of an older evolutionary model, readings chosen for their thematic and methodological pertinence to *The Age of Innocence*.

Like many people of "advanced culture" in her time, Wharton was also an avid reader of "Books on Primitive Man." The nature

---

[1]   Edith Wharton, *The Uncollected Critical Writings*, ed. Frederick Wegener (Princeton: Princeton University Press, 1996), pp. 200–01.

[2]   *A Backward Glance*, p. 60.

of her anthropological perspective remains, however, a subject for speculation. An early reviewer noted the similarities between Wharton's treatment of Old New York and the method of Elsie Clews Parsons,[1] another denizen, like Emma Goldman, of "new" New York's "Bohemian" enclave, Greenwich Village, and like Goldman, a radical critic of bourgeois marriage. In a series of books published in the teens, Parsons popularized an anthropological approach to contemporary social forms that challenged longstanding distinctions between "primitive" and "civilized," and made contemporary American customs, habits, and psychological attitudes seem as strange or foreign as those of any Fijian tribe. Parsons was influenced by Franz Boas's paradigm-shifting critique of the evolutionary assumptions underlying Victorian anthropology—in particular, the assumption that the "races" of the world were connected along an evolutionary scale at the top of which rests white, patriarchal, European "civilization." Boas's critique would significantly shape modern American ethnographic research; we hear one of its fundamental themes voiced in his popular disciple Ruth Benedict's emphasis on "the relativity of cultural habits." On the basis of *The Age of Innocence*, readers interested in Wharton's anthropological themes have tended to align her, loosely or otherwise, with this emerging "modernist" ethnographic perspective, or have tended to read her by the light of later ethnography.[2]

Still, while there is little evidence to suggest that Wharton was familiar with Boasian anthropology, there is considerable evidence that she was well-versed in the evolutionary anthropology it critiqued. As I have stated above, Wharton regarded highly the

---

[1]   Francis Hackett, "The Age of Innocence," *New Republic* 24 (17 November, 1920), p. 301.

[2]   For studies concerned with Wharton's use of anthropology, see Bentley, *The Ethnography of Manners*; Preston, *Edith Wharton's Social Register*; Fryer, *Felicitous Space*; and the essays by Knights and Bentley in *The Cambridge Companion to Edith Wharton* (all listed in the Select Bibliography in this volume). Also see Kenneth D. Pimple, "Edith Wharton's 'Inscrutable Totem Terrors': Ethnography and *The Age of Innocence*," *Southern Folklore* 51 (No. 2, 1994), pp. 137–52; Katie Trumpener and James M. Nyce, "The Recovered Fragments: Archaeological and Anthropological Perspectives in Edith Wharton's *The Age of Innocence*," in *Literary Anthropology*, ed. Fernando Poyatos (Philadelphia: John Benjamin, 1988), pp. 161–69; and Mary Ellis Gibson, "Edith Wharton and the Ethnography of Old New York," *Studies in American Fiction* 13 (Spring 1985), pp. 57–69.

achievement of Darwin and the now much-maligned Herbert Spencer. A recent catalogue of the remains of her library shows that she held volumes by the "father" of evolutionary anthropology, Edward B. Tylor (most notably *Primitive Man* [1865] and the "textbook" *Anthropology* [1894]), and by Edward Westermarck.[1] There is also much to suggest her familiarity with and admiration for Sir James Frazer's *The Golden Bough*[2]—in fact, she alludes to it in her 1919 poetic tribute to Roosevelt. And the evolutionary motif of "survivals" not only surfaces in *The Age of Innocence* but is explicitly drawn upon in *French Ways and Their Meaning*, which, like *In Morocco* (1920), falls back on ready-made distinctions between barbarism and civilization.

Nonetheless, Wharton's considerable knowledge of ethnographic "science" as underwritten by evolutionary (and from today's perspective, imperialistic) assumptions surely did not preclude her from discovering through her novelistic imagination what anthropologists, themselves trained in evolutionary paradigms, were discovering: namely, that the conditions for increasing "our" knowledge of primitive and foreign "others"—primarily through the method of field work—were estranging us from ourselves. In other words, in coming to know more and more different cultures through the process of globalization that is one of the fundamental aspects of modernity, "we" came to see our "local" cultures standing in greater relief as "different" cultures themselves—and perhaps as in danger of "dying" as those "tribes" more obviously facing extinction from modern forces. Some few years after writing *The Age of Innocence*, Wharton would meet and greatly admire the work of Bronislaw Malinowski, the Polish emigré and self-proclaimed founder of the "functional" method of anthropology,[3] whose pioneering and self-reflexive field work would impact

---

[1] See *Edith Wharton's Library: A Catalogue*, compiled by George Ramsden, with a Foreword by Hermione Lee (Settrington: Stone Trough Books, 1999), pp. 131, 136.

[2] *The Golden Bough*: this famous anthropological work was first published in two volumes in 1890, and later published in twelve volumes between 1911 and 1915. In it, Frazer theorized that humanity's mental development originated in a belief in magic and evolved to religious and finally scientific thought.

[3] See Bronislaw Malinowski, *The Sexual Life of Savages in North-Western Melanesia* (London: Routledge and Kegan Paul, 1929), pp. xxix–xxxii.

British anthropology in ways analogous to the impact Boas's work had on American anthropology. In identifying Victorian anthropology as the reading matter of a quaint people now themselves objectifiable as a "tribe" from the past, *The Age of Innocence* surely carries modernist implications. But vestiges of Wharton's own Victorian education surely leave their mark on the text as well.

"Appendix G: Wharton on Modernity and Tradition" provides readers with select passages from Wharton's other work of the late teens in which the tension between tradition and modernity, the broadest theme of *The Age of Innocence*, is in the foreground. Together they register the fact that Wharton's acceptance of change was inseparable from her struggle to find some principle of stability or some source of permanent value that might make otherwise chaotic change more akin to "growth," a word implying organic wholeness, a metaphor that makes commensurable the achievements of "civilization," past, present, and to come. Wharton was a remarkably adventurous woman who left her provincial world and embraced modernity, though not without reservations and a recognition of modernity's destructive aspects. As I suggested at the outset, the changes in her own life, coupled with the war experience and its aftermath, made her at turns anxious about the future and nostalgic about the past; but the predominant note of her work is one of fortitude and openness before inevitable processes. As she would write in the foreword to *A Backward Glance* when she was over seventy, "one can remain alive long past the usual date of disintegration if one is unafraid of change, insatiable in intellectual curiosity, interested in big things, and happy in small ways."[1]

---

[1]   *A Backward Glance*, p. xix.

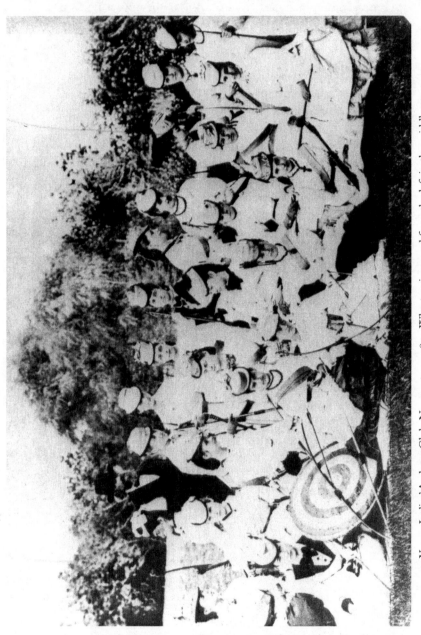

Young Ladies' Archery Club, Newport, ca. 1872. Wharton is second from the left in the middle row.

Edith Wharton: A Brief Chronology

1862 24 January: Edith Newbold Jones born, at 80 E. 21st St., New York City.

1866–71 Jones family lives in Europe, settling among other places in Rome, Paris, and Florence.

1872 Jones family returns to America, living at W. 23rd St., New York City and spending summers at Pencraig, the family estate in Newport, Rhode Island.

1878 *Verses*, a volume of poems, is privately printed at her mother's expense in Newport.

1879 Makes her social debut at the end of the year.

1882 Father dies in Cannes in March. In August she becomes engaged to Harry Stevens; the engagement is broken off in October.

1885 Marries Edward ("Teddy") Wharton in April.

1885–88 Lives at Pencraig Cottage on her mother's estate and spends several months of each year travelling in Europe, especially Italy. Makes four-month cruise of the Aegean Islands in 1888.

1891 Buys house in New York City (what would become 884 Park Avenue).

1893 Buys Land's End, a Newport estate. Three stories are accepted by *Scribner's Magazine*.

1897 *The Decoration of Houses*, co-authored with architect Ogden Codman, published by Scribner's.

1899 Settles briefly in Washington, D.C. Her first collection of stories, *The Greater Inclination*, is published by Scribner's.

1900 *The Touchstone*, a novella, published, first serially, then in book form, by Scribner's.

1901 Buys and begins developing what will become The Mount, a 113-acre property in Lenox, Massachusetts. *Crucial Instances*, her second collection of stories, published.

1902 *The Valley of Decision* published, a lengthy historical novel set in eighteenth-century Italy. Receives praise for it from Henry James, who encourages her to "*Do New York!*" Begins friendship with Theodore Roosevelt. Moves into The Mount.

1904   Buys her first automobile and travels first through France in it, and later through England with Henry James. *The Descent of Man*, her third collection of stories, published.

1905   *The House of Mirth* published, first serially, from January to November, and in book form in October. The novel is a huge commercial success.

1907   *The Fruit of the Tree* published, first serially then in book form.

1908-10   Divides her years between Paris and The Mount. High point of friendship with James. Enters into an intermittent but passionate love affair with William Morton Fullerton, a Paris correspondent for the London *Times*. Teddy Wharton confesses in 1909 to embezzling money from her trust funds and keeping a mistress. Her fourth collection of stories, *The Hermit and the Wild Woman,* and *A Motor-Flight Through France* published in 1908. A book of poetry, *Artemis to Actaeon,* published in 1909. *Tales of Men and Ghosts* published in 1910.

1911   *Ethan Frome* published serially, then in book form in September, by Scribner's.

1912   Sells The Mount in June. *The Reef* published by D. Appleton and Company.

1913   Divorces Edward Wharton in April. *The Custom of the Country* published serially, then in book form by Scribner's, in October.

1914   First visits Africa—Algeria and Tunisia. In Paris when the First World War breaks out, she establishes the first of her war charities, a workroom for seamstresses and other unemployed women. Establishes and presides over the American Hostels for Refugees.

1915   Makes several visits to the front—writes articles for *Scribner's* later collected as *Fighting France: From*

Dunkerque to Belfort. Organizes the Children of Flanders Rescue Committee to deal with refugee crisis. Puts together *The Book of the Homeless* to raise money for her charities: the book is made up of contributions by several prominent European and American writers and artists, and is introduced by Theodore Roosevelt.

1916   Henry James dies. French government makes her Chevalier of the Legion of Honor for her war-time services. *Xingu and Other Stories* published.

1917   *Summer* published, first serially in *McClure's*, then in book form by Appleton. Travels to French Morocco in September with Walter Berry, where among other things she visits a harem.

1918   Publishes *The Marne*, a war novella. Buys Pavillon Colombe, a home outside of Paris.

1919   First leases Ste. Claire du Vieux Château in Hyères in Southern France, which will become her permanent winter residence. Moves into Pavillon Colombe, which will become her permanent summer residence. *French Ways and Their Meaning*, a collection of previously published magazine articles, published by Appleton.

1920   *The Age of Innocence* published first serially in *The Pictorial Review* from July to October, then in book form by Appleton in October. *In Morocco* also published in October by Scribner's.

1921   Awarded Pulitzer Prize in May for *The Age of Innocence*.

1922   *Glimpses of the Moon* published serially in *The Pictorial Review*, then in book form by Appleton.

1923   *A Son at the Front* published by Scribner's.

1924   Four novellas, each covering a decade from 1840 to 1880, published in boxed set as *Old New York* by Appleton.

1925   *The Mother's Recompense* published serially in *The Pictorial Review*, then in book form by Appleton; *The Writing of Fiction* published by Scribner's.

1927 Buys the Hyères home. *Twilight Sleep* published by Appleton. Closest friend Walter Berry dies in October.

1928 *The Children* published serially in *The Pictorial Review*, then in book form by Appleton. *The Age of Innocence* (dramatization by Margaret Ayer Barnes) produced on Broadway.

1929 *Hudson River Bracketed*, her first novel about a writer, published first serially by *Delineator*, then in book form by Appleton. Receives a Gold Medal for "special distinction in literature" from the American Academy of Arts and Letters.

1930 Elected to the American Academy of Arts and Letters—only the second woman to receive this honor.

1932 *The Gods Arrive*, sequel to *Hudson River Bracketed*, published serially by *Delineator* after being rejected by other magazines; published in book form by Appleton.

1934 *A Backward Glance*, her autobiography, published by Appleton-Century (serialized beginning October 1933 in the *Ladies' Home Journal*).
Her last collection of stories, *The World Over*, published by Appleton-Century.

1937 11 August: dies at Saint-Brice-la-Forêt in France. Buried in the Cimetière des Gonards in Versailles, near Walter Berry.

1938 Posthumous publication of "A Little Girl's New York" in *Harper's Monthly* and of her unfinished novel, *The Buccaneers*, by Appleton-Century.

A Note on the Text

This edition follows the standard practice of using the sixth imprint of the first edition (1921) as its copytext. While Wharton cleared up her most embarrassing errors for the third imprint, she was bothered by printer's errors from the outset and was not entirely satisfied until the sixth imprint appeared, which incorporated all her corrections.

The AGE of INNOCENCE

BY

EDITH WHARTON

AUTHOR OF "THE HOUSE OF MIRTH,"
"THE REEF," "SUMMER," ETC.

D. APPLETON AND COMPANY

NEW YORK :: MCMXXI :: LONDON

BOOK ONE

I

On a January evening of the early seventies, Christine Nilsson was singing in *Faust* at the Academy of Music in New York.[1]

Though there was already talk of the erection, in remote metropolitan distances "above the Forties," of a new Opera House which should compete in costliness and splendour with those of the great European capitals, the world of fashion was still content to reassemble every winter in the shabby red and gold boxes of the sociable old Academy. Conservatives cherished it for being small and inconvenient, and thus keeping out the "new people" whom New York was beginning to dread and yet be drawn to; and the sentimental clung to it for its historic associations, and the musical for its excellent acoustics, always so problematic a quality in halls built for the hearing of music.[2]

It was Madame Nilsson's first appearance that winter, and what the daily press had already learned to describe as "an exceptionally brilliant audience" had gathered to hear her, transported through the slippery, snowy streets in private broughams, in the spacious family landau, or in the humbler but more convenient "Brown *coupé*."[3] To come to the Opera in a Brown *coupé* was

---

1   *Christine Nilsson* (1843–1921), Swedish soprano famous for playing Marguerite in Charles Gounod's opera *Faust* (first performed 1859). She toured America from 1870–1872, returning in 1873, 1874, and 1883. She played Marguerite on the inaugural night of the Metropolitan Opera House in 1883. *Faust*: one of the most popular operas of the nineteenth century, it focuses on the bargain Faust makes with Mephistopheles so that he may regain his youth and seduce the beautiful Marguerite. *Faust* first played in New York at the Academy of Music in 1863, where it was regularly performed thereafter.

2   The *Academy of Music* opened in 1854 and was situated at Fourteenth St. and Irving Place. It was destroyed by fire in 1866 but rebuilt in 1868. It was the main venue for touring foreign opera stars until the Metropolitan *Opera House* opened in 1883, at Broadway and Thirty-ninth St., forcing the Academy to close by 1886. *Above the forties*: parallel with Fifth Avenue, fashionable New York residences moved steadily northward (towards Central Park) with the advance of the nineteenth century.

3   *brougham*: an enclosed four-wheeled British carriage which had its body suspended on elliptical springs so that passengers could enter or exit in a single step; *landau*: a four-wheeled carriage with a top that could be opened for driving in mild weather; the *coupé*: a lightweight four-passenger carriage.

almost as honourable a way of arriving as in one's own carriage; and departure by the same means had the immense advantage of enabling one (with a playful allusion to democratic principles) to scramble into the first Brown conveyance in the line, instead of waiting till the cold-and-gin congested nose of one's own coachman gleamed under the portico of the Academy. It was one of the great livery-stableman's most masterly intuitions to have discovered that Americans want to get away from amusement even more quickly than they want to get to it.

When Newland Archer opened the door at the back of the club box the curtain had just gone up on the garden scene. There was no reason why the young man should not have come earlier, for he had dined at seven, alone with his mother and sister, and had lingered afterward over a cigar in the Gothic library with glazed black-walnut bookcases and finial-topped chairs which was the only room in the house where Mrs. Archer allowed smoking. But, in the first place, New York was a metropolis, and perfectly aware that in metropolises it was "not the thing" to arrive early at the opera; and what was or was "not the thing" played a part as important in Newland Archer's New York as the inscrutable totem terrors that had ruled the destinies of his forefathers thousands of years ago.

The second reason for his delay was a personal one. He had dawdled over his cigar because he was at heart a dilettante, and thinking over a pleasure to come often gave him a subtler satisfaction than its realisation. This was especially the case when the pleasure was a delicate one, as his pleasures mostly were; and on this occasion the moment he looked forward to was so rare and exquisite in quality that—well, if he had timed his arrival in accord with the prima donna's stage-manager he could not have entered the Academy at a more significant moment than just as she was singing: "He loves me—he loves me not—*he loves me!*" and sprinkling the falling daisy petals with notes as clear as dew.

She sang, of course, "*M'ama!*" and not "he loves me," since an unalterable and unquestioned law of the musical world required that the German text of French operas sung by Swedish artists should be translated into Italian for the clearer understanding of

English-speaking audiences.[1] This seemed as natural to Newland Archer as all the other conventions on which his life was moulded: such as the duty of using two silver-backed brushes with his monogram in blue enamel to part his hair, and of never appearing in society without a flower (preferably a gardenia) in his buttonhole.

"*M'ama ... non m'ama ...*" the prima donna sang, and "*M'ama!*", with a final burst of love triumphant, as she pressed the dishevelled daisy to her lips and lifted her large eyes to the sophisticated countenance of the little brown Faust-Capoul,[2] who was vainly trying, in a tight purple velvet doublet and plumed cap, to look as pure and true as his artless victim.

Newland Archer, leaning against the wall at the back of the club box, turned his eyes from the stage and scanned the opposite side of the house. Directly facing him was the box of old Mrs. Manson Mingott, whose monstrous obesity had long since made it impossible for her to attend the Opera, but who was always represented on fashionable nights by some of the younger members of the family. On this occasion, the front of the box was filled by her daughter-in-law, Mrs. Lovell Mingott, and her daughter, Mrs. Welland; and slightly withdrawn behind these brocaded matrons sat a young girl in white with eyes ecstatically fixed on the stage-lovers. As Madame Nilsson's "*M'ama!*" thrilled out above the silent house (the boxes always stopped talking during the Daisy Song)[3] a warm pink mounted to the girl's cheek, mantled her brow to the roots of her fair braids, and suffused the young slope of her breast to the line where it met a modest tulle tucker fastened with a single gardenia. She dropped her eyes to the immense bouquet of lilies-of-the-valley on her

---

[1] Though a French opera, *Faust* was regularly sung in Italian because Italian was considered the primary language of opera.

[2] Joseph-Amédée-Victor *Capoul* (1839–1924), French tenor who sang in Paris, London, and New York. He made his American debut in 1871 at the Academy of Music with Christine Nilsson in Ambroise Thomas's opera *Mignon*.

[3] *Daisy Song:* "*Duo*" (Act III, 18), about midway through the opera. At this point, the innocent Marguerite has fallen in love with Faust and is wondering whether or not he returns her love. Wharton highlights the idyllic moment in the opera before love brings tragedy and disillusionment.

knee, and Newland Archer saw her white-gloved finger-tips touch the flowers softly. He drew a breath of satisfied vanity and his eyes returned to the stage.

No expense had been spared on the setting, which was acknowledged to be very beautiful even by people who shared his acquaintance with the Opera houses of Paris and Vienna. The foreground, to the footlights, was covered with emerald green cloth. In the middle distance symmetrical mounds of woolly green moss bounded by croquet hoops formed the base of shrubs shaped like orange-trees but studded with large pink and red roses. Gigantic pansies, considerably larger than the roses, and closely resembling the floral penwipers made by female parishioners for fashionable clergymen, sprang from the moss beneath the rose-trees; and here and there a daisy grafted on a rose-branch flowered with a luxuriance prophetic of Mr. Luther Burbank's far-off prodigies.[1]

In the centre of this enchanted garden Madame Nilsson, in white cashmere slashed with pale blue satin, a reticule dangling from a blue girdle, and large yellow braids carefully disposed on each side of her muslin chemisette, listened with downcast eyes to M. Capoul's impassioned wooing, and affected a guileless incomprehension of his designs whenever, by word or glance, he persuasively indicated the ground floor window of the neat brick villa projecting obliquely from the right wing.

"The darling!" thought Newland Archer, his glance flitting back to the young girl with the lilies-of-the-valley. "She doesn't even guess what it's all about." And he contemplated her absorbed young face with a thrill of possessorship in which pride in his own masculine initiation was mingled with a tender reverence for her abysmal purity. "We'll read Faust together ... by the Italian lakes ..." he thought,[2] somewhat hazily confusing the scene of his projected honey-moon with the masterpieces of literature which it would be his manly privilege to reveal to his bride. It was only

---

[1] *Luther Burbank* (1849–1926), famed American nurseryman and horticulturalist.
[2] *Faust*: the verse tragedy by Johann Wolfgang von Goethe (1749–1832), published in two parts, in 1808 and 1832 respectively. Gounod based his opera on Part I of Goethe's play.

that afternoon that May Welland had let him guess that she "cared" (New York's consecrated phrase of maiden avowal), and already his imagination, leaping ahead of the engagement ring, the betrothal kiss and the march from Lohengrin,[1] pictured her at his side in some scene of old European witchery.

He did not in the least wish the future Mrs. Newland Archer to be a simpleton. He meant her (thanks to his enlightening companionship) to develop a social tact and readiness of wit enabling her to hold her own with the most popular married women of the "younger set," in which it was the recognised custom to attract masculine homage while playfully discouraging it. If he had probed to the bottom of his vanity (as he sometimes nearly did) he would have found there the wish that his wife should be as worldly-wise and as eager to please as the married lady whose charms had held his fancy through two mildly agitated years; without, of course, any hint of the frailty which had so nearly marred that unhappy being's life, and had disarranged his own plans for a whole winter.

How this miracle of fire and ice was to be created, and to sustain itself in a harsh world, he had never taken the time to think out; but he was content to hold his view without analysing it, since he knew it was that of all the carefully-brushed, white-waistcoated, buttonhole-flowered gentlemen who succeeded each other in the club box, exchanged friendly greetings with him, and turned their opera-glasses critically on the circle of ladies who were the product of the system. In matters intellectual and artistic Newland Archer felt himself distinctly the superior of these chosen specimens of old New York gentility; he had probably read more, thought more, and even seen a good deal more of the world, than any other man of the number. Singly they betrayed their inferiority; but grouped together they represented "New York," and the habit of masculine solidarity made him accept their doctrine on all the issues called moral. He instinctively felt that in this respect it would be troublesome—and also rather bad form—to strike out for himself.

---

[1]   Bridal March from Act III of Wagner's opera *Lohengrin*, informally known as "Here Comes the Bride."

"Well—upon my soul!" exclaimed Lawrence Lefferts, turning his opera-glass abruptly away from the stage. Lawrence Lefferts was, on the whole, the foremost authority on "form" in New York. He had probably devoted more time than any one else to the study of this intricate and fascinating question; but study alone could not account for his complete and easy competence. One had only to look at him, from the slant of his bald forehead and the curve of his beautiful fair moustache to the long patent-leather feet at the other end of his lean and elegant person, to feel that the knowledge of "form" must be congenital in any one who knew how to wear such good clothes so carelessly and carry such height with so much lounging grace. As a young admirer had once said of him: "If anybody can tell a fellow just when to wear a black tie with evening clothes and when not to, it's Larry Lefferts." And on the question of pumps versus patent-leather "Oxfords" his authority had never been disputed.

"My God!" he said; and silently handed his glass to old Sillerton Jackson.

Newland Archer, following Lefferts's glance, saw with surprise that his exclamation had been occasioned by the entry of a new figure into old Mrs. Mingott's box. It was that of a slim young woman, a little less tall than May Welland, with brown hair growing in close curls about her temples and held in place by a narrow band of diamonds. The suggestion of this headdress, which gave her what was then called a "Josephine look,"[1] was carried out in the cut of the dark blue velvet gown rather theatrically caught up under her bosom by a girdle with a large old-fashioned clasp. The wearer of this unusual dress, who seemed quite unconscious of the attention it was attracting, stood a moment in the centre of the box, discussing with Mrs. Welland the propriety of taking the latter's place in the front right-hand corner; then she yielded with a slight smile, and seated herself in line with Mrs. Welland's sister-in-law, Mrs. Lovell Mingott, who was installed in the opposite corner.

---

[1] After the Empress *Josephine*, wife of Napoleon Bonaparte. Her likeness was famously caught by Pierre-Paul Prud'hon (1758–1823) in the painting *Impératrice Joséphine* (1805) that depicts her wearing an empire-waisted dress with a gold girdle, curls clustered at her temples, and jeweled bands in her hair.

Mr. Sillerton Jackson had returned the opera-glass to Lawrence Lefferts. The whole of the club turned instinctively, waiting to hear what the old man had to say; for old Mr. Jackson was as great an authority on "family" as Lawrence Lefferts was on "form." He knew all the ramifications of New York's cousinships; and could not only elucidate such complicated questions as that of the connection between the Mingotts (through the Thorleys) with the Dallases of South Carolina, and that of the relationship of the elder branch of Philadelphia Thorleys to the Albany Chiverses (on no account to be confused with the Manson Chiverses of University Place), but could also enumerate the leading characteristics of each family: as, for instance, the fabulous stinginess of the younger lines of Leffertses (the Long Island ones); or the fatal tendency of the Rushworths to make foolish matches; or the insanity recurring in every second generation of the Albany Chiverses, with whom their New York cousins had always refused to intermarry—with the disastrous exception of poor Medora Manson, who, as everybody knew ... but then her mother was a Rushworth.

In addition to this forest of family trees, Mr. Sillerton Jackson carried between his narrow hollow temples, and under his soft thatch of silver hair, a register of most of the scandals and mysteries that had smouldered under the unruffled surface of New York society within the last fifty years. So far indeed did his information extend, and so acutely retentive was his memory, that he was supposed to be the only man who could have told you who Julius Beaufort, the banker, really was, and what had become of handsome Bob Spicer, old Mrs. Manson Mingott's father, who had disappeared so mysteriously (with a large sum of trust money) less than a year after his marriage, on the very day that a beautiful Spanish dancer who had been delighting thronged audiences in the old Opera-house on the Battery[1] had taken ship for Cuba. But these mysteries, and many others, were closely locked in Mr. Jackson's breast; for not only did his keen sense of honour forbid his repeating anything privately imparted, but he

---

[1] *old Opera-house on the Battery*: the Castle Garden (until 1855) in Battery Park, the once fashionable promenade at the bottom tip of Manhattan Island.

was fully aware that his reputation for discretion increased his opportunities of finding out what he wanted to know.

The club box, therefore, waited in visible suspense while Mr. Sillerton Jackson handed back Lawrence Lefferts's opera-glass. For a moment he silently scrutinised the attentive group out of his filmy blue eyes overhung by old veined lids; then he gave his moustache a thoughtful twist, and said simply: "I didn't think the Mingotts would have tried it on."

II

NEWLAND Archer, during this brief episode, had been thrown into a strange state of embarrassment.

It was annoying that the box which was thus attracting the undivided attention of masculine New York should be that in which his betrothed was seated between her mother and aunt; and for a moment he could not identify the lady in the Empire dress, nor imagine why her presence created such excitement among the initiated. Then light dawned on him, and with it came a momentary rush of indignation. No, indeed; no one would have thought the Mingotts would have tried it on!

But they had; they undoubtedly had; for the low-toned comments behind him left no doubt in Archer's mind that the young woman was May Welland's cousin, the cousin always referred to in the family as "poor Ellen Olenska." Archer knew that she had suddenly arrived from Europe a day or two previously; he had even heard from Miss Welland (not disapprovingly) that she had been to see poor Ellen, who was staying with old Mrs. Mingott. Archer entirely approved of family solidarity, and one of the qualities he most admired in the Mingotts was their resolute championship of the few black sheep that their blameless stock had produced. There was nothing mean or ungenerous in the young man's heart, and he was glad that his future wife should not be restrained by false prudery from being kind (in private) to her unhappy cousin; but to receive Countess Olenska in the family circle was a different thing from producing her in public, at the Opera of all places, and in the very box with the young girl whose engagement to him, Newland Archer, was to be announced within a few weeks. No, he felt as old Sillerton Jackson felt; he did not think the Mingotts would have tried it on!

He knew, of course, that whatever man dared (within Fifth Avenue's limits) that old Mrs. Manson Mingott, the Matriarch of the line, would dare. He had always admired the high and mighty old lady, who, in spite of having been only Catherine Spicer of Staten Island, with a father mysteriously discredited, and neither money nor position enough to make people forget it, had allied herself with the head of the wealthy Mingott line, married two of her daughters to "foreigners" (an Italian marquis and an English banker), and put the crowning touch to her audacities by building a large house of pale cream-coloured stone (when brown sandstone seemed as much the only wear as a frock-coat in the afternoon) in an inaccessible wilderness near the Central Park.[1]

Old Mrs. Mingott's foreign daughters had become a legend. They never came back to see their mother, and the latter being, like many persons of active mind and dominating will, sedentary and corpulent in her habit, had philosophically remained at home. But the cream-coloured house (supposed to be modelled on the private hotels of the Parisian aristocracy) was there as a visible proof of her moral courage; and she throned in it, among pre-Revolutionary furniture and souvenirs of the Tuileries of Louis Napoleon (where she had shone in her middle age),[2] as placidly as if there were nothing peculiar in living above Thirty-fourth Street, or in having French windows that opened like doors instead of sashes that pushed up.

Every one (including Mr. Sillerton Jackson) was agreed that old Catherine had never had beauty—a gift which, in the eyes of New York, justified every success, and excused a certain

---

[1] Mrs. Mingott is likely modeled on Wharton's great-aunt, Mary Mason Jones, who built her mansion in the then-unfashionable area of Fifty-seventh St. and Fifth Ave. in the 1860s, at which time open country could still be found north of Fifty-ninth St.

[2] *Tuileries of Louis Napoleon*: Charles *Louis Napoleon* Bonaparte (1808-1873), known as Louis Napoleon or Napoleon III, occupied the *Tuileries* Palace after crowning himself emperor in 1852, thus bringing to a definitive end the more democratic period instigated by the revolutionary uprisings of 1848. His rule from 1852-1871 marks the Second Empire. The Communards burned down the Tuileries during the uprising of 1871.

number of failings. Unkind people said that, like her Imperial namesake,[1] she had won her way to success by strength of will and hardness of heart, and a kind of haughty effrontery that was somehow justified by the extreme decency and dignity of her private life. Mr. Manson Mingott had died when she was only twenty-eight, and had "tied up" the money with an additional caution born of the general distrust of the Spicers; but his bold young widow went her way fearlessly, mingled freely in foreign society, married her daughters in heaven knew what corrupt and fashionable circles, hobnobbed with Dukes and Ambassadors, associated familiarly with Papists,[2] entertained Opera singers, and was the intimate friend of Mme. Taglioni;[3] and all the while (as Sillerton Jackson was the first to proclaim) there had never been a breath on her reputation; the only respect, he always added, in which she differed from the earlier Catherine.

Mrs. Manson Mingott had long since succeeded in untying her husband's fortune, and had lived in affluence for half a century; but memories of her early straits had made her excessively thrifty, and though, when she bought a dress or a piece of furniture, she took care that it should be of the best, she could not bring herself to spend much on the transient pleasures of the table. Therefore, for totally different reasons, her food was as poor as Mrs. Archer's, and her wines did nothing to redeem it. Her relatives considered that the penury of her table discredited the Mingott name, which had always been associated with good living; but people continued to come to her in spite of the "made dishes" and flat champagne, and in reply to the remonstrances of her son Lovell (who tried to retrieve the family credit by having the best *chef* in New York) she used to say laughingly: "What's the use of two good cooks in one family, now that I've married the girls and can't eat sauces?"

Newland Archer, as he mused on these things, had once more turned his eyes toward the Mingott box. He saw that Mrs. Welland

---

1   *her Imperial namesake*: Catherine II of Russia (1729-1796), known as Catherine the Great. She married the Grand Duke Peter of Russia in 1745, and deposed her husband in 1762, proclaiming herself ruler and wielding total authority.

2   *Papists*: Catholics.

3   Marie *Taglioni* (1804-1884), Italian ballerina who was idolized in Paris for her romantic style of dancing.

and her sister-in-law were facing their semi-circle of critics with the Mingottian *aplomb* which old Catherine had inculcated in all her tribe, and that only May Welland betrayed, by a heightened colour (perhaps due to the knowledge that he was watching her) a sense of the gravity of the situation. As for the cause of the commotion, she sat gracefully in her corner of the box, her eyes fixed on the stage, and revealing, as she leaned forward, a little more shoulder and bosom than New York was accustomed to seeing, at least in ladies who had reasons for wishing to pass unnoticed.

Few things seemed to Newland Archer more awful than an offence against "Taste," that far-off divinity of whom "Form" was the mere visible representative and vicegerent. Madame Olenska's pale and serious face appealed to his fancy as suited to the occasion and to her unhappy situation; but the way her dress (which had no tucker) sloped away from her thin shoulders shocked and troubled him. He hated to think of May Welland's being exposed to the influence of a young woman so careless of the dictates of Taste.

"After all," he heard one of the younger men begin behind him (everybody talked through the Mephistopheles-and-Martha scenes), "after all, just *what* happened?"

"Well—she left him; nobody attempts to deny that."

"He's an awful brute, isn't he?" continued the young enquirer, a candid Thorley, who was evidently preparing to enter the lists as the lady's champion.

"The very worst; I knew him at Nice," said Lawrence Lefferts with authority. "A half-paralysed white sneering fellow—rather handsome head, but eyes with a lot of lashes. Well, I'll tell you the sort: when he wasn't with women he was collecting china. Paying any price for both, I understand."

There was a general laugh, and the young champion said: "Well, then—?"

"Well, then; she bolted with his secretary."

"Oh, I see." The champion's face fell.

"It didn't last long, though: I heard of her a few months later living alone in Venice. I believe Lovell Mingott went out to get her. He said she was desperately unhappy. That's all right—but this parading her at the Opera's another thing."

"Perhaps," young Thorley hazarded, "she's too unhappy to be left at home."

This was greeted with an irreverent laugh, and the youth blushed deeply, and tried to look as if he had meant to insinuate what knowing people called a "*double entendre*."

"Well—it's queer to have brought Miss Welland, anyhow," some one said in a low tone, with a side-glance at Archer.

"Oh, that's part of the campaign: Granny's orders, no doubt," Lefferts laughed. "When the old lady does a thing she does it thoroughly."

The act was ending, and there was a general stir in the box. Suddenly Newland Archer felt himself impelled to decisive action. The desire to be the first man to enter Mrs. Mingott's box, to proclaim to the waiting world his engagement to May Welland, and to see her through whatever difficulties her cousin's anomalous situation might involve her in; this impulse had abruptly overruled all scruples and hesitations, and sent him hurrying through the red corridors to the farther side of the house.

As he entered the box his eyes met Miss Welland's, and he saw that she had instantly understood his motive, though the family dignity which both considered so high a virtue would not permit her to tell him so. The persons of their world lived in an atmosphere of faint implications and pale delicacies, and the fact that he and she understood each other without a word seemed to the young man to bring them nearer than any explanation would have done. Her eyes said: "You see why Mamma brought me," and his answered: "I would not for the world have had you stay away."

"You know my niece Countess Olenska?" Mrs. Welland enquired as she shook hands with her future son-in-law. Archer bowed without extending his hand, as was the custom on being introduced to a lady; and Ellen Olenska bent her head slightly, keeping her own pale-gloved hands clasped on her huge fan of eagle feathers. Having greeted Mrs. Lovell Mingott, a large blonde lady in creaking satin, he sat down beside his betrothed, and said in a low tone: "I hope you've told Madame Olenska that we're engaged? I want everybody to know—I want you to let me announce it this evening at the ball."

Miss Welland's face grew rosy as the dawn, and she looked at him with radiant eyes. "If you can persuade Mamma," she said; "but why should we change what is already settled?" He made no answer but that which his eyes returned, and she added, still more confidently smiling: "Tell my cousin yourself: I give you leave. She says she used to play with you when you were children."

She made way for him by pushing back her chair, and promptly, and a little ostentatiously, with the desire that the whole house should see what he was doing, Archer seated himself at the Countess Olenska's side.

"We *did* use to play together, didn't we?" she asked, turning her grave eyes to his. "You were a horrid boy, and kissed me once behind a door; but it was your cousin Vandie Newland, who never looked at me, that I was in love with." Her glance swept the horse-shoe curve of boxes. "Ah, how this brings it all back to me—I see everybody here in knickerbockers and pantalettes!" she said, with her trailing slightly foreign accent, her eyes returning to his face.

Agreeable as their expression was, the young man was shocked that they should reflect so unseemly a picture of the august tribunal before which, at that very moment, her case was being tried. Nothing could be in worse taste than misplaced flippancy; and he answered somewhat stiffly: "Yes, you have been away a very long time."

"Oh, centuries and centuries; so long," she said, "that I'm sure I'm dead and buried, and this dear old place is heaven;" which, for reasons he could not define, struck Newland Archer as an even more disrespectful way of describing New York society.

III

It invariably happened in the same way.

Mrs. Julius Beaufort, on the night of her annual ball, never failed to appear at the Opera; indeed, she always gave her ball on an Opera night in order to emphasise her complete superiority to household cares, and her possession of a staff of servants competent to organise every detail of the entertainment in her absence.

The Beauforts' house was one of the few in New York that possessed a ball-room (it antedated even Mrs. Manson Mingott's and the Headly Chiverses'); and at a time when it was beginning to be thought "provincial" to put a "crash" over the drawing-room floor and move the furniture upstairs, the possession of a ballroom that was used for no other purpose, and left for three-hundred-and-sixty-four days of the year to shuttered darkness, with its gilt chairs stacked in a corner and its chandelier in a bag; this undoubted superiority was felt to compensate for whatever was regrettable in the Beaufort past.

Mrs. Archer, who was fond of coining her social philosophy into axioms, had once said: "We all have our pet common people—" and though the phrase was a daring one, its truth was secretly admitted in many an exclusive bosom. But the Beauforts were not exactly common; some people said they were even worse. Mrs. Beaufort belonged indeed to one of America's most honoured families; she had been the lovely Regina Dallas (of the South Carolina branch), a penniless beauty introduced to New York society by her cousin, the imprudent Medora Manson, who was always doing the wrong thing from the right motive. When one was related to the Mansons and the Rushworths one had a "*droit de cité*" (as Mr. Sillerton Jackson, who had frequented the Tuileries, called it) in New York society; but did one not forfeit it in marrying Julius Beaufort?

The question was: who *was* Beaufort? He passed for an Englishman, was agreeable, handsome, ill-tempered, hospitable and witty. He had come to America with letters of recommendation from old Mrs. Manson Mingott's English son-in-law, the banker, and had speedily made himself an important position in the world of affairs; but his habits were dissipated, his tongue was bitter, his antecedents were mysterious; and when Medora Manson announced her cousin's engagement to him it was felt to be one more act of folly in poor Medora's long record of imprudences.

But folly is as often justified of her children as wisdom, and two years after young Mrs. Beaufort's marriage it was admitted that she had the most distinguished house in New York. No one knew exactly how the miracle was accomplished. She was indolent, passive, the caustic even called her dull; but dressed like an idol,

hung with pearls, growing younger and blonder and more beautiful each year, she throned in Mr. Beaufort's heavy brown-stone
palace, and drew all the world there without lifting her jewelled
little finger. The knowing people said it was Beaufort himself who
trained the servants, taught the *chef* new dishes, told the gardeners
what hot-house flowers to grow for the dinner-table and the
drawing-rooms, selected the guests, brewed the after-dinner punch
and dictated the little notes his wife wrote to her friends. If he did,
these domestic activities were privately performed, and he
presented to the world the appearance of a careless and hospitable
millionaire strolling into his own drawing-room with the detachment of an invited guest, and saying: "My wife's gloxinias are a
marvel, aren't they? I believe she gets them out from Kew."[1]

Mr. Beaufort's secret, people were agreed, was the way he
carried things off. It was all very well to whisper that he had been
"helped" to leave England by the international banking-house
in which he had been employed; he carried off that rumour as
easily as the rest—though New York's business conscience was
no less sensitive than its moral standard—he carried everything
before him, and all New York into his drawing rooms, and for
over twenty years now people had said they were "going to the
Beauforts'" with the same tone of security as if they had said
they were going to Mrs. Manson Mingott's, and with the added
satisfaction of knowing they would get hot canvas-back ducks
and vintage wines, instead of tepid Veuve Clicquot without a year
and warmed-up croquettes from Philadelphia.

Mrs. Beaufort, then, had as usual appeared in her box just
before the Jewel Song;[2] and when, again as usual, she rose at the
end of the third act, drew her opera cloak about her lovely shoulders, and disappeared, New York knew that meant that half an
hour later the ball would begin.

The Beaufort house was one that New Yorkers were proud to
show to foreigners, especially on the night of the annual ball. The

---

1 Royal Botanic Gardens at *Kew*, the site of a former royal estate in the London
   borough of Richmond.
2 *Jewel Song:* "Ô Dieu! que de bijoux," probably the most famous aria of the opera
   Faust. It occurs in Act III, just prior to the scene described in the opening pages of
   the novel.

Beauforts had been among the first people in New York to own
their own red velvet carpet and have it rolled down the steps by
their own footmen, under their own awning, instead of hiring it
with the supper and the ball-room chairs. They had also inaugurated the custom of letting the ladies take their cloaks off in the
hall, instead of shuffling up to the hostess's bedroom and recurling
their hair with the aid of the gas-burner; Beaufort was understood
to have said that he supposed all his wife's friends had maids who
saw to it that they were properly *coiffées* when they left home.

Then the house had been boldly planned with a ball-room,
so that, instead of squeezing through a narrow passage to get to
it (as at the Chiverses') one marched solemnly down a vista of
enfiladed drawing-rooms (the sea-green, the crimson and the
bouton d'or), seeing from afar the many-candled lustres reflected
in the polished parquetry, and beyond that the depths of a
conservatory where camellias and tree-ferns arched their costly
foliage over seats of black and gold bamboo.

Newland Archer, as became a young man of his position,
strolled in somewhat late. He had left his overcoat with the silk-
stockinged footmen (the stockings were one of Beaufort's few
fatuities), had dawdled a while in the library hung with Spanish
leather and furnished with Buhl and malachite, where a few men
were chatting and putting on their dancing-gloves, and had
finally joined the line of guests whom Mrs. Beaufort was receiving on the threshold of the crimson drawing-room.

Archer was distinctly nervous. He had not gone back to his
club after the Opera (as the young bloods usually did), but, the
night being fine, had walked for some distance up Fifth Avenue
before turning back in the direction of the Beauforts' house. He
was definitely afraid that the Mingotts might be going too far;
that, in fact, they might have Granny Mingott's orders to bring
the Countess Olenska to the ball.

From the tone of the club box he had perceived how grave a
mistake that would be; and, though he was more than ever determined to "see the thing through," he felt less chivalrously eager
to champion his betrothed's cousin than before their brief talk
at the Opera.

Wandering on to the *bouton d'or* drawing-room (where

Beaufort had had the audacity to hang "Love Victorious," the much-discussed nude of Bouguereau)[1] Archer found Mrs. Welland and her daughter standing near the ball-room door. Couples were already gliding over the floor beyond: the light of the wax candles fell on revolving tulle skirts, on girlish heads wreathed with modest blossoms, on the dashing aigrettes and ornaments of the young married women's *coiffures*, and on the glitter of highly glazed shirt-fronts and fresh glacé gloves.

Miss Welland, evidently about to join the dancers, hung on the threshold, her lilies-of-the-valley in her hand (she carried no other bouquet), her face a little pale, her eyes burning with a candid excitement. A group of young men and girls were gathered about her, and there was much hand-clasping, laughing and pleasantry on which Mrs. Welland, standing slightly apart, shed the beam of a qualified approval. It was evident that Miss Welland was in the act of announcing her engagement, while her mother affected the air of parental reluctance considered suitable to the occasion.

Archer paused a moment. It was at his express wish that the announcement had been made, and yet it was not thus that he would have wished to have his happiness known. To proclaim it in the heat and noise of a crowded ball-room was to rob it of the fine bloom of privacy which should belong to things nearest the heart. His joy was so deep that this blurring of the surface left its essence untouched; but he would have liked to keep the surface pure too. It was something of a satisfaction to find that May Welland shared this feeling. Her eyes fled to his beseechingly, and their look said: "Remember, we're doing this because it's right."

No appeal could have found a more immediate response in Archer's breast; but he wished that the necessity of their action had been represented by some ideal reason, and not simply by poor Ellen Olenska. The group about Miss Welland made way for him with significant smiles, and after taking his share of the

---

[1]   Adolphe William *Bouguereau* (1825–1905), French painter famous for nudes and religious subjects. There is no Bouguereau painting entitled "Love Victorious"; Wharton may have in mind the 1857 painting "Triumph of Venus" or the 1879 "Birth of Venus." See *A Backward Glance* (p. 61), where Wharton mentions Mr. William Astor's "audacious acquisition" of a Bouguereau Venus.

felicitations he drew his betrothed into the middle of the ball-room floor and put his arm about her waist.

"Now we shan't have to talk," he said, smiling into her candid eyes, as they floated away on the soft waves of the Blue Danube.[1]

She made no answer. Her lips trembled into a smile, but the eyes remained distant and serious, as if bent on some ineffable vision. "Dear," Archer whispered, pressing her to him: it was borne in on him that the first hours of being engaged, even if spent in a ball-room, had in them something grave and sacramental. What a new life it was going to be, with this whiteness, radiance, goodness at one's side!

The dance over, the two, as became an affianced couple, wandered into the conservatory; and sitting behind a tall screen of tree-ferns and camellias Newland pressed her gloved hand to his lips.

"You see I did as you asked me to," she said.

"Yes: I couldn't wait," he answered smiling. After a moment he added: "Only I wish it hadn't had to be at a ball."

"Yes, I know." She met his glance comprehendingly. "But after all—even here we're alone together, aren't we?"

"Oh, dearest—always!" Archer cried.

Evidently she was always going to understand; she was always going to say the right thing. The discovery made the cup of his bliss overflow, and he went on gaily: "The worst of it is that I want to kiss you and I can't." As he spoke he took a swift glance about the conservatory, assured himself of their momentary privacy, and catching her to him laid a fugitive pressure on her lips. To counteract the audacity of this proceeding he led her to a bamboo sofa in a less secluded part of the conservatory, and sitting down beside her broke a lily-of-the-valley from her bouquet. She sat silent, and the world lay like a sunlit valley at their feet.

"Did you tell my cousin Ellen?" she asked presently, as if she spoke through a dream.

He roused himself, and remembered that he had not done so. Some invincible repugnance to speak of such things to the strange foreign woman had checked the words on his lips.

---

[1] The *Blue Danube* Waltz (1867) by Johann Strauss, Jr. (1825-1899), Austrian composer.

"No—I hadn't the chance after all," he said, fibbing hastily.

"Ah." She looked disappointed, but gently resolved on gaining her point. "You must, then, for I didn't either; and I shouldn't like her to think—"

"Of course not. But aren't you, after all, the person to do it?"

She pondered on this. "If I'd done it at the right time, yes: but now that there's been a delay I think you must explain that I'd asked you to tell her at the Opera, before our speaking about it to everybody here. Otherwise she might think I had forgotten her. You see, she's one of the family, and she's been away so long that she's rather—sensitive."

Archer looked at her glowingly. "Dear and great angel! Of course I'll tell her." He glanced a trifle apprehensively toward the crowded ball-room. "But I haven't seen her yet. Has she come?"

"No; at the last minute she decided not to."

"At the last minute?" he echoed, betraying his surprise that she should ever have considered the alternative possible.

"Yes. She's awfully fond of dancing," the young girl answered simply. "But suddenly she made up her mind that her dress wasn't smart enough for a ball, though we thought it so lovely; and so my aunt had to take her home."

"Oh, well"—said Archer with happy indifference. Nothing about his betrothed pleased him more than her resolute determination to carry to its utmost limit that ritual of ignoring the "unpleasant" in which they had both been brought up.

"She knows as well as I do," he reflected, "the real reason of her cousin's staying away; but I shall never let her see by the least sign that I am conscious of there being a shadow of a shade on poor Ellen Olenska's reputation."

IV

In the course of the next day the first of the usual betrothal visits were exchanged. The New York ritual was precise and inflexible in such matters; and in conformity with it Newland Archer first went with his mother and sister to call on Mrs. Welland, after which he and Mrs. Welland and May drove out to old Mrs. Manson Mingott's to receive that venerable ancestress's blessing.

A visit to Mrs. Manson Mingott was always an amusing episode to the young man. The house in itself was already an historic document, though not, of course, as venerable as certain other old family houses in University Place and lower Fifth Avenue. Those were of the purest 1830, with a grim harmony of cabbage-rose-garlanded carpets, rosewood consoles, round-arched fire-places with black marble mantels, and immense glazed book-cases of mahogany; whereas old Mrs. Mingott, who had built her house later, had bodily cast out the massive furniture of her prime, and mingled with the Mingott heirlooms the frivolous upholstery of the Second Empire. It was her habit to sit in a window of her sitting-room on the ground floor, as if watching calmly for life and fashion to flow northward to her solitary doors. She seemed in no hurry to have them come, for her patience was equalled by her confidence. She was sure that presently the hoardings, the quarries, the one-story saloons, the wooden green-houses in ragged gardens, and the rocks from which goats surveyed the scene, would vanish before the advance of residences as stately as her own—perhaps (for she was an impartial woman) even statelier; and that the cobblestones over which the old clattering omnibuses bumped would be replaced by smooth asphalt, such as people reported having seen in Paris. Meanwhile, as every one she cared to see came to *her* (and she could fill her rooms as easily as the Beauforts, and without adding a single item to the *menu* of her suppers), she did not suffer from her geographic isolation.

The immense accretion of flesh which had descended on her in middle life like a flood of lava on a doomed city had changed her from a plump active little woman with a neatly-turned foot and ankle into something as vast and august as a natural phenomenon. She had accepted this submergence as philosophically as all her other trials, and now, in extreme old age, was rewarded by presenting to her mirror an almost unwrinkled expanse of firm pink and white flesh, in the centre of which the traces of a small face survived as if awaiting excavation. A flight of smooth double chins led down to the dizzy depths of a still-snowy bosom veiled in snowy muslins that were held in place by a miniature portrait of the late Mr. Mingott; and around and below, wave after wave of black silk surged away over the edges of a capacious armchair, with two tiny white hands poised like gulls on the surface of the billows. The burden of Mrs. Manson Mingott's flesh had long since made it impossible for her to go up and down stairs, and with characteristic independence she had made her reception rooms upstairs and established herself (in flagrant violation of all the New York proprieties) on the ground floor of her house; so that, as you sat in her sitting-room window with her, you caught (through a door that was always open, and a looped-back yellow damask portière) the unexpected vista of a bedroom with a huge low bed upholstered like a sofa, and a toilet-table with frivolous lace flounces and a gilt-framed mirror.

Her visitors were startled and fascinated by the foreignness of this arrangement, which recalled scenes in French fiction, and architectural incentives to immorality such as the simple American had never dreamed of. That was how women with lovers lived in the wicked old societies, in apartments with all the rooms on one floor, and all the indecent propinquities that their novels described. It amused Newland Archer (who had secretly situated the love-scenes of "Monsieur de Camors" in Mrs. Mingott's bedroom)[1] to picture her blameless life led in the stage-setting of adultery; but he said to himself, with considerable admiration, that if a lover had been what she wanted, the intrepid woman would have had him too.

To the general relief the Countess Olenska was not present in her grandmother's drawing-room during the visit of the betrothed couple. Mrs. Mingott said she had gone out; which, on a day of such glaring sunlight, and at the "shopping hour," seemed in itself an indelicate thing for a compromised woman to do. But at any rate it spared them the embarrassment of her presence, and the faint shadow that her unhappy past might seem to shed on their radiant future. The visit went off successfully, as was to have been expected. Old Mrs. Mingott was delighted with

---

1   *Monsieur de Camors* (1867), by popular French novelist Octave Feuillet (1821-1890). It deals with an adulterous liason.

the engagement, which, being long foreseen by watchful relatives, had been carefully passed upon in family council; and the engagement ring, a large thick sapphire set in invisible claws, met with her unqualified admiration.

"It's the new setting: of course it shows the stone beautifully, but it looks a little bare to old-fashioned eyes," Mrs. Welland had explained, with a conciliatory side-glance at her future son-in-law.

"Old-fashioned eyes? I hope you don't mean mine, my dear? I like all the novelties," said the ancestress, lifting the stone to her small bright orbs, which no glasses had ever disfigured. "Very handsome," she added, returning the jewel; "very liberal. In my time a cameo set in pearls was thought sufficient. But it's the hand that sets off the ring, isn't it, my dear Mr. Archer?" and she waved one of her tiny hands, with small pointed nails and rolls of aged fat encircling the wrist like ivory bracelets. "Mine was modelled in Rome by the great Ferrigiani. You should have May's done: no doubt he'll have it done, my child. Her hand is large—it's these modern sports that spread the joints—but the skin is white.—And when's the wedding to be?" she broke off, fixing her eyes on Archer's face.

"Oh—" Mrs. Welland murmured, while the young man, smiling at his betrothed, replied: "As soon as ever it can, if only you'll back me up, Mrs. Mingott."

"We must give them time to get to know each other a little better, mamma," Mrs. Welland interposed, with the proper affectation of reluctance; to which the ancestress rejoined: "Know each other? Fiddlesticks! Everybody in New York has always known everybody. Let the young man have his way, my dear; don't wait till the bubble's off the wine. Marry them before Lent; I may catch pneumonia any winter now, and I want to give the wedding-breakfast."

These successive statements were received with the proper expressions of amusement, incredulity and gratitude; and the visit was breaking up in a vein of mild pleasantry when the door opened to admit the Countess Olenska, who entered in bonnet and mantle followed by the unexpected figure of Julius Beaufort.

There was a cousinly murmur of pleasure between the ladies, and Mrs. Mingott held out Ferrigiani's model to the banker. "Ha!

Beaufort, this is a rare favour!" (She had an odd foreign way of addressing men by their surnames.)

"Thanks. I wish it might happen oftener," said the visitor in his easy arrogant way. "I'm generally so tied down; but I met the Countess Ellen in Madison Square, and she was good enough to let me walk home with her."

"Ah—I hope the house will be gayer, now that Ellen's here!" cried Mrs. Mingott with a glorious effrontery. "Sit down—sit down, Beaufort: push up the yellow armchair; now I've got you I want a good gossip. I hear your ball was magnificent; and I understand you invited Mrs. Lemuel Struthers? Well—I've a curiosity to see the woman myself."

She had forgotten her relatives, who were drifting out into the hall under Ellen Olenska's guidance. Old Mrs. Mingott had always professed a great admiration for Julius Beaufort, and there was a kind of kinship in their cool domineering way and their short-cuts through the conventions. Now she was eagerly curious to know what had decided the Beauforts to invite (for the first time) Mrs. Lemuel Struthers, the widow of Struthers's Shoe-polish, who had returned the previous year from a long initiatory sojourn in Europe to lay siege to the tight little citadel of New York. "Of course if you and Regina invite her the thing is settled. Well, we need new blood and new money—and I hear she's still very good-looking," the carnivorous old lady declared.

In the hall, while Mrs. Welland and May drew on their furs, Archer saw that the Countess Olenska was looking at him with a faintly questioning smile.

"Of course you know already—about May and me," he said, answering her look with a shy laugh. "She scolded me for not giving you the news last night at the Opera: I had her orders to tell you that we were engaged—but I couldn't, in that crowd."

The smile passed from Countess Olenska's eyes to her lips: she looked younger, more like the bold brown Ellen Mingott of his boyhood. "Of course I know; yes. And I'm so glad. But one doesn't tell such things first in a crowd." The ladies were on the threshold and she held out her hand.

"Good-bye; come and see me some day," she said, still looking at Archer.

In the carriage, on the way down Fifth Avenue, they talked pointedly of Mrs. Mingott, of her age, her spirit, and all her wonderful attributes. No one alluded to Ellen Olenska; but Archer knew that Mrs. Welland was thinking: "It's a mistake for Ellen to be seen, the very day after her arrival, parading up Fifth Avenue at the crowded hour with Julius Beaufort—" and the young man himself mentally added: "And she ought to know that a man who's just engaged doesn't spend his time calling on married women. But I daresay in the set she's lived in they do— they never do anything else." And, in spite of the cosmopolitan views on which he prided himself, he thanked heaven that he was a New Yorker, and about to ally himself with one of his own kind.

V

THE next evening old Mr. Sillerton Jackson came to dine with the Archers.

Mrs. Archer was a shy woman and shrank from society; but she liked to be well-informed as to its doings. Her old friend Mr. Sillerton Jackson applied to the investigation of his friends' affairs the patience of a collector and the science of a naturalist; and his sister, Miss Sophy Jackson, who lived with him, and was entertained by all the people who could not secure her much-sought-after brother, brought home bits of minor gossip that filled out usefully the gaps in his picture.

Therefore, whenever anything happened that Mrs. Archer wanted to know about, she asked Mr. Jackson to dine; and as she honoured few people with her invitations, and as she and her daughter Janey were an excellent audience, Mr. Jackson usually came himself instead of sending his sister. If he could have dictated all the conditions, he would have chosen the evenings when Newland was out; not because the young man was uncongenial to him (the two got on capitally at their club) but because the old anecdotist sometimes felt, on Newland's part, a tendency to weigh his evidence that the ladies of the family never showed.

Mr. Jackson, if perfection had been attainable on earth, would also have asked that Mrs. Archer's food should be a little better.

But then New York, as far back as the mind of man could travel, had been divided into the two great fundamental groups of the Mingotts and Mansons and all their clan, who cared about eating and clothes and money, and the Archer-Newland-van-der-Luyden tribe, who were devoted to travel, horticulture and the best fiction, and looked down on the grosser forms of pleasure. You couldn't have everything, after all. If you dined with the Lovell Mingotts you got canvas-back and terrapin and vintage wines; at Adeline Archer's you could talk about Alpine scenery and "The Marble Faun";[1] and luckily the Archer Madeira had gone round the Cape. Therefore when a friendly summons came from Mrs. Archer, Mr. Jackson, who was a true eclectic, would usually say to his sister: "I've been a little gouty since my last dinner at the Lovell Mingotts'—it will do me good to diet at Adeline's."

Mrs. Archer, who had long been a widow, lived with her son and daughter in West Twenty-eighth Street. An upper floor was dedicated to Newland, and the two women squeezed themselves into narrower quarters below. In an unclouded harmony of tastes and interests they cultivated ferns in Wardian cases, made macramé lace and wool embroidery on linen, collected American revolutionary glazed ware, subscribed to "Good Words," and read Ouida's novels for the sake of the Italian atmosphere.[2] (They preferred those about peasant life, because of the descriptions of scenery and the pleasanter sentiments, though in general they liked novels about people in society, whose motives and habits were more comprehensible, spoke severely of Dickens, who "had never drawn a gentleman," and considered Thackeray less at home in the great world than Bulwer—who, however, was beginning to be thought old-fashioned.)[3]

---

[1] *The Marble Faun* (1860), last novel by American writer Nathaniel Hawthorne (1804-1864).

[2] *Good Words*: a popular English monthly magazine (1860-1906) whose contributors included Anthony Trollope, Charles Kingsley, and Thomas Hardy. *Ouida*: pen name of Marie Louise de la Ramée (1839-1908), prolific and popular English novelist and journalist.

[3] The most prominent English novelists of the day: Charles *Dickens* (1812-1870), whose works include *Oliver Twist* (1837), *Bleak House* (1853), and *Great Expectations* (1861); William Makepeace *Thackeray* (1811-1863), author of *Vanity Fair* (1847) and *Pendennis* (1848-50); Edward George Earle *Bulwer*-Lytton (1803-1873).

Mrs. and Miss Archer were both great lovers of scenery. It was what they principally sought and admired on their occasional travels abroad; considering architecture and painting as subjects for men, and chiefly for learned persons who read Ruskin.[1] Mrs. Archer had been born a Newland, and mother and daughter, who were as like as sisters, were both, as people said, "true Newlands"; tall, pale, and slightly round-shouldered, with long noses, sweet smiles and a kind of drooping distinction like that in certain faded Reynolds portraits.[2] Their physical resemblance would have been complete if an elderly *embonpoint* had not stretched Mrs. Archer's black brocade, while Miss Archer's brown and purple poplins hung, as the years went on, more and more slackly on her virgin frame.

Mentally, the likeness between them, as Newland was aware, was less complete than their identical mannerisms often made it appear. The long habit of living together in mutually dependent intimacy had given them the same vocabulary, and the same habit of beginning their phrases "Mother thinks" or "Janey thinks," according as one or the other wished to advance an opinion of her own; but in reality, while Mrs. Archer's serene unimaginativeness rested easily in the accepted and familiar, Janey was subject to starts and aberrations of fancy welling up from springs of suppressed romance.

Mother and daughter adored each other and revered their son and brother; and Archer loved them with a tenderness made compunctious and uncritical by the sense of their exaggerated admiration, and by his secret satisfaction in it. After all, he thought it a good thing for a man to have his authority respected in his own house, even if his sense of humour sometimes made him question the force of his mandate.

On this occasion the young man was very sure that Mr. Jackson would rather have had him dine out; but he had his own reasons for not doing so.

---

[1]   John *Ruskin* (1819-1900), influential English art critic, famous for *Modern Painters* (1843, 1846, 1856), *Seven Lamps of Architecture* (1849), and *The Stones of Venice* (1853).

[2]   Sir Joshua *Reynolds* (1723-1792), English society portrait painter, whose paintings include "The Age of Innocence." This 1788 portrait features a young girl in profile sitting against a tree and clasping her hands to her breast.

Of course old Jackson wanted to talk about Ellen Olenska, and of course Mrs. Archer and Janey wanted to hear what he had to tell. All three would be slightly embarrassed by Newland's presence, now that his prospective relation to the Mingott clan had been made known; and the young man waited with an amused curiosity to see how they would turn the difficulty.

They began, obliquely, by talking about Mrs. Lemuel Struthers.

"It's a pity the Beauforts asked her," Mrs. Archer said gently. "But then Regina always does what he tells her; and *Beaufort*—"

"Certain *nuances* escape Beaufort," said Mr. Jackson, cautiously inspecting the broiled shad, and wondering for the thousandth time why Mrs. Archer's cook always burnt the roe to a cinder. (Newland, who had long shared his wonder, could always detect it in the older man's expression of melancholy disapproval.)

"Oh, necessarily; Beaufort is a vulgar man," said Mrs. Archer. "My grandfather Newland always used to say to my mother: 'Whatever you do, don't let that fellow Beaufort be introduced to the girls.' But at least he's had the advantage of associating with gentlemen; in England too, they say. It's all very mysterious—" She glanced at Janey and paused. She and Janey knew every fold of the Beaufort mystery, but in public Mrs. Archer continued to assume that the subject was not one for the unmarried.

"But this Mrs. Struthers," Mrs. Archer continued; "what did you say *she* was, Sillerton?"

"Out of a mine: or rather out of the saloon at the head of the pit. Then with Living Wax-Works, touring New England. After the police broke *that* up, they say she lived—" Mr. Jackson in his turn glanced at Janey, whose eyes began to bulge from under her prominent lids. There were still hiatuses for her in Mrs. Struthers's past.

"Then," Mr. Jackson continued (and Archer saw he was wondering why no one had told the butler never to slice cucumbers with a steel knife), "then Lemuel Struthers came along. They say his advertiser used the girl's head for the shoe-polish posters; her hair's intensely black, you know—the Egyptian style. Anyhow, he—eventually—married her." There were volumes of innuendo in the way the "eventually" was spaced, and each syllable given its due stress.

"Oh, well—at the pass we've come to nowadays, it doesn't matter," said Mrs. Archer indifferently. The ladies were not really interested in Mrs. Struthers just then; the subject of Ellen Olenska was too fresh and too absorbing to them. Indeed, Mrs. Struthers's name had been introduced by Mrs. Archer only that she might presently be able to say: "And Newland's new cousin—Countess Olenska? Was *she* at the ball too?"

There was a faint touch of sarcasm in the reference to her son, and Archer knew it and had expected it. Even Mrs. Archer, who was seldom unduly pleased with human events, had been altogether glad of her son's engagement. ("Especially after that silly business with Mrs. Rushworth," as she had remarked to Janey, alluding to what had once seemed to Newland a tragedy of which his soul would always bear the scar.) There was no better match in New York than May Welland, look at the question from whatever point you chose. Of course such a marriage was only what Newland was entitled to; but young men are so foolish and incalculable—and some women so ensnaring and unscrupulous—that it was nothing short of a miracle to see one's only son safe past the Siren Isle and in the haven of a blameless domesticity.[1]

All this Mrs. Archer felt, and her son knew she felt; but he knew also that she had been perturbed by the premature announcement of his engagement, or rather by its cause; and it was for that reason—because on the whole he was a tender and indulgent master—that he had stayed at home that evening. "It's not that I don't approve of the Mingotts' *esprit de corps*; but why Newland's engagement should be mixed up with that Olenska woman's comings and goings I don't see," Mrs. Archer grumbled to Janey, the only witness of her slight lapses from perfect sweetness.

She had behaved beautifully—and in beautiful behaviour she was unsurpassed—during the call on Mrs. Welland; but Newland knew (and his betrothed doubtless guessed) that all through the visit she and Janey were nervously on the watch for Madame Olenska's possible intrusion; and when they left the house together

---

[1] In Homer's *Odyssey*, the *Sirens* were enchantresses who lured sailors to their deaths with seductive songs. Odysseus saved his crew by stuffing his sailors' ears with wax.

she had permitted herself to say to her son: "I'm thankful that Augusta Welland received us alone."

These indications of inward disturbance moved Archer the more that he too felt that the Mingotts had gone a little too far. But, as it was against all the rules of their code that the mother and son should ever allude to what was uppermost in their thoughts, he simply replied: "Oh, well, there's always a phase of family parties to be gone through when one gets engaged, and the sooner it's over the better." At which his mother merely pursed her lips under the lace veil that hung down from her grey velvet bonnet trimmed with frosted grapes.

Her revenge, he felt—her lawful revenge—would be to "draw" Mr. Jackson that evening on the Countess Olenska; and, having publicly done his duty as a future member of the Mingott clan, the young man had no objection to hearing the lady discussed in private—except that the subject was already beginning to bore him.

Mr. Jackson had helped himself to a slice of the tepid *filet* which the mournful butler had handed him with a look as sceptical as his own, and had rejected the mushroom sauce after a scarcely perceptible sniff. He looked baffled and hungry, and Archer reflected that he would probably finish his meal on Ellen Olenska.

Mr. Jackson leaned back in his chair, and glanced up at the candlelit Archers, Newlands and van der Luydens hanging in dark frames on the dark walls.

"Ah, how your grandfather Archer loved a good dinner, my dear Newland!" he said, his eyes on the portrait of a plump full-chested young man in a stock and a blue coat, with a view of a white-columned country-house behind him. "Well—well—well ... I wonder what he would have said to all these foreign marriages!"

Mrs. Archer ignored the allusion to the ancestral *cuisine* and Mr. Jackson continued with deliberation: "No, she was *not* at the ball."

"Ah—" Mrs. Archer murmured, in a tone that implied: "She had that decency."

"Perhaps the Beauforts don't know her," Janey suggested, with her artless malice.

Mr. Jackson gave a faint sip, as if he had been tasting invisible

Madeira. "Mrs. Beaufort may not—but Beaufort certainly does, for she was seen walking up Fifth Avenue this afternoon with him by the whole of New York."

"Mercy—" moaned Mrs. Archer, evidently perceiving the uselessness of trying to ascribe the actions of foreigners to a sense of delicacy.

"I wonder if she wears a round hat or a bonnet in the afternoon," Janey speculated. "At the Opera I know she had on dark blue velvet, perfectly plain and flat—like a night-gown."

"Janey!" said her mother; and Miss Archer blushed and tried to look audacious.

"It was, at any rate, in better taste not to go to the ball," Mrs. Archer continued.

A spirit of perversity moved her son to rejoin: "I don't think it was a question of taste with her. May said she meant to go, and then decided that the dress in question wasn't smart enough."

Mrs. Archer smiled at this confirmation of her inference. "Poor Ellen," she simply remarked; adding compassionately: "We must always bear in mind what an eccentric bringing-up Medora Manson gave her. What can you expect of a girl who was allowed to wear black satin at her coming-out ball?"

"Ah—don't I remember her in it!" said Mr. Jackson; adding: "Poor girl!" in the tone of one who, while enjoying the memory, had fully understood at the time what the sight portended.

"It's odd," Janey remarked, "that she should have kept such an ugly name as Ellen. I should have changed it to Elaine." She glanced about the table to see the effect of this.

Her brother laughed. "Why Elaine?"

"I don't know; it sounds more—more Polish," said Janey, blushing.

"It sounds more conspicuous; and that can hardly be what she wishes," said Mrs. Archer distantly.

"Why not?" broke in her son, growing suddenly argumentative. "Why shouldn't she be conspicuous if she chooses? Why should she slink about as if it were she who had disgraced herself? She's 'poor Ellen' certainly, because she had the bad luck to make a wretched marriage; but I don't see that that's a reason for hiding her head as if she were the culprit."

"That, I suppose," said Mr. Jackson, speculatively, "is the line the Mingotts mean to take."

The young man reddened. "I didn't have to wait for their cue, if that's what you mean, sir. Madame Olenska has had an unhappy life: that doesn't make her an outcast."

"There are rumours," began Mr. Jackson, glancing at Janey.

"Oh, I know: the secretary," the young man took him up. "Nonsense, mother; Janey's grown-up. They say, don't they," he went on, "that the secretary helped her to get away from her brute of a husband, who kept her practically a prisoner? Well, what if he did? I hope there isn't a man among us who wouldn't have done the same in such a case."

Mr. Jackson glanced over his shoulder to say to the sad butler: "Perhaps ... that sauce ... just a little, after all—"; then, having helped himself, he remarked: "I'm told she's looking for a house. She means to live here."

"I hear she means to get a divorce," said Janey boldly.

"I hope she will!" Archer exclaimed.

The word had fallen like a bombshell in the pure and tranquil atmosphere of the Archer dining-room. Mrs. Archer raised her delicate eye-brows in the particular curve that signified: "The butler—" and the young man, himself mindful of the bad taste of discussing such intimate matters in public, hastily branched off into an account of his visit to old Mrs. Mingott.

After dinner, according to immemorial custom, Mrs. Archer and Janey trailed their long silk draperies up to the drawing-room, where, while the gentlemen smoked below stairs, they sat beside a Carcel lamp with an engraved globe, facing each other across a rosewood work-table with a green silk bag under it, and stitched at the two ends of a tapestry band of field-flowers destined to adorn an "occasional" chair in the drawing-room of young Mrs. Newland Archer.

While this rite was in progress in the drawing-room, Archer settled Mr. Jackson in an armchair near the fire in the Gothic library and handed him a cigar. Mr. Jackson sank into the armchair with satisfaction, lit his cigar with perfect confidence (it was Newland who bought them), and stretching his thin old ankles to the coals, said: "You say the secretary merely helped her to get away, my dear fellow? Well, he was still helping her a year later, then; for somebody met 'em living at Lausanne together." Newland reddened. "Living together? Well, why not? Who had the right to make her life over if she hadn't? I'm sick of the' hypocrisy that would bury alive a woman of her age if her husband prefers to live with harlots."

He stopped and turned away angrily to light his cigar. "Women ought to be free—as free as we are," he declared, making a discovery of which he was too irritated to measure the terrific consequences.

Mr. Sillerton Jackson stretched his ankles nearer the coals and emitted a sardonic whistle.

"Well," he said after a pause, "apparently Count Olenski takes your view; for I never heard of his having lifted a finger to get his wife back."

VI

THAT evening, after Mr. Jackson had taken himself away, and the ladies had retired to their chintz-curtained bedroom, Newland Archer mounted thoughtfully to his own study. A vigilant hand had, as usual, kept the fire alive and the lamp trimmed; and the room, with its rows and rows of books, its bronze and steel statuettes of "The Fencers" on the mantelpiece and its many photographs of famous pictures, looked singularly home-like and welcoming.

As he dropped into his armchair near the fire his eyes rested on a large photograph of May Welland, which the young girl had given him in the first days of their romance, and which had now displaced all the other portraits on the table. With a new sense of awe he looked at the frank forehead, serious eyes and gay innocent mouth of the young creature whose soul's custodian he was to be. That terrifying product of the social system he belonged to and believed in, the young girl who knew nothing and expected everything, looked back at him like a stranger through May Welland's familiar features; and once more it was borne in on him that marriage was not the safe anchorage he had been taught to think, but a voyage on uncharted seas.

The case of the Countess Olenska had stirred up old settled convictions and set them drifting dangerously through his mind. His own exclamation: "Women should be free—as free as we are," struck to the root of a problem that it was agreed in his world to regard as non-existent. "Nice" women, however wronged, would never claim the kind of freedom he meant, and generous-minded men like himself were therefore—in the heat of argument—the more chivalrously ready to concede it to them. Such verbal generosities were in fact only a humbugging disguise of the inexorable conventions that tied things together and bound people down to the old pattern. But here he was pledged to defend, on the part of his betrothed's cousin, conduct that, on his own wife's part, would justify him in calling down on her all the thunders of Church and State. Of course the dilemma was purely hypothetical; since he wasn't a blackguard Polish nobleman, it was absurd to speculate what his wife's rights would be if he *were*. But Newland Archer was too imaginative not to feel that, in his case and May's, the tie might gall for reasons far less gross and palpable. What could he and she really know of each other, since it was his duty, as a "decent" fellow, to conceal his past from her, and hers, as a marriageable girl, to have no past to conceal? What if, for some one of the subtler reasons that would tell with both of them, they should tire of each other, misunderstand or irritate each other? He reviewed his friends' marriages—the supposedly happy ones—and saw none that answered, even remotely, to the passionate and tender comradeship which he pictured as his permanent relation with May Welland. He perceived that such a picture presupposed, on her part, the experience, the versatility, the freedom of judgment, which she had been carefully trained not to possess; and with a shiver of foreboding he saw his marriage becoming what most of the other marriages about him were: a dull association of material and social interests held together by ignorance on the one side and hypocrisy on the other. Lawrence Lefferts occurred to him as the husband who had most completely realised this enviable ideal. As became the high-priest of form, he had formed a wife so completely to his own convenience that, in the most conspicuous moments of his frequent love-affairs with other men's wives, she went about in smiling unconsciousness, saying that "Lawrence was so frightfully strict"; and had been known to blush indignantly, and avert her gaze, when some one alluded in her presence to the fact that Julius Beaufort (as became a "foreigner" of doubtful origin) had what was known in New York as "another establishment."

Archer tried to console himself with the thought that he was not quite such an ass as Larry Lefferts, nor May such a simpleton as poor Gertrude; but the difference was after all one of intelligence and not of standards. In reality they all lived in a kind of hieroglyphic world, where the real thing was never said or done or even thought, but only represented by a set of arbitrary signs; as when Mrs. Welland, who knew exactly why Archer had pressed her to announce her daughter's engagement at the Beaufort ball (and had indeed expected him to do no less), yet felt obliged to simulate reluctance, and the air of having had her hand forced, quite as, in the books on Primitive Man that people of advanced culture were beginning to read, the savage bride is dragged with shrieks from her parents' tent.[1]

The result, of course, was that the young girl who was the centre of this elaborate system of mystification remained the more inscrutable for her very frankness and assurance. She was frank, poor darling, because she had nothing to conceal, assured because she knew of nothing to be on her guard against; and with no better preparation than this, she was to be plunged overnight into what people evasively called "the facts of life."

The young man was sincerely but placidly in love. He delighted in the radiant good looks of his betrothed, in her health, her horsemanship, her grace and quickness at games, and the shy interest in books and ideas that she was beginning to develop under his guidance. (She had advanced far enough to join him in ridiculing the Idylls of the King, but not to feel the beauty of Ulysses and the

---

1   *books on Primitive Man*: these might have included *Primitive Marriage: An Inquiry into the Origin of the Form of Capture in Marriage Ceremonies* by John F. McLennan (1865); *The Origin of Civilisation and the Primitive Condition of Man* by Sir John Lubbock (1870); *The Descent of Man* by Charles Darwin (1871); *Primitive Culture* by Edward B. Tylor (1871); *Systems of Consanguinity and Affinity of the Human Family* by Henry Lewis Morgan (1871); and *Descriptive Sociology: Lowest Races, Negrito Races, and Malayo-Polynesian Races* by Herbert Spencer (1874). See Appendix F2, for McLennan's analysis of bridal captivity rituals.

Lotus Eaters.)[1] She was straightforward, loyal and brave; she had a sense of humour (chiefly proved by her laughing at *his* jokes); and he suspected, in the depths of her innocently-gazing soul, a glow of feeling that it would be a joy to waken. But when he had gone the brief round of her he returned discouraged by the thought that all this frankness and innocence were only an artificial product. Untrained human nature was not frank and innocent; it was full of the twists and defences of an instinctive guile. And he felt himself oppressed by this creation of factitious purity, so cunningly manufactured by a conspiracy of mothers and aunts and grandmothers and long-dead ancestresses, because it was supposed to be what he wanted, what he had a right to, in order that he might exercise his lordly pleasure in smashing it like an image made of snow.

There was a certain triteness in these reflections: they were those habitual to young men on the approach of their wedding day. But they were generally accompanied by a sense of compunction and self-abasement of which Newland Archer felt no trace. He could not deplore (as Thackeray's heroes so often exasperated him by doing) that he had not a blank page to offer his bride in exchange for the unblemished one she was to give to him. He could not get away from the fact that if he had been brought up as she had they would have been no more fit to find their way about than the Babes in the Wood;[2] nor could he, for all his anxious cogitations, see any honest reason (any, that is, unconnected with his own momentary pleasure, and the passion of masculine vanity) why his bride should not have been allowed the same freedom of experience as himself.

Such questions, at such an hour, were bound to drift through his mind; but he was conscious that their uncomfortable persistence and precision were due to the inopportune arrival of the Countess Olenska. Here he was, at the very moment of his

---

[1] All poems by the very popular English poet laureate, Alfred, Lord Tennyson (1809-1892). May is learning to ridicule the more popular *Idylls of the King* (1859, 1872) of his middle and more established period, but not yet able to appreciate the earlier, more innovative "Ulysses" (1842) and "The Lotos Eaters" (1833).

[2] An old fable in which an evil uncle hires two men to kill his niece and nephew for their inheritance. The men take the children to the woods and abandon them, where they are unable to survive on their own and eventually die.

betrothal—a moment for pure thoughts and cloudless hopes—pitchforked into a coil of scandal which raised all the special problems he would have preferred to let lie. "Hang Ellen Olenska!" he grumbled, as he covered his fire and began to undress. He could not really see why her fate should have the least bearing on his; yet he dimly felt that he had only just begun to measure the risks of the championship which his engagement had forced upon him.

A few days later the bolt fell.

The Lovell Mingotts had sent out cards for what was known as "a formal dinner" (that is, three extra footmen, two dishes for each course, and a Roman punch[1] in the middle), and had headed their invitations with the words "To meet the Countess Olenska," in accordance with the hospitable American fashion, which treats strangers as if they were royalties, or at least as their ambassadors.

The guests had been selected with a boldness and discrimination in which the initiated recognised the firm hand of Catherine the Great. Associated with such immemorial standbys as the Selfridge Merrys, who were asked everywhere because they always had been, the Beauforts, on whom there was a claim of relationship, and Mr. Sillerton Jackson and his sister Sophy (who went wherever her brother told her to), were some of the most fashionable and yet most irreproachable of the dominant "young married" set; the Lawrence Leffertses, Mrs. Lefferts Rushworth (the lovely widow), the Harry Thorleys, the Reggie Chiverses and young Morris Dagonet and his wife (who was a van der Luyden). The company indeed was perfectly assorted, since all the members belonged to the little inner group of people who, during the long New York season, disported themselves together daily and nightly with apparently undiminished zest.

Forty-eight hours later the unbelievable had happened; every one had refused the Mingotts' invitation except the Beauforts and old Mr. Jackson and his sister. The intended slight was emphasised by the fact that even the Reggie Chiverses, who were of the

---

[1] *Roman punch*: a concoction of lemonade, champagne, rum, orange juice, and whipped egg whites with sugar.

Mingott clan, were among those inflicting it; and by the uniform wording of the notes, in all of which the writers "regretted that they were unable to accept," without the mitigating plea of a "previous engagement" that ordinary courtesy prescribed.

New York society was, in those days, far too small, and too scant in its resources, for every one in it (including livery-stable-keepers, butlers and cooks) not to know exactly on which evenings people were free; and it was thus possible for the recipients of Mrs. Lovell Mingott's invitations to make cruelly clear their determination not to meet the Countess Olenska.

The blow was unexpected; but the Mingotts, as their way was, met it gallantly. Mrs. Lovell Mingott confided the case to Mrs. Welland, who confided it to Newland Archer; who, aflame at the outrage, appealed passionately and authoritatively to his mother; who, after a painful period of inward resistance and outward temporising, succumbed to his instances (as she always did), and immediately embracing his cause with an energy redoubled by her previous hesitations, put on her grey velvet bonnet and said: "I'll go and see Louisa van der Luyden."

The New York of Newland Archer's day was a small and slippery pyramid, in which, as yet, hardly a fissure had been made or a foothold gained. At its base was a firm foundation of what Mrs. Archer called "plain people"; an honourable but obscure majority of respectable families who (as in the case of the Spicers or the Leffertses or the Jacksons) had been raised above their level by marriage with one of the ruling clans. People, Mrs. Archer always said, were not as particular as they used to be; and with old Catherine Spicer ruling one end of Fifth Avenue, and Julius Beaufort the other, you couldn't expect the old traditions to last much longer.

Firmly narrowing upward from this wealthy but inconspicuous substratum was the compact and dominant group which the Mingotts, Newlands, Chiverses and Mansons so actively represented. Most people imagined them to be the very apex of the pyramid; but they themselves (at least those of Mrs. Archer's generation) were aware that, in the eyes of the professional genealogist, only a still smaller number of families could lay claim to that eminence.

"Don't tell me," Mrs. Archer would say to her children, "all this modern newspaper rubbish about a New York aristocracy. If there is one, neither the Mingotts nor the Mansons belong to it; no, nor the Newlands or the Chiverses either. Our grandfathers and great-grandfathers were just respectable English or Dutch merchants, who came to the colonies to make their fortune, and stayed here because they did so well. One of your great-grandfathers signed the Declaration, and another was a general on Washington's staff, and received General Burgoyne's sword after the battle of Saratoga.[1] These are things to be proud of, but they have nothing to do with rank or class. New York has always been a commercial community, and there are not more than three families in it who can claim an aristocratic origin in the real sense of the word."[2]

Mrs. Archer and her son and daughter, like every one else in New York, knew who these privileged beings were: the Dagonets of Washington Square, who came of an old English county family allied with the Pitts and Foxes; the Lannings, who had intermarried with the descendants of Count de Grasse, and the van der Luydens, direct descendants of the first Dutch governor of Manhattan,[3] and related by pre-revolutionary marriages to several members of the French and British aristocracy.

The Lannings survived only in the person of two very old but lively Miss Lannings, who lived cheerfully and reminiscently

---

[1] Wharton in her memoir recalls her maternal great-grandfather featured in paintings commemorating Revolutionary victories ("Surrender of Burgoyne" and "Surrender of Cornwallis") at the Rotunda in Washington (see *A Backward Glance*, 10-11). General George *Washington* (1732-1799), Commander-in-Chief of the Colonial Army during the American Revolution and later first president of the United States. General John *Burgoyne*: British general forced to surrender at *Saratoga* Springs in 1777.

[2] *New York aristocracy*: the "modern newspaper rubbish" may owe something to the efforts of socialite Ward McAllister (1827-1895) to establish a recognizable social elite. With Mrs. Caroline Astor he helped foster "the Four Hundred," named for the number of guests who could fit into Mrs. Astor's ballroom. McAllister's *Society as I Have Found It* (1890) remains a crucial document for understanding New York "society" during the period. Wharton's sister-in-law diligently consulted it while researching the novel for Wharton.

[3] Captain Cornelis May brought the first families, mostly Walloons from Leyden, to settle in New Netherland in the summer of 1624. Willem Verhulst replaced May as the director of New Netherland in 1625, but he was replaced in 1626 by Peter Minuit, who allegedly purchased Manhattan Island from the Lenapes for $24.

among family portraits and Chippendale; the Dagonets were a considerable clan, allied to the best names in Baltimore and Philadelphia; but the van der Luydens, who stood above all of them, had faded into a kind of super-terrestrial twilight, from which only two figures impressively emerged; those of Mr. and Mrs. Henry van der Luyden.

Mrs. Henry van der Luyden had been Louisa Dagonet, and her mother had been the granddaughter of Colonel du Lac, of an old Channel Island family, who had fought under Cornwallis and had settled in Maryland,[1] after the war, with his bride, Lady Angelica Trevenna, fifth daughter of the Earl of St. Austrey. The tie between the Dagonets, the du Lacs of Maryland, and their aristocratic Cornish kinsfolk, the Trevennas, had always remained close and cordial. Mr. and Mrs. van der Luyden had more than once paid long visits to the present head of the house of Trevenna, the Duke of St. Austrey, at his country-seat in Cornwall and at St. Austrey in Gloucestershire; and his Grace had frequently announced his intention of some day returning their visit (without the Duchess, who feared the Atlantic).

Mr. and Mrs. van der Luyden divided their time between Trevenna, their place in Maryland, and Skuytercliff, the great estate on the Hudson which had been one of the colonial grants of the Dutch government to the famous first Governor, and of which Mr. van der Luyden was still "Patroon."[2] Their large solemn house in Madison Avenue was seldom opened, and when they came to town they received in it only their most intimate friends.

"I wish you would go with me, Newland," his mother said, suddenly pausing at the door of the Brown *coupé*. "Louisa is fond of you; and of course it's on account of dear May that I'm taking this step—and also because, if we don't all stand together, there'll be no such thing as Society left."

---

[1] Charles *Cornwallis* (1738–1805), British soldier and statesman, whose defeat at Yorktown, Virginia, in 1781 virtually ended the American War of Independence.
[2] *Patroon*: title given to Dutch landlords in the colony of New Netherland from 1629–1664. The British took control of the colony after this period.

VII

MRS. Henry Van Der Luyden listened in silence to her cousin Mrs. Archer's narrative.

It was all very well to tell yourself in advance that Mrs. van der Luyden was always silent, and that, though non-committal by nature and training, she was very kind to the people she really liked. Even personal experience of these facts was not always a protection from the chill that descended on one in the high-ceilinged white-walled Madison Avenue drawing-room, with the pale brocaded armchairs so obviously uncovered for the occasion, and the gauze still veiling the ormolu mantel ornaments and the beautiful old carved frame of Gainsborough's "Lady Angelica du Lac."

Mrs. van der Luyden's portrait by Huntington (in black velvet and Venetian point) faced that of her lovely ancestress. It was generally considered "as fine as a Cabanel,"[1] and, though twenty years had elapsed since its execution, was still "a perfect likeness." Indeed the Mrs. van der Luyden who sat beneath it listening to Mrs. Archer might have been the twin-sister of the fair and still youngish woman drooping against a gilt armchair before a green rep curtain. Mrs. van der Luyden still wore black velvet and Venetian point when she went into society—or rather (since she never dined out) when she threw open her own doors to receive it. Her fair hair, which had faded without turning grey, was still parted in flat overlapping points on her forehead, and the straight nose that divided her pale blue eyes was only a little more pinched about the nostrils than when the portrait had been painted. She always, indeed, struck Newland Archer as having been rather gruesomely preserved in the airless atmosphere of a perfectly irreproachable existence, as bodies caught in glaciers keep for years a rosy life-in-death.

Like all his family, he esteemed and admired Mrs. van der Luyden; but he found her gentle bending sweetness less

---

[1]   *Lady Angelica du Lac*: unidentified portrait by Thomas *Gainsborough* (1727-1788), British landscape and society portrait painter. Daniel *Huntington* (1816-1906), American portrait painter. Alexandre *Cabanel* (1823-1889), French painter whose fashionable portraits were extremely successful during the Second Empire.

approachable than the grimness of some of his mother's old aunts, fierce spinsters who said "No" on principle before they knew what they were going to be asked.

Mrs. van der Luyden's attitude said neither yes nor no, but always appeared to incline to clemency till her thin lips, wavering into the shadow of a smile, made the almost invariable reply: "I shall first have to talk this over with my husband."

She and Mr. van der Luyden were so exactly alike that Archer often wondered how, after forty years of the closest conjugality, two such merged identities ever separated themselves enough for anything as controversial as a talking-over. But as neither had ever reached a decision without prefacing it by this mysterious conclave, Mrs. Archer and her son, having set forth their case, waited resignedly for the familiar phrase.

Mrs. van der Luyden, however, who had seldom surprised any one, now surprised them by reaching her long hand toward the bell-rope.

"I think," she said, "I should like Henry to hear what you have told me."

A footman appeared, to whom she gravely added: "If Mr. van der Luyden has finished reading the newspaper, please ask him to be kind enough to come."

She said "reading the newspaper" in the tone in which a Minister's wife might have said: "Presiding at a Cabinet meeting"—not from any arrogance of mind, but because the habit of a life-time, and the attitude of her friends and relations, had led her to consider Mr. van der Luyden's least gesture as having an almost sacerdotal importance.

Her promptness of action showed that she considered the case as pressing as Mrs. Archer; but, lest she should be thought to have committed herself in advance, she added, with the sweetest look: "Henry always enjoys seeing you, dear Adeline; and he will wish to congratulate Newland."

The double doors had solemnly reopened and between them appeared Mr. Henry van der Luyden, tall, spare and frock-coated, with faded fair hair, a straight nose like his wife's and the same look of frozen gentleness in eyes that were merely pale grey instead of pale blue.

Mr. van der Luyden greeted Mrs. Archer with cousinly affability, proffered to Newland low-voiced congratulations couched in the same language as his wife's, and seated himself in one of the brocade armchairs with the simplicity of a reigning sovereign.

"I had just finished reading the Times," he said, laying his long finger-tips together. "In town my mornings are so much occupied that I find it more convenient to read the newspapers after luncheon."

"Ah, there's a great deal to be said for that plan—indeed I think my uncle Egmont used to say he found it less agitating not to read the morning papers till after dinner," said Mrs. Archer responsively.

"Yes: my good father abhorred hurry. But now we live in a constant rush," said Mr. van der Luyden in measured tones, looking with pleasant deliberation about the large shrouded room which to Archer was so complete an image of its owners.

"But I hope you *had* finished your reading, Henry?" his wife interposed.

"Quite—quite," he reassured her.

"Then I should like Adeline to tell you—"

"Oh, it's really Newland's story," said his mother smiling; and proceeded to rehearse once more the monstrous tale of the affront inflicted on Mrs. Lovell Mingott.

"Of course," she ended, "Augusta Welland and Mary Mingott both felt that, especially in view of Newland's engagement, you and Henry *ought to know*."

"Ah—" said Mr. van der Luyden, drawing a deep breath.

There was a silence during which the tick of the monumental ormolu clock on the white marble mantelpiece grew as loud as the boom of a minute-gun. Archer contemplated with awe the two slender faded figures, seated side by side in a kind of viceregal rigidity, mouth-pieces of some remote ancestral authority which fate compelled them to wield, when they would so much rather have lived in simplicity and seclusion, digging invisible weeds out of the perfect lawns of Skuytercliff, and playing Patience together in the evenings.

Mr. van der Luyden was the first to speak.

"You really think this is due to some—some intentional interference of Lawrence Lefferts's?" he enquired, turning to Archer.

"I'm certain of it, sir. Larry has been going it rather harder than usual lately—if cousin Louisa won't mind my mentioning it—having rather a stiff affair with the postmaster's wife in their village, or some one of that sort; and whenever poor Gertrude Lefferts begins to suspect anything, and he's afraid of trouble, he gets up a fuss of this kind, to show how awfully moral he is, and talks at the top of his voice about the impertinence of inviting his wife to meet people he doesn't wish her to know. He's simply using Madame Olenska as a lightning-rod; I've seen him try the same thing often before."

"The *Leffertses!*—" said Mrs. van der Luyden.

"The *Leffertses!*—" echoed Mrs. Archer. "What would uncle Egmont have said of Lawrence Lefferts's pronouncing on anybody's social position? It shows what Society has come to."

"We'll hope it has not quite come to that," said Mr. van der Luyden firmly.

"Ah, if only you and Louisa went out more!" sighed Mrs. Archer.

But instantly she became aware of her mistake. The van der Luydens were morbidly sensitive to any criticism of their secluded existence. They were the arbiters of fashion, the Court of last Appeal, and they knew it, and bowed to their fate. But being shy and retiring persons, with no natural inclination for their part, they lived as much as possible in the sylvan solitude of Skuytercliff, and when they came to town, declined all invitations on the plea of Mrs. van der Luyden's health.

Newland Archer came to his mother's rescue. "Everybody in New York knows what you and cousin Louisa represent. That's why Mrs. Mingott felt she ought not to allow this slight on Countess Olenska to pass without consulting you."

Mrs. van der Luyden glanced at her husband, who glanced back at her.

"It is the principle that I dislike," said Mr. van der Luyden. "As long as a member of a well-known family is backed up by that family it should be considered—final."

"It seems so to me," said his wife, as if she were producing a new thought.

"I had no idea," Mr. van der Luyden continued, "that things had come to such a pass." He paused, and looked at his wife again.

"It occurs to me, my dear, that the Countess Olenska is already a sort of relation—through Medora Manson's first husband. At any rate, she will be when Newland marries." He turned toward the young man. "Have you read this morning's Times, Newland?"

"Why, yes, sir," said Archer, who usually tossed off half a dozen papers with his morning coffee.

Husband and wife looked at each other again. Their pale eyes clung together in prolonged and serious consultation; then a faint smile fluttered over Mrs. van der Luyden's face. She had evidently guessed and approved.

Mr. van der Luyden turned to Mrs. Archer. "If Louisa's health allowed her to dine out—I wish you would say to Mrs. Lovell Mingott—she and I would have been happy to—er—fill the places of the Lawrence Leffertses at her dinner." He paused to let the irony of this sink in. "As you know, this is impossible." Mrs. Archer sounded a sympathetic assent. "But Newland tells me he has read this morning's Times; therefore he has probably seen that Louisa's relative, the Duke of St. Austrey, arrives next week on the Russia. He is coming to enter his new sloop, the Guinevere, in next summer's International Cup Race; and also to have a little canvas-back shooting at Trevenna." Mr. van der Luyden paused again, and continued with increasing benevolence: "Before taking him down to Maryland we are inviting a few friends to meet him here—only a little dinner—with a reception afterward. I am sure Louisa will be as glad as I am if Countess Olenska will let us include her among our guests." He got up, bent his long body with a stiff friendliness toward his cousin, and added: "I think I have Louisa's authority for saying that she will herself leave the invitation to dine when she drives out presently: with our cards—of course with our cards."

Mrs. Archer, who knew this to be a hint that the seventeen-hand chestnuts[1] which were never kept waiting were at the door, rose with a hurried murmur of thanks. Mrs. van der Luyden beamed on her with the smile of Esther interceding with Ahasuerus[2] but her husband raised a protesting hand.

---

[1] *seventeen-hand chestnuts*: deep reddish-brown horses the height of seventeen human hands.

[2] In the Old Testament book of *Esther*, Esther saves the Jews living in Persia by appearing before her husband King *Ahasuerus* and inviting him to a banquet.

"There is nothing to thank me for, dear Adeline; nothing whatever. This kind of thing must not happen in New York; it shall not, as long as I can help it," he pronounced with sovereign gentleness as he steered his cousins to the door.

Two hours later, every one knew that the great C-spring barouche in which Mrs. van der Luyden took the air at all seasons had been seen at old Mrs. Mingott's door, where a large square envelope was handed in; and that evening at the Opera Mr. Sillerton Jackson was able to state that the envelope contained a card inviting the Countess Olenska to the dinner which the van der Luydens were giving the following week for their cousin, the Duke of St. Austrey.

Some of the younger men in the club box exchanged a smile at this announcement, and glanced sideways at Lawrence Lefferts, who sat carelessly in the front of the box, pulling his long fair moustache, and who remarked with authority, as the soprano paused: "No one but Patti ought to attempt the Sonnambula."[1]

VIII

It was generally agreed in New York that the Countess Olenska had "lost her looks."

She had appeared there first, in Newland Archer's boyhood, as a brilliantly pretty little girl of nine or ten, of whom people said that she "ought to be painted." Her parents had been continental wanderers, and after a roaming babyhood she had lost them both, and been taken in charge by her aunt, Medora Manson, also a wanderer, who was herself returning to New York to "settle down."

Poor Medora, repeatedly widowed, was always coming home to settle down (each time in a less expensive house), and bringing with her a new husband or an adopted child; but after a few

---

[1] Adelina *Patti* (1943-1919), renowned Italian coloratura. *La Sonnambula* (1831), or *The Sleepwalker*, popular opera by Vincenzo Bellini (1801-1835), in which a sleepwalking maiden is suspected of infidelity when she unknowingly wanders into the bedroom of a nobleman. Patti first appeared in *La Sonnambula* at Covent Garden in 1861.

months she invariably parted from her husband or quarrelled with her ward, and, having got rid of her house at a loss, set out again on her wanderings. As her mother had been a Rushworth, and her last unhappy marriage had linked her to one of the crazy Chiverses, New York looked indulgently on her eccentricities; but when she returned with her little orphaned niece, whose parents had been popular in spite of their regrettable taste for travel, people thought it a pity that the pretty child should be in such hands.

Every one was disposed to be kind to little Ellen Mingott, though her dusky red cheeks and tight curls gave her an air of gaiety that seemed unsuitable in a child who should still have been in black for her parents. It was one of the misguided Medora's many peculiarities to flout the unalterable rules that regulated American mourning, and when she stepped from the steamer her family were scandalised to see that the crape veil she wore for her own brother was seven inches shorter than those of her sisters-in-law, while little Ellen was in crimson merino and amber beads, like a gipsy foundling.

But New York had so long resigned itself to Medora that only a few old ladies shook their heads over Ellen's gaudy clothes, while her other relations fell under the charm of her high colour and high spirits. She was a fearless and familiar little thing, who asked disconcerting questions, made precocious comments, and possessed outlandish arts, such as dancing a Spanish shawl dance and singing Neapolitan love-songs to a guitar. Under the direction of her aunt (whose real name was Mrs. Thorley Chivers, but who, having received a Papal title, had resumed her first husband's patronymic, and called herself the Marchioness Manson, because in Italy she could turn it into Manzoni) the little girl received an expensive but incoherent education, which included "drawing from the model," a thing never dreamed of before, and playing the piano in quintets with professional musicians.

Of course no good could come of this; and when, a few years later, poor Chivers finally died in a madhouse, his widow (draped in strange weeds) again pulled up stakes and departed with Ellen, who had grown into a tall bony girl with conspicuous eyes. For some time no more was heard of them; then news came of Ellen's marriage to an immensely rich Polish nobleman of legendary fame, whom she had met at a ball at the Tuileries, and who was said to have princely establishments in Paris, Nice and Florence, a yacht at Cowes, and many square miles of shooting in Transylvania. She disappeared in a kind of sulphurous apotheosis, and when a few years later Medora again came back to New York, subdued, impoverished, mourning a third husband, and in quest of a still smaller house, people wondered that her rich niece had not been able to do something for her. Then came the news that Ellen's own marriage had ended in disaster, and that she was herself returning home to seek rest and oblivion among her kinsfolk.

These things passed through Newland Archer's mind a week later as he watched the Countess Olenska enter the van der Luyden drawing-room on the evening of the momentous dinner. The occasion was a solemn one, and he wondered a little nervously how she would carry it off. She came rather late, one hand still ungloved, and fastening a bracelet about her wrist; yet she entered without any appearance of haste or embarrassment the drawing-room in which New York's most chosen company was somewhat awfully assembled.

In the middle of the room she paused, looking about her with a grave mouth and smiling eyes; and in that instant Newland Archer rejected the general verdict on her looks. It was true that her early radiance was gone. The red cheeks had paled; she was thin, worn, a little older-looking than her age, which must have been nearly thirty. But there was about her the mysterious authority of beauty, a sureness in the carriage of the head, the movement of the eyes, which, without being in the least theatrical, struck his as highly trained and full of a conscious power. At the same time she was simpler in manner than most of the ladies present, and many people (as he heard afterward from Janey) were disappointed that her appearance was not more "stylish"—for stylishness was what New York most valued. It was, perhaps, Archer reflected, because her early vivacity had disappeared; because she was so quiet—quiet in her movements, her voice, and the tones of her low-pitched voice. New York had expected something a good deal more resonant in a young woman with such a history.

The dinner was a somewhat formidable business. Dining with the van der Luydens was at best no light matter, and dining there with a Duke who was their cousin was almost a religious solemnity. It pleased Archer to think that only an old New Yorker could perceive the shade of difference (to New York) between being merely a Duke and being the van der Luydens' Duke. New York took stray noblemen calmly, and even (except in the Struthers set) with a certain distrustful *hauteur*; but when they presented such credentials as these they were received with an old-fashioned cordiality that they would have been greatly mistaken in ascribing solely to their standing in Debrett.[1] It was for just such distinctions that the young man cherished his old New York even while he smiled at it.

The van der Luydens had done their best to emphasise the importance of the occasion. The du Lac Sèvres and the Trevenna George II plate were out; so was the van der Luyden "Lowestoft" (East India Company) and the Dagonet Crown Derby. Mrs. van der Luyden looked more than ever like a Cabanel, and Mrs. Archer, in her grandmother's seed-pearls and emeralds, reminded her son of an Isabey miniature.[2] All the ladies had on their handsomest jewels, but it was characteristic of the house and the occasion that these were mostly in rather heavy old-fashioned settings; and old Miss Lanning, who had been persuaded to come, actually wore her mother's cameos and a Spanish blonde shawl.

The Countess Olenska was the only young woman at the dinner; yet, as Archer scanned the smooth plump elderly faces between their diamond necklaces and towering ostrich feathers, they struck him as curiously immature compared with hers. It frightened him to think what must have gone to the making of her eyes.

The Duke of St. Austrey, who sat at his hostess's right, was naturally the chief figure of the evening. But if the Countess

---

[1] *Debrett: Debrett's Peerage and Baronetage*, first published in London in 1802, contains information about the royal family, the peerage, privy counsellors, Scottish Lords of Session, barons, and chiefs of names and clans of Scotland.

[2] *Isabey miniature*: after Jean-Baptiste *Isabey* (1767-1855), French painter, draughtsman, and printer, whose society miniatures were recognizable by their similar pose: a woman with a melancholy smile is framed by roses and surrounded by fluttering veils.

Olenska was less conspicuous than had been hoped, the Duke was almost invisible. Being a well-bred man he had not (like another recent ducal visitor) come to the dinner in a shooting-jacket; but his evening clothes were so shabby and baggy, and he wore them with such an air of their being homespun, that (with his stooping way of sitting, and the vast beard spreading over his shirt-front) he hardly gave the appearance of being in dinner attire. He was short, round-shouldered, sunburnt, with a thick nose, small eyes and a sociable smile; but he seldom spoke, and when he did it was in such low tones that, despite the frequent silences of expectation about the table, his remarks were lost to all but his neighbours.

When the men joined the ladies after dinner the Duke went straight up to the Countess Olenska, and they sat down in a corner and plunged into animated talk. Neither seemed aware that the Duke should first have paid his respects to Mrs. Lovell Mingott and Mrs. Headly Chivers, and the Countess have conversed with that amiable hypochondriac, Mr. Urban Dagonet of Washington Square, who, in order to have the pleasure of meeting her, had broken through his fixed rule of not dining out between January and April. The two chatted together for nearly twenty minutes; then the Countess rose and, walking alone across the wide drawing-room, sat down at Newland Archer's side.

It was not the custom in New York drawing-rooms for a lady to get up and walk away from one gentleman in order to seek the company of another. Etiquette required that she should wait, immovable as an idol, while the men who wished to converse with her succeeded each other at her side. But the Countess was apparently unaware of having broken any rule; she sat at perfect ease in a corner of the sofa beside Archer, and looked at him with the kindest eyes.

"I want you to talk to me about May," she said. Instead of answering her he asked: "You knew the Duke before?"

"Oh, yes—we used to see him every winter at Nice. He's very fond of gambling—he used to come to the house a great deal." She said it in the simplest manner, as if she had said: "He's fond of wild-flowers"; and after a moment she added candidly: "I think he's the dullest man I ever met."

This pleased her companion so much that he forgot the slight shock her previous remark had caused him. It was undeniably exciting to meet a lady who found the van der Luydens' Duke dull, and dared to utter the opinion. He longed to question her, to hear more about the life of which her careless words had given him so illuminating a glimpse; but he feared to touch on distressing memories, and before he could think of anything to say she had strayed back to her original subject.

"May is a darling; I've seen no young girl in New York so handsome and so intelligent. Are you very much in love with her?"

Newland Archer reddened and laughed. "As much as a man can be."

She continued to consider him thoughtfully, as if not to miss any shade of meaning in what he said. "Do you think, then, there is a limit?"

"To being in love? If there is, I haven't found it!"

She glowed with sympathy. "Ah—it's really and truly a romance?"

"The most romantic of romances!"

"How delightful! And you found it all out for yourselves—it was not in the least arranged for you?"

Archer looked at her incredulously. "Have you forgotten," he asked with a smile, "that in our country we don't allow our marriages to be arranged for us?"

A dusky blush rose to her cheek, and he instantly regretted his words.

"Yes," she answered, "I'd forgotten. You must forgive me if I sometimes make these mistakes. I don't always remember that everything here is good that was—that was bad where I've come from." She looked down at her Viennese fan of eagle feathers, and he saw that her lips trembled.

"I'm so sorry," he said impulsively; "but you *are* among friends here, you know."

"Yes—I know. Wherever I go I have that feeling. That's why I came home. I want to forget everything else, to become a complete American again, like the Mingotts and Wellands, and you and your delightful mother, and all the other good people here tonight. Ah, here's May arriving, and you will want to hurry away to her," she added, but without moving; and her eyes turned back from the door to rest on the young man's face.

The drawing-rooms were beginning to fill up with after-dinner guests, and following Madame Olenska's glance Archer saw May Welland entering with her mother. In her dress of white and silver, with a wreath of silver blossoms in her hair, the tall girl looked like a Diana just alight from the chase.[1]

"Oh," said Archer, "I have so many rivals; you see she's already surrounded. There's the Duke being introduced."

"Then stay with me a little longer," Madame Olenska said in a low tone, just touching his knee with her plumed fan. It was the lightest touch, but it thrilled him like a caress.

"Yes, let me stay," he answered in the same tone, hardly knowing what he said; but just then Mr. van der Luyden came up, followed by old Mr. Urban Dagonet. The Countess greeted them with her grave smile, and Archer, feeling his host's admonitory glance on him, rose and surrendered his seat.

Madame Olenska held out her hand as if to bid him good-bye.

"Tomorrow, then, after five—I shall expect you," she said; and then turned back to make room for Mr. Dagonet.

"Tomorrow—" Archer heard himself repeating, though there had been no engagement, and during their talk she had given him no hint that she wished to see him again.

As he moved away he saw Lawrence Lefferts, tall and resplendent, leading his wife up to be introduced; and heard Gertrude Lefferts say, as she beamed on the Countess with her large unperceiving smile: "But I think we used to go to dancing-school together when we were children—." Behind her, waiting their turn to name themselves to the Countess, Archer noticed a number of the recalcitrant couples who had declined to meet her at Mrs. Lovell Mingott's. As Mrs. Archer remarked: when the

---

[1] *Diana*: the first of several allusions associating May with Diana, in Roman mythology the virgin huntress, goddess of the woodlands, protector of women, moon goddess. In Sir James George Frazer's *The Golden Bough*, a book Wharton seems to have been familiar with while writing the novel, Diana is described as "a goddess of nature in general and of fertility in particular" (see the chapter "The Sacred Marriage," in Volume I).

van der Luydens chose, they knew how to give a lesson. The wonder was that they chose so seldom.

The young man felt a touch on his arm and saw Mrs. van der Luyden looking down on him from the pure eminence of black velvet and the family diamonds. "It was good of you, dear Newland, to devote yourself so unselfishly to Madame Olenska. I told your cousin Henry he must really come to the rescue."

He was aware of smiling at her vaguely, and she added, as if condescending to his natural shyness: "I've never seen May looking lovelier. The Duke thinks her the handsomest girl in the room."

IX

THE Countess Olenska had said "after five"; and at half after the hour Newland Archer rang the bell of the peeling stucco house with a giant wisteria throttling its feeble cast-iron balcony, which she had hired, far down West Twenty-third Street,[1] from the vagabond Medora.

It was certainly a strange quarter to have settled in. Small dressmakers, bird-stuffers and "people who wrote" were her nearest neighbours; and further down the dishevelled street Archer recognised a dilapidated wooden house, at the end of a paved path, in which a writer and journalist called Winsett, whom he used to come across now and then, had mentioned that he lived. Winsett did not invite people to his house; but he had once pointed it out to Archer in the course of a nocturnal stroll, and the latter had asked himself, with a little shiver, if the humanities were so meanly housed in other capitals.

Madame Olenska's own dwelling was redeemed from the same appearance only by a little more paint about the window-frames; and as Archer mustered its modest front he said to himself that the Polish Count must have robbed her of her fortune as well as of her illusions.

The young man had spent an unsatisfactory day. He had lunched with the Wellands, hoping afterward to carry off May

---

[1]   Wharton herself lived at 14 West Twenty-third Street near Fifth Avenue in the 1870s.

for a walk in the Park. He wanted to have her to himself, to tell her how enchanting she had looked the night before, and how proud he was of her, and to press her to hasten their marriage. But Mrs. Welland had firmly reminded him that the round of family visits was not half over, and, when he hinted at advancing the date of the wedding, had raised reproachful eye-brows and sighed out: "Twelve dozen of everything—hand-embroidered—"

Packed in the family landau they rolled from one tribal doorstep to another, and Archer, when the afternoon's round was over, parted from his betrothed with the feeling that he had been shown off like a wild animal cunningly trapped. He supposed that his readings in anthropology caused him to take such a coarse view of what was after all a simple and natural demonstration of family feeling; but when he remembered that the Wellands did not expect the wedding to take place till the following autumn, and pictured what his life would be till then, a dampness fell upon his spirit.

"Tomorrow," Mrs. Welland called after him, "we'll do the Chiverses and the Dallases"; and he perceived that she was going through their two families alphabetically, and that they were only in the first quarter of the alphabet.

He had meant to tell May of the Countess Olenska's request—her command, rather—that he should call on her that afternoon; but in the brief moments when they were alone he had had more pressing things to say. Besides, it struck him as a little absurd to allude to the matter. He knew that May most particularly wanted him to be kind to her cousin; was it not that wish which had hastened the announcement of their engagement? It gave him an odd sensation to reflect that, but for the Countess's arrival, he might have been, if not still a free man, at least a man less irrevocably pledged. But May had willed it so, and he felt himself somehow relieved of further responsibility—and therefore at liberty, if he chose, to call on her cousin without telling her.

As he stood on Madame Olenska's threshold curiosity was his uppermost feeling. He was puzzled by the tone in which she had summoned him; he concluded that she was less simple than she seemed.

The door was opened by a swarthy foreign-looking maid, with a prominent bosom under a gay neckerchief, whom he vaguely fancied to be Sicilian. She welcomed him with all her white teeth, and answering his enquiries by a head-shake of incomprehension led him through the narrow hall into a low firelit drawing-room. The room was empty, and she left him, for an appreciable time, to wonder whether she had gone to find her mistress, or whether she had not understood what he was there for, and thought it might be to wind the clocks—of which he perceived that the only visible specimen had stopped. He knew that the southern races communicated with each other in the language of pantomime, and was mortified to find her shrugs and smiles so unintelligible. At length she returned with a lamp; and Archer, having meanwhile put together a phrase out of Dante and Petrarch evoked the answer: "*La signora è fuori; ma verrà subito*";[1] which he took to mean: "She's out—but you'll soon see."

What he saw, meanwhile, with the help of the lamp, was the faded shadowy charm of a room unlike any room he had known. He knew that the Countess Olenska had brought some of her possessions with her—bits of wreckage, she called them—and these, he supposed, were represented by some small slender tables of dark wood, a delicate little Greek bronze on the chimney-piece, and a stretch of red damask nailed on the discoloured wallpaper behind a couple of Italian-looking pictures in old frames.

Newland Archer prided himself on his knowledge of Italian art. His boyhood had been saturated with Ruskin, and he had read all the latest books: John Addington Symonds, Vernon Lee's "Euphorion," the essays of P. G. Hamerton, and a wonderful new volume called "The Renaissance" by Walter Pater. He talked easily of Botticelli, and spoke of Fra Angelico with a faint conde-

---

[1] *Dante* Alighieri (1265-1321), Italian poet, author of *Vita Nuova* (1290-94) and *La Divina Commedia* (1307-14). Francesco *Petrarca* (1304-1374), Italian poet famous for his series of sonnets dedicated to Laura. *La signora ... subito*: Italian for "The lady is outside; but she will come right away."

scension.[1] But these pictures bewildered him, for they were like nothing that he was accustomed to look at (and therefore able to see) when he travelled in Italy; and perhaps, also, his powers of observation were impaired by the oddness of finding himself in this strange empty house, where apparently no one expected him. He was sorry that he had not told May Welland of Countess Olenska's request, and a little disturbed by the thought that his betrothed might come in to see her cousin. What would she think if she found him sitting there with the air of intimacy implied by waiting alone in the dusk at a lady's fireside?

But since he had come he meant to wait; and he sank into a chair and stretched his feet to the logs.

It was odd to have summoned him in that way, and then forgotten him; but Archer felt more curious than mortified. The atmosphere of the room was so different from any he had ever breathed that self-consciousness vanished in the sense of adventure. He had been before in drawing-rooms hung with red damask, with pictures "of the Italian school"; what struck him was the way in which Medora Manson's shabby hired house, with its blighted background of pampas grass and Rogers statuettes,[2] had, by a turn of the hand, and the skilful use of a few properties, been transformed into something intimate, "foreign," subtly suggestive of old romantic scenes and sentiments. He tried to analyse the trick, to find a clue to it in the way the chairs and tables were grouped, in the fact that only two Jacqueminot roses (of which nobody ever bought less than a dozen) had been

---

[1] *John Addington Symonds* (1840-1893), English poet and critic, author of *History of the Renaissance in Italy* (1875-86), which Wharton greatly admired. *Euphorion*: novel by *Vernon Lee*, pen-name of Violet Paget (1856-1935), English essayist and novelist who lived mostly in Italy. *Philip Gilbert Hamerton* (1834-1894), English essayist, who became art critic for the *Saturday Review* and was responsible for the revival of interest in etching after publishing *Etching and Etchers* in 1868. *Walter Pater* (1839-1894), English scholar and writer, author of one of the aestheticist movement's most influential texts, *Studies in the History of the Renaissance* (1873). Sandro *Botticelli* (1444/5-1510), Florentine painter of religious and mythological pictures, creator of such famous works as *Primavera* and *The Birth of Venus*. Fra Angelico, or Guido di Pietro (circa 1395-1455), Dominican friar, Florentine painter of frescoes, alterpieces, manuscripts, and religious pictures. Both Botticelli and Fra Angelico were admired by Ruskin.

[2] *Rogers statuettes*: popular plaster statues of a sentimental character produced by American sculptor John Rogers (1829-1904).

placed in the slender vase at his elbow, and in the vague pervading perfume that was not what one put on handkerchiefs, but rather like the scent of some far-off bazaar, a smell made up of Turkish coffee and ambergris and dried roses.

His mind wandered away to the question of what May's drawing-room would look like. He knew that Mr. Welland, who was behaving "very handsomely," already had his eye on a newly built house in East Thirty-ninth Street. The neighbourhood was thought remote, and the house was built in a ghastly greenish-yellow stone that the younger architects were beginning to employ as a protest against the brownstone of which the uniform hue coated New York like a cold chocolate sauce; but the plumbing was perfect. Archer would have liked to travel, to put off the housing question; but, though the Wellands approved of an extended European honeymoon (perhaps even a winter in Egypt), they were firm as to the need of a house for the returning couple. The young man felt that his fate was sealed: for the rest of his life he would go up every evening between the cast-iron railings of that greenish-yellow doorstep, and pass through a Pompeian vestibule into a hall with a wainscoting of varnished yellow wood. But beyond that his imagination could not travel. He knew the drawing-room above had a bay window, but he could not fancy how May would deal with it. She submitted cheerfully to the purple satin and yellow tuftings of the Welland drawing-room, to its sham Buhl tables and gilt vitrines full of modern Saxe. He saw no reason to suppose that she would want anything different in her own house; and his only comfort was to reflect that she would probably let him arrange his library as he pleased—which would be, of course, with "sincere" Eastlake furniture,[1] and the plain new book-cases without glass doors.

---

[1] *Buhl*: a style of decorative inlay using tortoiseshell and metal, usually silver or brass. *Vitrines full of modern Saxe*: display cabinet for collections of Meissen porcelain, known as Saxe in France and Dresden in England. *Eastlake furniture*: after Charles Locke Eastlake (1836-1906), English architect and furniture designer who proposed a return to plain, simply-constructed furniture. His *Hints on Household Taste* (1868) became very popular in both England and America.

The round-bosomed maid came in, drew the curtains, pushed back a log, and said consolingly: "*Verrà—verrà.*"[1] When she had gone Archer stood up and began to wander about. Should he wait any longer? His position was becoming rather foolish. Perhaps he had misunderstood Madame Olenska—perhaps she had not invited him after all.

Down the cobblestones of the quiet street came the ring of a stepper's hoofs; they stopped before the house, and he caught the opening of a carriage door. Parting the curtains he looked out into the early dusk. A street-lamp faced him, and in its light he saw Julius Beaufort's compact English brougham, drawn by a big roan, and the banker descending from it, and helping out Madame Olenska.

Beaufort stood, hat in hand, saying something which his companion seemed to negative; then they shook hands, and he jumped into his carriage while she mounted the steps.

When she entered the room she showed no surprise at seeing Archer there; surprise seemed the emotion that she was least addicted to.

"How do you like my funny house?" she asked. "To me it's like heaven."

As she spoke she untied her little velvet bonnet and tossing it away with her long cloak stood looking at him with meditative eyes.

"You've arranged it delightfully," he rejoined, alive to the flatness of the words, but imprisoned in the conventional by his consuming desire to be simple and striking.

"Oh, it's a poor little place. My relations despise it. But at any rate it's less gloomy than the van der Luydens'."

The words gave him an electric shock, for few were the rebellious spirits who would have dared to call the stately home of the van der Luydens gloomy. Those privileged to enter it shivered there, and spoke of it as "handsome." But suddenly he was glad that she had given voice to the general shiver.

"It's delicious—what you've done here," he repeated.

"I like the little house," she admitted; "but I suppose what I like is the blessedness of its being here, in my own country and

---

[1] "*Verrà* ...": Italian for "she will come—she will come."

my own town; and then, of being alone in it." She spoke so low that he hardly heard the last phrase; but in his awkwardness he took it up.

"You like so much to be alone?"

"Yes; as long as my friends keep me from feeling lonely." She sat down near the fire, said: "Nastasia will bring the tea presently," and signed to him to return to his armchair, adding: "I see you've already chosen your corner."

Leaning back, she folded her arms behind her head, and looked at the fire under drooping lids.

"This is the hour I like best—don't you?"

A proper sense of his dignity caused him to answer: "I was afraid you'd forgotten the hour. Beaufort must have been very engrossing."

She looked amused. "Why—have you waited long? Mr. Beaufort took me to see a number of houses—since it seems I'm not to be allowed to stay in this one." She appeared to dismiss both Beaufort and himself from her mind, and went on: "I've never been in a city where there seems to be such a feeling against living in *des quartiers excentriques*. What does it matter where one lives? I'm told this street is respectable."

"It's not fashionable."

"Fashionable! Do you all think so much of that? Why not make one's own fashions? But I suppose I've lived too independently; at any rate, I want to do what you all do—I want to feel cared for and safe."

He was touched, as he had been the evening before when she spoke of her need of guidance.

"That's what your friends want you to feel. New York's an awfully safe place," he added with a flash of sarcasm.

"Yes, isn't it? One feels that," she cried, missing the mockery. "Being here is like—like—being taken on a holiday when one has been a good little girl and done all one's lessons."

The analogy was well meant, but did not altogether please him. He did not mind being flippant about New York, but disliked to hear any one else take the same tone. He wondered if she did not begin to see what a powerful engine it was, and how nearly it had crushed her. The Lovell Mingotts' dinner, patched up *in extremis* out of all sorts of social odds and ends, ought to have taught her the narrowness of her escape; but either she had been all along unaware of having skirted disaster, or else she had lost sight of it in the triumph of the van der Luyden evening. Archer inclined to the former theory; he fancied that her New York was still completely undifferentiated, and the conjecture nettled him.

"Last night," he said, "New York laid itself out for you. The van der Luydens do nothing by halves."

"No: how kind they are! It was such a nice party. Every one seems to have such an esteem for them."

The terms were hardly adequate; she might have spoken in that way of a tea-party at the dear old Miss Lannings'.

"The van der Luydens," said Archer, feeling himself pompous as he spoke, "are the most powerful influence in New York society. Unfortunately—owing to her health—they receive very seldom."

She unclasped her hands from behind her head, and looked at him meditatively.

"Isn't that perhaps the reason?"

"The reason—?"

"For their great influence; that they make themselves so rare."

He coloured a little, stared at her—and suddenly felt the penetration of the remark. At a stroke she had pricked the van der Luydens and they collapsed. He laughed, and sacrificed them.

Nastasia brought the tea, with handleless Japanese cups and little covered dishes, placing the tray on a low table.

"But you'll explain these things to me—you'll tell me all I ought to know," Madame Olenska continued, leaning forward to hand him his cup.

"It's you who are telling me; opening my eyes to things I'd looked at so long that I'd ceased to see them."

She detached a small gold cigarette-case from one of her bracelets, held it out to him, and took a cigarette herself. On the chimney were long spills for lighting them.

"Ah, then we can both help each other. But I want help so much more. You must tell me just what to do."

It was on the tip of his tongue to reply: "Don't be seen driving about the streets with Beaufort—" but he was being too deeply drawn into the atmosphere of the room, which was her atmosphere, and to give advice of that sort would have been like telling some one who was bargaining for attar-of-roses in Samarkand that one should always be provided with arctics for a New York winter.[1] New York seemed much farther off than Samarkand, and if they were indeed to help each other she was rendering what might prove the first of their mutual services by making him look at his native city objectively. Viewed thus, as through the wrong end of a telescope, it looked disconcertingly small and distant; but then from Samarkand it would.

A flame darted from the logs and she bent over the fire, stretching her thin hands so close to it that a faint halo shone about the oval nails. The light touched to russet the rings of dark hair escaping from her braids, and made her pale face paler.

"There are plenty of people to tell you what to do," Archer rejoined, obscurely envious of them.

"Oh—all my aunts? And my dear old Granny?" She considered the idea impartially. "They're all a little vexed with me for setting up for myself—poor Granny especially. She wanted to keep me with her; but I had to be free—" He was impressed by this light way of speaking of the formidable Catherine, and moved by the thought of what must have given Madame Olenska this thirst for even the loneliest kind of freedom. But the idea of Beaufort gnawed him.

"I think I understand how you feel," he said. "Still, your family can advise you; explain differences; show you the way."

She lifted her thin black eyebrows. "Is New York such a labyrinth? I thought it so straight up and down—like Fifth Avenue. And with all the cross streets numbered!" She seemed to guess his faint disapproval of this, and added, with the rare smile that enchanted her whole face: "If you knew how I like it for just *that*—the straight-up-and-downness, and the big honest labels on everything!"

He saw his chance. "Everything may be labelled—but everybody is not."

"Perhaps. I may simplify too much—but you'll warn me if I

---

[1] *Attar-of-roses*: essential oil obtained from rose petals. *Samarkand*: a city in Uzbekistan, a country north of Afghanistan. *Arctics*: rubber coverings for shoes.

do." She turned from the fire to look at him. "There are only two people here who make me feel as if they understood what I mean and could explain things to me: you and Mr. Beaufort."

Archer winced at the joining of the names, and then, with a quick readjustment, understood, sympathised and pitied. So close to the powers of evil she must have lived that she still breathed more freely in their air. But since she felt that he understood her also, his business would be to make her see Beaufort as he really was, with all he represented—and abhor it.

He answered gently: "I understand. But just at first don't let go of your old friends' hands: I mean the older women, your Granny Mingott, Mrs. Welland, Mrs. van der Luyden. They like and admire you—they want to help you."

She shook her head and sighed. "Oh, I know—I know! But on condition that they don't hear anything unpleasant. Aunt Welland put it in those very words when I tried .... Does no one want to know the truth here, Mr. Archer? The real loneliness is living among all these kind people who only ask one to pretend!" She lifted her hands to her face, and he saw her thin shoulders shaken by a sob.

"Madame Olenska!—Oh, don't, Ellen," he cried, starting up and bending over her. He drew down one of her hands, clasping and chafing it like a child's while he murmured reassuring words; but in a moment she freed herself, and looked up at him with wet lashes.

"Does no one cry here, either? I suppose there's no need to, in heaven," she said, straightening her loosened braids with a laugh, and bending over the tea-kettle. It was burnt into his consciousness that he had called her "Ellen"—called her so twice; and that she had not noticed it. Far down the inverted telescope he saw the faint white figure of May Welland—in New York.

Suddenly Nastasia put her head in to say something in her rich Italian.

Madame Olenska, again with a hand at her hair, uttered an exclamation of assent—a flashing "*Già—già*"—and the Duke of St. Austrey entered, piloting a tremendous black-wigged and red-plumed lady in overflowing furs.

"My dear Countess, I've brought an old friend of mine to see you—Mrs. Struthers. She wasn't asked to the party last night, and she wants to know you."

The Duke beamed on the group, and Madame Olenska advanced with a murmur of welcome toward the queer couple. She seemed to have no idea how oddly matched they were, nor what a liberty the Duke had taken in bringing his companion— and to do him justice, as Archer perceived, the Duke seemed as unaware of it himself.

"Of course I want to know you, my dear," cried Mrs. Struthers in a round rolling voice that matched her bold feathers and her brazen wig. "I want to know everybody who's young and interesting and charming. And the Duke tells me you like music— didn't you, Duke? You're a pianist yourself, I believe? Well, do you want to hear Sarasate play tomorrow evening at my house?[1] You know I've something going on every Sunday evening—it's the day when New York doesn't know what to do with itself, and so I say to it: 'Come and be amused.' And the Duke thought you'd be tempted by Sarasate. You'll find a number of your friends."

Madame Olenska's face grew brilliant with pleasure. "How kind! How good of the Duke to think of me!" She pushed a chair up to the tea-table and Mrs. Struthers sank into it delectably. "Of course I shall be too happy to come."

"That's all right, my dear. And bring your young gentleman with you." Mrs. Struthers extended a hail-fellow hand to Archer. "I can't put a name to you—but I'm sure I've met you—I've met everybody, here, or in Paris or London. Aren't you in diplomacy? All the diplomatists come to me. You like music too? Duke, you must be sure to bring him."

The Duke said "Rather" from the depths of his beard, and Archer withdrew with a stiffly circular bow that made him feel as full of spine as a self-conscious school-boy among careless and unnoticing elders.

He was not sorry for the *dénouement* of his visit: he only wished it had come sooner, and spared him a certain waste of emotion. As he went out into the wintry night, New York again became vast and imminent, and May Welland the loveliest

---

[1] Pablo de *Sarasate* (1844-1908), Spanish composer and violinist.

woman in it. He turned into his florist's to send her the daily box of lilies-of-the-valley which, to his confusion, he found he had forgotten that morning.

As he wrote a word on his card and waited for an envelope he glanced about the embowered shop, and his eye lit on a cluster of yellow roses. He had never seen any as sun-golden before, and his first impulse was to send them to May instead of the lilies. But they did not look like her—there was something too rich, too strong, in their fiery beauty. In a sudden revulsion of mood, and almost without knowing what he did, he signed to the florist to lay the roses in another long box, and slipped his card into a second envelope, on which he wrote the name of the Countess Olenska; then, just as he was turning away, he drew the card out again, and left the empty envelope on the box.

"They'll go at once?" he enquired, pointing to the roses.

The florist assured him that they would.

<h1 style="text-align:center">X</h1>

THE next day he persuaded May to escape for a walk in the Park after luncheon. As was the custom in old-fashioned Episcopalian New York, she usually accompanied her parents to church on Sunday afternoons; but Mrs. Welland condoned her truancy, having that very morning won her over to the necessity of a long engagement, with time to prepare a hand-embroidered trousseau containing the proper number of dozens.

The day was delectable. The bare vaulting of trees along the Mall was ceiled with lapis lazuli, and arched above snow that shone like splintered crystals. It was the weather to call out May's radiance, and she burned like a young maple in the frost. Archer was proud of the glances turned on her, and the simple joy of possessorship cleared away his underlying perplexities.

"It's so delicious—waking every morning to smell lilies-of-the-valley in one's room!" she said.

"Yesterday they came late. I hadn't time in the morning—"

"But your remembering each day to send them makes me love them so much more than if you'd given a standing order, and they came every morning on the minute, like one's music-teacher—as I know Gertrude Lefferts's did, for instance, when she and Lawrence were engaged."

"Ah—they would!" laughed Archer, amused at her keenness. He looked sideways at her fruit-like cheek and felt rich and secure enough to add: "When I sent your lilies yesterday afternoon I saw some rather gorgeous yellow roses and packed them off to Madame Olenska. Was that right?"

"How dear of you! Anything of that kind delights her. It's odd she didn't mention it: she lunched with us today, and spoke of Mr. Beaufort's having sent her wonderful orchids, and cousin Henry van der Luyden a whole hamper of carnations from Skuytercliff. She seems so surprised to receive flowers. Don't people send them in Europe? She thinks it such a pretty custom."

"Oh, well, no wonder mine were overshadowed by Beaufort's," said Archer irritably. Then he remembered that he had not put a card with the roses, and was vexed at having spoken of them. He wanted to say: "I called on your cousin yesterday," but hesitated. If Madame Olenska had not spoken of his visit it might seem awkward that he should. Yet not to do so gave the affair an air of mystery that he disliked. To shake off the question he began to talk of their own plans, their future, and Mrs. Welland's insistence on a long engagement.

"If you call it long! Isabel Chivers and Reggie were engaged for two years: Grace and Thorley for nearly a year and a half. Why aren't we very well off as we are?"

It was the traditional maidenly interrogation, and he felt ashamed of himself for finding it singularly childish. No doubt she simply echoed what was said for her; but she was nearing her twenty-second birthday, and he wondered at what age "nice" women began to speak for themselves.

"Never, if we won't let them, I suppose," he mused, and recalled his mad outburst to Mr. Sillerton Jackson: "Women ought to be as free as we are—"

It would presently be his task to take the bandage from this young woman's eyes, and bid her look forth on the world. But how many generations of the women who had gone to her making had descended bandaged to the family vault? He shivered a little, remembering some of the new ideas in his scientific books, and the much-cited instance of the Kentucky cave-fish, which had ceased to develop eyes because they had no use for them.[1] What if, when he had bidden May Welland to open hers, they could only look out blankly at blankness?

"We might be much better off. We might be altogether together—we might travel."

Her face lit up. "That would be lovely," she owned: she would love to travel. But her mother would not understand their wanting to do things so differently.

"As if the mere 'differently' didn't account for it!" the wooer insisted.

"Newland! You're so original!" she exulted.

His heart sank, for he saw that he was saying all the things that young men in the same situation were expected to say, and that she was making the answers that instinct and tradition taught her to make—even to the point of calling him original.

"Original! We're all as like each other as those dolls cut out of the same folded paper. We're like patterns stencilled on a wall. Can't you and I strike out for ourselves, May?"

He had stopped and faced her in the excitement of their discussion, and her eyes rested on him with a bright unclouded admiration.

"Mercy—shall we elope?" she laughed.

"If you would—"

"You *do* love me, Newland! I'm so happy."

"But then—why not be happier?"

"We can't behave like people in novels, though, can we?"

"Why not—why not—why not?"

She looked a little bored by his insistence. She knew very well that they couldn't, but it was troublesome to have to produce a reason. "I'm not clever enough to argue with you. But that kind of thing is rather—vulgar, isn't it?" she suggested, relieved to have hit on a word that would assuredly extinguish the whole subject.

"Are you so much afraid, then, of being vulgar?"

---

[1] See Chapter 5, "Laws of Variation: Effects of Use and Disuse," in Charles Darwin's *The Origin of Species* (1859).

She was evidently staggered by this. "Of course I should hate it—so would you," she rejoined, a trifle irritably.

He stood silent, beating his stick nervously against his boot-top; and feeling that she had indeed found the right way of closing the discussion, she went on light-heartedly: "Oh, did I tell you that I showed Ellen my ring? She thinks it the most beautiful setting she ever saw. There's nothing like it in the rue de la Paix, she said. I do love you, Newland, for being so artistic!"

The next afternoon, as Archer, before dinner, sat smoking sullenly in his study, Janey wandered in on him. He had failed to stop at his club on the way up from the office where he exercised the profession of the law in the leisurely manner common to well-to-do New Yorkers of his class. He was out of spirits and slightly out of temper, and a haunting horror of doing the same thing every day at the same hour besieged his brain.

"Sameness—sameness!" he muttered, the word running through his head like a persecuting tune as he saw the familiar tall-hatted figures lounging behind the plate-glass; and because he usually dropped in at the club at that hour he had gone home instead. He knew not only what they were likely to be talking about, but the part each one would take in the discussion. The Duke of course would be their principal theme; though the appearance in Fifth Avenue of a golden-haired lady in a small canary-coloured brougham with a pair of black cobs (for which Beaufort was generally thought responsible) would also doubt-less be thoroughly gone into. Such "women" (as they were called) were few in New York, those driving their own carriages still fewer, and the appearance of Miss Fanny Ring in Fifth Avenue at the fashionable hour had profoundly agitated society. Only the day before, her carriage had passed Mrs. Lovell Mingott's, and the latter had instantly rung the little bell at her elbow and ordered the coachman to drive her home. "What if it had happened to Mrs. van der Luyden?" people asked each other with a shudder.[1] Archer could hear Lawrence Lefferts, at that very hour, holding forth on the disintegration of society.

---

[1]   See selection from "A Little Girl's New York," Appendix D.

He raised his head irritably when his sister Janey entered, and then quickly bent over his book (Swinburne's "Chastelard"— just out)[1] as if he had not seen her. She glanced at the writing-table heaped with books, opened a volume of the "Contes Drôlatiques,"[2] made a wry face over the archaic French, and sighed: "What learned things you read!"

"Well—?" he asked, as she hovered Cassandra-like before him.[3]

"Mother's very angry."

"Angry? With whom? About what?"

"Miss Sophy Jackson has just been here. She brought word that her brother would come in after dinner: she couldn't say very much, because he forbade her to: he wishes to give all the details himself. He's with cousin Louisa van der Luyden now."

"For heaven's sake, my dear girl, try a fresh start. It would take an omniscient Deity to know what you're talking about."

"It's not a time to be profane, Newland.... Mother feels badly enough about your not going to church ..."

With a groan he plunged back into his book.

"*Newland*! Do listen. Your friend Madame Olenska was at Mrs. Lemuel Struthers's party last night: she went there with the Duke and Mr. Beaufort."

At the last clause of this announcement a senseless anger swelled the young man's breast. To smother it he laughed. "Well, what of it? I knew she meant to."

Janey paled and her eyes began to project. "You knew she meant to—and you didn't try to stop her? To warn her?"

"Stop her? Warn her?" He laughed again. "I'm not engaged to be married to the Countess Olenska!" The words had a fantastic sound in his own ears.

"You're marrying into her family."

---

[1]   *Chastelard* (1865) is the first of three dramas about Mary, Queen of Scots by Algernon Charles *Swinburne* (1837-1909), controversial British poet, playwright, and critic.

[2]   *Les Contes Drôlatiques* (1832-1837) by Honoré de Balzac (1799-1850), prolific French novelist, author of the interconnected novels known collectively as the *Comédie Humaine*.

[3]   *Cassandra*: in classical literature, a young woman gifted with prophecy fated to go unheeded.

"Oh, family—family!" he jeered.

"Newland—don't you care about Family?"

"Not a brass farthing."

"Nor about what cousin Louisa van der Luyden will think?"

"Not the half of one—if she thinks such old maid's rubbish."

"Mother is not an old maid," said his virgin sister with pinched lips.

He felt like shouting back: "Yes, she is, and so are the van der Luydens, and so we all are, when it comes to being so much as brushed by the wing-tip of Reality." But he saw her long gentle face puckering into tears, and felt ashamed of the useless pain he was inflicting.

"Hang Countess Olenska! Don't be a goose, Janey—I'm not her keeper."

"No; but you *did* ask the Wellands to announce your engagement sooner so that we might all back her up; and if it hadn't been for that cousin Louisa would never have invited her to the dinner for the Duke."

"Well—what harm was there in inviting her? She was the best-looking woman in the room; she made the dinner a little less funereal than the usual van der Luyden banquet."

"You know cousin Henry asked her to please you: he persuaded cousin Louisa. And now they're so upset that they're going back to Skuytercliff tomorrow. I think, Newland, you'd better come down. You don't seem to understand how mother feels."

In the drawing-room Newland found his mother. She raised a troubled brow from her needlework to ask: "Has Janey told you?"

"Yes." He tried to keep his tone as measured as her own. "But I can't take it very seriously."

"Not the fact of having offended cousin Louisa and cousin Henry?"

"The fact that they can be offended by such a trifle as Countess Olenska's going to the house of a woman they consider common."

"*Consider—!*"

"Well, who is; but who has good music, and amuses people on Sunday evenings, when the whole of New York is dying of inanition."

"Good music? All I know is, there was a woman who got up

on a table and sang the things they sing at the places you go to in Paris. There was smoking and champagne."

"Well—that kind of thing happens in other places, and the world still goes on."

"I don't suppose, dear, you're really defending the French Sunday?"

"I've heard you often enough, mother, grumble at the English Sunday when we've been in London."

"New York is neither Paris nor London."

"Oh, no, it's not!" her son groaned.

"You mean, I suppose, that society here is not as brilliant? You're right, I daresay; but we belong here, and people should respect our ways when they come among us. Ellen Olenska especially: she came back to get away from the kind of life people lead in brilliant societies."

Newland made no answer, and after a moment his mother ventured: "I was going to put on my bonnet and ask you to take me to see cousin Louisa for a moment before dinner." He frowned, and she continued: "I thought you might explain to her what you've just said: that society abroad is different ... that people are not as particular, and that Madame Olenska may not have realised how we feel about such things. It would be, you know, dear," she added with an innocent adroitness, "in Madame Olenska's interest if you did."

"Dearest mother, I really don't see how we're concerned in the matter. The Duke took Madame Olenska to Mrs. Struthers's—in fact he brought Mrs. Struthers to call on her. I was there when they came. If the van der Luydens want to quarrel with anybody, the real culprit is under their own roof."

"Quarrel? Newland, did you ever know of cousin Henry's quarrelling? Besides, the Duke's his guest; and a stranger too. Strangers don't discriminate: how should they? Countess Olenska is a New Yorker, and should have respected the feelings of New York."

"Well, then, if they must have a victim, you have my leave to throw Madame Olenska to them," cried her son, exasperated. "I don't see myself—or you either—offering ourselves up to expiate her crimes."

"Oh, of course you see only the Mingott side," his mother answered, in the sensitive tone that was her nearest approach to anger.

The sad butler drew back the drawing-room portières and announced: "Mr. Henry van der Luyden."

Mrs. Archer dropped her needle and pushed her chair back with an agitated hand.

"Another lamp," she cried to the retreating servant, while Janey bent over to straighten her mother's cap.

Mr. van der Luyden's figure loomed on the threshold, and Newland Archer went forward to greet his cousin.

"We were just talking about you, sir," he said.

Mr. van der Luyden seemed overwhelmed by the announcement. He drew off his glove to shake hands with the ladies, and smoothed his tall hat shyly, while Janey pushed an arm-chair forward, and Archer continued: "And the Countess Olenska."

Mrs. Archer paled.

"Ah—a charming woman. I have just been to see her," said Mr. van der Luyden, complacency restored to his brow. He sank into the chair, laid his hat and gloves on the floor beside him in the old-fashioned way, and went on: "She has a real gift for arranging flowers. I had sent her a few carnations from Skuytercliff, and I was astonished. Instead of massing them in big bunches as our head-gardener does, she had scattered them about loosely, here and there ... I can't say how. The Duke had told me: he said: 'Go and see how cleverly she's arranged her drawing-room.' And she has. I should really like to take Louisa to see her, if the neighbourhood were not so—unpleasant."

A dead silence greeted this unusual flow of words from Mr. van der Luyden. Mrs. Archer drew her embroidery out of the basket into which she had nervously tumbled it, and Newland, leaning against the chimney-place and twisting a humming-bird-feather screen in his hand, saw Janey's gaping countenance lit up by the coming of the second lamp.

"The fact is," Mr. van der Luyden continued, stroking his long grey leg with a bloodless hand weighed down by the Patroon's great signet-ring, "the fact is, I dropped in to thank her for the very pretty note she wrote me about my flowers; and also—but this is between ourselves, of course—to give her a friendly warning about allowing the Duke to carry her off to parties with him. I don't know if you've heard—"

Mrs. Archer produced an indulgent smile. "Has the Duke been carrying her off to parties?"

"You know what these English grandees are. They're all alike. Louisa and I are very fond of our cousin—but it's hopeless to expect people who are accustomed to the European courts to trouble themselves about our little republican distinctions. The Duke goes where he's amused." Mr. van der Luyden paused, but no one spoke. "Yes—it seems he took her with him last night to Mrs. Lemuel Struthers's. Sillerton Jackson has just been to us with the foolish story, and Louisa was rather troubled. So I thought the shortest way was to go straight to Countess Olenska and explain—by the merest hint, you know—how we feel in New York about certain things. I felt I might, without indelicacy, because the evening she dined with us she rather suggested ... rather let me see that she would be grateful for guidance. And she *was*."

Mr. van der Luyden looked about the room with what would have been self-satisfaction on features less purged of the vulgar passions. On his face it became a mild benevolence which Mrs. Archer's countenance dutifully reflected.

"How kind you both are, dear Henry—always! Newland will particularly appreciate what you have done because of dear May and his new relations."

She shot an admonitory glance at her son, who said: "Immensely, sir. But I was sure you'd like Madame Olenska."

Mr. van der Luyden looked at him with extreme gentleness. "I never ask to my house, my dear Newland," he said, "any one whom I do not like. And so I have just told Sillerton Jackson." With a glance at the clock he rose and added: "But Louisa will be waiting. We are dining early, to take the Duke to the Opera."

After the portières had solemnly closed behind their visitor a silence fell upon the Archer family.

"Gracious—how romantic!" at last broke explosively from Janey. No one knew exactly what inspired her elliptic comments, and her relations had long since given up trying to interpret them.

Mrs. Archer shook her head with a sigh. "Provided it all turns out for the best," she said, in the tone of one who knows how surely it will not. "Newland, you must stay and see Sillerton Jackson when he comes this evening: I really shan't know what to say to him."

"Poor mother! But he won't come—" her son laughed, stooping to kiss away her frown.

XI

SOME two weeks later, Newland Archer, sitting in abstracted idleness in his private compartment of the office of Letterblair, Lamson and Low, attorneys at law, was summoned by the head of the firm.

Old Mr. Letterblair, the accredited legal adviser of three generations of New York gentility, throned behind his mahogany desk in evident perplexity. As he stroked his close-clipped white whiskers and ran his hand through the rumpled grey locks above his jutting brows, his disrespectful junior partner thought how much he looked like the Family Physician annoyed with a patient whose symptoms refuse to be classified.

"My dear sir—" he always addressed Archer as "sir"—"I have sent for you to go into a little matter; a matter which, for the moment, I prefer not to mention either to Mr. Skipworth or Mr. Redwood." The gentlemen he spoke of were the other senior partners of the firm; for, as was always the case with legal associations of old standing in New York, all the partners named on the office letter-head were long since dead; and Mr. Letterblair, for example, was, professionally speaking, his own grandson.

He leaned back in his chair with a furrowed brow. "For family reasons—" he continued.

Archer looked up.

"The Mingott family," said Mr. Letterblair with an explanatory smile and bow. "Mrs. Manson Mingott sent for me yesterday. Her grand-daughter the Countess Olenska wishes to sue her husband for divorce. Certain papers have been placed in my hands." He paused and drummed on his desk. "In view of your prospective alliance with the family I should like to consult you—to consider the case with you—before taking any farther steps."

Archer felt the blood in his temples. He had seen the Countess Olenska only once since his visit to her, and then at the Opera, in the Mingott box. During this interval she had become a less vivid and importunate image, receding from his foreground as May Welland resumed her rightful place in it. He had not heard her divorce spoken of since Janey's first random allusion to it, and had dismissed the tale as unfounded gossip. Theoretically, the idea of divorce was almost as distasteful to him as to his mother; and he was annoyed that Mr. Letterblair (no doubt prompted by old Catherine Mingott) should be so evidently planning to draw him into the affair. After all, there were plenty of Mingott men for such jobs, and as yet he was not even a Mingott by marriage.

He waited for the senior partner to continue. Mr. Letterblair unlocked a drawer and drew out a packet. "If you will run your eye over these papers—"

Archer frowned. "I beg your pardon, sir; but just because of the prospective relationship, I should prefer your consulting Mr. Skipworth or Mr. Redwood."

Mr. Letterblair looked surprised and slightly offended. It was unusual for a junior to reject such an opening.

He bowed. "I respect your scruple, sir; but in this case I believe true delicacy requires you to do as I ask. Indeed, the suggestion is not mine but Mrs. Manson Mingott's and her son's. I have seen Lovell Mingott; and also Mr. Welland. They all named you."

Archer felt his temper rising. He had been somewhat languidly drifting with events for the last fortnight, and letting May's fair looks and radiant nature obliterate the rather importunate pressure of the Mingott claims. But this behest of old Mrs. Mingott's roused him to a sense of what the clan thought they had the right to exact from a prospective son-in-law; and he chafed at the rôle.

"Her uncles ought to deal with this," he said.

"They have. The matter has been gone into by the family. They are opposed to the Countess's idea; but she is firm, and insists on a legal opinion."

The young man was silent: he had not opened the packet in his hand.

"Does she want to marry again?"

"I believe it is suggested; but she denies it."

"Then—"

"Will you oblige me, Mr. Archer, by first looking through these papers? Afterward, when we have talked the case over, I will give you my opinion."

Archer withdrew reluctantly with the unwelcome documents. Since their last meeting he had half-unconsciously collaborated with events in ridding himself of the burden of Madame Olenska. His hour alone with her by the firelight had drawn them into a momentary intimacy on which the Duke of St. Austrey's intrusion with Mrs. Lemuel Struthers, and the Countess's joyous greeting of them, had rather providentially broken. Two days later Archer had assisted at the comedy of her reinstatement in the van der Luydens' favour, and had said to himself, with a touch of tartness, that a lady who knew how to thank all-powerful elderly gentlemen to such good purpose for a bunch of flowers did not need either the private consolations or the public championship of a young man of his small compass. To look at the matter in this light simplified his own case and surprisingly furbished up all the dim domestic virtues. He could not picture May Welland, in whatever conceivable emergency, hawking about her private difficulties and lavishing her confidences on strange men; and she had never seemed to him finer or fairer than in the week that followed. He had even yielded to her wish for a long engagement, since she had found the one disarming answer to his plea for haste.

"You know, when it comes to the point, your parents have always let you have your way ever since you were a little girl," he argued; and she had answered, with her clearest look: "Yes; and that's what makes it so hard to refuse the very last thing they'll ever ask of me as a little girl."

That was the old New York note; that was the kind of answer he would like always to be sure of his wife's making. If one had habitually breathed the New York air there were times when anything less crystalline seemed stifling.

The papers he had retired to read did not tell him much in fact; but they plunged him into an atmosphere in which he choked and spluttered. They consisted mainly of an exchange of letters between Count Olenski's solicitors and a French legal firm to whom the Countess had applied for the settlement of her financial situation. There was also a short letter from the Count to his wife: after reading it, Newland Archer rose, jammed the papers back into their envelope, and reëntered Mr. Letterblair's office.

"Here are the letters, sir. If you wish I'll see Madame Olenska," he said in a constrained voice.

"Thank you—thank you, Mr. Archer. Come and dine with me tonight if you're free, and we'll go into the matter afterward: in case you wish to call on our client tomorrow."

Newland Archer walked straight home again that afternoon. It was a winter evening of transparent clearness, with an innocent young moon above the house-tops; and he wanted to fill his soul's lungs with the pure radiance, and not exchange a word with any one till he and Mr. Letterblair were closeted together after dinner. It was impossible to decide otherwise than he had done: he must see Madame Olenska himself rather than let her secrets be bared to other eyes. A great wave of compassion had swept away his indifference and impatience: she stood before him as an exposed and pitiful figure, to be saved at all costs from farther wounding herself in her mad plunges against fate.

He remembered what she had told him of Mrs. Welland's request to be spared whatever was "unpleasant" in her history, and winced at the thought that it was perhaps this attitude of mind which kept the NewYork air so pure. "Are we only Pharisees after all?" he wondered,[1] puzzled by the effort to reconcile his instinctive disgust at human vileness with his equally instinctive pity for human frailty.

For the first time he perceived how elementary his own principles had always been. He passed for a young man who had not been afraid of risks, and he knew that his secret love-affair with poor silly Mrs. Thorley Rushworth had not been too secret to

---

[1] *Pharisees*: in the New Testament, the Jewish religious leaders who strictly observed the traditional and written law.

invest him with a becoming air of adventure. But Mrs. Rushworth was "that kind of woman"; foolish, vain, clandestine by nature, and far more attracted by the secrecy and peril of the affair than by such charms and qualities as he possessed. When the fact dawned on him it nearly broke his heart, but now it seemed the redeeming feature of the case. The affair, in short, had been of the kind that most of the young men of his age had been through, and emerged from with calm consciences and an undisturbed belief in the abysmal distinction between the women one loved and respected and those one enjoyed—and pitied. In this view they were sedulously abetted by their mothers, aunts and other elderly female relatives, who all shared Mrs. Archer's belief that when "such things happened" it was undoubtedly foolish of the man, but somehow always criminal of the woman. All the elderly ladies whom Archer knew regarded any woman who loved imprudently as necessarily unscrupulous and designing, and mere simple-minded man as powerless in her clutches. The only thing to do was to persuade him, as early as possible, to marry a nice girl, and then trust to her to look after him.

In the complicated old European communities, Archer began to guess, love-problems might be less simple and less easily classified. Rich and idle and ornamental societies must produce many more such situations; and there might even be one in which a woman naturally sensitive and aloof would yet, from the force of circumstances, from sheer defencelessness and loneliness, be drawn into a tie inexcusable by conventional standards.

On reaching home he wrote a line to the Countess Olenska, asking at what hour of the next day she could receive him, and despatched it by a messenger-boy, who returned presently with a word to the effect that she was going to Skuytercliff the next morning to stay over Sunday with the van der Luydens, but that he would find her alone that evening after dinner. The note was written on a rather untidy half-sheet, without date or address, but her hand was firm and free. He was amused at the idea of her week-ending in the stately solitude of Skuytercliff, but immediately afterward felt that there, of all places, she would most feel the chill of minds rigorously averted from the "unpleasant."

He was at Mr. Letterblair's punctually at seven, glad of the pretext for excusing himself soon after dinner. He had formed his own opinion from the papers entrusted to him, and did not especially want to go into the matter with his senior partner. Mr. Letterblair was a widower, and they dined alone, copiously and slowly, in a dark shabby room hung with yellowing prints of "The Death of Chatham" and "The Coronation of Napoleon."[1] On the sideboard, between fluted Sheraton knife-cases, stood a decanter of Haut Brion, and another of the old Lanning port (the gift of a client), which the wastrel Tom Lanning had sold off a year or two before his mysterious and discreditable death in San Francisco— an incident less publicly humiliating to the family than the sale of the cellar.

After a velvety oyster soup came shad and cucumbers, then a young broiled turkey with corn fritters, followed by a canvasback with currant jelly and a celery mayonnaise. Mr. Letterblair, who lunched on a sandwich and tea, dined deliberately and deeply, and insisted on his guest's doing the same. Finally, when the closing rites had been accomplished, the cloth was removed, cigars were lit, and Mr. Letterblair, leaning back in his chair and pushing the port westward, said, spreading his back agreeably to the coal fire behind him: "The whole family are against a divorce. And I think rightly."

Archer instantly felt himself on the other side of the argument. "But why, sir? If there ever was a case—"

"Well—what's the use? *She's* here—he's there; the Atlantic's between them. She'll never get back a dollar more of her money than what he's voluntarily returned to her: their damned heathen marriage settlements take precious good care of that. As things go over there, Olenski's acted generously: he might have turned her out without a penny."

The young man knew this and was silent.

"I understand, though," Mr. Letterblair continued, "that she

---

[1] *The Death of Chatham* (1779), a painting by American artist of the colonial period, John Singleton Copley (1738-1815). *The Coronation of Napoleon in Notre Dame* (1805-07), a painting by French artist Jacques-Louis David (1748-1825), the Premier Peintre for Napoleon Bonaparte.

attaches no importance to the money. Therefore, as the family say, why not let well enough alone?"

Archer had gone to the house an hour earlier in full agreement with Mr. Letterblair's view; but put into words by this selfish, well-fed and supremely indifferent old man it suddenly became the Pharisaic voice of a society wholly absorbed in barricading itself against the unpleasant.

"I think that's for her to decide."

"H'm—have you considered the consequences if she decides for divorce?"

"You mean the threat in her husband's letter? What weight would that carry? It's no more than the vague charge of an angry blackguard."

"Yes; but it might make some unpleasant talk if he really defends the suit."

"Unpleasant—!" said Archer explosively.

Mr. Letterblair looked at him from under enquiring eyebrows, and the young man, aware of the uselessness of trying to explain what was in his mind, bowed acquiescently while his senior continued: "Divorce is always unpleasant."

"You agree with me?" Mr. Letterblair resumed, after a waiting silence.

"Naturally," said Archer.

"Well, then, I may count on you; the Mingotts may count on you; to use your influence against the idea?"

Archer hesitated. "I can't pledge myself till I've seen the Countess Olenska," he said at length.

"Mr. Archer, I don't understand you. Do you want to marry into a family with a scandalous divorce-suit hanging over it?"

"I don't think that has anything to do with the case."

Mr. Letterblair put down his glass of port and fixed on his young partner a cautious and apprehensive gaze.

Archer understood that he ran the risk of having his mandate withdrawn, and for some obscure reason he disliked the prospect. Now that the job had been thrust on him he did not propose to relinquish it; and, to guard against the possibility, he saw that he must reassure the unimaginative old man who was the legal conscience of the Mingotts.

"You may be sure, sir, that I shan't commit myself till I've reported to you; what I meant was that I'd rather not give an opinion till I've heard what Madame Olenska has to say."

Mr. Letterblair nodded approvingly at an excess of caution worthy of the best New York tradition, and the young man, glancing at his watch, pleaded an engagement and took leave.

XII

OLD-FASHIONED New York dined at seven, and the habit of after-dinner calls, though derided in Archer's set, still generally prevailed. As the young man strolled up Fifth Avenue from Waverley Place, the long thoroughfare was deserted but for a group of carriages standing before the Reggie Chiverses' (where there was a dinner for the Duke), and the occasional figure of an elderly gentleman in heavy overcoat and muffler ascending a brownstone doorstep and disappearing into a gas-lit hall. Thus, as Archer crossed Washington Square, he remarked that old Mr. du Lac was calling on his cousins the Dagonets, and turning down the corner of West Tenth Street he saw Mr. Skipworth, of his own firm, obviously bound on a visit to the Miss Lannings. A little farther up Fifth Avenue, Beaufort appeared on his doorstep, darkly projected against a blaze of light, descended to his private brougham, and rolled away to a mysterious and probably unmentionable destination. It was not an Opera night, and no one was giving a party, so that Beaufort's outing was undoubtedly of a clandestine nature. Archer connected it in his mind with a little house beyond Lexington Avenue in which beribboned window curtains and flower-boxes had recently appeared, and before whose newly painted door the canary-coloured brougham of Miss Fanny Ring was frequently seen to wait.

Beyond the small and slippery pyramid which composed Mrs. Archer's world lay the almost unmapped quarter inhabited by artists, musicians and "people who wrote." These scattered fragments of humanity had never shown any desire to be amalgamated with the social structure. In spite of odd ways they were said to be, for the most part, quite respectable; but they preferred to keep to themselves. Medora Manson, in her prosperous days, had inaugurated a "literary salon"; but it had soon died out owing to the reluctance of the literary to frequent it.

Others had made the same attempt, and there was a household of Blenkers—an intense and voluble mother, and three blowsy daughters who imitated her—where one met Edwin Booth and Patti and William Winter, and the new Shakespearian actor George Rignold,[1] and some of the magazine editors and musical and literary critics.

Mrs. Archer and her group felt a certain timidity concerning these persons. They were odd, they were uncertain, they had things one didn't know about in the background of their lives and minds. Literature and art were deeply respected in the Archer set, and Mrs. Archer was always at pains to tell her children how much more agreeable and cultivated society had been when it included such figures as Washington Irving, Fitz-Greene Halleck and the poet of "The Culprit Fay."[2] The most celebrated authors of that generation had been "gentlemen"; perhaps the unknown persons who succeeded them had gentlemanly sentiments, but their origin, their appearance, their hair, their intimacy with the stage and the Opera, made any old New York criterion inapplicable to them.

"When I was a girl," Mrs. Archer used to say, "we knew everybody between the Battery and Canal Street; and only the people one knew had carriages. It was perfectly easy to place any one then; now one can't tell, and I prefer not to try."

---

[1]   Edwin Booth (1833-1893), successful American actor and theatre manager, considered the finest American tragedian of his time and among the greatest Shakespearean actors. William Winter (1836-1917), prolific American author, theatre historian, and critic, chief drama critic for the New York Tribune from 1865-1909. George Rignold (1838-1912), English actor, famous throughout Europe, North America, and Australia for playing Shakespeare's Henry V.

[2]   All respectable New York writers approved of by Wharton's mother. Washington Irving (1783-1859), author and diplomat to Spain and England, most famous for The Sketch-Book (1820), which included "Rip van Winkle" and "The Legend of Sleepy Hollow." Fitz-Greene Halleck (1790-1867), American poet and member of the writers' circle known as the Knickerbocker Group (so-named from Irving's History of New York). "The Culprit Fay": a poem by Joseph Rodman Drake (1795-1820), member of the Knickerbocker Group, co-author of "The Croaker Papers" with Halleck. It recounts the adventures of a fairy who loves a mortal woman amidst the backdrop of Hudson River scenery.

Only old Catherine Mingott, with her absence of moral prejudices and almost *parvenu* indifference to the subtler distinctions, might have bridged the abyss; but she had never opened a book or looked at a picture, and cared for music only because it reminded her of gala nights at the *Italiens*,[1] in the days of her triumph at the Tuileries. Possibly Beaufort, who was her match in daring, would have succeeded in bringing about a fusion; but his grand house and silk-stockinged footmen were an obstacle to informal sociability. Moreover, he was as illiterate as old Mrs. Mingott, and considered "fellows who wrote" as the mere paid purveyors of rich men's pleasures; and no one rich enough to influence his opinion had ever questioned it.

Newland Archer had been aware of these things ever since he could remember, and had accepted them as part of the structure of his universe. He knew that there were societies where painters and poets and novelists and men of science, and even great actors, were as sought after as Dukes; he had often pictured to himself what it would have been to live in the intimacy of drawing-rooms dominated by the talk of Mérimée (whose "Lettres à une Inconnue" was one of his inseparables), of Thackeray, Browning or William Morris.[2] But such things were inconceivable in New York, and unsettling to think of. Archer knew most of the "fellows who wrote," the musicians and the painters: he met them at the Century,[3] or at the little musical and theatrical clubs that were beginning to come into existence. He enjoyed them there, and was bored with them at the Blenkers', where they were mingled with fervid and dowdy women who passed them about like captured curiosities; and even after his most exciting talks with Ned Winsett

---

[1] *Italiens*: famed theatre in Paris on the Boulevard des Italiens.

[2] Prosper *Mérimée* (1803-1870), French novelist, dramatist and historian whose *Lettres à une Inconnue* (1873) is a collection of the correspondence with Mlle. Jenny Dacquin between 1831 and 1870. Robert *Browning* (1812-1889), English poet, author of *Men and Women* (1855) and *The Ring and the Book* (1868-9), who innovatively developed the dramatic monologue. *William Morris* (1834-1896), English writer, artist, and social reformer associated with the Pre-Raphaelite Brotherhood, author of *The Defense of Guenevere and Other Poems* (1858).

[3] The *Century* Association: a prestigious New York City club founded in 1846 by William Cullen Bryant to promote interest in literature and the arts. Its name derives from the original membership limit of 100 authors and artists and their supporters.

he always came away with the feeling that if his world was small, so was theirs, and that the only way to enlarge either was to reach a stage of manners where they would naturally merge.

He was reminded of this by trying to picture the society in which the Countess Olenska had lived and suffered, and also—perhaps—tasted mysterious joys. He remembered with what amusement she had told him that her grandmother Mingott and the Wellands objected to her living in a "Bohemian" quarter given over to "people who wrote." It was not the peril but the poverty that her family disliked; but that shade escaped her, and she supposed they considered literature compromising.

She herself had no fears of it, and the books scattered about her drawing-room (a part of the house in which books were usually supposed to be "out of place"), though chiefly works of fiction, had whetted Archer's interest with such new names as those of Paul Bourget, Huysmans, and the Goncourt brothers.[1] Ruminating on these things as he approached her door, he was once more conscious of the curious way in which she reversed his values, and of the need of thinking himself into conditions incredibly different from any that he knew if he were to be of use in her present difficulty.

Nastasia opened the door, smiling mysteriously. On the bench in the hall lay a sable-lined overcoat, a folded opera hat of dull silk with a gold J. B. on the lining, and a white silk muffler: there was no mistaking the fact that these costly articles were the property of Julius Beaufort.

Archer was angry: so angry that he came near scribbling a word on his card and going away; then he remembered that in writing to Madame Olenska he had been kept by excess of discretion from saying that he wished to see her privately. He had therefore no one but himself to blame if she had opened her

---

[1] *Paul Bourget* (1852-1932), French novelist and man of letters, and close friend of Wharton. Joris-Karl *Huysmans* (1848-1907), French novelist associated with aestheticism, author of *Marthe, Histoire d'une Fille* (1876), a scandalous story of a young prostitute, loosely modelled on the life of Huysmann's own mistress. Edmond (1822-1896) and Jules de *Goncourt* (1830-70), French novelists and critics, collaborators on *L'Art du Dix-Huitième Siècle* (1859-75) and several novels.

doors to other visitors; and he entered the drawing-room with the dogged determination to make Beaufort feel himself in the way, and to outstay him.

The banker stood leaning against the mantelshelf, which was draped with an old embroidery held in place by brass candelabra containing church candles of yellowish wax. He had thrust his chest out, supporting his shoulders against the mantel and resting his weight on one large patent-leather foot. As Archer entered he was smiling and looking down on his hostess, who sat on a sofa placed at right angles to the chimney. A table banked with flowers formed a screen behind it, and against the orchids and azaleas which the young man recognised as tributes from the Beaufort hot-houses, Madame Olenska sat half-reclined, her head propped on a hand and her wide sleeve leaving the arm bare to the elbow.

It was usual for ladies who received in the evening to wear what were called "simple dinner dresses": a close-fitting armour of whale-boned silk, slightly open in the neck, with lace ruffles filling in the crack, and tight sleeves with a flounce uncovering just enough wrist to show an Etruscan gold bracelet or a velvet band. But Madame Olenska, heedless of tradition, was attired in a long robe of red velvet bordered about the chin and down the front with glossy black fur. Archer remembered, on his last visit to Paris, seeing a portrait by the new painter, Carolus Duran,[1] whose pictures were the sensation of the Salon, in which the lady wore one of these bold sheath-like robes with her chin nestling in fur. There was something perverse and provocative in the notion of fur worn in the evening in a heated drawing-room, and in the combination of a muffled throat and bare arms; but the effect was undeniably pleasing.

"Lord love us—three whole days at Skuytercliff!" Beaufort was saying in his loud sneering voice as Archer entered. "You'd better take all your furs, and a hot-water-bottle."

"Why? Is the house so cold?" she asked, holding out her left hand to Archer in a way mysteriously suggesting that she expected him to kiss it.

---

[1]   Charles-Emile-Auguste *Duran* (1837-1917), fashionable French portrait painter, who opened a Parisian studio in 1870 at which many Americans studied, including John Singer Sargent.

"No; but the missus is," said Beaufort, nodding carelessly to the young man.

"But I thought her so kind. She came herself to invite me. Granny says I must certainly go."

"Granny would, of course. And *I* say it's a shame you're going to miss the little oyster supper I'd planned for you at Delmonico's next Sunday, with Campanini and Scalchi and a lot of jolly people."[1] She looked doubtfully from the banker to Archer.

"Ah—that does tempt me! Except the other evening at Mrs. Struthers's I've not met a single artist since I've been here."

"What kind of artists? I know one or two painters, very good fellows, that I could bring to see you if you'd allow me," said Archer boldly.

"Painters? Are there painters in New York?" asked Beaufort, in a tone implying that there could be none since he did not buy their pictures; and Madame Olenska said to Archer, with her grave smile: "That would be charming. But I was really thinking of dramatic artists, singers, actors, musicians. My husband's house was always full of them."

She said the words "my husband" as if no sinister associations were connected with them, and in a tone that seemed almost to sigh over the lost delights of her married life. Archer looked at her perplexedly, wondering if it were lightness or dissimulation that enabled her to touch so easily on the past at the very moment when she was risking her reputation in order to break with it.

"I do think," she went on, addressing both men, "that the *imprévu*[2] adds to one's enjoyment. It's perhaps a mistake to see the same people every day."

"It's confoundedly dull, anyhow; New York is dying of dulness," Beaufort grumbled. "And when I try to liven it up for

---

[1] *Delmonico's*: a fashionable New York restaurant which opened in 1827 on William Street. Moving several times to ever-more fashionable addresses, it was the site of many of the fabulous dances and parties of the Gilded Age. In 1870, it was the site of the first débutante ball held outside of a private home. Italo *Campanini* (1845-1896), Italian tenor who made his American debut at the New York Academy of Music in 1873 and appeared in *Faust* at the opening of the Metropolitan Opera in 1883. Sofia *Scalchi* (1850-1922), Italian mezzo-soprano who visited the United States in 1882 and sang in the opening season of the Metropolitan Opera in 1883.

[2] *imprévu*: French for "unforseen" or "unexpected."

you, you go back on me. Come—think better of it! Sunday is your last chance, for Campanini leaves next week for Baltimore and Philadelphia; and I've a private room, and a Steinway, and they'll sing all night for me."

"How delicious! May I think it over, and write to you tomorrow morning?"

She spoke amiably, yet with the least hint of dismissal in her voice. Beaufort evidently felt it, and being unused to dismissals, stood staring at her with an obstinate line between his eyes.

"Why not now?"

"It's too serious a question to decide at this late hour."

"Do you call it late?"

She returned his glance coolly. "Yes; because I have still to talk business with Mr. Archer for a little while."

"Ah," Beaufort snapped. There was no appeal from her tone, and with a slight shrug he recovered his composure, took her hand, which he kissed with a practised air, and calling out from the threshold: "I say, Newland, if you can persuade the Countess to stop in town of course you're included in the supper," left the room with his heavy important step.

For a moment Archer fancied that Mr. Letterblair must have told her of his coming; but the irrelevance of her next remark made him change his mind.

"You know painters, then? You live in their *milieu?*" she asked, her eyes full of interest.

"Oh, not exactly. I don't know that the arts have a *milieu* here, any of them; they're more like a very thinly settled outskirt."

"But you care for such things?"

"Immensely. When I'm in Paris or London I never miss an exhibition. I try to keep up."

She looked down at the tip of the little satin boot that peeped from her long draperies.

"I used to care immensely too: my life was full of such things. But now I want to try not to."

"You want to try not to?"

"Yes: I want to cast off all my old life, to become just like everybody else here."

Archer reddened. "You'll never be like everybody else," he said.

She raised her straight eyebrows a little. "Ah, don't say that. If you knew how I hate to be different!"

Her face had grown as sombre as a tragic mask. She leaned forward, clasping her knee in her thin hands, and looking away from him into remote dark distances.

"I want to get away from it all," she insisted.

He waited a moment and cleared his throat. "I know. Mr. Letterblair has told me."

"Ah?"

"That's the reason I've come. He asked me to—you see I'm in the firm."

She looked slightly surprised, and then her eyes brightened. "You mean you can manage it for me? I can talk to you instead of Mr. Letterblair? Oh, that will be so much easier!"

Her tone touched him, and his confidence grew with his self-satisfaction. He perceived that she had spoken of business to Beaufort simply to get rid of him; and to have routed Beaufort was something of a triumph.

"I am here to talk about it," he repeated.

She sat silent, her head still propped by the arm that rested on the back of the sofa. Her face looked pale and extinguished, as if dimmed by the rich red of her dress. She struck Archer, of a sudden, as a pathetic and even pitiful figure.

"Now we're coming to hard facts," he thought, conscious in himself of the same instinctive recoil that he had so often criticised in his mother and her contemporaries. How little practice he had had in dealing with unusual situations! Their very vocabulary was unfamiliar to him, and seemed to belong to fiction and the stage. In face of what was coming he felt as awkward and embarrassed as a boy.

After a pause Madame Olenska broke out with unexpected vehemence: "I want to be free; I want to wipe out all the past."

"I understand that."

Her face warmed. "Then you'll help me?"

"First—" he hesitated—"perhaps I ought to know a little more."

She seemed surprised. "You know about my husband—my life with him?"

He made a sign of assent.

"Well—then—what more is there? In this country are such things tolerated? I'm a Protestant—our church does not forbid divorce in such cases."

"Certainly not."

They were both silent again, and Archer felt the spectre of Count Olenski's letter grimacing hideously between them. The letter filled only half a page, and was just what he had described it to be in speaking of it to Mr. Letterblair: the vague charge of an angry blackguard. But how much truth was behind it? Only Count Olenski's wife could tell.

"I've looked through the papers you gave to Mr. Letterblair," he said at length.

"Well—can there be anything more abominable?"

"No."

She changed her position slightly, screening her eyes with her lifted hand.

"Of course you know," Archer continued, "that if your husband chooses to fight the case—as he threatens to—"

"Yes—?"

"He can say things—things that might be unpl—might be disagreeable to you: say them publicly, so that they would get about, and harm you even if—"

"If—?"

"I mean: no matter how unfounded they were."

She paused for a long interval; so long that, not wishing to keep his eyes on her shaded face, he had time to imprint on his mind the exact shape of her other hand, the one on her knee, and every detail of the three rings on her fourth and fifth fingers; among which, he noticed, a wedding ring did not appear.

"What harm could such accusations, even if he made them publicly, do me here?"

It was on his lips to exclaim: "My poor child—far more harm than anywhere else!" Instead, he answered, in a voice that sounded in his ears like Mr. Letterblair's: "New York society is a very small world compared with the one you've lived in. And it's ruled, in spite of appearances, by a few people with—well, rather old-fashioned ideas."

She said nothing, and he continued: "Our ideas about marriage and divorce are particularly old-fashioned. Our legislation favours divorce—our social customs don't."

"Never?"

"Well—not if the woman, however injured, however irreproachable, has appearances in the least degree against her, has exposed herself by any unconventional action to—to offensive insinuations—"

She drooped her head a little lower, and he waited again, intensely hoping for a flash of indignation, or at least a brief cry of denial. None came.

A little travelling clock ticked purringly at her elbow, and a log broke in two and sent up a shower of sparks. The whole hushed and brooding room seemed to be waiting silently with Archer.

"Yes," she murmured at length, "that's what my family tell me."

He winced a little. "It's not unnatural—"

"*Our* family," she corrected herself; and Archer coloured. "For you'll be my cousin soon," she continued gently.

"I hope so."

"And you take their view?"

He stood up at this, wandered across the room, stared with void eyes at one of the pictures against the old red damask, and came back irresolutely to her side. How could he say: "Yes, if what your husband hints is true, or if you've no way of disproving it?"

"Sincerely—" she interjected, as he was about to speak.

He looked down into the fire. "Sincerely, then—what should you gain that would compensate for the possibility—the certainty—of a lot of beastly talk?"

"But my freedom—is that nothing?"

It flashed across him at that instant that the charge in the letter was true, and that she hoped to marry the partner of her guilt. How was he to tell her that, if she really cherished such a plan, the laws of the State were inexorably opposed to it? The mere suspicion that the thought was in her mind made him feel harshly and impatiently toward her. "But aren't you as free as air as it is?" he returned. "Who can touch you? Mr Letterblair tells me the financial question has been settled—"

"Oh, yes," she said indifferently.

"Well, then: is it worth while to risk what may be infinitely disagreeable and painful? Think of the newspapers—their vileness! It's all stupid and narrow and unjust—but one can't make over society."

"No," she acquiesced; and her tone was so faint and desolate that he felt a sudden remorse for his own hard thoughts.

"The individual, in such cases, is nearly always sacrificed to what is supposed to be the collective interest: people cling to any convention that keeps the family together—protects the children, if there are any," he rambled on, pouring out all the stock phrases that rose to his lips in his intense desire to cover over the ugly reality which her silence seemed to have laid bare. Since she would not or could not say the one word that would have cleared the air, his wish was not to let her feel that he was trying to probe into her secret. Better keep on the surface, in the prudent old New York way, than risk uncovering a wound he could not heal.

"It's my business, you know," he went on, "to help you to see these things as the people who are fondest of you see them. The Mingotts, the Wellands, the van der Luydens, all your friends and relations: if I didn't show you honestly how they judge such questions, it wouldn't be fair of me, would it?" He spoke insistently, almost pleading with her in his eagerness to cover up that yawning silence.

She said slowly: "No; it wouldn't be fair."

The fire had crumbled down to greyness, and one of the lamps made a gurgling appeal for attention. Madame Olenska rose, wound it up and returned to the fire, but without resuming her seat.

Her remaining on her feet seemed to signify that there was nothing more for either of them to say, and Archer stood up also.

"Very well; I will do what you wish," she said abruptly. The blood rushed to his forehead; and, taken aback by the suddenness of her surrender, he caught her two hands awkwardly in his.

"I—I do want to help you," he said.

"You do help me. Good night, my cousin."

He bent and laid his lips on her hands, which were cold and lifeless. She drew them away, and he turned to the door, found his coat and hat under the faint gas-light of the hall, and plunged out into the winter night bursting with the belated eloquence of the inarticulate.

XIII

IT was a crowded night at Wallack's theatre.[1]

The play was "The Shaughraun," with Dion Boucicault in the title rôle and Harry Montague and Ada Dyas as the lovers. The popularity of the admirable English company was at its height, and the Shaughraun always packed the house. In the galleries the enthusiasm was unreserved; in the stalls and boxes, people smiled a little at the hackneyed sentiments and clap-trap situations, and enjoyed the play as much as the galleries did.[2]

There was one episode, in particular, that held the house from floor to ceiling. It was that in which Harry Montague, after a sad, almost monosyllabic scene of parting with Miss Dyas, bade her good-bye, and turned to go. The actress, who was standing near the mantelpiece and looking down into the fire, wore a gray cashmere dress without fashionable loopings or trimmings, moulded to her tall figure and flowing in long lines about her feet. Around her neck was a narrow black velvet ribbon with the ends falling down her back.

When her wooer turned from her she rested her arms against the mantel-shelf and bowed her face in her hands. On the threshold he paused to look at her; then he stole back, lifted one of the ends of velvet ribbon, kissed it, and left the room without

---

1   *Wallack's Theatre*, at Broadway and Thirteenth Street from 1861 to 1901.

2   *The Shaughraun*: three-act play which ran 143 nights at Wallack's Theatre in 1874, by popular playwright and actor Dion *Boucicault* (1820-1890). The scene highlighted takes place at the end of Act II, where the British officer Captain Molyneux takes leave of his beloved Claire, who says they cannot speak of their love until her brother, an Irish rebel, is released from prison. Though Wharton highlights the renunciation the lovers must endure here, the play ends happily for the two sets of lovers it deals with. The "shaughraun" is an Irish trickster, wanderer figure, who helps bring about the comic ending. *Harry Montague* (1844-1878), American actor who worked in London during the 1860s, but returned to New York in 1874 to spend the rest of his career with producer Lester Wallack. *Ada Dyas* (1844-1908), leading actress in Wallack's company. *Galleries*: cheaper seats for lower class audience.

her hearing him or changing her attitude. And on this silent parting the curtain fell.

It was always for the sake of that particular scene that Newland Archer went to see "The Shaughraun." He thought the adieux of Montague and Ada Dyas as fine as anything he had ever seen Croisette and Bressant do in Paris, or Madge Robertson and Kendal in London;[1] in its reticence, its dumb sorrow, it moved him more than the most famous histrionic outpourings.

On the evening in question the little scene acquired an added poignancy by reminding him—he could not have said why—of his leave-taking from Madame Olenska after their confidential talk a week or ten days earlier.

It would have been as difficult to discover any resemblance between the two situations as between the appearance of the persons concerned. Newland Archer could not pretend to anything approaching the young English actor's romantic good looks, and Miss Dyas was a tall red-haired woman of monumental build whose pale and pleasantly ugly face was utterly unlike Ellen Olenska's vivid countenance. Nor were Archer and Madame Olenska two lovers parting in heart-broken silence; they were client and lawyer separating after a talk which had given the lawyer the worst possible impression of the client's case. Wherein, then, lay the resemblance that made the young man's heart beat with a kind of retrospective excitement? It seemed to be in Madame Olenska's mysterious faculty of suggesting tragic and moving possibilities outside the daily run of experience. She had hardly ever said a word to him to produce this impression, but it was a part of her, either a projection of her mysterious and outlandish background or of something inherently dramatic, passionate and unusual in herself. Archer had always been inclined to think that

---

[1] Sophie *Croizette* (1847-1901), French actress, popular member of the Comédie Française from 1870 to 1883. Jean-Baptiste *Bressant* (1815-1886), famous French actor, member of the Comédie Française for 23 years, and teacher of Sophie Croizette. Dame Margaret *(Madge) Robertson* (1848-1935), English actress and stage manager who established a reputation for society comedy. Robertson married William Hunter *Kendal* (1843-1917), English actor and stage manager, in 1874, and they starred thereafter as "The Kendals" in Shakespeare and Gilbert and Sullivan operettas, and jointly managed St. James's Theatre from 1879-88.

chance and circumstance played a small part in shaping people's lots compared with their innate tendency to have things happen to them. This tendency he had felt from the first in Madame Olenska. The quiet, almost passive young woman struck him as exactly the kind of person to whom things were bound to happen, no matter how much she shrank from them and went out of her way to avoid them. The exciting fact was her having lived in an atmosphere so thick with drama that her own tendency to provoke it had apparently passed unperceived. It was precisely the odd absence of surprise in her that gave him the sense of her having been plucked out of a very maelstrom: the things she took for granted gave the measure of those she had rebelled against.

Archer had left her with the conviction that Count Olenski's accusation was not unfounded. The mysterious person who figured in his wife's past as "the secretary" had probably not been unrewarded for his share in her escape. The conditions from which she had fled were intolerable, past speaking of, past believing: she was young, she was frightened, she was desperate—what more natural than that she should be grateful to her rescuer? The pity was that her gratitude put her, in the law's eyes and the world's, on a par with her abominable husband. Archer had made her understand this, as he was bound to do; he had also made her understand that simple-hearted kindly New York, on whose larger charity she had apparently counted, was precisely the place where she could least hope for indulgence.

To have to make this fact plain to her—and to witness her resigned acceptance of it—had been intolerably painful to him. He felt himself drawn to her by obscure feelings of jealousy and pity, as if her dumbly-confessed error had put her at his mercy, humbling yet endearing her. He was glad it was to him she had revealed her secret, rather than to the cold scrutiny of Mr. Letterblair, or the embarrassed gaze of her family. He immediately took it upon himself to assure them both that she had given up her idea of seeking a divorce, basing her decision on the fact that she had understood the uselessness of the proceeding; and with infinite relief they had all turned their eyes from the "unpleasantness" she had spared them.

"I was sure Newland would manage it," Mrs. Welland had said proudly of her future son-in-law; and old Mrs. Mingott, who had summoned him for a confidential interview, had congratulated him on his cleverness, and added impatiently: "Silly goose! I told her myself what nonsense it was. Wanting to pass herself off as Ellen Mingott and an old maid, when she has the luck to be a married woman and a Countess!"

These incidents had made the memory of his last talk with Madame Olenska so vivid to the young man that as the curtain fell on the parting of the two actors his eyes filled with tears, and he stood up to leave the theatre.

In doing so, he turned to the side of the house behind him, and saw the lady of whom he was thinking seated in a box with the Beauforts, Lawrence Lefferts and one or two other men. He had not spoken with her alone since their evening together, and had tried to avoid being with her in company; but now their eyes met, and as Mrs. Beaufort recognised him at the same time, and made her languid little gesture of invitation, it was impossible not to go into the box.

Beaufort and Lefferts made way for him, and after a few words with Mrs. Beaufort, who always preferred to look beautiful and not have to talk, Archer seated himself behind Madame Olenska. There was no one else in the box but Mr. Sillerton Jackson, who was telling Mrs. Beaufort in a confidential undertone about Mrs. Lemuel Struthers's last Sunday reception (where some people reported that there had been dancing). Under cover of this circumstantial narrative, to which Mrs. Beaufort listened with her perfect smile, and her head at just the right angle to be seen in profile from the stalls, Madame Olenska turned and spoke in a low voice.

"Do you think," she asked, glancing toward the stage, "he will send her a bunch of yellow roses tomorrow morning?"

Archer reddened, and his heart gave a leap of surprise. He had called only twice on Madame Olenska, and each time he had sent her a box of yellow roses, and each time without a card. She had never before made any allusion to the flowers, and he supposed she had never thought of him as the sender. Now her sudden recognition of the gift, and her associating it with the tender leave-taking on the stage, filled him with an agitated pleasure.

"I was thinking of that too—I was going to leave the theatre in order to take the picture away with me," he said.

To his surprise her colour rose, reluctantly and duskily. She looked down at the mother-of-pearl opera-glass in her smoothly gloved hands, and said, after a pause: "What do you do while May is away?"

"I stick to my work," he answered, faintly annoyed by the question.

In obedience to a long-established habit, the Wellands had left the previous week for St. Augustine, where, out of regard for the supposed susceptibility of Mr. Welland's bronchial tubes, they always spent the latter part of the winter. Mr. Welland was a mild and silent man, with no opinions but with many habits. With these habits none might interfere; and one of them demanded that his wife and daughter should always go with him on his annual journey to the south. To preserve an unbroken domesticity was essential to his peace of mind; he would not have known where his hair-brushes were, or how to provide stamps for his letters, if Mrs. Welland had not been there to tell him.

As all the members of the family adored each other, and as Mr. Welland was the central object of their idolatry, it never occurred to his wife and May to let him go to St. Augustine alone; and his sons, who were both in the law, and could not leave New York during the winter, always joined him for Easter and travelled back with him.

It was impossible for Archer to discuss the necessity of May's accompanying her father. The reputation of the Mingotts' family physician was largely based on the attack of pneumonia which Mr. Welland had never had; and his insistence on St. Augustine was therefore inflexible. Originally, it had been intended that May's engagement should not be announced till her return from Florida, and the fact that it had been made known sooner could not be expected to alter Mr. Welland's plans. Archer would have liked to join the travellers and have a few weeks of sunshine and boating with his betrothed; but he too was bound by custom and conventions. Little arduous as his professional duties were, he would have been convicted of frivolity by the whole Mingott clan if he had suggested asking for a holiday in mid-winter; and he accepted May's departure with the resignation which he perceived would have to be one of the principal constituents of married life.

He was conscious that Madame Olenska was looking at him under lowered lids. "I have done what you wished—what you advised," she said abruptly.

"Ah—I'm glad," he returned, embarrassed by her broaching the subject at such a moment.

"I understand—that you were right," she went on a little breathlessly; "but sometimes life is difficult ... perplexing ... "

"I know."

"And I wanted to tell you that I *do* feel you were right; and that I'm grateful to you," she ended, lifting her opera-glass quickly to her eyes as the door of the box opened and Beaufort's resonant voice broke in on them.

Archer stood up, and left the box and the theatre.

Only the day before he had received a letter from May Welland in which, with characteristic candour, she had asked him to "be kind to Ellen" in their absence. "She likes you and admires you so much—and you know, though she doesn't show it, she's still very lonely and unhappy. I don't think Granny understands her, or uncle Lovell Mingott either; they really think she's much worldlier and fonder of society than she is. And I can quite see that New York must seem dull to her, though the family won't admit it. I think she's been used to lots of things we haven't got; wonderful music, and picture shows, and celebrities—artists and authors and all the clever people you admire. Granny can't understand her wanting anything but lots of dinners and clothes—but I can see that you're almost the only person in New York who can talk to her about what she really cares for."

His wise May—how he had loved her for that letter! But he had not meant to act on it; he was too busy, to begin with, and he did not care, as an engaged man, to play too conspicuously the part of Madame Olenska's champion. He had an idea that she knew how to take care of herself a good deal better than the ingenuous May imagined. She had Beaufort at her feet, Mr. van der Luyden hovering above her like a protecting deity, and any number of candidates (Lawrence Lefferts among them) waiting their opportunity in the middle distance. Yet he never saw her, or exchanged a word with her, without feeling that, after all,

May's ingenuousness almost amounted to a gift of divination. Ellen Olenska was lonely and she was unhappy.

XIV

As he came out into the lobby Archer ran across his friend Ned Winsett, the only one among what Janey called his "clever people" with whom he cared to probe into things a little deeper than the average level of club and chop-house banter.

He had caught sight, across the house, of Winsett's shabby round-shouldered back, and had once noticed his eyes turned toward the Beaufort box. The two men shook hands, and Winsett proposed a bock at a little German restaurant around the corner. Archer, who was not in the mood for the kind of talk they were likely to get there, declined on the plea that he had work to do at home; and Winsett said: "Oh, well so have I for that matter, and I'll be the Industrious Apprentice too."

They strolled along together, and presently Winsett said: "Look here, what I'm really after is the name of the dark lady in that swell box of yours—with the Beauforts, wasn't she? The one your friend Lefferts seems so smitten by."

Archer, he could not have said why, was slightly annoyed. What the devil did Ned Winsett want with Ellen Olenska's name? And above all, why did he couple it with Lefferts's? It was unlike Winsett to manifest such curiosity; but after all, Archer remembered, he was a journalist.

"It's not for an interview, I hope?" he laughed.

"Well—not for the press; just for myself," Winsett rejoined. "The fact is she's a neighbour of mine—queer quarter for such a beauty to settle in—and she's been awfully kind to my little boy, who fell down her area chasing his kitten, and gave himself a nasty cut. She rushed in bareheaded, carrying him in her arms, with his knee all beautifully bandaged, and was so sympathetic and beautiful that my wife was too dazzled to ask her name."

A pleasant glow dilated Archer's heart. There was nothing extraordinary in the tale: any woman would have done as much for a neighbour's child. But it was just like Ellen, he felt, to have rushed in bareheaded, carrying the boy in her arms, and to have dazzled poor Mrs. Winsett into forgetting to ask who she was.

"That is the Countess Olenska—a granddaughter of old Mrs. Mingott's."

"Whew—a Countess!" whistled Ned Winsett. "Well, I didn't know Countesses were so neighbourly. Mingotts ain't."

"They would be, if you'd let them."

"Ah, well—" It was their old interminable argument as to the obstinate unwillingness of the "clever people" to frequent the fashionable, and both men knew that there was no use in prolonging it.

"I wonder," Winsett broke off, "how a Countess happens to live in our slum?"

"Because she doesn't care a hang about where she lives—or about any of our little social sign-posts," said Archer, with a secret pride in his own picture of her.

"H'm—been in bigger places, I suppose," the other commented. "Well, here's my corner."

He slouched off across Broadway, and Archer stood looking after him and musing on his last words.

Ned Winsett had those flashes of penetration; they were the most interesting thing about him, and always made Archer wonder why they had allowed him to accept failure so stolidly at an age when most men are still struggling.

Archer had known that Winsett had a wife and child, but he had never seen them. The two men always met at the Century, or at some haunt of journalists and theatrical people, such as the restaurant where Winsett had proposed to go for a bock. He had given Archer to understand that his wife was an invalid; which might be true of the poor lady, or might merely mean that she was lacking in social gifts or in evening clothes, or in both. Winsett himself had a savage abhorrence of social observances: Archer, who dressed in the evening because he thought it cleaner and more comfortable to do so, and who had never stopped to consider that cleanliness and comfort are two of the costliest items in a modest budget, regarded Winsett's attitude as part of the boring "Bohemian" pose that always made fashionable people, who changed their clothes without talking about it, and were not forever harping on the number of servants one kept, seem so much simpler and less self-conscious than the others. Nevertheless, he was always stimulated by Winsett, and whenever he caught sight of the journalist's lean bearded face and melancholy eyes he would rout him out of his corner and carry him off for a long talk.

Winsett was not a journalist by choice. He was a pure man of letters, untimely born in a world that had no need of letters; but after publishing one volume of brief and exquisite literary appreciations, of which one hundred and twenty copies were sold, thirty given away, and the balance eventually destroyed by the publishers (as per contract) to make room for more marketable material, he had abandoned his real calling, and taken a sub-editorial job on a women's weekly, where fashion-plates and paper patterns alternated with New England love-stories and advertisements of temperance drinks.

On the subject of "Hearth-fires" (as the paper was called) he was inexhaustibly entertaining; but beneath his fun lurked the sterile bitterness of the still young man who has tried and given up. His conversation always made Archer take the measure of his own life, and feel how little it contained; but Winsett's, after all, contained still less, and though their common fund of intellectual interests and curiosities made their talks exhilarating, their exchange of views usually remained within the limits of a pensive dilettantism.

"The fact is, life isn't much a fit for either of us," Winsett had once said. "I'm down and out; nothing to be done about it. I've got only one ware to produce, and there's no market for it here, and won't be in my time. But you're free and you're well-off. Why don't *you* get into touch? There's only one way to do it: to go into politics."

Archer threw his head back and laughed. There one saw at a flash the unbridgeable difference between men like Winsett and the others—Archer's kind. Every one in polite circles knew that, in America, "a gentleman couldn't go into politics." But, since he could hardly put it in that way to Winsett, he answered evasively: "Look at the career of the honest man in American politics! They don't want us."

"Who's 'they'? Why don't you all get together and be 'they' yourselves?"

Archer's laugh lingered on his lips in a slightly condescending smile. It was useless to prolong the discussion: everybody knew the melancholy fate of the few gentlemen who had risked their clean linen in municipal or state politics in New York. The day was past when that sort of thing was possible: the country was in possession of the bosses and the emigrant, and decent people had to fall back on sport or culture.[1]

"Culture! Yes—if we had it! But there are just a few little local patches, dying out here and there for lack of—well, hoeing and cross-fertilising: the last remnants of the old European tradition that your forebears brought with them. But you're in a pitiful little minority: you've got no centre, no competition, no audience. You're like the pictures on the walls of a deserted house: 'The Portrait of a Gentleman.' You'll never amount to anything, any of you, till you roll up your sleeves and get right down into the muck. That, or emigrate ... God! If I could emigrate ... "

Archer mentally shrugged his shoulders and turned the conversation back to books, where Winsett, if uncertain, was always interesting. Emigrate! As if a gentleman could abandon his own country! One could no more do that than one could roll up one's sleeves and go down into the muck. A gentleman simply stayed at home and abstained. But you couldn't make a man like Winsett see that; and that was why the New York of literary clubs and exotic restaurants, though a first shake made it seem more of a kaleidoscope, turned out, in the end, to be a smaller box, with a more monotonous pattern, than the assembled atoms of Fifth Avenue.

The next morning Archer scoured the town in vain for more yellow roses. In consequence of this search he arrived late at the

---

[1] *bosses and the emigrant*: probably a reference to Tammany Hall, headquarters of the powerful and disciplined Democratic Party political machine, which actively recruited European immigrants, particularly the Irish. New York City politics was notoriously corrupt; one prominent political figure, William Marcy Tweed (1823-1878), known as "Boss Tweed," was arrested on charges of forgery and larceny in 1871 and sent to prison in 1873.

office, perceived that his doing so made no difference whatever to any one, and was filled with sudden exasperation at the elaborate futility of his life. Why should he not be, at that moment, on the sands of St. Augustine with May Welland? No one was deceived by his pretense of professional activity. In old-fashioned legal firms like that of which Mr. Letterblair was the head, and which were mainly engaged in the management of large estates and "conservative" investments, there were always two or three young men, fairly well-off, and without professional ambition, who, for a certain number of hours of each day, sat at their desks accomplishing trivial tasks, or simply reading the newspapers. Though it was supposed to be proper for them to have an occupation, the crude fact of money-making was still regarded as derogatory, and the law, being a profession, was accounted a more gentlemanly pursuit than business. But none of these young men had much hope of really advancing in his profession, or any earnest desire to do so; and over many of them the green mould of the perfunctory was already perceptibly spreading.

It made Archer shiver to think that it might be spreading over him too. He had, to be sure, other tastes and interests; he spent his vacations in European travel, cultivated the "clever people" May spoke of, and generally tried to "keep up," as he had somewhat wistfully put it to Madame Olenska. But once he was married, what would become of this narrow margin of life in which his real experiences were lived? He had seen enough of other young men who had dreamed his dream, though perhaps less ardently, and who had gradually sunk into the placid and luxurious routine of their elders.

From the office he sent a note by messenger to Madame Olenska, asking if he might call that afternoon, and begging her to let him find a reply at his club; but at the club he found nothing, nor did he receive any letter the following day. This unexpected silence mortified him beyond reason, and though the next morning he saw a glorious cluster of yellow roses behind a florist's window-pane, he left it there. It was only on the third morning that he received a line by post from the Countess Olenska. To his surprise it was dated from Skuytercliff, whither the van der Luydens had promptly retreated after putting the Duke on board his steamer.

"I ran away," the writer began abruptly (without the usual preliminaries), "the day after I saw you at the play, and these kind friends have taken me in. I wanted to be quiet, and think things over. You were right in telling me how kind they were; I feel myself so safe here. I wish that you were with us." She ended with a conventional "Yours sincerely," and without any allusion to the date of her return.

The tone of the note surprised the young man. What was Madame Olenska running away from, and why did she feel the need to be safe? His first thought was of some dark menace from abroad; then he reflected that he did not know her epistolary style, and that it might run to picturesque exaggeration. Women always exaggerated; and moreover she was not wholly at her ease in English, which she often spoke as if she were translating from the French. "Je me suis évadée—" put in that way, the opening sentence immediately suggested that she might merely have wanted to escape from a boring round of engagements; which was very likely true, for he judged her to be capricious, and easily wearied of the pleasure of the moment.

It amused him to think of the van der Luydens' having carried her off to Skuytercliff on a second visit, and this time for an indefinite period. The doors of Skuytercliff were rarely and grudgingly opened to visitors, and a chilly week-end was the most ever offered to the few thus privileged. But Archer had seen, on his last visit to Paris, the delicious play of Labiche, "Le Voyage de M. Perrichon," and he remembered M. Perrichon's dogged and undiscouraged attachment to the young man whom he had pulled out of the glacier.[1] The van der Luydens had rescued Madame Olenska from a doom almost as icy; and though there were many other reasons for being attracted to her, Archer knew that beneath them all lay the gentle and obstinate determination to go on rescuing her.

He felt a distinct disappointment on learning that she was away; and almost immediately remembered that, only the day before, he had refused an invitation to spend the following

---

[1]   Le Voyage de M. Perrichon, a light comedy by French dramatist Eugène Labiche (1815-1888).

Sunday with the Reggie Chiverses at their house on the Hudson, a few miles below Skuytercliff.

He had had his fill long ago of the noisy friendly parties at Highbank, with coasting, ice-boating, sleighing, long tramps in the snow, and a general flavour of mild flirting and milder practical jokes. He had just received a box of new books from his London bookseller, and had preferred the prospect of a quiet Sunday at home with his spoils. But he now went into the club writing-room, wrote a hurried telegram, and told the servant to send it immediately. He knew that Mrs. Reggie didn't object to her visitors' suddenly changing their minds, and that there was always a room to spare in her elastic house.

XV

NEWLAND Archer arrived at the Chiverses' on Friday evening, and on Saturday went conscientiously through all the rites appertaining to a week-end at Highbank.

In the morning he had a spin in the ice-boat with his hostess and a few of the hardier guests; in the afternoon he "went over the farm" with Reggie, and listened, in the elaborately appointed stables, to long and impressive disquisitions on the horse; after tea he talked in a corner of the firelit hall with a young lady who had professed herself broken-hearted when his engagement was announced, but was now eager to tell him of her own matrimonial hopes; and finally, about midnight, he assisted in putting a gold-fish in one visitor's bed, dressed up a burglar in the bathroom of a nervous aunt, and saw in the small hours by joining in a pillow-fight that ranged from the nurseries to the basement. But on Sunday after luncheon he borrowed a cutter, and drove over to Skuytercliff.

People had always been told that the house at Skuytercliff was an Italian villa. Those who had never been to Italy believed it; so did some who had. The house had been built by Mr. van der Luyden in his youth, on his return from the "grand tour," and in anticipation of his approaching marriage with Miss Louisa Dagonet. It was a large square wooden structure, with tongued and grooved walls painted pale green and white, a Corinthian portico, and fluted pilasters between the windows. From the high ground on which it stood a series of terraces bordered by balustrades and urns descended in the steel-engraving style to a small irregular lake with an asphalt edge overhung by rare weeping conifers. To the right and left, the famous weedless lawns studded with "specimen" trees (each of a different variety) rolled away to long ranges of grass crested with elaborate cast-iron ornaments; and below, in a hollow, lay the four-roomed stone house which the first Patroon had built on the land granted him in 1612.

Against the uniform sheet of snow and the greyish winter sky the Italian villa loomed up rather grimly; even in summer it kept its distance, and the boldest coleus bed had never ventured nearer than thirty feet from its awful front. Now, as Archer rang the bell, the long tinkle seemed to echo through a mausoleum; and the surprise of the butler who at length responded to the call was as great as though he had been summoned from his final sleep.

Happily Archer was of the family, and therefore, irregular though his arrival was, entitled to be informed that the Countess Olenska was out, having driven to afternoon service with Mrs. van der Luyden exactly three quarters of an hour earlier.

"Mr. van der Luyden," the butler continued, "is in, sir; but my impression is that he is either finishing his nap or else reading yesterday's Evening Post. I heard him say, sir, on his return from church this morning, that he intended to look through the Evening Post after luncheon; if you like, sir, I might go to the library door and listen—"

But Archer, thanking him, said that he would go and meet the ladies; and the butler, obviously relieved, closed the door on him majestically.

A groom took the cutter to the stables, and Archer struck through the park to the high-road. The village of Skuytercliff was only a mile and a half away, but he knew that Mrs. van der Luyden never walked, and that he must keep to the road to meet the carriage. Presently, however, coming down a foot-path that crossed the highway, he caught sight of a slight figure in a red cloak, with a big dog running ahead. He hurried forward, and Madame Olenska stopped short with a smile of welcome.

"Ah, you've come!" she said, and drew her hand from her muff. The red cloak made her look gay and vivid, like the Ellen Mingott of old days; and he laughed as he took her hand, and answered: "I came to see what you were running away from."

Her face clouded over, but she answered: "Ah, well—you will see, presently."

The answer puzzled him. "Why—do you mean that you've been overtaken?"

She shrugged her shoulders, with a little movement like Nastasia's, and rejoined in a lighter tone: "Shall we walk on? I'm so cold after the sermon. And what does it matter, now you're here to protect me?"

The blood rose to his temples and he caught a fold of her cloak. "Ellen—what is it? You must tell me."

"Oh, presently—let's run a race first: my feet are freezing to the ground," she cried; and gathering up the cloak she fled away across the snow, the dog leaping about her with challenging barks. For a moment Archer stood watching, his gaze delighted by the flash of the red meteor against the snow; then he started after her, and they met, panting and laughing, at a wicket that led into the park.

She looked up at him and smiled. "I knew you'd come!"

"That shows you wanted me to," he returned, with a disproportionate joy in their nonsense. The white glitter of the trees filled the air with its own mysterious brightness, and as they walked on over the snow the ground seemed to sing under their feet.

"Where did you come from?" Madame Olenska asked.

He told her, and added: "It was because I got your note."

After a pause she said, with a just perceptible chill in her voice: "May asked you to take care of me."

"I didn't need any asking."

"You mean—I'm so evidently helpless and defenceless? What a poor thing you must all think me! But women here seem not—seem never to feel the need: any more than the blessed in heaven."

He lowered his voice to ask: "What sort of a need?"

"Ah, don't ask me! I don't speak your language," she retorted petulantly.

The answer smote him like a blow, and he stood still in the path, looking down at her.

"What did I come for, if I don't speak yours?"

"Oh, my friend—!" She laid her hand lightly on his arm, and he pleaded earnestly: "Ellen—why won't you tell me what's happened?"

She shrugged again. "Does anything ever happen in heaven?" He was silent, and they walked on a few yards without exchanging a word. Finally she said: "I will tell you—but where, where, where? One can't be alone for a minute in that great seminary of a house, with all the doors wide open, and always a servant bringing tea, or a log for the fire, or the newspaper! Is there nowhere in an American house where one may be by one's self? You're so shy, and yet you're so public. I always feel as if I were in the convent again—or on the stage, before a dreadfully polite audience that never applauds."

"Ah, you don't like us!" Archer exclaimed.

They were walking past the house of the old Patroon, with its squat walls and small square windows compactly grouped about a central chimney. The shutters stood wide, and through one of the newly-washed windows Archer caught the light of a fire.

"Why—the house is open!" he said.

She stood still. "No; only for today, at least. I wanted to see it, and Mr. van der Luyden had the fire lit and the windows opened, so that we might stop there on the way back from church this morning." She ran up the steps and tried the door. "It's still unlocked—what luck! Come in and we can have a quiet talk. Mrs. van der Luyden has driven over to see her old aunts at Rhinebeck and we shan't be missed at the house for another hour."

He followed her into the narrow passage. His spirits, which had dropped at her last words, rose with an irrational leap. The homely little house stood there, its panels and brasses shining in the firelight, as if magically created to receive them. A big bed of embers still gleamed in the kitchen chimney, under an iron pot hung from an ancient crane. Rush-bottomed arm-chairs faced each other across the tiled hearth, and rows of Delft plates stood on shelves against the walls. Archer stooped over and threw a log upon the embers.

Madame Olenska, dropping her cloak, sat down in one of the chairs. Archer leaned against the chimney and looked at her.

"You're laughing now; but when you wrote me you were unhappy," he said.

"Yes." She paused. "But I can't feel unhappy when you're here."

"I sha'n't be here long," he rejoined, his lips stiffening with the effort to say just so much and no more.

"No; I know. But I'm improvident: I live in the moment when I'm happy."

The words stole through him like a temptation, and to close his senses to it he moved away from the hearth and stood gazing out at the black tree-boles against the snow. But it was as if she too had shifted her place, and he still saw her, between himself and the trees, drooping over the fire with her indolent smile. Archer's heart was beating insubordinately. What if it were from him that she had been running away, and if she had waited to tell him so till they were here alone together in this secret room?

"Ellen, if I'm really a help to you—if you really wanted me to come—tell me what's wrong, tell me what it is you're running away from," he insisted.

He spoke without shifting his position, without even turning to look at her: if the thing was to happen, it was to happen in this way, with the whole width of the room between them, and his eyes still fixed on the outer snow.

For a long moment she was silent; and in that moment Archer imagined her, almost heard her, stealing up behind him to throw her light arms about his neck. While he waited, soul and body throbbing with the miracle to come, his eyes mechanically received the image of a heavily-coated man with his fur collar turned up who was advancing along the path to the house. The man was Julius Beaufort.

"Ah—!" Archer cried, bursting into a laugh.

Madame Olenska had sprung up and moved to his side, slipping her hand into his; but after a glance through the window her face paled and she shrank back.

"So that was it?" Archer said derisively.

"I didn't know he was here," Madame Olenska murmured. Her hand still clung to Archer's; but he drew away from her, and walking out into the passage threw open the door of the house.

"Hallo, Beaufort—this way! Madame Olenska was expecting you," he said.

During his journey back to New York the next morning, Archer relived with a fatiguing vividness his last moments at Skuytercliff. Beaufort, though clearly annoyed at finding him with Madame Olenska, had, as usual, carried off the situation high-handedly. His way of ignoring people whose presence inconvenienced him actually gave them, if they were sensitive to it, a feeling of invisibility, of non-existence. Archer, as the three strolled back through the park, was aware of this odd sense of disembodiment; and humbling as it was to his vanity it gave him the ghostly advantage of observing unobserved.

Beaufort had entered the little house with his usual easy assurance; but he could not smile away the vertical line between his eyes. It was fairly clear that Madame Olenska had not known that he was coming, though her words to Archer had hinted at the possibility; at any rate, she had evidently not told him where she was going when she left New York, and her unexplained departure had exasperated him. The ostensible reason of his appearance was the discovery, the very night before, of a "perfect little house," not in the market, which was really just the thing for her, but would be snapped up instantly if she didn't take it; and he was loud in mock-reproaches for the dance she had led him in running away just as he had found it.

"If only this new dodge for talking along a wire had been a little bit nearer perfection I might have told you all this from town, and been toasting my toes before the club fire at this minute, instead of tramping after you through the snow," he grumbled, disguising a real irritation under the pretence of it; and at this opening Madame Olenska twisted the talk away to the fantastic possibility that they might one day actually converse with each other from street to street, or even—incredible dream!—from one town to another.[1] This struck

---

[1]   Alexander Graham Bell exhibited his telephone at the 1876 Centennial Exposition in Philadelphia; the first telephone line and switchboard were installed in Boston in 1877. A central switching office opened in Manhattan in 1878.

from all three allusions to Edgar Poe and Jules Verne,[1] and such platitudes as naturally rise to the lips of the most intelligent when they are talking against time, and dealing with a new invention in which it would seem ingenuous to believe too soon; and the question of the telephone carried them safely back to the big house.

Mrs. van der Luyden had not yet returned; and Archer took his leave and walked off to fetch the cutter, while Beaufort followed the Countess Olenska indoors. It was probable that, little as the van der Luydens encouraged unannounced visits, he could count on being asked to dine, and sent back to the station to catch the nine o'clock train; but more than that he would certainly not get, for it would be inconceivable to his hosts that a gentleman travelling without luggage should wish to spend the night, and distasteful to them to propose it to a person with whom they were on terms of such limited cordiality as Beaufort.

Beaufort knew all this, and must have foreseen it; and his taking the long journey for so small a reward gave the measure of his impatience. He was undeniably in pursuit of the Countess Olenska; and Beaufort had only one object in view in his pursuit of pretty women. His dull and childless home had long since palled on him; and in addition to more permanent consolations he was always in quest of amorous adventures in his own set. This was the man from whom Madame Olenska was avowedly flying: the question was whether she had fled because his importunities displeased her, or because she did not wholly trust herself to resist them; unless, indeed, all her talk of flight had been a blind, and her departure no more than a manœuvre.

Archer did not really believe this. Little as he had actually seen of Madame Olenska, he was beginning to think that he could read her face, and if not her face, her voice; and both had betrayed annoyance, and even dismay, at Beaufort's sudden appearance. But,

---

[1] *Edgar Allen Poe* (1809-1849), American short-story writer and poet, and *Jules Verne* (1828-1905), popular French writer who wrote adventure novels informed by popular science. Both are associated here with wild imaginations and for writing early instances of what we think of today as "science fiction."

after all, if this were the case, was it not worse than if she had left New York for the express purpose of meeting him? If she had done that, she ceased to be an object of interest, she threw in her lot with the vulgarest of dissemblers: a woman engaged in a love affair with Beaufort "classed" herself irretrievably.

No, it was worse a thousand times if, judging Beaufort, and probably despising him, she was yet drawn to him by all that gave him an advantage over the other men about her: his habit of two continents and two societies, his familiar association with artists and actors and people generally in the world's eye, and his careless contempt for local prejudices. Beaufort was vulgar, he was uneducated, he was purse-proud; but the circumstances of his life, and a certain native shrewdness, made him better worth talking to than many men, morally and socially his betters, whose horizon was bounded by the Battery and the Central Park. How should any one coming from a wider world not feel the difference and be attracted by it?

Madame Olenska, in a burst of irritation, had said to Archer that he and she did not talk the same language; and the young man knew that in some respects this was true. But Beaufort understood every turn of her dialect, and spoke it fluently: his view of life, his tone, his attitude, were merely a coarser reflection of those revealed in Count Olenski's letter. This might seem to be to his disadvantage with Count Olenski's wife; but Archer was too intelligent to think that a young woman like Ellen Olenska would necessarily recoil from everything that reminded her of her past. She might believe herself wholly in revolt against it; but what had charmed her in it would still charm her, even though it were against her will.

Thus, with a painful impartiality, did the young man make out the case for Beaufort, and for Beaufort's victim. A longing to enlighten her was strong in him; and there were moments when he imagined that all she asked was to be enlightened.

That evening he unpacked his books from London. The box was full of things he had been waiting for impatiently; a new volume of Herbert Spencer, another collection of the prolific Alphonse Daudet's brilliant tales, and a novel called "Middlemarch," as to which there had lately been interesting things said in the reviews.[1] He had declined three dinner invitations in favour of this feast; but though he turned the pages with the sensuous joy of the book-lover, he did not know what he was reading, and one book after another dropped from his hand. Suddenly, among them, he lit on a small volume of verse which he had ordered because the name had attracted him: "The House of Life."[2] He took it up, and found himself plunged in an atmosphere unlike any he had ever breathed in books; so warm, so rich, and yet so ineffably tender, that it gave a new and haunting beauty to the most elementary of human passions. All through the night he pursued through those enchanted pages the vision of a woman who had the face of Ellen Olenska; but when he woke the next morning, and looked out at the brownstone houses across the street, and thought of his desk in Mr. Letterblair's office, and the family pew in Grace Church, his hour in the park of Skuytercliff became as far outside the pale of probability as the visions of the night.

"Mercy, how pale you look, Newland!" Janey commented over the coffee-cups at breakfast; and his mother added: "Newland, dear, I've noticed lately that you've been coughing; I do hope you're not letting yourself be overworked?" For it was the conviction of both ladies that, under the iron despotism of his senior partners, the young man's life was spent in the most exhausting professional labours—and he had never thought it necessary to undeceive them.

The next two or three days dragged by heavily. The taste of

---

[1]   *Herbert Spencer* (1820-1903), English philosopher, author of *Principles of Psychology* (1855 and 1870-2), *First Principles* (1862), and *Descriptive Sociology* (1874). He was famous for systematic thinking, and for applying Darwin's ideas to social matters and thus lending intellectual authority to "social Darwinist" formulae popularized in the late nineteenth and early twentieth centuries. *Alphonse Daudet* (1840-1897), popular French novelist and short story writer. *Middlemarch* (1870–1871), one of the masterpieces of nineteeth-century literary realism, by English novelist George Eliot, pen-name of Mary Ann Evans (1819-1880). It explores marital relations and domestic issues with as backdrop the social and political upheavals resulting from the first Reform Bill.

[2]   *The House of Life*: sequence of love sonnets by Dante Gabriel Rossetti (1828-1882), English poet and painter, and founding member of the Pre-Raphaelite Brotherhood. It did not appear with this title until 1881; in Rossetti's *Poems* of 1871, the group appears under the title, "Sonnets and Songs, towards a work to be called 'The House of Life'."

the usual was like cinders in his mouth, and there were moments when he felt as if he were being buried alive under his future. He heard nothing of the Countess Olenska, or of the perfect little house, and though he met Beaufort at the club they merely nodded at each other across the whist-tables. It was not till the fourth evening that he found a note awaiting him on his return home. "Come late tomorrow: I must explain to you. Ellen." These were the only words it contained.

The young man, who was dining out, thrust the note into his pocket, smiling a little at the Frenchness of the "to you." After dinner he went to a play; and it was not until his return home, after midnight, that he drew Madame Olenska's missive out again and re-read it slowly a number of times. There were several ways of answering it, and he gave considerable thought to each one during the watches of an agitated night. That on which, when morning came, he finally decided was to pitch some clothes into a portmanteau and jump on board a boat that was leaving that very afternoon for St. Augustine.

XVI

WHEN Archer walked down the sandy main street of St. Augustine to the house which had been pointed out to him as Mr. Welland's, and saw May Welland standing under a magnolia with the sun in her hair, he wondered why he had waited so long to come.

Here was the truth, here was reality, here was the life that belonged to him; and he, who fancied himself so scornful of arbitrary restraints, had been afraid to break away from his desk because of what people might think of his stealing a holiday!

Her first exclamation was: "Newland—has anything happened?" and it occurred to him that it would have been more "feminine" if she had instantly read in his eyes why he had come. But when he answered: "Yes—I found I had to see you," her happy blushes took the chill from her surprise, and he saw how easily he would be forgiven, and how soon even Mr. Letterblair's mild disapproval would be smiled away by a tolerant family.

Early as it was, the main street was no place for any but formal greetings, and Archer longed to be alone with May, and to pour out all his tenderness and his impatience. It still lacked an hour to the late Welland breakfast-time, and instead of asking him to come in she proposed that they should walk out to an old orange-garden beyond the town. She had just been for a row on the river, and the sun that netted the little waves with gold seemed to have caught her in its meshes. Across the warm brown of her cheek her blown hair glittered like silver wire; and her eyes too looked lighter, almost pale in their youthful limpidity. As she walked beside Archer with her long swinging gait her face wore the vacant serenity of a young marble athlete.

To Archer's strained nerves the vision was as soothing as the sight of the blue sky and the lazy river. They sat down on a bench under the orange-trees and he put his arm about her and kissed her. It was like drinking at a cold spring with the sun on it; but his pressure may have been more vehement than he had intended, for the blood rose to her face and she drew back as if he had startled her.

"What is it?" he asked, smiling; and she looked at him with surprise, and answered: "Nothing."

A slight embarrassment fell on them, and her hand slipped out of his. It was the only time that he had kissed her on the lips except for their fugitive embrace in the Beaufort conservatory, and he saw that she was disturbed, and shaken out of her cool boyish composure.

"Tell me what you do all day," he said, crossing his arms under his tilted-back head, and pushing his hat forward to screen the sun-dazzle. To let her talk about familiar and simple things was the easiest way of carrying on his own independent train of thought; and he sat listening to her simple chronicle of swimming, sailing and riding, varied by an occasional dance at the primitive inn when a man-of-war came in. A few pleasant people from Philadelphia and Baltimore were picknicking at the inn, and the Selfridge Merrys had come down for three weeks because Kate Merry had had bronchitis. They were planning to lay out a lawn tennis court on the sands; but no one but Kate and May had racquets, and most of the people had not even heard of the game.[1]

All this kept her very busy, and she had not had time to do more than look at the little vellum book that Archer had sent her the week before (the "Sonnets from the Portuguese"); but she was learning by heart "How they brought the Good News from Ghent to Aix," because it was one of the first things he had ever read to her; and it amused her to be able to tell him that Kate Merry had never even heard of a poet called Robert Browning.[2]

Presently she started up, exclaiming that they would be late for breakfast; and they hurried back to the tumble-down house with its paintless porch and unpruned hedge of plumbago and pink geraniums where the Wellands were installed for the winter. Mr. Welland's sensitive domesticity shrank from the discomforts of the slovenly southern hotel, and at immense expense, and in face of almost insuperable difficulties, Mrs. Welland was obliged, year after year, to improvise an establishment partly made up of discontented New York servants and partly drawn from the local African supply.

"The doctors want my husband to feel that he is in his own home; otherwise he would be so wretched that the climate would not do him any good," she explained, winter after winter, to the sympathising Philadelphians and Baltimoreans; and Mr. Welland, beaming across a breakfast table miraculously supplied with the most varied delicacies, was presently saying to Archer: "You see, my dear fellow, we camp—we literally camp. I tell my wife and May that I want to teach them how to rough it."

Mr. and Mrs. Welland had been as much surprised as their daughter by the young man's sudden arrival; but it had occurred to him to explain that he had felt himself on the verge of a nasty cold, and this seemed to Mr. Welland an all-sufficient reason for abandoning any duty.

---

[1] Englishman Major W. C. Wingfield patented the equipment and rules for the modern version of tennis in 1874; that same year, the game was brought to the United States by Mary Ewing Outerbridge.

[2] *Sonnets From the Portuguese* (1847, 1850) by popular English poet Elizabeth Barrett Browning (1806-1861) is a collection of forty-four love poems to her husband, poet Robert Browning. *"How they ... Aix"*: poem by Robert Browning.

"You can't be too careful, especially toward spring," he said, heaping his plate with straw-coloured griddle-cakes and drowning them in golden syrup. "If I'd only been as prudent at your age May would have been dancing at the Assemblies now,[1] instead of spending her winters in a wilderness with an old invalid."

"Oh, but I love it here, Papa; you know I do. If only Newland could stay I should like it a thousand times better than New York."

"Newland must stay till he has quite thrown off his cold," said Mrs. Welland indulgently; and the young man laughed, and said he supposed there was such a thing as one's profession.

He managed, however, after an exchange of telegrams with the firm, to make his cold last a week; and it shed an ironic light on the situation to know that Mr. Letterblair's indulgence was partly due to the satisfactory way in which his brilliant young junior partner had settled the troublesome matter of the Olenski divorce. Mr. Letterblair had let Mrs. Welland know that Mr. Archer had "rendered an invaluable service" to the whole family, and that old Mrs. Manson Mingott had been particularly pleased; and one day when May had gone for a drive with her father in the only vehicle the place produced Mrs. Welland took occasion to touch on a topic which she always avoided in her daughter's presence.

"I'm afraid Ellen's ideas are not at all like ours. She was barely eighteen when Medora Manson took her back to Europe—you remember the excitement when she appeared in black at her coming-out ball? Another of Medora's fads—really this time it was almost prophetic! That must have been at least twelve years ago; and since then Ellen has never been to America. No wonder she is completely Europeanised."

"But European society is not given to divorce: Countess Olenska thought she would be conforming to American ideas in asking for her freedom." It was the first time that the young man had pronounced her name since he had left Skuytercliff, and he felt the colour rise to his cheek.

Mrs. Welland smiled compassionately. "That is just like the extraordinary things that foreigners invent about us. They think we dine at two o'clock and countenance divorce! That is why it

<hr>

[1]   *Assemblies*: fashionable City Assembly balls held regularly.

seems to me so foolish to entertain them when they come to New York. They accept our hospitality, and then they go home and repeat the same stupid stories."

Archer made no comment on this, and Mrs. Welland continued: "But we do most thoroughly appreciate your persuading Ellen to give up the idea. Her grandmother and her uncle Lovell could do nothing with her; both of them have written that her changing her mind was entirely due to your influence—in fact she said so to her grandmother. She has an unbounded admiration for you. Poor Ellen—she was always a wayward child. I wonder what her fate will be?"

"What we've all contrived to make it," he felt like answering. "If you'd all of you rather she should be Beaufort's mistress than some decent fellow's wife you've certainly gone the right way about it."

He wondered what Mrs. Welland would have said if he had uttered the words instead of merely thinking them. He could picture the sudden decomposure of her firm placid features, to which a lifelong mastery over trifles had given an air of factitious authority. Traces still lingered on them of a fresh beauty like her daughter's; and he asked himself if May's face was doomed to thicken into the same middle-aged image of invincible innocence.

Ah, no, he did not want May to have that kind of innocence, the innocence that seals the mind against imagination and the heart against experience!

"I verily believe," Mrs. Welland continued, "that if the horrible business had come out in the newspapers it would have been my husband's death-blow. I don't know any of the details; I only ask not to, as I told poor Ellen when she tried to talk to me about it. Having an invalid to care for, I have to keep my mind bright and happy. But Mr. Welland was terribly upset; he had a slight temperature every morning while we were waiting to hear what had been decided. It was the horror of his girl's learning that such things were possible—but of course, dear Newland, you felt that too. We all knew that you were thinking of May."

"I'm always thinking of May," the young man rejoined, rising to cut short the conversation.

He had meant to seize the opportunity of his private talk with Mrs. Welland to urge her to advance the date of his marriage. But .

he could think of no arguments that would move her, and with a sense of relief he saw Mr. Welland and May driving up to the door.

His only hope was to plead again with May, and on the day before his departure he walked with her to the ruinous garden of the Spanish Mission. The background lent itself to allusions to European scenes; and May, who was looking her loveliest under a wide-brimmed hat that cast a shadow of mystery over her too-clear eyes, kindled into eagerness as he spoke of Granada and the Alhambra.[1]

"We might be seeing it all this spring—even the Easter ceremonies at Seville," he urged, exaggerating his demands in the hope of a larger concession.

"Easter in Seville? And it will be Lent next week!" she laughed.

"Why shouldn't we be married in Lent?" he rejoined; but she looked so shocked that he saw his mistake.[2]

"Of course I didn't mean that, dearest; but soon after Easter—so that we could sail at the end of April. I know I could arrange it at the office."

She smiled dreamily upon the possibility; but he perceived that to dream of it sufficed her. It was like hearing him read aloud out of his poetry books the beautiful things that could not possibly happen in real life.

"Oh, do go on, Newland; I do love your descriptions."

"But why should they be only descriptions? Why shouldn't we make them real?"

"We shall, dearest, of course; next year." Her voice lingered over it.

"Don't you want them to be real sooner? Can't I persuade you to break away now?"

She bowed her head, vanishing from him under her conniving hat-brim.

---

[1] *Alhambra*: a thirteenth-century palace built on a mountain in Granada, one of the finest examples of Moorish architecture in Spain.

[2] *Lent*: period of 40 weekdays from Ash Wednesday to Easter evening, Lent is a time of penitential preparation to commemorate Jesus's 40-day fast in the wilderness. For practicing Episcopalians, Lent would have been a time to avoid worldly pleasures.

"Why should we dream away another year? Look at me, dear! Don't you understand how I want you for my wife?"

For a moment she remained motionless; then she raised on him eyes of such despairing clearness that he half-released her waist from his hold. But suddenly her look changed and deepened inscrutably. "I'm not sure if I *do* understand," she said. "Is it—is it because you're not certain of continuing to care for me?"

Archer sprang up from his seat. "My God—perhaps—I don't know," he broke out angrily.

May Welland rose also; as they faced each other she seemed to grow in womanly stature and dignity. Both were silent for a moment, as if dismayed by the unforeseen trend of their words: then she said in a low voice: "If that is it—is there some one else?"

"Some one else—between you and me?" He echoed her words slowly, as though they were only half-intelligible and he wanted time to repeat the question to himself. She seemed to catch the uncertainty of his voice, for she went on in a deepening tone: "Let us talk frankly, Newland. Sometimes I've felt a difference in you; especially since our engagement has been announced."

"Dear—what madness!" he recovered himself to exclaim.

She met his protest with a faint smile. "If it is, it won't hurt us to talk about it." She paused, and added, lifting her head with one of her noble movements: "Or even if it's true: why shouldn't we speak of it? You might so easily have made a mistake."

He lowered his head, staring at the black leaf-pattern on the sunny path at their feet. "Mistakes are always easy to make; but if I had made one of the kind you suggest, is it likely that I should be imploring you to hasten our marriage?"

She looked downward too, disturbing the pattern with the point of her sunshade while she struggled for expression. "Yes," she said at length. "You might want—once for all—to settle the question: it's one way."

Her quiet lucidity startled him, but did not mislead him into thinking her insensible. Under her hat-brim he saw the pallor of her profile, and a slight tremor of the nostril above her resolutely steadied lips.

"Well—?" he questioned, sitting down on the bench, and looking up at her with a frown that he tried to make playful.

She dropped back into her seat and went on: "You mustn't think that a girl knows as little as her parents imagine. One hears and one notices—one has one's feelings and ideas. And of course, long before you told me that you cared for me, I'd known that there was some one else you were interested in; every one was talking about it two years ago at Newport. And once I saw you sitting together on the verandah at a dance—and when she came back into the house her face was sad, and I felt sorry for her; I remembered it afterward, when we were engaged."

Her voice had sunk almost to a whisper, and she sat clasping and unclasping her hands about the handle of her sunshade. The young man laid his upon them with a gentle pressure; his heart dilated with an inexpressible relief.

"My dear child—was *that* it? If you only knew the truth!"

She raised her head quickly. "Then there is a truth I don't know?"

He kept his hand over hers. "I meant, the truth about the old story you speak of."

"But that's what I want to know, Newland—what I ought to know. I couldn't have my happiness made out of a wrong—an unfairness—to somebody else. And I want to believe that it would be the same with you. What sort of a life could we build on such foundations?"

Her face had taken on a look of such tragic courage that he felt like bowing himself down at her feet. "I've wanted to say this for a long time," she went on. "I've wanted to tell you that, when two people really love each other, I understand that there may be situations which make it right that they should—should go against public opinion. And if you feel yourself in any way pledged ... pledged to the person we've spoken of ... and if there is any way ... any way in which you can fulfill your pledge ... even by her getting a divorce ... Newland, don't give her up because of me!"

His surprise at discovering that her fears had fastened upon an episode so remote and so completely of the past as his love affair with Mrs. Thorley Rushworth gave way to wonder at the generosity of her view. There was something superhuman in an attitude so recklessly unorthodox, and if other problems had not pressed on him he would have been lost in wonder at the prodigy of the Wellands' daughter urging him to marry his former mistress. But he was still dizzy with the glimpse of the precipice they had skirted, and full of a new awe at the mystery of young-girlhood.

For a moment he could not speak; then he said: "There is no pledge—no obligation whatever—of the kind you think. Such cases don't always—present themselves quite as simply as ... But that's no matter ... I love your generosity, because I feel as you do about those things ... I feel that each case must be judged individually, on its own merits ... irrespective of stupid conventionalities ... I mean, each woman's right to her liberty—" He pulled himself up, startled by the turn his thoughts had taken, and went on, looking at her with a smile: "Since you understand so many things, dearest, can't you go a little farther, and understand the uselessness of our submitting to another form of the same foolish conventionalities? If there's no one and nothing between us, isn't that an argument for marrying quickly, rather than for more delay?"

She flushed with joy and lifted her face to his; as he bent to it he saw that her eyes were full of happy tears. But in another moment she seemed to have descended from her womanly eminence to helpless and timorous girlhood; and he understood that her courage and initiative were all for others, and that she had none for herself. It was evident that the effort of speaking had been much greater than her studied composure betrayed, and that at his first word of reassurance she had dropped back into the usual, as a too-adventurous child takes refuge in its mother's arms.

Archer had no heart to go on pleading with her; he was too much disappointed at the vanishing of the new being who had cast that one deep look at him from her transparent eyes. May seemed to be aware of his disappointment, but without knowing how to alleviate it; and they stood up and walked silently home.

XVII

"YOUR cousin the Countess called on mother while you were away," Janey Archer announced to her brother on the evening of his return.

The young man, who was dining alone with his mother and sister, glanced up in surprise and saw Mrs. Archer's gaze demurely bent on her plate. Mrs. Archer did not regard her seclusion from the world as a reason for being forgotten by it; and Newland guessed that she was slightly annoyed that he should be surprised by Madame Olenska's visit.

"She had on a black velvet polonaise with jet buttons, and a tiny green monkey muff; I never saw her so stylishly dressed," Janey continued. "She came alone, early on Sunday afternoon; luckily the fire was lit in the drawing-room. She had one of those new card-cases. She said she wanted to know us because you'd been so good to her."

Newland laughed. "Madame Olenska always takes that tone about her friends. She's very happy at being among her own people again."

"Yes, so she told us," said Mrs. Archer. "I must say she seems thankful to be here."

"I hope you liked her, mother."

Mrs. Archer drew her lips together. "She certainly lays herself out to please, even when she is calling on an old lady."

"Mother doesn't think her simple," Janey interjected, her eyes screwed upon her brother's face.

"It's just my old-fashioned feeling; dear May is my ideal," said Mrs. Archer.

"Ah," said her son, "they're not alike."

Archer had left St. Augustine charged with many messages for old Mrs. Mingott; and a day or two after his return to town he called on her.

The old lady received him with unusual warmth; she was grateful to him for persuading the Countess Olenska to give up the idea of a divorce; and when he told her that he had deserted the office without leave, and rushed down to St. Augustine simply because he wanted to see May, she gave an adipose chuckle and patted his knee with her puff-ball hand.

"Ah, ah—so you kicked over the traces, did you? And I suppose Augusta and Welland pulled long faces, and behaved as if the end of the world had come? But little May—she knew better, I'll be bound?"

"I hoped she did; but after all she wouldn't agree to what I'd gone down to ask for."

"Wouldn't she indeed? And what was that?"

"I wanted to get her to promise that we should be married in April. What's the use of our wasting another year?"

Mrs. Manson Mingott screwed up her little mouth into a grimace of mimic prudery and twinkled at him through malicious lids. "'Ask Mamma,' I suppose—the usual story. Ah, these Mingotts—all alike! Born in a rut, and you can't root 'em out of it. When I built this house you'd have thought I was moving to California! Nobody ever *had* built above Fortieth Street—no, says I, nor above the Battery either, before Christopher Columbus discovered America. No, no; not one of them wants to be different; they're as scared of it as the small-pox. Ah, my dear Mr. Archer, I thank my stars I'm nothing but a vulgar Spicer; but there's not one of my own children that takes after me but my little Ellen." She broke off, still twinkling at him, and asked, with the casual irrelevance of old age: "Now, why in the world didn't you marry my little Ellen?"

Archer laughed. "For one thing, she wasn't there to be married."

"No—to be sure; more's the pity. And now it's too late; her life is finished." She spoke with the cold-blooded complacency of the aged throwing earth into the grave of young hopes. The young man's heart grew chill, and he said hurriedly: "Can't I persuade you to use your influence with the Wellands, Mrs. Mingott? I wasn't made for long engagements."

Old Catherine beamed on him approvingly. "No; I can see that. You've got a quick eye. When you were a little boy I've no doubt you liked to be helped first." She threw back her head with a laugh that made her chins ripple like little waves. "Ah, here's my Ellen now!" she exclaimed, as the portières parted behind her.

Madame Olenska came forward with a smile. Her face looked

vivid and happy, and she held out her hand gaily to Archer while she stooped to her grandmother's kiss.

"I was just saying to him, my dear: 'Now, why didn't you marry my little Ellen?'"

Madame Olenska looked at Archer, still smiling. "And what did he answer?"

"Oh, my darling, I leave you to find that out! He's been down to Florida to see his sweetheart."

"Yes, I know." She still looked at him. "I went to see your mother, to ask where you'd gone. I sent a note that you never answered, and I was afraid you were ill."

He muttered something about leaving unexpectedly, in a great hurry, and having intended to write to her from St. Augustine.

"And of course once you were there you never thought of me again!" She continued to beam on him with a gaiety that might have been a studied assumption of indifference.

"If she still needs me, she's determined not to let me see it," he thought, stung by her manner. He wanted to thank her for having been to see his mother, but under the ancestress's malicious eye he felt himself tongue-tied and constrained.

"Look at him—in such hot haste to get married that he took French leave and rushed down to implore the silly girl on his knees! That's something like a lover—that's the way handsome Bob Spicer carried off my poor mother; and then got tired of her before I was weaned—though they only had to wait eight months for me! But there—you're not a Spicer, young man; luckily for you and for May. It's only my poor Ellen that has kept any of their wicked blood; the rest of them are all model Mingotts," cried the old lady scornfully.

Archer was aware that Madame Olenska, who had seated herself at her grandmother's side, was still thoughtfully scrutinising him. The gaiety had faded from her eyes, and she said with great gentleness: "Surely, Granny, we can persuade them between us to do as he wishes."

Archer rose to go, and as his hand met Madame Olenska's he felt that she was waiting for him to make some allusion to her unanswered letter.

"When can I see you?" he asked, as she walked with him to the door of the room.

"Whenever you like; but it must be soon if you want to see the little house again. I am moving next week."

A pang shot through him at the memory of his lamplit hours in the low-studded drawing-room. Few as they had been, they were thick with memories.

"Tomorrow evening?"

She nodded. "Tomorrow; yes; but early. I'm going out."

The next day was a Sunday, and if she were "going out" on a Sunday evening it could, of course, be only to Mrs. Lemuel Struthers's. He felt a slight movement of annoyance, not so much at her going there (for he rather liked her going where she pleased in spite of the van der Luydens), but because it was the kind of house at which she was sure to meet Beaufort, where she must have known beforehand that she would meet him—and where she was probably going for that purpose.

"Very well; tomorrow evening," he repeated, inwardly resolved that he would not go early, and that by reaching her door late he would either prevent her from going to Mrs. Struthers's, or else arrive after she had started—which, all things considered, would no doubt be the simplest solution.

It was only half-past eight, after all, when he rang the bell under the wisteria; not as late as he had intended by half an hour—but a singular restlessness had driven him to her door. He reflected, however, that Mrs. Struthers's Sunday evenings were not like a ball, and that her guests, as if to minimise their delinquency, usually went early.

The one thing he had not counted on, in entering Madame Olenska's hall, was to find hats and overcoats there. Why had she bidden him to come early if she was having people to dine? On a closer inspection of the garments besides which Nastasia was laying his own, his resentment gave way to curiosity. The overcoats were in fact the very strangest he had ever seen under a polite roof; and it took but a glance to assure himself that neither of them belonged to Julius Beaufort. One was a shaggy yellow ulster of "reach-me-down" cut, the other a very old and rusty cloak with a cape—something like what the French called a "Macfarlane." This garment, which appeared to be made for a person of prodigious size, had evidently seen long and hard wear, and its greenish-black folds gave out a moist sawdusty smell suggestive of prolonged sessions against bar-room walls. On it lay a ragged grey scarf and an odd felt hat of semiclerical shape.

Archer raised his eyebrows enquiringly at Nastasia, who raised hers in return with a fatalistic "Già!" as she threw open the draw-ing-room door.

The young man saw at once that his hostess was not in the room; then, with surprise, he discovered another lady standing by the fire. This lady, who was long, lean and loosely put together, was clad in raiment intricately looped and fringed, with plaids and stripes and bands of plain colour disposed in a design to which the clue seemed missing. Her hair, which had tried to turn white and only succeeded in fading, was surmounted by a Spanish comb and black lace scarf, and silk mittens, visibly darned, covered her rheumatic hands.

Beside her, in a cloud of cigar-smoke, stood the owners of the two overcoats, both in morning clothes that they had evidently not taken off since morning. In one of the two, Archer, to his surprise, recognised Ned Winsett; the other and older, who was unknown to him, and whose gigantic frame declared him to be the wearer of the "Macfarlane," had a feeble leonine head with crumpled grey hair, and moved his arms with large pawing gestures, as though he were distributing lay blessings to a kneeling multitude.

These three persons stood together on the hearth-rug, their eyes fixed on an extraordinarily large bouquet of crimson roses, with a knot of purple pansies at their base, that lay on the sofa where Madame Olenska usually sat.

"What they must have cost at this season—though of course it's the sentiment one cares about!" the lady was saying in a sigh-ing staccato as Archer came in.

The three turned with surprise at his appearance, and the lady, advancing, held out her hand.

"Dear Mr. Archer—almost my cousin Newland!" she said. "I am the Marchioness Manson."

Archer bowed, and she continued: "My Ellen has taken me in for a few days. I came from Cuba, where I have been spending the winter with Spanish friends—such delightful distinguished people: the highest nobility of old Castile—how I wish you could know them! But I was called away by our dear great friend here, Dr. Carver. You don't know Dr. Agathon Carver, founder of the Valley of Love Community?"[1]

Dr. Carver inclined his leonine head, and the Marchioness continued: "Ah, New York—New York—how little the life of the spirit has reached it! But I see you do know Mr. Winsett."

"Oh, yes—*I* reached him some time ago; but not by that route," Winsett said with his dry smile.

The Marchioness shook her head reprovingly. "How do you know, Mr. Winsett? The spirit bloweth where it listeth."[2]

"List—oh, list!" interjected Dr. Carver in a stentorian murmur.[3]

"But do sit down, Mr. Archer. We four have been having a delightful little dinner together, and my child has gone up to dress. She expects you; she will be down in a moment. We were just admiring these marvellous flowers, which will surprise her when she reappears."

Winsett remained on his feet. "I'm afraid I must be off. Please tell Madame Olenska that we shall all feel lost when she abandons our street. This house has been an oasis."

"Ah, but she won't abandon *you*. Poetry and art are the breath of life to her. It *is* poetry you write, Mr. Winsett?"

"Well, no; but I sometimes read it," said Winsett, including the group in a general nod and slipping out of the room.

---

1 *Valley of Love Community*: utopian "free love" communities were notorious if relatively rare in nineteenth-century America. "Free love" advocates typically defended themselves against charges of promiscuity and immorality by appealing to the radically spiritual character of true love; they often practiced forms of socialism or communism, and were generally drawn to esoteric spiritualist doctrines. Wharton may have had in mind, in particular, the Oneida community in upstate New York, founded in 1848 and led by John Humphrey Noyes. The community survived until 1881, though Noyes fled to Canada to avoid prosecution for immorality.

2 John 3:8: "The wind bloweth where it listeth, and thou hearest the sound thereof, but canst not tell whence it cometh, and whither it goeth: so is every one that is born of the Spirit."

3 "*List—oh, list!*": spoken by the ghost of Hamlet's father in William Shakespeare's *Hamlet*, Act I, V. 22-23 ("List, list, O, list!/ If thou didst ever thy dear father love—").

"A caustic spirit—*un peu sauvage*. But so witty; Dr. Carver, you *do* think him witty?"

"I never think of wit," said Dr. Carver severely.

"Ah—ah—you never think of wit! How merciless he is to us weak mortals, Mr. Archer! But he lives only in the life of the spirit; and tonight he is mentally preparing the lecture he is to deliver presently at Mrs. Blenker's. Dr. Carver, would there be time, before you start for the Blenkers' to explain to Mr. Archer your illuminating discovery of the Direct Contact? But no; I see it is nearly nine o'clock, and we have no right to detain you while so many are waiting for your message."

Dr. Carver looked slightly disappointed at this conclusion, but, having compared his ponderous gold time-piece with Madame Olenska's little travelling-clock, he reluctantly gathered up his mighty limbs for departure.

"I shall see you later, dear friend?" he suggested to the Marchioness, who replied with a smile: "As soon as Ellen's carriage comes I will join you; I do hope the lecture won't have begun."

Dr. Carver looked thoughtfully at Archer. "Perhaps, if this young gentleman is interested in my experiences, Mrs. Blenker might allow you to bring him with you?"

"Oh, dear friend, if it were possible—I am sure she would be too happy. But I fear my Ellen counts on Mr. Archer herself."

"That," said Dr. Carver, "is unfortunate—but here is my card." He handed it to Archer, who read on it, in Gothic characters:

> ### Agathon Carver
> ### The Valley of Love
> ### Kittasquattamy, N.Y.

Dr. Carver bowed himself out, and Mrs. Manson, with a sigh that might have been either of regret or relief, again waved Archer to a seat.

"Ellen will be down in a moment; and before she comes, I am so glad of this quiet moment with you."

Archer murmured his pleasure at their meeting, and the Marchioness continued, in her low sighing accents: "I know everything, dear Mr. Archer—my child has told me all you have done for her. Your wise advice: your courageous firmness—thank heaven it was not too late!"

The young man listened with considerable embarrassment. Was there any one, he wondered, to whom Madame Olenska had not proclaimed his intervention in her private affairs?

"Madame Olenska exaggerates; I simply gave her a legal opinion, as she asked me to."

"Ah, but in doing it—in doing it you were the unconscious instrument of—of—what word have we moderns for Providence, Mr. Archer?" cried the lady, tilting her head on one side and drooping her lids mysteriously. "Little did you know that at that very moment I was being appealed to: being approached, in fact—from the other side of the Atlantic!"

She glanced over her shoulder, as though fearful of being overheard, and then, drawing her chair nearer, and raising a tiny ivory fan to her lips, breathed behind it: "By the Count himself—my poor, mad, foolish Olenski; who asks only to take her back on her own terms."

"Good God!" Archer exclaimed, springing up.

"You are horrified? Yes, of course; I understand. I don't defend poor Stanislas, though he has always called me his best friend. He does not defend himself—he casts himself at her feet: in my person." She tapped her emaciated bosom. "I have his letter here."

"A letter?—Has Madame Olenska seen it?" Archer stammered, his brain whirling with the shock of the announcement.

The Marchioness Manson shook her head softly. "Time—time; I must have time. I know my Ellen—haughty, intractable; shall I say, just a shade unforgiving?"

"But, good heavens, to forgive is one thing; to go back into that hell—"

"Ah, yes," the Marchioness acquiesced. "So she describes it—my sensitive child! But on the material side, Mr. Archer, if one may stoop to consider such things; do you know what she is giving up? Those roses there on the sofa—acres like them, under glass and in the open, in his matchless terraced gardens at Nice! Jewels—historic pearls: the Sobieski emeralds—sables—but she cares nothing for all these! Art and beauty, those she does care for, she lives for, as I always have; and those also surrounded her. Pictures, priceless furniture, music, brilliant conversation—ah, that, my dear young man, if you'll excuse me, is what you've no conception of here! And she had it all; and the homage of the greatest. She tells me she is not thought handsome in New York— good heavens! Her portrait has been painted nine times; the greatest artists in Europe have begged for the privilege. Are these things nothing? And the remorse of an adoring husband?"

As the Marchioness Manson rose to her climax her face assumed an expression of ecstatic retrospection which would have moved Archer's mirth had he not been numb with amazement.

He would have laughed if any one had foretold to him that his first sight of poor Medora Manson would have been in the guise of a messenger of Satan; but he was in no mood for laughing now, and she seemed to him to come straight out of the hell from which Ellen Olenska had just escaped.

"She knows nothing yet—of all this?" he asked abruptly.

Mrs. Manson laid a purple finger on her lips. "Nothing directly— but does she suspect? Who can tell? The truth is, Mr. Archer, I have been waiting to see you. From the moment I heard of the firm stand you had taken, and of your influence over her, I hoped it might be possible to count on your support—to convince you ... "

"That she ought to go back? I would rather see her dead!" cried the young man violently.

"Ah," the Marchioness murmured, without visible resentment. For a while she sat in her arm-chair, opening and shutting the absurd ivory fan between her mittened fingers; but suddenly she lifted her head and listened.

"Here she comes," she said in a rapid whisper; and then, pointing to the bouquet on the sofa: "Am I to understand that you prefer *that*, Mr. Archer? After all, marriage is marriage ... and my niece is still a wife...."

XVIII

"WHAT are you two plotting together, aunt Medora?" Madame Olenska cried as she came into the room.

She was dressed as if for a ball. Everything about her shimmered and glimmered softly, as if her dress had been woven out of candle-beams; and she carried her head high, like a pretty woman challenging a roomful of rivals.

"We were saying, my dear, that here was something beautiful to surprise you with," Mrs. Manson rejoined, rising to her feet and pointing archly to the flowers.

Madame Olenska stopped short and looked at the bouquet. Her colour did not change, but a sort of white radiance of anger ran over her like summer lightning. "Ah," she exclaimed, in a shrill voice that the young man had never heard, "who is ridiculous enough to send me a bouquet? Why a bouquet? And why tonight of all nights? I am not going to a ball; I am not a girl engaged to be married. But some people are always ridiculous."

She turned back to the door, opened it, and called out: "Nastasia!"

The ubiquitous handmaiden promptly appeared, and Archer heard Madame Olenska say, in an Italian that she seemed to pronounce with intentional deliberateness in order that he might follow it: "Here—throw this into the dust-bin!" and then, as Nastasia stared protestingly: "But no—it's not the fault of the poor flowers. Tell the boy to carry them to the house three doors away, the house of Mr. Winsett, the dark gentleman who dined here. His wife is ill—they may give her pleasure ... The boy is out, you say? Then, my dear one, run yourself; here, put my cloak over you and fly. I want the thing out of the house immediately! And, as you live, don't say they come from me!"

She flung her velvet opera cloak over the maid's shoulders and turned back into the drawing-room, shutting the door sharply. Her bosom was rising high under its lace, and for a moment Archer thought she was about to cry; but she burst into a laugh instead, and looking from the Marchioness to Archer, asked abruptly: "And you two—have you made friends!"

"It's for Mr. Archer to say, darling; he has waited patiently while you were dressing."

"Yes—I gave you time enough: my hair wouldn't go," Madame Olenska said, raising her hand to the heaped-up curls of her *chignon*. "But that reminds me: I see Dr. Carver is gone, and you'll be late at the Blenkers'. Mr. Archer, will you put my aunt in the carriage?"

She followed the Marchioness into the hall, saw her fitted into a miscellaneous heap of overshoes, shawls and tippets, and called from the doorstep: "Mind, the carriage is to be back for me at ten!" Then she returned to the drawing-room, where Archer, on re-entering it, found her standing by the mantelpiece, examining herself in the mirror. It was not usual, in New York society, for a lady to address her parlour-maid as "my dear one," and send her out on an errand wrapped in her own opera-cloak; and Archer, through all his deeper feelings, tasted the pleasurable excitement of being in a world where action followed on emotion with such Olympian speed.

Madame Olenska did not move when he came up behind her, and for a second their eyes met in the mirror; then she turned, threw herself into her sofa-corner, and sighed out: "There's time for a cigarette."

He handed her the box and lit a spill for her; and as the flame flashed up into her face she glanced at him with laughing eyes and said: "What do you think of me in a temper?"

Archer paused a moment; then he answered with sudden resolution: "It makes me understand what your aunt has been saying about you."

"I knew she'd been talking about me. Well?"

"She said you were used to all kinds of things—splendours and amusements and excitements—that we could never hope to give you here."

Madame Olenska smiled faintly into the circle of smoke about her lips.

"Medora is incorrigibly romantic. It has made up to her for so many things!"

Archer hesitated again, and again took his risk. "Is your aunt's romanticism always consistent with accuracy?"

"You mean: does she speak the truth?" Her niece considered. "Well, I'll tell you: in almost everything she says, there's something true and something untrue. But why do you ask? What has she been telling you?"

He looked away into the fire, and then back at her shining presence. His heart tightened with the thought that this was their last evening by that fireside, and that in a moment the carriage would come to carry her away.

"She says—she pretends that Count Olenski has asked her to persuade you to go back to him."

Madame Olenska made no answer. She sat motionless, holding her cigarette in her half-lifted hand. The expression of her face had not changed; and Archer remembered that he had before noticed her apparent incapacity for surprise.

"You knew, then?" he broke out.

She was silent for so long that the ash dropped from her cigarette. She brushed it to the floor. "She has hinted about a letter: poor darling! Medora's hints—"

"Is it at your husband's request that she has arrived here suddenly?"

Madame Olenska seemed to consider this question also. "There again: one can't tell. She told me she had had a 'spiritual summons,' whatever that is, from Dr. Carver. I'm afraid she's going to marry Dr. Carver ... poor Medora, there's always some one she wants to marry. But perhaps the people in Cuba just got tired of her! I think she was with them as a sort of paid companion. Really, I don't know why she came."

"But you do believe she has a letter from your husband?"

Again Madame Olenska brooded silently; then she said: "After all, it was to be expected."

The young man rose and went to lean against the fireplace. A sudden restlessness possessed him, and he was tongue-tied by the sense that their minutes were numbered, and that at any moment he might hear the wheels of the returning carriage.

"You know that your aunt believes you will go back?"

Madame Olenska raised her head quickly. A deep blush rose to her face and spread over her neck and shoulders. She blushed seldom and painfully, as if it hurt her like a burn.

"Many cruel things have been believed of me," she said.

"Oh, Ellen—forgive me; I'm a fool and a brute!"

She smiled a little. "You are horribly nervous; you have your own troubles. I know you think the Wellands are unreasonable about your marriage, and of course I agree with you. In Europe people don't understand our long American engagements; I suppose they are not as calm as we are." She pronounced the "we" with a faint emphasis that gave it an ironic sound.

Archer felt the irony but did not dare to take it up. After all, she had perhaps purposely deflected the conversation from her own affairs, and after the pain his last words had evidently caused her he felt that all he could do was to follow her lead. But the sense of the waning hour made him desperate: he could not bear the thought that a barrier of words should drop between them again.

"Yes," he said abruptly; "I went south to ask May to marry me after Easter. There's no reason why we shouldn't be married then."

"And May adores you—and yet you couldn't convince her? I thought her too intelligent to be the slave of such absurd superstitions."

"She *is* too intelligent—she's not their slave."

Madame Olenska looked at him. "Well, then—I don't understand."

Archer reddened, and hurried on with a rush. "We had a frank talk—almost the first. She thinks my impatience a bad sign."

"Merciful heavens—a bad sign?"

"She thinks it means that I can't trust myself to go on caring for her. She thinks, in short, I want to marry her at once to get away from some one that I—care for more."

Madame Olenska examined this curiously. "But if she thinks that—why isn't she in a hurry too?"

"Because she's not like that: she's so much nobler. She insists all the more on the long engagement, to give me time—"

"Time to give her up for the other woman?"

"If I want to."

Madame Olenska leaned toward the fire and gazed into it with fixed eyes. Down the quiet street Archer heard the approaching trot of her horses.

"That *is* noble," she said, with a slight break in her voice.

"Yes. But it's ridiculous."

"Ridiculous? Because you don't care for any one else?"

"Because I don't mean to marry any one else."

"Ah." There was another long interval. At length she looked up at him and asked: "This other woman—does she love you?"

"Oh, there's no other woman; I mean, the person that May was thinking of is—was never—"

"Then, why, after all, are you in such haste?"

"There's your carriage," said Archer.

She half-rose and looked about her with absent eyes. Her fan and gloves lay on the sofa beside her and she picked them up mechanically.

"Yes; I suppose I must be going."

"You're going to Mrs. Struthers's?"

"Yes." She smiled and added: "I must go where I am invited, or I should be too lonely. Why not come with me?"

Archer felt that at any cost he must keep her beside him, must make her give him the rest of her evening. Ignoring her question, he continued to lean against the chimney-piece, his eyes fixed on the hand in which she held her gloves and fan, as if watching to see if he had the power to make her drop them.

"May guessed the truth," he said. "There is another woman—but not the one she thinks."

Ellen Olenska made no answer, and did not move. After a moment he sat down beside her, and, taking her hand, softly unclasped it, so that the gloves and fan fell on the sofa between them.

She started up, and freeing herself from him moved away to the other side of the hearth. "Ah, don't make love to me! Too many people have done that," she said, frowning.

Archer, changing colour, stood up also: it was the bitterest rebuke she could have given him. "I have never made love to you," he said, "and I never shall. But you are the woman I would have married if it had been possible for either of us."

"Possible for either of us?" She looked at him with unfeigned astonishment. "And you say that—when it's you who've made it impossible?"

He stared at her, groping in a blackness through which a single arrow of light tore its blinding way.

"*I've* made it impossible—?"

"You, you, *you*!" she cried, her lip trembling like a child's on the verge of tears. "Isn't it you who made me give up divorcing—give it up because you showed me how selfish and wicked it was, how one must sacrifice one's self to preserve the dignity of marriage ... and to spare one's family the publicity, the scandal? And because my family was going to be your family—for May's sake and for yours—I did what you told me, what you proved to me that I ought to do. Ah," she broke out with a sudden laugh, "I've made no secret of having done it for you!"

She sank down on the sofa again, crouching among the festive ripples of her dress like a stricken masquerader; and the young man stood by the fireplace and continued to gaze at her without moving.

"Good God," he groaned. "When I thought—"

"You thought?"

"Ah, don't ask me what I thought!"

Still looking at her, he saw the same burning flush creep up her neck to her face. She sat upright, facing him with a rigid dignity.

"I do ask you."

"Well, then: there were things in that letter you asked me to read—"

"My husband's letter?"

"Yes."

"I had nothing to fear from that letter: absolutely nothing! All I feared was to bring notoriety, scandal, on the family—on you and May."

"Good God," he groaned again, bowing his face in his hands.

The silence that followed lay on them with the weight of things final and irrevocable. It seemed to Archer to be crushing him down like his own grave-stone; in all the wide future he saw nothing that would ever lift that load from his heart. He did not move from his place, or raise his head from his hands; his hidden eyeballs went on staring into utter darkness.

"At least I loved you—" he brought out.

On the other side of the hearth, from the sofa-corner where he supposed that she still crouched, he heard a faint stifled crying like a child's. He started up and came to her side.

"Ellen! What madness! Why are you crying? Nothing's done that can't be undone. I'm still free, and you're going to be." He had her in his arms, her face like a wet flower at his lips, and all their vain terrors shrivelling up like ghosts at sunrise. The one thing that astonished him now was that he should have stood for five minutes arguing with her across the width of the room, when just touching her made everything so simple.

She gave him back all his kiss, but after a moment he felt her stiffening in his arms, and she put him aside and stood up.

"Ah, my poor Newland—I suppose this had to be. But it doesn't in the least alter things," she said, looking down at him in her turn from the hearth.

"It alters the whole of life for me."

"No, no—it mustn't, it can't. You're engaged to May Welland; and I'm married."

He stood up too, flushed and resolute. "Nonsense! It's too late for that sort of thing. We've no right to lie to other people or to ourselves. We won't talk of your marriage; but do you see me marrying May after this?"

She stood silent, resting her thin elbows on the mantelpiece, her profile reflected in the glass behind her. One of the locks of her *chignon* had become loosened and hung on her neck; she looked haggard and almost old.

"I don't see you," she said at length, "putting that question to May. Do you?"

He gave a reckless shrug. "It's too late to do anything else."

"You say that because it's the easiest thing to say at this moment—not because it's true. In reality it's too late to do anything but what we'd both decided on."

"Ah, I don't understand you!"

She forced a pitiful smile that pinched her face instead of smoothing it. "You don't understand because you haven't yet guessed how you've changed things for me: oh, from the first— long before I knew all you'd done."

"All I'd done?"

"Yes. I was perfectly unconscious at first that people here were shy of me—that they thought I was a dreadful sort of person. It seems they had even refused to meet me at dinner. I found that out afterward; and how you'd made your mother go with you to the van der Luydens'; and how you'd insisted on announcing your engagement at the Beaufort ball, so that I might have two families to stand by me instead of one—"

At that he broke into a laugh.

"Just imagine," she said, "how stupid and unobservant I was! I knew nothing of all this till Granny blurted it out one day. New York simply meant peace and freedom to me: it was coming home. And I was so happy at being among my own people that every one I met seemed kind and good, and glad to see me. But from the very beginning," she continued, "I felt there was no one as kind as you; no one who gave me reasons that I understood for doing what at first seemed so hard and—unnecessary. The very good people didn't convince me; I felt they'd never been tempted. But you knew; you understood; you had felt the world outside tugging at one with all its golden hands—and yet you hated the things it asks of one; you hated happiness bought by disloyalty and cruelty and indifference. That was what I'd never known before—and it's better than anything I've known."

She spoke in a low even voice, without tears or visible agitation; and each word, as it dropped from her, fell into his breast like burning lead. He sat bowed over, his head between his hands, staring at the hearth-rug, and at the tip of the satin shoe that showed under her dress. Suddenly he knelt down and kissed the shoe.

She bent over him, laying her hands on his shoulders, and looking at him with eyes so deep that he remained motionless under her gaze.

"Ah, don't let us undo what you've done!" she cried. "I can't go back now to that other way of thinking. I can't love you unless I give you up."

His arms were yearning up to her; but she drew away, and they remained facing each other, divided by the distance that her words had created. Then, abruptly, his anger overflowed.

"And Beaufort? Is he to replace me?"

As the words sprang out he was prepared for an answering flare of anger; and he would have welcomed it as fuel for his own. But Madame Olenska only grew a shade paler, and stood with her arms hanging down before her, and her head slightly bent, as her way was when she pondered a question.

"He's waiting for you now at Mrs. Struthers's; why don't you go to him?" Archer sneered.

She turned to ring the bell. "I shall not go out this evening; tell the carriage to go and fetch the Signora Marchesa," she said when the maid came.

After the door had closed again Archer continued to look at her with bitter eyes. "Why this sacrifice? Since you tell me that you're lonely I've no right to keep you from your friends."

She smiled a little under her wet lashes. "I shan't be lonely now. I *was* lonely; I *was* afraid. But the emptiness and the darkness are gone; when I turn back into myself now I'm like a child going at night into a room where there's always a light."

Her tone and her look still enveloped her in a soft inaccessibility, and Archer groaned out again: "I don't understand you!"

"Yet you understand May!"

He reddened under the retort, but kept his eyes on her. "May is ready to give me up."

"What! Three days after you've entreated her on your knees to hasten your marriage?"

"She's refused; that gives me the right—"

"Ah, you've taught me what an ugly word that is," she said.

He turned away with a sense of utter weariness. He felt as though he had been struggling for hours up the face of a steep precipice, and now, just as he had fought his way to the top, his hold had given way and he was pitching down headlong into darkness.

If he could have got her in his arms again he might have swept away her arguments; but she still held him at a distance by something inscrutably aloof in her look and attitude, and by his own awed sense of her sincerity. At length he began to plead again.

"If we do this now it will be worse afterward—worse for every one—"

"No—no—no!" she almost screamed, as if he frightened her.

At that moment the bell sent a long tinkle through the house. They had heard no carriage stopping at the door, and they stood motionless, looking at each other with startled eyes.

Outside, Nastasia's step crossed the hall, the outer door opened, and a moment later she came in carrying a telegram which she handed to the Countess Olenska.

"The lady was very happy at the flowers," Nastasia said,

smoothing her apron. "She thought it was her *signor marito* who had sent them,[1] and she cried a little and said it was a folly."

Her mistress smiled and took the yellow envelope. She tore it open and carried it to the lamp; then, when the door had closed again, she handed the telegram to Archer.

It was dated from St. Augustine, and addressed to the Countess Olenska. In it he read: "Granny's telegram successful. Papa and Mamma agree marriage after Easter. Am telegraphing Newland. Am too happy for words and love you dearly. Your grateful May."

Half an hour later, when Archer unlocked his own front-door, he found a similar envelope on the hall-table on top of his pile of notes and letters. The message inside the envelope was also from May Welland, and ran as follows: "Parents consent wedding Tuesday after Easter at twelve Grace Church eight bridesmaids please see Rector so happy love May."

Archer crumpled up the yellow sheet as if the gesture could annihilate the news it contained. Then he pulled out a small pocket-diary and turned over the pages with trembling fingers; but he did not find what he wanted, and cramming the telegram into his pocket he mounted the stairs.

A light was shining through the door of the little hall-room which served Janey as a dressing-room and boudoir, and her brother rapped impatiently on the panel. The door opened, and his sister stood before him in her immemorial purple flannel dressing-gown, with her hair "on pins." Her face looked pale and apprehensive.

"Newland! I hope there's no bad news in that telegram? I waited on purpose, in case—" (No item of his correspondence was safe from Janey.)

He took no notice of her question. "Look here—what day is Easter this year?"

She looked shocked at such unchristian ignorance. "Easter? Newland! Why, of course, the first week in April. Why?"

"The first week?" He turned again to the pages of his diary, calculating rapidly under his breath. "The first week, did you say?" He threw back his head with a long laugh.

---

1 *Signor marito*: Italian for "husband."

"For mercy's sake what's the matter?"

"Nothing's the matter, except that I'm going to be married in a month."

Janey fell upon his neck and pressed him to her purple flannel breast. "Oh Newland, how wonderful! I'm so glad! But, dearest, why do you keep on laughing? Do hush, or you'll wake Mamma."

BOOK TWO

XIX

THE day was fresh, with a lively spring wind full of dust. All the old ladies in both families had got out their faded sables and yellowing ermines, and the smell of camphor from the front pews almost smothered the faint spring scent of the lilies banking the altar.

Newland Archer, at a signal from the sexton, had come out of the vestry and placed himself with his best man on the chancel step of Grace Church.[1]

The signal meant that the brougham bearing the bride and her father was in sight; but there was sure to be a considerable interval of adjustment and consultation in the lobby, where the bridesmaids were already hovering like a cluster of Easter blossoms. During this unavoidable lapse of time the bridegroom, in proof of his eagerness was expected to expose himself alone to the gaze of the assembled company; and Archer had gone through this formality as resignedly as through all the others which made of a nineteenth century New York wedding a rite that seemed to belong to the dawn of history. Everything was equally easy—or equally painful, as one chose to put it—in the path he was committed to tread, and he had obeyed the flurried injunctions of his best man as piously as other bridegrooms had obeyed his own, in the days when he had guided them through the same labyrinth.

So far he was reasonably sure of having fulfilled all his obligations. The bridesmaids' eight bouquets of white lilac and lilies-of-the-valley had been sent in due time, as well as the gold and sapphire sleeve-links of the eight ushers and the best man's cat's-eye scarf-pin; Archer had sat up half the night trying to vary the wording of his thanks for the last batch of presents from men friends and ex-lady-loves; the fees for the Bishop and the Rector were safely in the

---

[1]   *Grace Church*: The fashionable Episcopal Church on Broadway at Tenth Street. Edith Wharton was baptized in this church.

pocket of his best man; his own luggage was already at Mrs. Manson Mingott's, where the wedding-breakfast was to take place, and so were the travelling clothes into which he was to change; and a private compartment had been engaged in the train that was to carry the young couple to their unknown destination—concealment of the spot in which the bridal night was to be spent being one of the most sacred taboos of the prehistoric ritual.

"Got the ring all right?" whispered young van der Luyden Newland, who was inexperienced in the duties of a best man, and awed by the weight of his responsibility.

Archer made the gesture which he had seen so many bridegrooms make: with his ungloved right hand he felt in the pocket of his dark grey waistcoat, and assured himself that the little gold circlet (engraved inside: *Newland to May, April —, 187—*) was in its place; then, resuming his former attitude, his tall hat and pearl-grey gloves with black stitchings grasped in his left hand, he stood looking at the door of the church.

Overhead, Handel's March swelled pompously through the imitation stone vaulting,[1] carrying on its waves the faded drift of the many weddings at which, with cheerful indifference, he had stood on the same chancel step watching other brides float up the nave toward other bridegrooms.

"How like a first night at the Opera!" he thought, recognising all the same faces in the same boxes (no, pews), and wondering if, when the Last Trump sounded, Mrs. Selfridge Merry would be there with the same towering ostrich feathers in her bonnet, and Mrs. Beaufort with the same diamond earrings and the same smile—and whether suitable proscenium seats were already prepared for them in another world.

After that there was still time to review, one by one, the familiar countenances in the first rows; the women's sharp with curiosity and excitement, the men's sulky with the obligation of having to put on their frock-coats before luncheon, and fight for food at the wedding-breakfast.

"Too bad the breakfast is at old Catherine's," the bridegroom

---

[1] *Handel's March*: possibly from the popular *Water Music* (1717), written by George Friedrich *Handel* (1685-1759) for a royal fête on the Thames River.

could fancy Reggie Chivers saying. "But I'm told that Lovell Mingott insisted on its being cooked by his own *chef,* so it ought to be good if one can only get at it." And he could imagine Sillerton Jackson adding with authority: "My dear fellow, haven't you heard? It's to be served at small tables, in the new English fashion."

Archer's eyes lingered a moment on the left-hand pew, where his mother, who had entered the church on Mr. Henry van der Luyden's arm, sat weeping softly under her Chantilly veil, her hands in her grandmother's ermine muff.

"Poor Janey!" he thought, looking at his sister, "even by screwing her head around she can see only the people in the few front pews; and they're mostly dowdy Newlands and Dagonets."

On the hither side of the white ribbon dividing off the seats reserved for the families he saw Beaufort, tall and red-faced, scrutinising the women with his arrogant stare. Beside him sat his wife, all silvery chinchilla and violets; and on the far side of the ribbon, Lawrence Lefferts's sleekly brushed head seemed to mount guard over the invisible deity of "Good Form" who presided at the ceremony.

Archer wondered how many flaws Lefferts's keen eyes would discover in the ritual of his divinity; then he suddenly recalled that he too had once thought such questions important. The things that had filled his days seemed now like a nursery parody of life, or like the wrangles of mediæval schoolmen over metaphysical terms that nobody had ever understood. A stormy discussion as to whether the wedding presents should be "shown" had darkened the last hours before the wedding; and it seemed inconceivable to Archer that grown-up people should work themselves into a state of agitation over such trifles, and that the matter should have been decided (in the negative) by Mrs. Welland's saying, with indignant tears: "I should as soon turn the reporters loose in my house." Yet there was a time when Archer had had definite and rather aggressive opinions on all such problems, and when everything concerning the manners and customs of his little tribe had seemed to him fraught with world-wide significance.

"And all the while, I suppose," he thought, "real people were living somewhere, and real things happening to them ... "

"*There they come!*" breathed the best man excitedly; but the bridegroom knew better.

The cautious opening of the door of the church meant only that Mr. Brown the livery-stable keeper (gowned in black in his intermittent character of sexton) was taking a preliminary survey of the scene before marshalling his forces. The door was softly shut again; then after another interval it swung majestically open, and a murmur ran through the church: "The family!"

Mrs. Welland came first, on the arm of her eldest son. Her large pink face was appropriately solemn, and her plum-coloured satin with pale blue side-panels, and blue ostrich plumes in a small satin bonnet, met with general approval; but before she had settled herself with a stately rustle in the pew opposite Mrs. Archer's the spectators were craning their necks to see who was coming after her. Wild rumours had been abroad the day before to the effect that Mrs. Manson Mingott, in spite of her physical disabilities, had resolved on being present at the ceremony; and the idea was so much in keeping with her sporting character that bets ran high at the clubs as to her being able to walk up the nave and squeeze into a seat. It was known that she had insisted on sending her own carpenter to look into the possibility of taking down the end panel of the front pew, and to measure the space between the seat and the front; but the result had been discouraging, and for one anxious day her family had watched her dallying with the plan of being wheeled up the nave in her enormous Bath chair[1] and sitting enthroned in it at the foot of the chancel.

The idea of this monstrous exposure of her person was so painful to her relations that they could have covered with gold the ingenious person who suddenly discovered that the chair was too wide to pass between the iron uprights of the awning which extended from the church door to the curbstone. The idea of doing away with this awning, and revealing the bride to the mob of dressmakers and newspaper reporters who stood outside fighting to get near the joints of the canvas, exceeded

---

[1] *Bath chair:* a wheeled chair that could be pushed from behind or pulled from the front. During the Victorian period, these chairs were highly decorated and upholstered.

even old Catherine's courage, though for a moment she had weighed the possibility. "Why, they might take a photograph of my child *and put it in the papers!*" Mrs. Welland exclaimed when her mother's last plan was hinted to her; and from this unthinkable indecency the clan recoiled with a collective shudder. The ancestress had had to give in; but her concession was bought only by the promise that the wedding-breakfast should take place under her roof, though (as the Washington Square connection said) with the Wellands' house in easy reach it was hard to have to make a special price with Brown to drive one to the other end of nowhere.

Though all these transactions had been widely reported by the Jacksons a sporting minority still clung to the belief that old Catherine would appear in church, and there was a distinct lowering of the temperature when she was found to have been replaced by her daughter-in-law. Mrs. Lovell Mingott had the high colour and glassy stare induced in ladies of her age and habit by the effort of getting into a new dress; but once the disappointment occasioned by her mother-in-law's non-appearance had subsided, it was agreed that her black Chantilly over lilac satin, with a bonnet of Parma violets, formed the happiest contrast to Mrs. Welland's blue and plum-colour. Far different was the impression produced by the gaunt and mincing lady who followed on Mr. Mingott's arm, in a wild dishevelment of stripes and fringes and floating scarves; and as this last apparition glided into view Archer's heart contracted and stopped beating.

He had taken it for granted that the Marchioness Manson was still in Washington, where she had gone some four weeks previously with her niece, Madame Olenska. It was generally understood that their abrupt departure was due to Madame Olenska's desire to remove her aunt from the baleful eloquence of Dr. Agathon Carver, who had nearly succeeded in enlisting her as a recruit for the Valley of Love; and in the circumstances no one had expected either of the ladies to return for the wedding. For a moment Archer stood with his eyes fixed on Medora's fantastic figure, straining to see who came behind her; but the little procession was at an end, for all the lesser members of the family had taken their seats, and the eight tall ushers, gathering themselves together like birds or insects preparing for some migratory manœuvre, were already slipping through the side doors into the lobby.

"Newland—I say: *she's here!*" the best man whispered.

Archer roused himself with a start.

A long time had apparently passed since his heart had stopped beating, for the white and rosy procession was in fact half way up the nave, the Bishop, the Rector and two white-winged assistants were hovering about the flower-banked altar, and the first chords of the Spohr symphony[1] were strewing their flower-like notes before the bride.

Archer opened his eyes (but could they really have been shut, as he imagined?), and felt his heart beginning to resume its usual task. The music, the scent of the lilies on the altar, the vision of the cloud of tulle and orange-blossoms floating nearer and nearer, the sight of Mrs. Archer's face suddenly convulsed with happy sobs, the low benedictory murmur of the Rector's voice, the ordered evolutions of the eight pink bridesmaids and the eight black ushers: all these sights, sounds and sensations, so familiar in themselves, so unutterably strange and meaningless in his new relation to them, were confusedly mingled in his brain.

"My God," he thought, "*have* I got the ring?"—and once more he went through the bridegroom's convulsive gesture.

Then, in a moment, May was beside him, such radiance streaming from her that it sent a faint warmth through his numbness, and he straightened himself and smiled into her eyes.

"Dearly beloved, we are gathered together here," the Rector began ... [2]

The ring was on her hand, the Bishop's benediction had been given, the bridesmaids were a-poise to resume their place in the procession, and the organ was showing preliminary symptoms of breaking out into the Mendelssohn March,[3] without which no

---

[1]   Symphony by Ludwig (Louis) *Spohr* (1784-1859), German composer and violinist, popular in the nineteenth century.

[2]   Wharton originally wrote "Forasmuch as it hath pleased Almighty God," the opening lines of the funeral service from the *Book of Common Prayer*. It was immediately changed after catching the attention of several first readers.

[3]   *Mendelssohn March*: the "Wedding March" from *A Midsummer Night's Dream* (1842) by Felix Mendelssohn (1809-1847) became very fashionable for use at weddings after it was used in a royal wedding in 1858. It is traditionally used today.

newly-wedded couple had ever emerged upon New York.

"Your arm—*I say, give her your arm*!" young Newland nervously hissed; and once more Archer became aware of having been adrift far off in the unknown. What was it that had sent him there, he wondered? Perhaps the glimpse, among the anonymous spectators in the transept, of a dark coil of hair under a hat which, a moment later, revealed itself as belonging to an unknown lady with a long nose, so laughably unlike the person whose image she had evoked that he asked himself if he were becoming subject to hallucinations.

And now he and his wife were pacing slowly down the nave, carried forward on the light Mendelssohn ripples, the spring day beckoning to them through widely opened doors, and Mrs. Welland's chestnuts, with big white favours on their frontlets, curvetting and showing off at the far end of the canvas tunnel.

The footman, who had a still bigger white favour on his lapel, wrapped May's white cloak about her, and Archer jumped into the brougham at her side. She turned to him with a triumphant smile and their hands clasped under her veil.

"Darling!" Archer said—and suddenly the same black abyss yawned before him and he felt himself sinking into it, deeper and deeper, while his voice rambled on smoothly and cheerfully: "Yes, of course I thought I'd lost the ring; no wedding would be complete if the poor devil of a bridegroom didn't go through that. But you *did* keep me waiting, you know! I had time to think of every horror that might possibly happen."

She surprised him by turning, in full Fifth Avenue, and flinging her arms about his neck. "But none ever *can* happen now, can it, Newland, as long as we two are together?"

Every detail of the day had been so carefully thought out that the young couple, after the wedding-breakfast, had ample time to put on their travelling-clothes, descend the wide Mingott stairs between laughing bridesmaids and weeping parents, and get into the brougham under the traditional shower of rice and satin slippers; and there was still half an hour left in which to drive to the station, buy the last weeklies at the bookstall with the air of seasoned travellers, and settle themselves in the reserved compartment in which May's maid had already placed her dove-coloured travelling cloak and glaringly new dressing-bag from London.

The old du Lac aunts at Rhinebeck had put their house at the disposal of the bridal couple, with a readiness inspired by the prospect of spending a week in New York with Mrs. Archer; and Archer, glad to escape the usual "bridal suite" in a Philadelphia or Baltimore hotel, had accepted with an equal alacrity.

May was enchanted at the idea of going to the country, and childishly amused at the vain efforts of the eight bridesmaids to discover where their mysterious retreat was situated. It was thought "very English" to have a country-house lent to one, and the fact gave a last touch of distinction to what was generally conceded to be the most brilliant wedding of the year; but where the house was no one was permitted to know, except the parents of bride and groom, who, when taxed with the knowledge, pursed their lips and said mysteriously: "Ah, they didn't tell us—" which was manifestly true, since there was no need to.

Once they were settled in their compartment, and the train, shaking off the endless wooden suburbs, had pushed out into the pale landscape of spring, talk became easier than Archer had expected. May was still, in look and tone, the simple girl of yesterday, eager to compare notes with him as to the incidents of the wedding, and discussing them as impartially as a bridesmaid talking it all over with an usher. At first Archer had fancied that this detachment was the disguise of an inward tremor; but her clear eyes revealed only the most tranquil unawareness. She was alone for the first time with her husband; but her husband was only the charming comrade of yesterday. There was no one whom she liked as much, no one whom she trusted as completely, and the culminating "lark" of the whole delightful adventure of engagement and marriage was to be off with him alone on a journey, like a grown-up person, like a "married woman," in fact.

It was wonderful that—as he had learned in the Mission garden at St. Augustine—such depths of feeling could co-exist with such absence of imagination. But he remembered how, even then, she had surprised him by dropping back to inexpressive girlishness as soon as her conscience had been eased of its burden; and he saw that she would probably go through life dealing to the best of her ability with each experience as it came, but never anticipating any by so much as a stolen glance.

Perhaps that faculty of unawareness was what gave her eyes their transparency, and her face the look of representing a type rather than a person; as if she might have been chosen to pose for a Civic Virtue or a Greek goddess.[1] The blood that ran so close to her fair skin might have been a preserving fluid rather than a ravaging element; yet her look of indestructible youthfulness made her seem neither hard nor dull, but only primitive and pure. In the thick of this meditation Archer suddenly felt himself looking at her with the startled gaze of a stranger, and plunged into a reminiscence of the wedding-breakfast and of Granny Mingott's immense and triumphant pervasion of it.

May settled down to frank enjoyment of the subject. "I was surprised, though—weren't you?—that aunt Medora came after all. Ellen wrote that they were neither of them well enough to take the journey; I do wish it had been she who had recovered! Did you see the exquisite old lace she sent me?"

He had known that the moment must come sooner or later, but he had somewhat imagined that by force of willing he might hold it at bay.

"Yes—I—no: yes, it was beautiful," he said, looking at her blindly, and wondering if, whenever he heard those two syllables, all his carefully built-up world would tumble about him like a house of cards.

"Aren't you tired? It will be good to have some tea when we arrive—I'm sure the aunts have got everything beautifully ready," he rattled on, taking her hand in his; and her mind rushed away instantly to the magnificent tea and coffee service of Baltimore silver which the Beauforts had sent, and which "went" so perfectly with uncle Lovell Mingott's trays and side-dishes.

In the spring twilight the train stopped at the Rhinebeck station, and they walked along the platform to the waiting carriage.

---

[1] *Civic Virtue or a Greek goddess*: an allegorical statue designed to encourage public virtue, popular in the late nineteenth century; the Greek goddess Wharton likely has in mind is Diana, a popular figure in nineteenth-century America for embodying both chastity and natural energy and grace.

"Ah, how awfully kind of the van der Luydens—they've sent their man over from Skuytercliff to meet us," Archer exclaimed, as a sedate person out of livery approached them and relieved the maid of her bags.

"I'm extremely sorry, sir," said this emissary, "that a little accident has occurred at the Miss du Lacs': a leak in the water-tank. It happened yesterday, and Mr. van der Luyden, who heard of it this morning, sent a house-maid up by the early train to get the Patroon's house ready. It will be quite comfortable, I think you'll find, sir; and the Miss du Lacs have sent their cook over, so that it will be exactly the same as if you'd been at Rhinebeck."

Archer stared at the speaker so blankly that he repeated in still more apologetic accents: "It'll be exactly the same, sir, I do assure you—" and May's eager voice broke out, covering the embarrassed silence: "The same as Rhinebeck? The Patroon's house? But it will be a hundred thousand times better—won't it, Newland? It's too dear and kind of Mr. van der Luyden to have thought of it."

And as they drove off, with the maid beside the coachman, and their shining bridal bags on the seat before them, she went on excitedly: "Only fancy, I've never been inside it—have you? The van der Luydens show it to so few people. But they opened it for Ellen, it seems, and she told me what a darling little place it was: she says it's the only house she's seen in America that she could imagine being perfectly happy in."

"Well—that's what we're going to be, isn't it?" cried her husband gaily; and she answered with her boyish smile: "Ah, it's just our luck beginning—the wonderful luck we're always going to have together!"

XX

"OF course we must dine with Mrs. Carfry, dearest," Archer said; and his wife looked at him with an anxious frown across the monumental Britannia ware[1] of their lodging house breakfast-table.

---

[1]   *Britannia ware*: a nineteenth-century Glasgow earthenware produced for the North and South American markets.

In all the rainy desert of autumnal London there were only two people whom the Newland Archers knew; and these two they had sedulously avoided, in conformity with the old New York tradition that it was not "dignified" to force one's self on the notice of one's acquaintances in foreign countries.

Mrs. Archer and Janey, in the course of their visits to Europe, had so unflinchingly lived up to this principle, and met the friendly advances of their fellow-travellers with an air of such impenetrable reserve, that they had almost achieved the record of never having exchanged a word with a "foreigner" other than those employed in hotels and railway-stations. Their own compatriots—save those previously known or properly accredited—they treated with an even more pronounced disdain; so that, unless they ran across a Chivers, a Dagonet or a Mingott, their months abroad were spent in an unbroken *tête-à-tête*. But the utmost precautions are sometimes unavailing; and one night at Botzen one of the two English ladies in the room across the passage (whose names, dress and social situation were already intimately known to Janey) had knocked on the door and asked if Mrs. Archer had a bottle of liniment. The other lady—the intruder's sister, Mrs. Carfry—had been seized with a sudden attack of bronchitis; and Mrs. Archer, who never travelled without a complete family pharmacy, was fortunately able to produce the required remedy.

Mrs. Carfry was very ill, and as she and her sister Miss Harle were travelling alone they were profoundly grateful to the Archer ladies, who supplied them with ingenious comforts and whose efficient maid helped to nurse the invalid back to health.

When the Archers left Botzen they had no idea of ever seeing Mrs. Carfry and Miss Harle again. Nothing, to Mrs. Archer's mind, would have been more "undignified" than to force one's self on the notice of a "foreigner" to whom one had happened to render an accidental service. But Mrs. Carfry and her sister, to whom this point of view was unknown, and who would have found it utterly incomprehensible, felt themselves linked by an eternal gratitude to the "delightful Americans" who had been so kind at Botzen. With touching fidelity they seized every chance of meeting Mrs. Archer and Janey in the course of their continental travels, and displayed a supernatural acuteness in finding out when they were to pass through London on their way to or from the States. The intimacy became indissoluble, and Mrs. Archer and Janey, whenever they alighted at Brown's Hotel, found themselves awaited by two affectionate friends who, like themselves, cultivated ferns in Wardian cases, made macramé lace, read the memoirs of the Baroness Bunsen[1] and had views about the occupants of the leading London pulpits. As Mrs. Archer said, it made "another thing of London" to know Mrs. Carfry and Miss Harle; and by the time that Newland became engaged the tie between the families was so firmly established that it was thought "only right" to send a wedding invitation to the two English ladies, who sent, in return, a pretty bouquet of pressed Alpine flowers under glass. And on the dock, when Newland and his wife sailed for England, Mrs. Archer's last word had been: "You must take May to see Mrs. Carfry."

Newland and his wife had had no idea of obeying this injunction; but Mrs. Carfry, with her usual acuteness, had run them down and sent them an invitation to dine; and it was over this invitation that May Archer was wrinkling her brows across the tea and muffins.

"It's all very well for you, Newland; you *know* them. But I shall feel so shy among a lot of people I've never met. And what shall I wear?"

Newland leaned back in his chair and smiled at her. She looked handsomer and more Diana-like than ever. The moist English air seemed to have deepened the bloom of her cheeks and softened the slight hardness of her virginal features; or else it was simply the inner glow of happiness, shining through like a light under ice.

"Wear, dearest? I thought a trunkful of things had come from Paris last week."

"Yes, of course. I meant to say that I shan't know *which* to wear." She pouted a little. "I've never dined out in London; and I don't want to be ridiculous."

---

[1] Frances *Bunsen* (1791-1876), wife of Baron Christian Bunsen, the German ambassador to England from 1841-1854, published *A Memoir of Baron Bunsen, Drawn Chiefly From Family Papers, By His Widow* in 1868.

He tried to enter into her perplexity. "But don't Englishwomen dress just like everybody else in the evening?"

"Newland! How can you ask such funny questions? When they go to the theatre in old ball-dresses and bare heads."

"Well, perhaps they wear new ball-dresses at home; but at any rate Mrs. Carfry and Miss Harle won't. They'll wear caps like my mother's—and shawls; very soft shawls."

"Yes; but how will the other women be dressed?"

"Not as well as you, dear," he rejoined, wondering what had suddenly developed in her Janey's morbid interest in clothes.

She pushed back her chair with a sigh. "That's dear of you, Newland; but it doesn't help me much."

He had an inspiration. "Why not wear your wedding-dress? That can't be wrong, can it?"

"Oh, dearest! If I only had it here! But it's gone to Paris to be made over for next winter, and Worth hasn't sent it back."

"Oh, well—" said Archer, getting up. "Look here—the fog's lifting. If we made a dash for the National Gallery we might manage to catch a glimpse of the pictures."

The Newland Archers were on their way home, after a three months' wedding-tour which May, in writing to her girl friends, vaguely summarised as "blissful."

They had not gone to the Italian Lakes: on reflection, Archer had not been able to picture his wife in that particular setting. Her own inclination (after a month with the Paris dressmakers) was for mountaineering in July and swimming in August. This plan they punctually fulfilled, spending July at Interlaken and Grindelwald, and August at a little place called Etretat, on the Normandy coast, which some one had recommended as quaint and quiet. Once or twice, in the mountains, Archer had pointed southward and said: "There's Italy"; and May, her feet in a gentian-bed, had smiled cheerfully, and replied: "It would be lovely to go there next winter, if only you didn't have to be in New York."

But in reality travelling interested her even less than he had expected. She regarded it (once her clothes were ordered) as merely an enlarged opportunity for walking, riding, swimming, and trying her hand at the fascinating new game of lawn tennis; and when they finally got back to London (where they were to spend a fortnight while he ordered *his* clothes) she no longer concealed the eagerness with which she looked forward to sailing.

In London nothing interested her but the theatres and the shops; and she found the theatres less exciting than the Paris *cafés chantants* where, under the blossoming horse-chestnuts of the Champs Élysées, she had had the novel experience of looking down from the restaurant terrace on an audience of "cocottes,"[1] and having her husband interpret to her as much of the songs as he thought suitable for bridal ears.

Archer had reverted to all his old inherited ideas about marriage. It was less trouble to conform with the tradition and treat May exactly as all his friends treated their wives than to try to put into practice the theories with which his untrammelled bachelorhood had dallied. There was no use in trying to emancipate a wife who had not the dimmest notion that she was not free; and he had long since discovered that May's only use of the liberty she supposed herself to possess would be to lay it on the altar of her wifely adoration. Her innate dignity would always keep her from making the gift abjectly; and a day might even come (as it once had) when she would find strength to take it altogether back if she thought she were doing it for his own good. But with a conception of marriage so uncomplicated and incurious as hers such a crisis could be brought about only by something visibly outrageous in his own conduct; and the fineness of her feeling for him made that unthinkable. Whatever happened, he knew, she would always be loyal, gallant and unresentful; and that pledged him to the practice of the same virtues.

All this tended to draw him back into his old habits of mind. If her simplicity had been the simplicity of pettiness he would have chafed and rebelled; but since the lines of her character, though so few, were on the same fine mould as her face, she became the tutelary divinity of all his old traditions and reverences.

Such qualities were scarcely of the kind to enliven foreign travel, though they made her so easy and pleasant a companion;

---

[1]   *cafés chantants*: cafés featuring singing, sometimes of a bawdy nature; *cocottes*: French slang for "loose woman."

but he saw at once how they would fall into place in their proper setting. He had no fear of being oppressed by them, for his artistic and intellectual life would go on, as it always had, outside the domestic circle; and within it there would be nothing small and stifling—coming back to his wife would never be like entering a stuffy room after a tramp in the open. And when they had children the vacant corners in both their lives would be filled.

All these things went through his mind during their long slow drive from Mayfair to South Kensington, where Mrs. Carfry and her sister lived. Archer too would have preferred to escape their friends' hospitality: in conformity with the family tradition he had always travelled as a sight-seer and looker-on, affecting a haughty unconsciousness of the presence of his fellow-beings. Once only, just after Harvard, he had spent a few gay weeks at Florence with a band of queer Europeanised Americans, dancing all night with titled ladies in palaces, and gambling half the day with the rakes and dandies of the fashionable club; but it had all seemed to him, though the greatest fun in the world, as unreal as a carnival. These queer cosmopolitan women, deep in complicated love-affairs which they appeared to feel the need of retailing to every one they met, and the magnificent young officers and elderly dyed wits who were the subjects or the recipients of their confidences, were too different from the people Archer had grown up among, too much like expensive and rather malodorous hot-house exotics, to detain his imagination long. To introduce his wife into such a society was out of the question; and in the course of his travels no other had shown any marked eagerness for his company.

Not long after their arrival in London he had run across the Duke of St. Austrey, and the Duke, instantly and cordially recognising him, had said: "Look me up, won't you?"—but no proper-spirited American would have considered that a suggestion to be acted on, and the meeting was without a sequel. They had even managed to avoid May's English aunt, the banker's wife, who was still in Yorkshire; in fact, they had purposely postponed going to London till the autumn in order that their arrival during the season might not appear pushing and snobbish to these unknown relatives.

"Probably there'll be nobody at Mrs. Carfry's—London's a

desert at this season, and you've made yourself much too beautiful," Archer said to May, who sat at his side in the hansom so spotlessly splendid in her sky-blue cloak edged with swansdown that it seemed wicked to expose her to the London grime.

"I don't want them to think that we dress like savages," she replied, with a scorn that Pocahontas might have resented; and he was struck again by the religious reverence of even the most unworldly American women for the social advantages of dress.

"It's their armour," he thought, "their defence against the unknown, and their defiance of it." And he understood for the first time the earnestness with which May, who was incapable of tying a ribbon in her hair to charm him, had gone through the solemn rite of selecting and ordering her extensive wardrobe.

He had been right in expecting the party at Mrs. Carfry's to be a small one. Besides their hostess and her sister, they found, in the long chilly drawing-room, only another shawled lady, a genial Vicar who was her husband, a silent lad whom Mrs. Carfry named as her nephew, and a small dark gentleman with lively eyes whom she introduced as his tutor, pronouncing a French name as she did so.

Into this dimly-lit and dim-featured group May Archer floated like a swan with the sunset on her: she seemed larger, fairer, more voluminously rustling than her husband had ever seen her; and he perceived that the rosiness and rustlingness were the tokens of an extreme and infantile shyness.

"What on earth will they expect me to talk about?" her helpless eyes implored him, at the very moment that her dazzling apparition was calling forth the same anxiety in their own bosoms. But beauty, even when distrustful of itself, awakens confidence in the manly heart; and the Vicar and the French-named tutor were soon manifesting to May their desire to put her at her ease.

In spite of their best efforts, however, the dinner was a languishing affair. Archer noticed that his wife's way of showing herself at her ease with foreigners was to become more uncompromisingly local in her references, so that, though her loveliness was an encouragement to admiration, her conversation was a chill to repartee. The Vicar soon abandoned the struggle; but the tutor, who spoke the most fluent and accomplished English, gallantly continued to pour it out to her until the ladies, to the manifest relief of all concerned, went up to the drawing-room. The Vicar, after a glass of port, was obliged to hurry away to a meeting, and the shy nephew, who appeared to be an invalid, was packed off to bed. But Archer and the tutor continued to sit over their wine, and suddenly Archer found himself talking as he had not done since his last symposium with Ned Winsett. The Carfry nephew, it turned out, had been threatened with consumption, and had had to leave Harrow for Switzerland, where he had spent two years in the milder air of Lake Leman. Being a bookish youth, he had been entrusted to M. Rivière, who had brought him back to England, and was to remain with him till he went up to Oxford the following spring; and M. Rivière added with simplicity that he should then have to look out for another job.

It seemed impossible, Archer thought, that he should be long without one, so varied were his interests and so many his gifts. He was a man of about thirty, with a thin ugly face (May would certainly have called him common-looking) to which the play of his ideas gave an intense expressiveness; but there was nothing frivolous or cheap in his animation.

His father, who had died young, had filled a small diplomatic post, and it had been intended that the son should follow the same career; but an insatiable taste for letters had thrown the young man into journalism, then into authorship (apparently unsuccessful), and at length—after other experiments and vicissitudes which he spared his listener—into tutoring English youths in Switzerland. Before that, however, he had lived much in Paris, frequented the Goncourt *grenier*, been advised by Maupassant not to attempt to write (even that seemed to Archer a dazzling honour!),[1] and had often talked with Mérimée in his mother's house. He had obviously always been desperately poor and anxious (having a mother and an unmarried sister to provide for), and it was apparent that his literary ambitions had failed. His situation, in fact, seemed, materially speaking, no more brilliant

---

[1] *grenier*: French for "attic." "Le Grenier" was the name of a house in Auteuil where, beginning in 1885, Edmond de Goncourt held Sunday salons frequented by young writers and artists. Guy de *Maupassant* (1850-1893), very successful French short story writer.

than Ned Winsett's; but he had lived in a world in which, as he said, no one who loved ideas need hunger mentally. As it was precisely of that love that poor Winsett was starving to death, Archer looked with a sort of vicarious envy at this eager impecunious young man who had fared so richly in his poverty.

"You see, Monsieur, it's worth everything, isn't it, to keep one's intellectual liberty, not to enslave one's powers of appreciation, one's critical independence? It was because of that that I abandoned journalism, and took to so much duller work: tutoring and private secretaryship. There is a good deal of drudgery, of course; but one preserves one's moral freedom, what we call in French one's *quant à soi*. And when one hears good talk one can join in it without compromising any opinions but one's own; or one can listen, and answer it inwardly. Ah, good conversation—there's nothing like it, is there? The air of ideas is the only air worth breathing. And so I have never regretted giving up either diplomacy or journalism—two different forms of the same self-abdication." He fixed his vivid eyes on Archer as he lit another cigarette. "*Voyez-vous*, Monsieur, to be able to look life in the face: that's worth living in a garret for, isn't it? But, after all, one must earn enough to pay for the garret; and I confess that to grow old as a private tutor—or a 'private' anything—is almost as chilling to the imagination as a second secretaryship at Bucharest. Sometimes I feel I must make a plunge: an immense plunge. Do you suppose, for instance, there would be any opening for me in America—in New York?"

Archer looked at him with startled eyes. New York, for a young man who had frequented the Goncourts and Flaubert,[1] and who thought the life of ideas the only one worth living! He continued to stare at M. Rivière perplexedly, wondering how to tell him that his very superiorities and advantages would be the surest hindrance to success.

"New York—New York—but must it be especially New York?" he stammered, utterly unable to imagine what lucrative

---

[1] Gustave *Flaubert* (1821-1880), French novelist, author of *Madame Bovary* (1857) and *L'Education Sentimentale* (1869). Flaubert strove to produce an objective and impersonal work of art, and is credited with raising the aesthetic standards of the novel.

opening his native city could offer to a young man to whom good conversation appeared to be the only necessity.

A sudden flush rose under M. Rivière's sallow skin. "I—I thought it your metropolis: is not the intellectual life more active there?" he rejoined; then, as if fearing to give his hearer the impression of having asked a favour, he went on hastily: "One throws out random suggestions—more to one's self than to others. In reality, I see no immediate prospect—" and rising from his seat he added, without a trace of constraint: "But Mrs. Carfry will think that I ought to be taking you upstairs."

During the homeward drive Archer pondered deeply on this episode. His hour with M. Rivière had put new air into his lungs, and his first impulse had been to invite him to dine the next day; but he was beginning to understand why married men did not always immediately yield to their first impulses.

"That young tutor is an interesting fellow: we had some awfully good talk after dinner about books and things," he threw out tentatively in the hansom.

May roused herself from one of the dreamy silences into which he had read so many meanings before six months of marriage had given him the key to them.

"The little Frenchman? Wasn't he dreadfully common?" she questioned coldly; and he guessed that she nursed a secret disappointment at having been invited out in London to meet a clergyman and a French tutor. The disappointment was not occasioned by the sentiment ordinarily defined as snobbishness, but by old New York's sense of what was due to it when it risked its dignity in foreign lands. If May's parents had entertained the Carfrys in Fifth Avenue they would have offered them something more substantial than a parson and a schoolmaster.

But Archer was on edge, and took her up.

"Common—common *where*?" he queried; and she returned with unusual readiness: "Why, I should say anywhere but in his school-room. Those people are always awkward in society. But then," she added disarmingly, "I suppose I shouldn't have known if he was clever."

Archer disliked her use of the word "clever" almost as much as her use of the word "common"; but he was beginning to fear his tendency to dwell on the things he disliked in her. After all, her point of view had always been the same. It was that of all the people he had grown up among, and he had always regarded it as necessary but negligible. Until a few months ago he had never known a "nice" woman who looked at life differently; and if a man married it must necessarily be among the nice.

"Ah—then I won't ask him to dine!" he concluded with a laugh; and May echoed, bewildered: "Goodness—ask the Carfrys' tutor?"

"Well, not on the same day with the Carfrys, if you prefer I shouldn't. But I did rather want another talk with him. He's looking for a job in New York."

Her surprise increased with her indifference: he almost fancied that she suspected him of being tainted with "foreignness."

"A job in New York? What sort of a job? People don't have French tutors: what does he want to do?"

"Chiefly to enjoy good conversation, I understand," her husband retorted perversely; and she broke into an appreciative laugh. "Oh, Newland, how funny! Isn't that *French*?"

On the whole, he was glad to have the matter settled for him by her refusing to take seriously his wish to invite M. Rivière. Another after-dinner talk would have made it difficult to avoid the question of New York; and the more Archer considered it the less he was able to fit M. Rivière into any conceivable picture of New York as he knew it.

He perceived with a flash of chilling insight that in future many problems would be thus negatively solved for him; but as he paid the hansom and followed his wife's long train into the house he took refuge in the comforting platitude that the first six months were always the most difficult in marriage. "After that I suppose we shall have pretty nearly finished rubbing off each other's angles," he reflected; but the worst of it was that May's pressure was already bearing on the very angles whose sharpness he most wanted to keep.

XXI

THE small bright lawn stretched away smoothly to the big bright sea.

The turf was hemmed with an edge of scarlet geranium and coleus, and cast-iron vases painted in chocolate colour, standing at intervals along the winding path that led to the sea, looped their garlands of petunia and ivy geranium above the neatly raked gravel.

Half way between the edge of the cliff and the square wooden house (which was also chocolate-coloured, but with the tin roof of the verandah striped in yellow and brown to represent an awning) two large targets had been placed against a background of shrubbery. On the other side of the lawn, facing the targets, was pitched a real tent, with benches and garden-seats about it. A number of ladies in summer dresses and gentlemen in grey frock-coats and tall hats stood on the lawn or sat upon the benches; and every now and then a slender girl in starched muslin would step from the tent, bow in hand, and speed her shaft at one of the targets, while the spectators interrupted their talk to watch the result.

Newland Archer, standing on the verandah of the house, looked curiously down upon this scene. On each side of the shiny painted steps was a large blue china flower-pot on a bright yellow china stand. A spiky green plant filled each pot, and below the verandah ran a wide border of blue hydrangeas edged with more red geraniums. Behind him, the French windows of the drawing-rooms through which he had passed gave glimpses, between swaying lace curtains, of glassy parquet floors islanded with chintz *poufs*, dwarf arm-chairs, and velvet tables covered with trifles in silver.

The Newport Archery Club always held its August meeting at the Beauforts'. The sport, which had hitherto known no rival but croquet, was beginning to be discarded in favour of lawn-tennis; but the latter game was still considered too rough and inelegant for social occasions, and as an opportunity to show off pretty dresses and graceful attitudes the bow and arrow held their own.

Archer looked down with wonder at the familiar spectacle. It surprised him that life should be going on in the old way when his own reactions to it had so completely changed. It was

Newport that had first brought home to him the extent of the change. In New York, during the previous winter, after he and May had settled down in the new greenish-yellow house with the bow-window and the Pompeian vestibule, he had dropped back with relief into the old routine of the office, and the renewal of this daily activity had served as a link with his former self. Then there had been the pleasurable excitement of choosing a showy grey stepper for May's brougham (the Wellands had given the carriage), and the abiding occupation and interest of arranging his new library, which, in spite of family doubts and disapprovals, had been carried out as he had dreamed, with a dark embossed paper, Eastlake book-cases and "sincere" arm-chairs and tables. At the Century he had found Winsett again, and at the Knicker-bocker the fashionable young men of his own set;[1] and what with the hours dedicated to the law and those given to dining out or entertaining friends at home, with an occasional evening at the Opera or the play, the life he was living had still seemed a fairly real and inevitable sort of business.

But Newport represented the escape from duty into an atmosphere of unmitigated holiday-making. Archer had tried to persuade May to spend the summer on a remote island off the coast of Maine (called, appropriately enough, Mount Desert),[2] where a few hardy Bostonians and Philadelphians were camping in "native" cottages, and whence came reports of enchanting scenery and a wild, almost trapper-like existence amid woods and waters.

But the Wellands always went to Newport, where they owned one of the square boxes on the cliffs, and their son-in-law could adduce no good reason why he and May should not join them there. As Mrs. Welland rather tartly pointed out, it was hardly worth while for May to have worn herself out trying on summer clothes in Paris if she was not to be allowed to wear them; and this argument was of a kind to which Archer had as yet found no answer.

May herself could not understand his obscure reluctance to fall in with so reasonable and pleasant a way of spending the summer.

---

[1] The *Knickerbocker* Club: a distinguished gentlemen's club formed in 1871.

[2] An island off the coast of Maine, *Mount Desert* Island became a popular resort destination after several American artists 'discovered' it in the 1840s.

She reminded him that he had always liked Newport in his bachelor days, and as this was indisputable he could only profess that he was sure he was going to like it better than ever now that they were to be there together. But as he stood on the Beaufort verandah and looked out on the brightly peopled lawn it came home to him with a shiver that he was not going to like it at all.

It was not May's fault, poor dear. If, now and then, during their travels, they had fallen slightly out of step, harmony had been restored by their return to the conditions she was used to. He had always foreseen that she would not disappoint him; and he had been right. He had married (as most young men did) because he had met a perfectly charming girl at the moment when a series of rather aimless sentimental adventures were ending in premature disgust; and she had represented peace, stability, comradeship, and the steadying sense of an unescapable duty.

He could not say that he had been mistaken in his choice, for she had fulfilled all that he had expected. It was undoubtedly gratifying to be the husband of one of the handsomest and most popular young married women in New York, especially when she was also one of the sweetest-tempered and most reasonable of wives; and Archer had never been insensible to such advantages. As for the momentary madness which had fallen upon him on the eve of his marriage, he had trained himself to regard it as the last of his discarded experiments. The idea that he could ever, in his senses, have dreamed of marrying the Countess Olenska had become almost unthinkable, and she remained in his memory simply as the most plaintive and poignant of a line of ghosts.

But all these abstractions and eliminations made of his mind a rather empty and echoing place, and he supposed that was one of the reasons why the busy animated people on the Beaufort lawn shocked him as if they had been children playing in a grave-yard.

He heard a murmur of skirts beside him, and the Marchioness Manson fluttered out of the drawing-room window. As usual, she was extraordinarily festooned and bedizened, with a limp Leghorn hat anchored to her head by many windings of faded gauze, and a little black velvet parasol on a carved ivory handle absurdly balanced over her much larger hat-brim.

"My dear Newland, I had no idea that you and May had arrived! You yourself came only yesterday, you say? Ah, business—business—professional duties ... I understand. Many husbands, I know, find it impossible to join their wives here except for the week-end." She cocked her head on one side and languished at him through screwed-up eyes. "But marriage is one long sacrifice, as I used often to remind my Ellen—"

Archer's heart stopped with the queer jerk which it had given once before, and which seemed suddenly to slam a door between himself and the outer world; but this break of continuity must have been of the briefest, for he presently heard Medora answering a question he had apparently found voice to put.

"No, I am not staying here, but with the Blenkers, in their delicious solitude at Portsmouth. Beaufort was kind enough to send his famous trotters for me this morning, so that I might have at least a glimpse of one of Regina's garden-parties; but this evening I go back to rural life. The Blenkers, dear original beings, have hired a primitive old farm-house at Portsmouth where they gather about them representative people ... " She drooped slightly beneath her protecting brim, and added with a faint blush: "This week Dr. Agathon Carver is holding a series of Inner Thought meetings there. A contrast indeed to this gay scene of worldly pleasure—but then I have always lived on contrasts! To me the only death is monotony. I always say to Ellen: Beware of monotony; it's the mother of all the deadly sins. But my poor child is going through a phase of exaltation, of abhorrence of the world. You know, I suppose, that she has declined all invitations to stay at Newport, even with her grandmother Mingott? I could hardly persuade her to come with me to the Blenkers', if you will believe it! The life she leads is morbid, unnatural. Ah, if she had only listened to me when it was still possible ...When the door was still open ... But shall we go down and watch this absorbing match? I hear your May is one of the competitors."

Strolling toward them from the tent Beaufort advanced over the lawn, tall, heavy, too tightly buttoned into a London frock-coat, with one of his own orchids in its buttonhole. Archer, who had not seen him for two or three months, was struck by the change in his appearance. In the hot summer light his floridness seemed heavy and bloated, and but for his erect square-shouldered walk he would have looked like an over-fed and over-dressed old man.

There were all sorts of rumours afloat about Beaufort. In the spring he had gone off on a long cruise to the West Indies in his new steam-yacht, and it was reported that, at various points where he had touched, a lady resembling Miss Fanny Ring had been seen in his company. The steam-yacht, built in the Clyde,[1] and fitted with tiled bath-rooms and other unheard-of luxuries, was said to have cost him half a million; and the pearl necklace which he had presented to his wife on his return was as magnificent as such expiatory offerings are apt to be. Beaufort's fortune was substantial enough to stand the strain; and yet the disquieting rumours persisted, not only in Fifth Avenue but in Wall Street. Some people said he had speculated unfortunately in railways, others that he was being bled by one of the most insatiable members of her profession; and to every report of threatened insolvency Beaufort replied by a fresh extravagance: the building of a new row of orchid-houses, the purchase of a new string of race-horses, or the addition of a new Meissonnier[2] or Cabanel to his picture-gallery.

He advanced toward the Marchioness and Newland with his usual half-sneering smile. "Hullo, Medora! Did the trotters do their business? Forty minutes, eh? ... Well, that's not so bad, considering your nerves had to be spared." He shook hands with Archer, and then, turning back with them, placed himself on Mrs. Manson's other side, and said, in a low voice, a few words which their companion did not catch.

The Marchioness replied by one of her queer foreign jerks, and a "*Que voulez-vous?*"[3] which deepened Beaufort's frown; but he produced a good semblance of a congratulatory smile as he glanced at Archer to say: "You know May's going to carry off the first prize."

---

1   The *Clyde* River runs from Glasgow to Greenock where it widens into the Firth of Clyde. The area has long been associated with shipbuilding.

2   Ernest *Meissonnier* (1815-1891), French painter famous for his very small scenes with intricate details of costumes and accessories. His work was considered by such people as Balzac, Zola, and Baudelaire to represent the poor taste of the nouveaux-riches.

3   *Que voulez-vous*: French for "What can one do?"

"Ah, then it remains in the family," Medora rippled; and at that moment they reached the tent and Mrs. Beaufort met them in a girlish cloud of mauve muslin and floating veils.

May Welland was just coming out of the tent. In her white dress, with a pale green ribbon about the waist and a wreath of ivy on her hat, she had the same Diana-like aloofness as when she had entered the Beaufort ball-room on the night of her engagement. In the interval not a thought seemed to have passed behind her eyes or a feeling through her heart; and though her husband knew that she had the capacity for both he marvelled afresh at the way in which experience dropped away from her.

She had her bow and arrow in her hand, and placing herself on the chalk-mark traced on the turf she lifted the bow to her shoulder and took aim. The attitude was so full of a classic grace that a murmur of appreciation followed her appearance, and Archer felt the glow of proprietorship that so often cheated him into momentary well-being. Her rivals—Mrs. Reggie Chivers, the Merry girls, and divers rosy Thorleys, Dagonets and Mingotts, stood behind her in a lovely anxious group, brown heads and golden bent above the scores, and pale muslins and flower-wreathed hats mingled in a tender rainbow. All were young and pretty, and bathed in summer bloom; but not one had the nymph-like ease of his wife, when, with tense muscles and happy frown, she bent her soul upon some feat of strength.

"Gad," Archer heard Lawrence Lefferts say, "not one of the lot holds the bow as she does;" and Beaufort retorted: "Yes; but that's the only kind of target she'll ever hit."

Archer felt irrationally angry. His host's contemptuous tribute to May's "niceness" was just what a husband should have wished to hear said of his wife. The fact that a coarse-minded man found her lacking in attraction was simply another proof of her quality; yet the words sent a faint shiver through his heart. What if "niceness" carried to that supreme degree were only a negation, the curtain dropped before an emptiness? As he looked at May, returning flushed and calm from her final bull's-eye, he had the feeling that he had never yet lifted that curtain.

She took the congratulations of her rivals and of the rest of the company with the simplicity that was her crowning grace. No one could ever be jealous of her triumphs because she managed to give the feeling that she would have been just as serene if she had missed them. But when her eyes met her husband's her face glowed with the pleasure she saw in his.

Mrs. Welland's basket-work pony-carriage was waiting for them, and they drove off among the dispersing carriages, May handling the reins and Archer sitting at her side.

The afternoon sunlight still lingered upon the bright lawns and shrubberies, and up and down Bellevue Avenue rolled a double line of victorias, dog-carts, landaus and "vis-à-vis," carrying well-dressed ladies and gentlemen away from the Beaufort garden-party, or homeward from their daily afternoon turn along the Ocean Drive.

"Shall we go to see Granny?" May suddenly proposed. "I should like to tell her myself that I've won the prize. There's lots of time before dinner."

Archer acquiesced, and she turned the ponies down Narragansett Avenue, crossed Spring Street and drove out toward the rocky moorland beyond. In this unfashionable region Catherine the Great, always indifferent to precedent and thrifty of purse, had built herself in her youth a many-peaked and cross-beamed *cottage-orné* on a bit of cheap land overlooking the bay. Here, in a thicket of stunted oaks, her verandahs spread themselves above the island-dotted waters. A winding drive led up between iron stags and blue glass balls embedded in mounds of geraniums to a front door of highly-varnished walnut under a striped verandah-roof; and behind it ran a narrow hall with a black and yellow star-patterned parquet floor, upon which opened four small square rooms with heavy flock-papers under ceilings on which an Italian house-painter had lavished all the divinities of Olympus.[1] One of these rooms had been turned into a bedroom by Mrs. Mingott when the burden of flesh descended on her, and in the adjoining one she spent her days, enthroned in a large arm-chair between the open door and window, and perpetually waving a palm-leaf

---

[1]   *divinities of Olympus*: the classical Greek gods such as Zeus, Poseiden, Hades, Demeter, Apollo, Aphrodite, Hermes, etc., were traditionally believed to have their home at Mount Olympus.

fan which the prodigious projection of her bosom kept so far from the rest of her person that the air it set in motion stirred only the fringe of the anti-macassars on the chair-arms.

Since she had been the means of hastening his marriage old Catherine had shown to Archer the cordiality which a service rendered excites toward the person served. She was persuaded that irrepressible passion was the cause of his impatience; and being an ardent admirer of impulsiveness (when it did not lead to the spending of money) she always received him with a genial twinkle of complicity and a play of allusion to which May seemed fortunately impervious.

She examined and appraised with much interest the diamond-tipped arrow which had been pinned on May's bosom at the conclusion of the match, remarking that in her day a filigree brooch would have been thought enough, but that there was no denying that Beaufort did things handsomely.

"Quite an heirloom, in fact, my dear," the old lady chuckled. "You must leave it in fee to your eldest girl." She pinched May's white arm and watched the colour flood her face. "Well, well, what have I said to make you shake out the red flag? Ain't there going to be any daughters—only boys, eh? Good gracious, look at her blushing again all over her blushes! What—can't I say that either? Mercy me—when my children beg me to have all those gods and goddesses painted out overhead I always say I'm too thankful to have somebody about me that *nothing* can shock!"

Archer burst into a laugh, and May echoed it, crimson to the eyes.

"Well, now tell me all about the party, please, my dears, for I shall never get a straight word about it out of that silly Medora," the ancestress continued; and, as May exclaimed: "Cousin Medora? But I thought she was going back to Portsmouth?" she answered placidly: "So she is—but she's got to come here first to pick up Ellen. Ah—you didn't know Ellen had come to spend the day with me? Such fol-de-rol, her not coming for the summer; but I gave up arguing with young people about fifty years ago. Ellen—*Ellen!*" she cried in her shrill old voice, trying to bend forward far enough to catch a glimpse of the lawn beyond the verandah.

There was no answer, and Mrs. Mingott rapped impatiently with her stick on the shiny floor. A mulatto maid-servant in a bright turban, replying to the summons, informed her mistress that she had seen "Miss Ellen" going down the path to the shore; and Mrs. Mingott turned to Archer.

"Run down and fetch her, like a good grandson; this pretty lady will describe the party to me," she said; and Archer stood up as if in a dream.

He had heard the Countess Olenska's name pronounced often enough during the year and a half since they had last met, and was even familiar with the main incidents of her life in the interval. He knew that she had spent the previous summer at Newport, where she appeared to have gone a great deal into society, but that in the autumn she had suddenly sub-let the "perfect house" which Beaufort had been at such pains to find for her, and decided to establish herself in Washington. There, during the winter, he had heard of her (as one always heard of pretty women in Washington) as shining in the "brilliant diplomatic society" that was supposed to make up for the social short-comings of the Administration.[1] He had listened to these accounts, and to various contradictory reports on her appearance, her conversation, her point of view and her choice of friends, with the detachment with which one listens to reminiscences of some one long since dead; not till Medora suddenly spoke her name at the archery match had Ellen Olenska become a living presence to him again. The Marchioness's foolish lisp had called up a vision of the little fire-lit drawing-room and the sound of the carriage-wheels returning down the deserted street. He thought of a story he had read, of some peasant children in Tuscany lighting a bunch of straw in a wayside cavern, and revealing old silent images in their painted tomb ...

The way to the shore descended from the bank on which the house was perched to a walk above the water planted with weeping willows. Through their veil Archer caught the glint of the Lime Rock, with its white-washed turret and the tiny house in which

---

[1]   Most likely the notoriously corrupt administration of Ulysses S. Grant, president of the United States from 1869 to 1877.

the heroic light-house keeper, Ida Lewis,[1] was living her last venerable years. Beyond it lay the flat reaches and ugly government chimneys of Goat Island, the bay spreading northward in a shimmer of gold to Prudence Island with its low growth of oaks, and the shores of Conanicut faint in the sunset haze.

From the willow walk projected a slight wooden pier ending in a sort of pagoda-like summer-house; and in the pagoda a lady stood, leaning against the rail, her back to the shore. Archer stopped at the sight as if he had waked from sleep. That vision of the past was a dream, and the reality was what awaited him in the house on the bank overhead: was Mrs. Welland's pony-carriage circling around and around the oval at the door, was May sitting under the shameless Olympians and glowing with secret hopes, was the Welland villa at the far end of Bellevue Avenue, and Mr. Welland, already dressed for dinner, and pacing the drawing-room floor, watch in hand, with dyspeptic impatience—for it was one of the houses in which one always knew exactly what is happening at a given hour.

"What am I? A son-in-law—" Archer thought.

The figure at the end of the pier had not moved. For a long moment the young man stood half way down the bank, gazing at the bay furrowed with the coming and going of sail-boats, yacht-launches, fishing-craft and the trailing black coal-barges hauled by noisy tugs. The lady in the summer-house seemed to be held by the same sight. Beyond the grey bastions of Fort Adams a long-drawn sunset was splintering up into a thousand fires, and the radiance caught the sail of a cat-boat as it beat out through the channel between the Lime Rock and the shore. Archer, as he watched, remembered the scene in the Shaughraun, and Montague lifting Ada Dyas's ribbon to his lips without her knowing that he was in the room.

"She doesn't know—she hasn't guessed. Shouldn't I know if she came up behind me, I wonder?" he mused; and suddenly he said to himself: "If she doesn't turn before that sail crosses the Lime Rock light I'll go back."

---

[1] *Ida Lewis* Wilson (1841-1911), keeper of the Lime Rock Lighthouse in Newport, Rhode Island.

The boat was gliding out on the receding tide. It slid before the Lime Rock, blotted out Ida Lewis's little house, and passed across the turret in which the light was hung. Archer waited till a wide space of water sparkled between the last reef of the island and the stern of the boat; but still the figure in the summer-house did not move.

He turned and walked up the hill.

"I'm sorry you didn't find Ellen—I should have liked to see her again," May said as they drove home through the dusk. "But perhaps she wouldn't have cared—she seems so changed."

"Changed?" echoed her husband in a colourless voice, his eyes fixed on the ponies' twitching ears.

"So indifferent to her friends, I mean; giving up New York and her house, and spending her time with such queer people. Fancy how hideously uncomfortable she must be at the Blenkers'! She says she does it to keep Cousin Medora out of mischief: to prevent her marrying dreadful people. But I sometimes think we've always bored her."

Archer made no answer, and she continued, with a tinge of hardness that he had never before noticed in her frank fresh voice: "After all, I wonder if she wouldn't be happier with her husband."

He burst into a laugh. "Sancta simplicitas!" he exclaimed;[1] and as she turned a puzzled frown on him he added: "I don't think I ever heard you say a cruel thing before."

"Cruel?"

"Well—watching the contortions of the damned is supposed to be a favourite sport of the angels; but I believe even they don't think people happier in hell."

"It's a pity she ever married abroad then," said May, in the placid tone with which her mother met Mr. Welland's vagaries; and Archer felt himself gently relegated to the category of unreasonable husbands.

They drove down Bellevue Avenue and turned in between the chamfered wooden gate-posts surmounted by cast-iron

---

[1] *Sancta simplicitas*: Latin for "sacred simplicity."

lamps which marked the approach to the Welland villa. Lights were already shining through its windows, and Archer, as the carriage stopped, caught a glimpse of his father-in-law, exactly as he had pictured him, pacing the drawing-room, watch in hand and wearing the pained expression that he had long since found to be much more efficacious than anger.

The young man, as he followed his wife into the hall, was conscious of a curious reversal of mood. There was something about the luxury of the Welland house and the density of the Welland atmosphere, so charged with minute observances and exactions, that always stole into his system like a narcotic. The heavy carpets, the watchful servants, the perpetually reminding tick of disciplined clocks, the perpetually renewed stack of cards and invitations on the hall table, the whole chain of tyrannical trifles binding one hour to the next, and each member of the household to all the others, made any less systematised and affluent existence seem unreal and precarious. But now it was the Welland house, and the life he was expected to lead in it, that had become unreal and irrelevant, and the brief scene on the shore, when he had stood irresolute, half-way down the bank, was as close to him as the blood in his veins.

All night he lay awake in the big chintz bedroom at May's side, watching the moonlight slant along the carpet, and thinking of Ellen Olenska driving home across the gleaming beaches behind Beaufort's trotters.

XXII

"A party for the Blenkers—the Blenkers?"

Mr. Welland laid down his knife and fork and looked anxiously and incredulously across the luncheon-table at his wife, who, adjusting her gold eye-glasses, read aloud, in the tone of high comedy: "Professor and Mrs. Emerson Sillerton request the pleasure of Mr. and Mrs. Welland's company at the meeting of the Wednesday Afternoon Club on August 25th at 3 o'clock punctually. To meet Mrs. and the Misses Blenker.

"Red Gables, Catherine Street. R. S. V. P."

"Good gracious—" Mr. Welland gasped, as if a second reading had been necessary to bring the monstrous absurdity of the thing home to him.

"Poor Amy Sillerton—you never can tell what her husband will do next," Mrs. Welland sighed. "I suppose he's just discovered the Blenkers."

Professor Emerson Sillerton was a thorn in the side of Newport society; and a thorn that could not be plucked out, for it grew on a venerable and venerated family tree. He was, as people said, a man who had had "every advantage." His father was Sillerton Jackson's uncle, his mother a Pennilow of Boston; on each side there was wealth and position, and mutual suitability. Nothing—as Mrs. Welland had often remarked—nothing on earth obliged Emerson Sillerton to be an archaeologist, or indeed a Professor of any sort, or to live in Newport in winter, or do any of the other revolutionary things that he did. But at least, if he was going to break with tradition and flout society in the face, he need not have married poor Amy Dagonet, who had a right to expect "something different," and money enough to keep her own carriage.

No one in the Mingott set could understand why Amy Sillerton had submitted so tamely to the eccentricities of a husband who filled the house with long-haired men and short-haired women, and, when he travelled, took her to explore tombs in Yucatan instead of going to Paris or Italy. But there they were, set in their ways, and apparently unaware that they were different from other people; and when they gave one of their dreary annual garden-parties every family on the Cliffs, because of the Sillerton-Pennilow-Dagonet connection, had to draw lots and send an unwilling representative.

"It's a wonder," Mrs. Welland remarked, "that they didn't choose the Cup Race day! Do you remember, two years ago, their giving a party for a black man on the day of Julia Mingott's *thé dansant*? Luckily this time there's nothing else going on that I know of—for of course some of us will have to go."

Mr. Welland sighed nervously. "'Some of us,' my dear—more than one? Three o'clock is such a very awkward hour. I have to be here at half-past three to take my drops: it's really no use trying to follow Bencomb's new treatment if I don't do it systematically;

and if I join you later, of course I shall miss my drive." At the thought he laid down his knife and fork again, and a flush of anxiety rose to his finely-wrinkled cheek.

"There's no reason why you should go at all, my dear," his wife answered with a cheerfulness that had become automatic. "I have some cards to leave at the other end of Bellevue Avenue, and I'll drop in at about half-past three and stay long enough to make poor Amy feel that she hasn't been slighted." She glanced hesitatingly at her daughter. "And if Newland's afternoon is provided for perhaps May can drive you out with the ponies, and try their new russet harness."

It was a principle in the Welland family that people's days and hours should be what Mrs. Welland called "provided for." The melancholy possibility of having to "kill time" (especially for those who did not care for whist or solitaire) was a vision that haunted her as the spectre of the unemployed haunts the philanthropist. Another of her principles was that parents should never (at least visibly) interfere with the plans of their married children; and the difficulty of adjusting this respect for May's independence with the exigency of Mr. Welland's claims could be overcome only by the exercise of an ingenuity which left not a second of Mrs. Welland's own time unprovided for.

"Of course I'll drive with Papa—I'm sure Newland will find something to do," May said, in a tone that gently reminded her husband of his lack of response. It was a cause of constant distress to Mrs. Welland that her son-in-law showed so little foresight in planning his days. Often already, during the fortnight that he had passed under her roof, when she enquired how he meant to spend his afternoon, he had answered paradoxically: "Oh, I think for a change I'll just save it instead of spending it—" and once, when she and May had had to go on a long-postponed round of afternoon calls, he had confessed to having lain all the afternoon under a rock on the beach below the house.

"Newland never seems to look ahead," Mrs. Welland once ventured to complain to her daughter; and May answered serenely: "No; but you see it doesn't matter, because when there's nothing particular to do he reads a book."

"Ah, yes—like his father!" Mrs. Welland agreed, as if allowing for an inherited oddity; and after that the question of Newland's unemployment was tacitly dropped.

Nevertheless, as the day for the Sillerton reception approached, May began to show a natural solicitude for his welfare, and to suggest a tennis match at the Chiverses', or a sail on Julius Beaufort's cutter, as a means of atoning for her temporary desertion. "I shall be back by six, you know, dear: Papa never drives later than that—" and she was not reassured till Archer said that he thought of hiring a run-about and driving up the island to a stud-farm to look at a second horse for her brougham. They had been looking for this horse for some time, and the suggestion was so acceptable that May glanced at her mother as if to say: "You see he knows how to plan out his time as well as any of us."

The idea of the stud-farm and the brougham horse had germinated in Archer's mind on the very day when the Emerson Sillerton invitation had first been mentioned; but he had kept it to himself as if there were something clandestine in the plan, and discovery might prevent its execution. He had, however, taken the precaution to engage in advance a run-about with a pair of old livery-stable trotters that could still do their eighteen miles on level roads; and at two o'clock, hastily deserting the luncheon-table, he sprang into the light carriage and drove off.

The day was perfect. A breeze from the north drove little puffs of white cloud across an ultramarine sky, with a bright sea running under it. Bellevue Avenue was empty at that hour, and after dropping the stable-lad at the corner of Mill Street Archer turned down the Old Beach Road and drove across Eastman's Beach.

He had the feeling of unexplained excitement with which, on half-holidays at school, he used to start off into the unknown. Taking his pair at an easy gait, he counted on reaching the stud-farm, which was not far beyond Paradise Rocks, before three o'clock; so that, after looking over the horse (and trying him if he seemed promising) he would still have four golden hours to dispose of.

As soon as he heard of the Sillerton's party he had said to himself that the Marchioness Manson would certainly come to Newport with the Blenkers, and that Madame Olenska might again take the opportunity of spending the day with her grandmother. At any rate, the Blenker habitation would probably be deserted, and he would be able, without indiscretion, to satisfy a vague curiosity concerning it. He was not sure that he wanted to see the Countess Olenska again; but ever since he had looked at her from the path above the bay he had wanted, irrationally and indescribably, to see the place she was living in, and to follow the movements of her imagined figure as he had watched the real one in the summer-house. The longing was with him day and night, an incessant undefinable craving, like the sudden whim of a sick man for food or drink once tasted and long since forgotten. He could not see beyond the craving, or picture what it might lead to, for he was not conscious of any wish to speak to Madame Olenska or to hear her voice. He simply felt that if he could carry away the vision of the spot of earth she walked on, and the way the sky and sea enclosed it, the rest of the world might seem less empty.

When he reached the stud-farm a glance showed him that the horse was not what he wanted; nevertheless he took a turn behind it in order to prove to himself that he was not in a hurry. But at three o'clock he shook out the reins over the trotters and turned into the by-roads leading to Portsmouth. The wind had dropped and a faint haze on the horizon showed that a fog was waiting to steal up the Saconnet on the turn of the tide; but all about him fields and woods were steeped in golden light.

He drove past grey-shingled farm-houses in orchards, past hay-fields and groves of oak, past villages with white steeples rising sharply into the fading sky; and at last, after stopping to ask the way of some men at work in a field, he turned down a lane between high banks of goldenrod and brambles. At the end of the lane was the blue glimmer of the river; to the left, standing in front of a clump of oaks and maples, he saw a long tumble-down house with white paint peeling from its clapboards.

On the road-side facing the gateway stood one of the open sheds in which the New Englander shelters his farming implements and visitors "hitch" their "teams." Archer, jumping down, led his pair into the shed, and after tying them to a post turned toward the house. The patch of lawn before it had relapsed into a hay-field; but to the left an overgrown box-garden full of dahlias and rusty rose-bushes encircled a ghostly summer-house of trellis-work that had once been white, surmounted by a wooden Cupid who had lost his bow and arrow but continued to take ineffectual aim.

Archer leaned for a while against the gate. No one was in sight, and not a sound came from the open windows of the house: a grizzled Newfoundland dozing before the door seemed as ineffectual a guardian as the arrowless Cupid. It was strange to think that this place of silence and decay was the home of the turbulent Blenkers; yet Archer was sure that he was not mistaken.

For a long time he stood there, content to take in the scene, and gradually falling under its drowsy spell; but at length he roused himself to the sense of the passing time. Should he look his fill and then drive away? He stood irresolute, wishing suddenly to see the inside of the house, so that he might picture the room that Madame Olenska sat in. There was nothing to prevent his walking up to the door and ringing the bell; if, as he supposed, she was away with the rest of the party, he could easily give his name, and ask permission to go into the sitting-room to write a message.

But instead, he crossed the lawn and turned toward the box-garden. As he entered it he caught sight of something bright-coloured in the summer-house, and presently made it out to be a pink parasol. The parasol drew him like a magnet: he was sure it was hers. He went into the summer-house, and sitting down on the rickety seat picked up the silken thing and looked at its carved handle, which was made of some rare wood that gave out an aromatic scent. Archer lifted the handle to his lips.

He heard a rustle of skirts against the box, and sat motionless, leaning on the parasol handle with clasped hands, and letting the rustle come nearer without lifting his eyes. He had always known that this must happen ...

"Oh, Mr. Archer!" exclaimed a loud young voice; and looking up he saw before him the youngest and largest of the Blenker girls, blonde and blowsy, in bedraggled muslin. A red blotch on one of her cheeks seemed to show that it had recently been pressed against a pillow, and her half-awakened eyes stared at him hospitably but confusedly.

"Gracious—where did you drop from? I must have been sound asleep in the hammock. Everybody else has gone to Newport. Did you ring?" she incoherently enquired.

Archer's confusion was greater than hers. "I—no—that is, I was just going to. I had to come up the island to see about a horse, and I drove over on a chance of finding Mrs. Blenker and your visitors. But the house seemed empty—so I sat down to wait."

Miss Blenker, shaking off the fumes of sleep, looked at him with increasing interest. "The house *is* empty. Mother's not here, or the Marchioness—or anybody but me." Her glance became faintly reproachful. "Didn't you know that Professor and Mrs. Sillerton are giving a garden-party for mother and all of us this afternoon? It was too unlucky that I couldn't go; but I've had a sore throat, and mother was afraid of the drive home this evening. Did you ever know anything so disappointing? Of course," she added gaily, "I shouldn't have minded half as much if I'd known you were coming."

Symptoms of a lumbering coquetry became visible in her, and Archer found the strength to break in: "But Madame Olenska— has she gone to Newport too?"

Miss Blenker looked at him with surprise. "Madame Olenska—didn't you know she'd been called away?"

"Called away?—"

"Oh, my best parasol! I lent it to that goose of a Katie, because it matched her ribbons, and the careless thing must have dropped it here. We Blenkers are all like that ... real Bohemians!" Recovering the sunshade with a powerful hand she unfurled it and suspended its rosy dome above her head. "Yes, Ellen was called away yesterday: she lets us call her Ellen, you know. A telegram came from Boston: she said she might be gone for two days. I do *love* the way she does her hair, don't you?" Miss Blenker rambled on.

Archer continued to stare through her as though she had been transparent. All he saw was the trumpery parasol that arched its pinkness above her giggling head.

After a moment he ventured: "You don't happen to know why Madame Olenska went to Boston? I hope it was not on account of bad news?"

Miss Blenker took this with a cheerful incredulity. "Oh, I don't believe so. She didn't tell us what was in the telegram. I think she didn't want the Marchioness to know. She's so romantic-looking, isn't she? Doesn't she remind you of Mrs. Scott-Siddons when she reads 'Lady Geraldine's Courtship'?[1] Did you never hear her?"

Archer was dealing hurriedly with crowding thoughts. His whole future seemed suddenly to be unrolled before him; and passing down its endless emptiness he saw the dwindling figure of a man to whom nothing was ever to happen. He glanced about him at the unpruned garden, the tumble-down house, and the oak-grove under which the dusk was gathering. It had seemed so exactly the place in which he ought to have found Madame Olenska; and she was far away, and even the pink sunshade was not hers ...

He frowned and hesitated. "You don't know, I suppose—I shall be in Boston tomorrow. If I could manage to see her—"

He felt that Miss Blenker was losing interest in him, though her smile persisted. "Oh, of course; how lovely of you! She's staying at the Parker House; it must be horrible there in this weather."

After that Archer was but intermittently aware of the remarks they exchanged. He could only remember stoutly resisting her entreaty that he should await the returning family and have high tea with them before he drove home. At length, with his hostess still at his side, he passed out of range of the wooden Cupid, unfastened his horses and drove off. At the turn of the lane he saw Miss Blenker standing at the gate and waving the pink parasol.

XXIII

THE next morning, when Archer got out of the Fall River train, he emerged upon a steaming midsummer Boston. The streets near the station were full of the smell of beer and coffee and decaying fruit and a shirt-sleeved populace moved through them with the intimate abandon of boarders going down the passage to the bathroom.

---

[1] Mary Francis *Scott-Siddens* (1844–1896), English actress; "*Lady Geraldine's Courtship: A Romance of the Age*," a poem by Elizabeth Barrett Browning.

Archer found a cab and drove to the Somerset Club for break-fast.[1] Even the fashionable quarters had the air of untidy domes-ticity to which no excess of heat ever degrades the European cities. Care-takers in calico lounged on the door-steps of the wealthy, and the Common looked like a pleasure-ground on the morrow of a Masonic picnic. If Archer had tried to imagine Ellen Olenska in improbable scenes he could not have called up any into which it was more difficult to fit her than this heat-pros-trated and deserted Boston.

He breakfasted with appetite and method, beginning with a slice of melon, and studying a morning paper while he waited for his toast and scrambled eggs. A new sense of energy and activity had possessed him ever since he had announced to May the night before that he had business in Boston, and should take the Fall River boat that night and go on to New York the following evening. It had always been understood that he would return to town early in the week, and when he got back from his expedition to Portsmouth a letter from the office, which fate had conspicuously placed on a corner of the hall table, sufficed to justify his sudden change of plan. He was even ashamed of the ease with which the whole thing had been done: it reminded him, for an uncomfortable moment, of Lawrence Lefferts's masterly contrivances for securing his freedom. But this did not long trouble him, for he was not in an analytic mood.

After breakfast he smoked a cigarette and glanced over the Commercial Advertiser. While he was thus engaged two or three men he knew came in, and the usual greetings were exchanged: it was the same world after all, though he had such a queer sense of having slipped through the meshes of time and space.

He looked at his watch, and finding that it was half-past nine got up and went into the writing-room. There he wrote a few lines, and ordered a messenger to take a cab to the Parker House and wait for the answer. He then sat down behind another news-paper and tried to calculate how long it would take a cab to get to the Parker House.[2]

---

[1] the *Somerset Club*: very exclusive private club founded in 1851, located at 42 Beacon Street in Boston.

[2] *Parker House*: elegant Boston hotel at the corner of School and Tremont streets near Boston Common.

"The lady was out, sir," he suddenly heard a waiter's voice at his elbow; and he stammered: "Out?—" as if it were a word in a strange language.

He got up and went into the hall. It must be a mistake: she could not be out at that hour. He flushed with anger at his own stupidity: why had he not sent the note as soon as he arrived?

He found his hat and stick and went forth into the street. The city had suddenly become as strange and vast and empty as if he were a traveller from distant lands. For a moment he stood on the door-step hesitating; then he decided to go to the Parker House. What if the messenger had been misinformed, and she were still there?

He started to walk across the Common; and on the first bench, under a tree, he saw her sitting. She had a grey silk sunshade over her head—how could he ever have imagined her with a pink one? As he approached he was struck by her listless attitude: she sat there as if she had nothing else to do. He saw her drooping profile, and the knot of hair fastened low in the neck under her dark hat, and the long wrinkled glove on the hand that held the sunshade. He came a step or two nearer, and she turned and looked at him.

"Oh"—she said; and for the first time he noticed a startled look on her face; but in another moment it gave way to a slow smile of wonder and contentment.

"Oh"—she murmured again, on a different note, as he stood looking down at her; and without rising she made a place for him on the bench.

"I'm here on business—just got here," Archer explained; and, without knowing why, he suddenly began to feign astonishment at seeing her. "But what on earth are *you* doing in this wilderness?" He had really no idea what he was saying: he felt as if he were shouting at her across endless distances, and she might vanish again before he could overtake her.

"I? Oh, I'm here on business too," she answered, turning her head toward him so that they were face to face. The words hardly reached him: he was aware only of her voice, and of the startling fact that not an echo of it had remained in his memory. He had not even remembered that it was low-pitched, with a faint roughness on the consonants.

"You do your hair differently," he said, his heart beating as if he had uttered something irrevocable.

"Differently? No—it's only that I do it as best I can when I'm without Nastasia."

"Nastasia; but isn't she with you?"

"No; I'm alone. For two days it was not worth while to bring her."

"You're alone—at the Parker House?"

She looked at him with a flash of her old malice. "Does it strike you as dangerous?"

"No; not dangerous—"

"But unconventional? I see; I suppose it is." She considered a moment. "I hadn't thought of it, because I've just done something so much more unconventional." The faint tinge of irony lingered in her eyes. "I've just refused to take back a sum of money—that belonged to me."

Archer sprang up and moved a step or two away. She had furled her parasol and sat absently drawing patterns on the gravel. Presently he came back and stood before her.

"Some one—has come here to meet you?"

"Yes."

"With this offer?"

She nodded.

"And you refused—because of the conditions?"

"I refused," she said after a moment.

He sat down by her again. "What were the conditions?"

"Oh, they were not onerous: just to sit at the head of his table now and then."

There was another interval of silence. Archer's heart had slammed itself shut in the queer way it had, and he sat vainly groping for a word.

"He wants you back—at any price?"

"Well—a considerable price. At least the sum is considerable for me."

He paused again, beating about the question he felt he must put.

"It was to meet him here that you came?"

She stared, and then burst into a laugh. "Meet him—my husband? *Here?* At this season he's always at Cowes or Baden."[1]

"He sent some one?"

"Yes."

"With a letter?"

She shook her head. "No; just a message. He never writes. I don't think I've had more than one letter from him." The allusion brought the colour to her cheek, and it reflected itself in Archer's vivid blush.

"Why does he never write?"

"Why should he? What does one have secretaries for?"

The young man's blush deepened. She had pronounced the word as if it had no more significance than any other in her vocabulary. For a moment it was on the tip of his tongue to ask: "Did he send his secretary, then?" But the remembrance of Count Olenski's only letter to his wife was too present to him. He paused again, and then took another plunge.

"And the person?"—

"The emissary? The emissary," Madame Olenska rejoined, still smiling, "might, for all I care, have left already; but he has insisted on waiting till this evening ... in case ... on the chance ... "

"And you came out here to think the chance over?"

"I came out to get a breath of air. The hotel's too stifling. I'm taking the afternoon train back to Portsmouth."

They sat silent, not looking at each other, but straight ahead at the people passing along the path. Finally she turned her eyes again to his face and said: "You're not changed."

He felt like answering: "I was, till I saw you again;" but instead he stood up abruptly and glanced about him at the untidy sweltering park.

"This is horrible. Why shouldn't we go out a little on the bay? There's a breeze, and it will be cooler. We might take the steamboat down to Point Arley." She glanced up at him hesitatingly and

---

[1] *Cowes* Castle on the Isle of Wight has been the headquarters of the Royal Yacht Squadron since 1856, and various yachting competitions are held during Cowes Week in early August. *Baden-Baden,* famed for its hot mineral springs and located in Germany's Black Forest, is one of the world's greatest spas.

he went on: "On a Monday morning there won't be anybody on the boat. My train doesn't leave till evening: I'm going back to New York. Why shouldn't we?" he insisted, looking down at her; and suddenly he broke out: "Haven't we done all we could?"

"Oh"—she murmured again. She stood up and re-opened her sunshade, glancing about her as if to take counsel of the scene, and assure herself of the impossibility of remaining in it. Then her eyes returned to his face. "You mustn't say things like that to me," she said.

"I'll say anything you like; or nothing. I won't open my mouth unless you tell me to. What harm can it do to anybody? All I want is to listen to you," he stammered.

She drew out a little gold-faced watch on an enamelled chain. "Oh, don't calculate," he broke out; "give me the day! I want to get you away from that man. At what time was he coming?"

Her colour rose again. "At eleven."

"Then you must come at once."

"You needn't be afraid—if I don't come."

"Nor you either—if you do. I swear I only want to hear about you, to know what you've been doing. It's a hundred years since we've met—it may be another hundred before we meet again."

She still wavered, her anxious eyes on his face. "Why didn't you come down to the beach to fetch me, the day I was at Granny's?" she asked.

"Because you didn't look round—because you didn't know I was there. I swore I wouldn't unless you looked round." He laughed as the childishness of the confession struck him.

"But I didn't look round on purpose."

"On purpose?"

"I knew you were there; when you drove in I recognised the ponies. So I went down to the beach."

"To get away from me as far as you could?"

She repeated in a low voice: "To get away from you as far as I could."

He laughed out again, this time in boyish satisfaction. "Well, you see it's no use. I may as well tell you," he added, "that the business I came here for was just to find you. But, look here, we must start or we shall miss our boat."

"Our boat?" She frowned perplexedly, and then smiled. "Oh, but I must go back to the hotel first: I must leave a note—"

"As many notes as you please. You can write here." He drew out a note-case and one of the new stylographic pens.[1] "I've even got an envelope—you see how everything's predestined! There—steady the thing on your knee, and I'll get the pen going in a second. They have to be humoured; wait—" He banged the hand that held the pen against the back of the bench. "It's like jerking down the mercury in a thermometer: just a trick. Now try—"

She laughed, and bending over the sheet of paper which he had laid on his note-case, began to write. Archer walked away a few steps, staring with radiant unseeing eyes at the passers-by, who, in their turn, paused to stare at the unwonted sight of a fashionably-dressed lady writing a note on her knee on a bench in the Common.

Madame Olenska slipped the sheet into the envelope, wrote a name on it, and put it into her pocket. Then she too stood up.

They walked back toward Beacon Street, and near the club Archer caught sight of the plush-lined "herdic"[2] which had carried his note to the Parker House, and whose driver was reposing from this effort by bathing his brow at the corner hydrant.

"I told you everything was predestined! Here's a cab for us. You see!" They laughed, astonished at the miracle of picking up a public conveyance at that hour, and in that unlikely spot, in a city where cab-stands were still a "foreign" novelty.

Archer, looking at his watch, saw that there was time to drive to the Parker House before going to the steamboat landing. They rattled through the hot streets and drew up at the door of the hotel.

Archer held out his hand for the letter. "Shall I take it in?" he asked; but Madame Olenska, shaking her head, sprang out and disappeared through the glazed doors. It was barely half-past ten;

---

[1] *stylographic pens*: fountain pen with a perforated writing point fed with ink from the stem. Duncan MacKinnon patented it in Canada and England in 1875 and in America in 1876.

[2] *herdic*: a two or four-wheeled cab with a low-slung body, a back entrance, and seats along the sides.

but what if the emissary, impatient for her reply, and not knowing how else to employ his time, were already seated among the travellers with cooling drinks at their elbows of whom Archer had caught a glimpse as she went in?

He waited, pacing up and down before the herdic. A Sicilian youth with eyes like Nastasia's offered to shine his boots, and an Irish matron to sell him peaches; and every few moments the doors opened to let out hot men with straw hats tilted far back, who glanced at him as they went by. He marvelled that the door should open so often, and that all the people it let out should look so like each other, and so like all the other hot men who, at that hour, through the length and breadth of the land, were passing continuously in and out of the swinging doors of hotels.

And then, suddenly, came a face that he could not relate to the other faces. He caught but a flash of it, for his pacings had carried him to the farthest point of his beat, and it was in turning back to the hotel that he saw, in a group of typical countenances—the lank and weary, the round and surprised, the lantern-jawed and mild—this other face that was so many more things at once, and things so different. It was that of a young man, pale too, and half-extinguished by the heat, or worry, or both, but somehow, quicker, vivider, more conscious; or perhaps seeming so because he was so different. Archer hung a moment on a thin thread of memory, but it snapped and floated off with the disappearing face—apparently that of some foreign business man, looking doubly foreign in such a setting. He vanished in the stream of passers-by, and Archer resumed his patrol.

He did not care to be seen watch in hand within view of the hotel, and his unaided reckoning of the lapse of time led him to conclude that, if Madame Olenska was so long in reappearing, it could only be because she had met the emissary and been waylaid by him. At the thought Archer's apprehension rose to anguish.

"If she doesn't come soon I'll go in and find her," he said.

The doors swung open again and she was at his side. They got into the herdic, and as it drove off he took out his watch and saw that she had been absent just three minutes. In the clatter of loose windows that made talk impossible they bumped over the disjointed cobblestones to the wharf.

Seated side by side on a bench of the half-empty boat they found that they had hardly anything to say to each other, or rather that what they had to say communicated itself best in the blessed silence of their release and their isolation.

As the paddle-wheels began to turn, and wharves and shipping to recede through the veil of heat, it seemed to Archer that everything in the old familiar world of habit was receding also. He longed to ask Madame Olenska if she did not have the same feeling: the feeling that they were starting on some long voyage from which they might never return. But he was afraid to say it, or anything else that might disturb the delicate balance of her trust in him. In reality he had no wish to betray that trust. There had been days and nights when the memory of their kiss had burned and burned on his lips; the day before even, on the drive to Portsmouth, the thought of her had run through him like fire; but now that she was beside him, and they were drifting forth into this unknown world, they seemed to have reached the kind of deeper nearness that a touch may sunder.

As the boat left the harbour and turned seaward a breeze stirred about them and the bay broke up into long oily undulations, then into ripples tipped with spray. The fog of sultriness still hung over the city, but ahead lay a fresh world of ruffled waters, and distant promontories with light-houses in the sun. Madame Olenska, leaning back against the boat-rail, drank in the coolness between parted lips. She had wound a long veil about her hat, but it left her face uncovered, and Archer was struck by the tranquil gaiety of her expression. She seemed to take their adventure as a matter of course, and to be neither in fear of unexpected encounters, nor (what was worse) unduly elated by their possibility.

In the bare dining-room of the inn, which he had hoped they would have to themselves, they found a strident party of innocent-looking young men and women—school-teachers on a holiday, the landlord told them—and Archer's heart sank at the idea of having to talk through their noise.

"This is hopeless—I'll ask for a private room," he said; and Madame Olenska, without offering any objection, waited while he went in search of it. The room opened on a long wooden verandah, with the sea coming in at the windows. It was bare and cool, with a table covered with a coarse checkered cloth and adorned by a bottle of pickles and a blueberry pie under a cage. No more guileless-looking *cabinet particulier* ever offered its shelter to a clandestine couple:[1] Archer fancied he saw the sense of its reassurance in the faintly amused smile with which Madame Olenska sat down opposite to him. A woman who had run away from her husband—and reputedly with another man—was likely to have mastered the art of taking things for granted; but something in the quality of her composure took the edge from his irony. By being so quiet, so unsurprised and so simple she had managed to brush away the conventions and make him feel that to seek to be alone was the natural thing for two old friends who had so much to say to each other ...

XXIV

THEY lunched slowly and meditatively, with mute intervals between rushes of talk; for, the spell once broken, they had much to say, and yet moments when saying became the mere accompaniment to long duologues of silence. Archer kept the talk from his own affairs, not with conscious intention but because he did not want to miss a word of her history; and leaning on the table, her chin resting on her clasped hands, she talked to him of the year and a half since they had met.

She had grown tired of what people called "society"; New York was kind, it was almost oppressively hospitable; she should never forget the way in which it had welcomed her back; but after the first flush of novelty she had found herself, as she phrased it, too "different" to care for the things it cared about— and so she had decided to try Washington, where one was supposed to meet more varieties of people and of opinion. And on the whole she should probably settle down in Washington, and make a home there for poor Medora, who had worn out the patience of all her other relations just at the time when she most needed looking after and protecting from matrimonial perils.

---

[1]   *Cabinet particulier.* French for "private dining room."

"But Dr. Carver—aren't you afraid of Dr. Carver? I hear he's been staying with you at the Blenkers'."

She smiled. "Oh, the Carver danger is over. Dr. Carver is a very clever man. He wants a rich wife to finance his plans, and Medora is simply a good advertisement as a convert."

"A convert to what?"

"To all sorts of new and crazy social schemes. But, do you know, they interest me more than the blind conformity to tradition—somebody else's tradition—that I see among our own friends. It seems stupid to have discovered America only to make it into a copy of another country." She smiled across the table. "Do you suppose Christopher Columbus would have taken all that trouble just to go to the Opera with the Selfridge Merrys?"

Archer changed colour. "And Beaufort—do you say these things to Beaufort?" he asked abruptly.

"I haven't see him for a long time. But I used to; and he understands."

"Ah, it's what I've always told you; you don't like us. And you like Beaufort because he's so unlike us." He looked about the bare room and out at the bare beach and the row of stark white village houses strung along the shore. "We're damnably dull. We've no character, no colour, no variety.—I wonder," he broke out, "why you don't go back?"

Her eyes darkened, and he expected an indignant rejoinder. But she sat silent, as if thinking over what he had said, and he grew frightened lest she should answer that she wondered too.

At length she said: "I believe it's because of you."

It was impossible to make the confession more dispassionately, or in a tone less encouraging to the vanity of the person addressed. Archer reddened to the temples, but dared not move or speak: it was as if her words had been some rare butterfly that the least motion might drive off on startled wings, but that might gather a flock about it if it were left undisturbed.

"At least," she continued, "it was you who made me understand that under the dullness there are things so fine and sensitive and delicate that even those I most cared for in my other life look cheap in comparison. I don't know how to explain myself"—she drew together her troubled brows—"but it seems as if I'd never before understood with how much that is hard and shabby and base the most exquisite pleasures may be paid."

"Exquisite pleasures—it's something to have had them!" he felt like retorting; but the appeal in her eyes kept him silent.

"I want," she went on, "to be perfectly honest with you—and with myself. For a long time I've hoped this chance would come: that I might tell you how you've helped me, what you've made of me—"

Archer sat staring beneath frowning brows. He interrupted her with a laugh. "And what do you make out that you've made of me?"

She paled a little. "Of you?"

"Yes: for I'm of your making much more than you ever were of mine. I'm the man who married one woman because another one told him to."

Her paleness turned to a fugitive flush. "I thought—you promised—you were not to say such things today."

"Ah—how like a woman! None of you will ever see a bad business through!"

She lowered her voice. "*Is* it a bad business—for May?"

He stood in the window, drumming against the raised sash, and feeling in every fibre the wistful tenderness with which she had spoken her cousin's name.

"For that's the thing we've always got to think of—haven't we—by your own showing?" she insisted.

"My own showing?" he echoed, his blank eyes still on the sea.

"Or if not," she continued, pursuing her own thought with a painful application, "if it's not worth while to have given up, to have missed things, so that others may be saved from disillusionment and misery—then everything I came home for, everything that made my other life seem by contrast so bare and so poor because no one there took account of them—all these things are a sham or a dream—"

He turned around without moving from his place. "And in that case there's no reason on earth why you shouldn't go back?" he concluded for her.

Her eyes were clinging to him desperately. "Oh, *is* there no reason?"

"Not if you staked your all on the success of my marriage. My marriage," he said savagely, "isn't going to be a sight to keep you here." She made no answer, and he went on: "What's the use? You gave me my first glimpse of a real life, and at the same moment you asked me to go on with a sham one. It's beyond human enduring—that's all."

"Oh, don't say that; when I'm enduring it!" she burst out, her eyes filling.

Her arms had dropped along the table, and she sat with her face abandoned to his gaze as if in the recklessness of a desperate peril. The face exposed her as much as if it had been her whole person, with the soul behind it: Archer stood dumb, overwhelmed by what it suddenly told him.

"You too—oh, all this time, you too?"

For answer, she let the tears on her lids overflow and run slowly downward.

Half the width of the room was still between them, and neither made any show of moving. Archer was conscious of a curious indifference to her bodily presence: he would hardly have been aware of it if one of the hands she had flung out on the table had not drawn his gaze as on the occasion when, in the little Twenty-third Street house, he had kept his eye on it in order not to look at her face. Now his imagination spun about the hand as about the edge of a vortex; but still he made no effort to draw nearer. He had known the love that is fed on caresses and feeds them; but this passion that was closer than his bones was not to be superficially satisfied. His one terror was to do anything which might efface the sound and impression of her words; his one thought, that he should never again feel quite alone.

But after a moment the sense of waste and ruin overcame him. There they were, close together and safe and shut in; yet so chained to their separate destinies that they might as well have been half the world apart.

"What's the use—when you will go back?" he broke out, a great hopeless *How on earth can I keep you?* crying out to her beneath his words.

She sat motionless, with lowered lids. "Oh—I shan't go yet!"

"Not yet? Some time, then? Some time that you already foresee?"

At that she raised her clearest eyes. "I promise you: not as long as you hold out. Not as long as we can look straight at each other like this."

He dropped into his chair. What her answer really said was: "If you lift a finger you'll drive me back: back to all the abominations you know of, and all the temptations you half guess." He understood it as clearly as if she had uttered the words, and the thought kept him anchored to his side of the table in a kind of moved and sacred submission.

"What a life for you!—" he groaned.

"Oh—as long as it's a part of yours."

"And mine a part of yours?"

She nodded.

"And that's to be all—for either of us?"

"Well; it *is* all, isn't it?"

At that he sprang up, forgetting everything but the sweetness of her face. She rose too, not as if to meet him or to flee from him, but quietly, as though the worst of the task were done and she had only to wait; so quietly that, as he came close, her outstretched hands acted not as a check but as a guide to him. They fell into his, while her arms, extended but not rigid, kept him far enough off to let her surrendered face say the rest.

They may have stood in that way for a long time, or only for a few moments; but it was long enough for her silence to communicate all she had to say, and for him to feel that only one thing mattered. He must do nothing to make this meeting their last; he must leave their future in her care, asking only that she should keep fast hold of it.

"Don't—don't be unhappy," she said, with a break in her voice, as she drew her hands away; and he answered: "You won't go back—you won't go back?" as if it were the one possibility he could not bear.

"I won't go back," she said; and turning away she opened the door and led the way into the public dining-room.

The strident school-teachers were gathering up their possessions preparatory to a straggling flight to the wharf; across the beach lay the white steam-boat at the pier; and over the sunlit waters Boston loomed in a line of haze.

XXV

ONCE more on the boat, and in the presence of others, Archer felt a tranquillity of spirit that surprised as much as it sustained him. The day, according to any current valuation, had been a rather ridiculous failure; he had not so much as touched Madame Olenska's hand with his lips, or extracted one word from her that gave promise of farther opportunities. Nevertheless, for a man sick with unsatisfied love, and parting for an indefinite period from the object of his passion, he felt himself almost humiliatingly calm and comforted. It was the perfect balance she had held between their loyalty to others and their honesty to themselves that had so stirred and yet tranquillized him; a balance not artfully calculated, as her tears and her falterings showed, but resulting naturally from her unabashed sincerity. It filled him with a tender awe, now the danger was over, and made him thank the fates that no personal vanity, no sense of playing a part before sophisticated witnesses, had tempted him to tempt her. Even after they had clasped hands for good-bye at the Fall River station, and he had turned away alone, the conviction remained with him of having saved out of their meeting much more than he had sacrificed.

He wandered back to the club, and went and sat alone in the deserted library, turning and turning over in his thoughts every separate second of their hours together. It was clear to him, and it grew more clear under closer scrutiny, that if she should finally decide on returning to Europe—returning to her husband—it would not be because her old life tempted her, even on the new terms offered. No: she would go only if she felt herself becoming a temptation to Archer, a temptation to fall away from the standard they had both set up. Her choice would be to stay near him as long as he did not ask her to come nearer; and it depended on himself to keep her just there, safe but secluded.

In the train these thoughts were still with him. They enclosed him in a kind of golden haze, through which the faces about him looked remote and indistinct: he had a feeling that if he spoke to his fellow-travellers they would not understand what he was saying. In this state of abstraction he found himself, the following morning, waking to the reality of a stifling September day in

New York. The heat-withered faces in the long train streamed past him, and he continued to stare at them through the same golden blur; but suddenly, as he left the station, one of the faces detached itself, came closer and forced itself upon his consciousness. It was, as he instantly recalled, the face of the young man he had seen, the day before, passing out of the Parker House, and had noted as not conforming to type, as not having an American hotel face.

The same thing struck him now; and again he became aware of a dim stir of former associations. The young man stood looking about him with the dazed air of the foreigner flung upon the harsh mercies of American travel; then he advanced toward Archer, lifted his hat, and said in English: "Surely, Monsieur, we met in London?"

"Ah, to be sure: in London!" Archer grasped his hand with curiosity and sympathy. "So you *did* get here, after all?" he exclaimed, casting a wondering eye on the astute and haggard little countenance of young Carfry's French tutor.

"Oh, I got here—yes," M. Rivière smiled with drawn lips. "But not for long; I return the day after tomorrow.". He stood grasping his light valise in one neatly gloved hand, and gazing anxiously, perplexedly, almost appealingly, into Archer's face.

"I wonder, Monsieur, since I've had the good luck to run across you, if I might—"

"I was just going to suggest it: come to luncheon, won't you? Down town, I mean: if you'll look me up in my office I'll take you to a very decent restaurant in that quarter."

M. Rivière was visibly touched and surprised. "You're too kind. But I was only going to ask if you would tell me how to reach some sort of conveyance. There are no porters, and no one here seems to listen—"

"I know: our American stations must surprise you. When you ask for a porter they give you chewing-gum. But if you'll come along I'll extricate you; and you must really lunch with me, you know."

The young man, after a just perceptible hesitation, replied, with profuse thanks, and in a tone that did not carry complete conviction, that he was already engaged; but when they had reached the comparative reassurance of the street he asked if he might call that afternoon.

Archer, at ease in the midsummer leisure of the office, fixed an hour and scribbled his address, which the Frenchman pocketed with reiterated thanks and a wide flourish of his hat. A horse-car received him, and Archer walked way.

Punctually at the hour M. Rivière appeared, shaved, smoothed-out, but still unmistakably drawn and serious. Archer was alone in his office, and the young man, before accepting the seat he proffered, began abruptly: "I believe I saw you, sir, yesterday in Boston."

The statement was insignificant enough, and Archer was about to frame an assent when his words were checked by something mysterious yet illuminating in his visitor's insistent gaze.

"It is extraordinary, very extraordinary," M. Rivière continued, "that we should have met in the circumstances in which I find myself."

"What circumstances?" Archer asked, wondering a little crudely if he needed money.

M. Rivière continued to study him with tentative eyes. "I have come, not to look for employment, as I spoke of doing when we last met, but on a special mission—"

"Ah—!" Archer exclaimed. In a flash the two meetings had connected themselves in his mind. He paused to take in the situation thus suddenly lighted up for him, and M. Rivière also remained silent, as if aware that what he had said was enough.

"A special mission," Archer at length repeated.

The young Frenchman, opening his palms, raised them slightly, and the two men continued to look at each other across the office-desk till Archer roused himself to say: "Do sit down"; whereupon M. Rivière bowed, took a distant chair, and again waited.

"It was about this mission that you wanted to consult me?" Archer finally asked.

M. Rivière bent his head. "Not in my own behalf: on that score I—I have fully dealt with myself. I should like—if I may—to speak to you about the Countess Olenska."

Archer had known for the last few minutes that the words were coming; but when they came they sent the blood rushing to his temples as if he had been caught by a bent-back branch in a thicket.

"And on whose behalf," he said, "do you wish to do this?"

M. Rivière met the question sturdily. "Well—I might say *hers*, if it did not sound like a liberty. Shall I say instead: on behalf of abstract justice?"

Archer considered him ironically. "In other words: you are Count Olenski's messenger?"

He saw his blush more darkly reflected in M. Rivière's sallow countenance. "Not to *you*, Monsieur. If I come to you, it is on quite other grounds."

"What right have you, in the circumstances, to *be* on any other ground?" Archer retorted. "If you're an emissary you're an emissary."

The young man considered. "My mission is over: as far as the Countess Olenska goes, it has failed."

"I can't help that," Archer rejoined on the same note of irony.

"No: but you can help—" M. Rivière paused, turned his hat about in his still carefully gloved hands, looked into its lining and then back at Archer's face. "You can help, Monsieur, I am convinced, to make it equally a failure with her family."

Archer pushed back his chair and stood up. "Well—and by God I will!" he exclaimed. He stood with his hands in his pockets, staring down wrathfully at the little Frenchman, whose face, though he too had risen, was still an inch or two below the line of Archer's eyes.

M. Rivière paled to his normal hue: paler than that his complexion could hardly turn.

"Why the devil," Archer explosively continued, "should you have thought—since I suppose you're appealing to me on the ground of my relationship to Madame Olenska—that I should take a view contrary to the rest of her family?"

The change of expression in M. Rivière's face was for a time his only answer. His look passed from timidity to absolute distress: for a young man of his usually resourceful mien it would have been difficult to appear more disarmed and defenceless. "Oh, Monsieur—"

"I can't imagine," Archer continued, "why you should have come to me when there are others so much nearer to the Countess; still less why you thought I should be more accessible to the arguments I suppose you were sent over with."

M. Rivière took this onslaught with a disconcerting humility. "The arguments I want to present to you, Monsieur, are my own and not those I was sent over with."

"Then I see still less reason for listening to them."

M. Rivière again looked into his hat, as if considering whether these last words were not a sufficiently broad hint to put it on and be gone. Then he spoke with sudden decision. "Monsieur—will you tell me one thing? Is it my right to be here that you question? Or do you perhaps believe the whole matter to be already closed?"

His quiet insistence made Archer feel the clumsiness of his own bluster. M. Rivière had succeeded in imposing himself: Archer, reddening slightly, dropped into his chair again, and signed to the young man to be seated.

"I beg your pardon: but why isn't the matter closed?"

M. Rivière gazed back at him with anguish. "You do, then, agree with the rest of the family that, in face of the new proposals I have brought, it is hardly possible for Madame Olenska not to return to her husband?"

"Good God!" Archer exclaimed; and his visitor gave out a low murmur of confirmation.

"Before seeing her, I saw—at Count Olenski's request—Mr. Lovell Mingott, with whom I had several talks before going to Boston. I understand that he represents his mother's view; and that Mrs. Manson Mingott's influence is great throughout her family."

Archer sat silent, with the sense of clinging to the edge of a sliding precipice. The discovery that he had been excluded from a share in these negotiations, and even from the knowledge that they were on foot, caused him a surprise hardly dulled by the acuter wonder of what he was learning. He saw in a flash that if the family had ceased to consult him it was because some deep tribal instinct warned them that he was no longer on their side; and he recalled, with a start of comprehension, a remark of May's during their drive home from Mrs. Manson Mingott's on the day of the Archery Meeting: "Perhaps, after all, Ellen would be happier with her husband."

Even in the tumult of new discoveries Archer remembered his indignant exclamation, and the fact that since then his wife had never named Madame Olenska to him. Her careless allusion had no doubt been the straw held up to see which way the wind blew; the result had been reported to the family, and thereafter Archer had been tacitly omitted from their counsels. He admired the tribal discipline which made May bow to this decision. She would not have done so, he knew, had her conscience protested; but she probably shared the family view that Madame Olenska would be better off as an unhappy wife than as a separated one, and that there was no use in discussing the case with Newland, who had an awkward way of suddenly not seeming to take the most fundamental things for granted.

Archer looked up and met his visitor's anxious gaze. "Don't you know, Monsieur—is it possible you don't know—that the family begin to doubt if they have the right to advise the Countess to refuse her husband's last proposals?"

"The proposals you brought?"

"The proposals I brought."

It was on Archer's lips to exclaim that whatever he knew or did not know was no concern of M. Rivière's; but something in the humble and yet courageous tenacity of M. Rivière's gaze made him reject this conclusion, and he met the young man's question with another. "What is your object in speaking to me of this?"

He had not to wait a moment for the answer. "To beg you, Monsieur—to beg you with all the force I'm capable of—not to let her go back—Oh, don't let her!" M. Rivière exclaimed.

Archer looked at him with increasing astonishment. There was no mistaking the sincerity of his distress or the strength of his determination: he had evidently resolved to let everything go by the board but the supreme need of thus putting himself on record. Archer considered.

"May I ask," he said at length, "if this is the line you took with the Countess Olenska?"

M. Rivière reddened, but his eyes did not falter. "No, Monsieur: I accepted my mission in good faith. I really believed—for reasons I need not trouble you with—that it would be better for Madame Olenska to recover her situation, her fortune, the social consideration that her husband's standing gives her."

"So I supposed: you could hardly have accepted such a mission otherwise."

"I should not have accepted it."

"Well, then—?" Archer paused again, and their eyes met in another protracted scrutiny.

"Ah, Monsieur, after I had seen her, after I had listened to her, I knew she was better off here."

"You knew—?"

"Monsieur, I discharged my mission faithfully: I put the Count's arguments, I stated his offers, without adding any comment of my own. The Countess was good enough to listen patiently; she carried her goodness so far as to see me twice; she considered impartially all I had come to say. And it was in the course of these two talks that I changed my mind, that I came to see things differently."

"May I ask what led to this change?"

"Simply seeing the change in *her*," M. Rivière replied.

"The change in her? Then you knew her before?"

The young man's colour again rose. "I used to see her in her husband's house. I have known Count Olenski for many years. You can imagine that he would not have sent a stranger on such a mission."

Archer's gaze, wandering away to the blank walls of the office, rested on a hanging calendar surmounted by the rugged features of the President of the United States.[1] That such a conversation should be going on anywhere within the millions of square miles subject to his rule seemed as strange as anything that the imagination could invent.

"The change—what sort of a change?"

"Ah, Monsieur, if I could tell you!" M. Rivière paused. "*Tenez*—the discovery, I suppose, of what I'd never thought of before: that she's an American. And that if you're an American of *her* kind—of your kind—things that are accepted in certain other societies, or at least put up with as part of a general convenient give-and-take—become unthinkable, simply unthinkable. If Madame Olenska's relations understood what these things were, their opposition to her returning would no doubt be as unconditional as her own; but they seem to regard her husband's wish to have her back as proof of an irresistible longing for domestic life."

---

[1] *President of the United States*: most likely Ulysses S. Grant, president from 1869 to 1877.

M. Rivière paused, and then added: "Whereas it's far from being as simple as that."

Archer looked back to the President of the United States, and then down at his desk and at the papers scattered on it. For a second or two he could not trust himself to speak. During this interval he heard M. Rivière's chair pushed back, and was aware that the young man had risen. When he glanced up again he saw that his visitor was as moved as himself.

"Thank you," Archer said simply.

"There's nothing to thank me for, Monsieur: it is I, rather—" M. Rivière broke off, as if speech for him too were difficult. "I should like, though," he continued in a firmer voice, "to add one thing. You asked me if I was in Count Olenski's employ. I am at this moment: I returned to him, a few months ago, for reasons of private necessity such as may happen to any one who has persons, ill and older persons, dependent on him. But from the moment that I have taken the step of coming here to say these things to you I consider myself discharged, and I shall tell him so on my return, and give him the reasons. That's all, Monsieur."

M. Rivière bowed and drew back a step.

"Thank you," Archer said again, as their hands met.

XXVI

EVERY year on the fifteenth of October Fifth Avenue opened its shutters, unrolled its carpets and hung up its triple layer of window-curtains.

By the first of November this household ritual was over, and society had begun to look about and take stock of itself. By the fifteenth the season was in full blast, Opera and theatres were putting forth their new attractions, dinner-engagements were accumulating, and dates for dances being fixed. And punctually at about this time Mrs. Archer always said that New York was very much changed.

Observing it from the lofty stand-point of a non-participant, she was able, with the help of Mr. Sillerton Jackson and Miss Sophy, to trace each new crack in its surface, and all the strange weeds pushing up between the ordered rows of social vegetables. It had been one of the amusements of Archer's youth to wait for this annual pronouncement of his mother's, and to hear her enumerate the minute signs of disintegration that his careless gaze had overlooked. For New York, to Mrs. Archer's mind, never changed without changing for the worse; and in this view Miss Sophy Jackson heartily concurred.

Mr. Sillerton Jackson, as became a man of the world, suspended his judgment and listened with an amused impartiality to the lamentations of the ladies. But even he never denied that New York had changed; and Newland Archer, in the winter of the second year of his marriage, was himself obliged to admit that if it had not actually changed it was certainly changing.

These points had been raised, as usual, at Mrs. Archer's Thanksgiving dinner. At the date when she was officially enjoined to give thanks for the blessings of the year it was her habit to take a mournful though not embittered stock of her world, and wonder what there was to be thankful for. At any rate, not the state of society; society, if it could be said to exist, was rather a spectacle on which to call down Biblical imprecations—and in fact, every one knew what the Reverend Dr. Ashmore meant when he chose a text from Jeremiah (chap. ii., verse 25) for his Thanksgiving sermon.[1] Dr. Ashmore, the new Rector of St. Matthew's, had been chosen because he was very "advanced": his sermons were considered bold in thought and novel in language. When he fulminated against fashionable society he always spoke of its "trend"; and to Mrs. Archer it was terrifying and yet fascinating to feel herself part of a community that was trending.

"There's no doubt that Dr. Ashmore is right: there *is* a marked trend," she said, as if it were something visible and measurable, like a crack in a house.

"It was odd, though, to preach about it on Thanksgiving," Miss Jackson opined; and her hostess drily rejoined: "Oh, he means us to give thanks for what's left."

Archer had been wont to smile at these annual vaticinations

---

[1]   *Jeremiah 2:25*: "Withhold thy foot from being unshod, and thy throat from thirst: but thou saidst, There is no hope: no; for I have loved strangers, and after them will I go."

of his mother's; but this year even he was obliged to acknowledge, as he listened to an enumeration of the changes, that the "trend" was visible.

"The extravagance in dress—" Miss Jackson began. "Sillerton took me to the first night of the Opera, and I can only tell you that Jane Merry's dress was the only one I recognised from last year; and even that had had the front panel changed. Yet I know she got it out from Worth only two years ago, because my seamstress always goes in to make over her Paris dresses before she wears them."

"Ah, Jane Merry is one of *us*," said Mrs. Archer sighing, as if it were not such an enviable thing to be in an age when ladies were beginning to flaunt abroad their Paris dresses as soon as they were out of the Custom House, instead of letting them mellow under lock and key, in the manner of Mrs. Archer's contemporaries.

"Yes; she's one of the few. In my youth," Miss Jackson rejoined, "it was considered vulgar to dress in the newest fashions; and Amy Sillerton has always told me that in Boston the rule was to put away one's Paris dresses for two years. Old Mrs. Baxter Pennilow, who did everything handsomely, used to import twelve a year, two velvet, two satin, two silk, and the other six of poplin and the finest cashmere. It was a standing order, and as she was ill for two years before she died they found forty-eight Worth dresses that had never been taken out of tissue paper; and when the girls left off their mourning they were able to wear the first lot at the Symphony concerts without looking in advance of the fashion."

"Ah, well, Boston is more conservative than New York; but I always think it's a safe rule for a lady to lay aside her French dresses for one season," Mrs. Archer conceded.

"It was Beaufort who started the new fashion by making his wife clap her new clothes on her back as soon as they arrived: I must say at times it takes all Regina's distinction not to look like ... like ..." Miss Jackson glanced around the table, caught Janey's bulging gaze, and took refuge in an unintelligible murmur.

"Like her rivals," said Mr. Sillerton Jackson, with the air of producing an epigram.

"Oh,—" the ladies murmured; and Mrs. Archer added, partly to distract her daughter's attention from forbidden topics: "Poor

Regina! Her Thanksgiving hasn't been a very cheerful one, I'm afraid. Have you heard the rumours about Beaufort's speculations, Sillerton?"

Mr. Jackson nodded carelessly. Every one had heard the rumours in question, and he scorned to confirm a tale that was already common property.

A gloomy silence fell upon the party. No one really liked Beaufort, and it was not wholly unpleasant to think the worst of his private life; but the idea of his having brought financial dishonour on his wife's family was too shocking to be enjoyed even by his enemies. Archer's New York tolerated hypocrisy in private relations; but in business matters it exacted a limpid and impeccable honesty. It was a long time since any well-known banker had failed discreditably; but every one remembered the social extinction visited on the heads of the firm when the last event of the kind had happened. It would be the same with the Beauforts, in spite of his power and her popularity; not all the leagued strength of the Dallas connection would save poor Regina if there were any truth in the reports of her husband's unlawful speculations.

The talk took refuge in less ominous topics; but everything they touched on seemed to confirm Mrs. Archer's sense of an accelerated trend.

"Of course, Newland, I know you let dear May go to Mrs. Struthers's Sunday evenings—" she began; and May interposed gaily: "Oh, you know, everybody goes to Mrs. Struthers's now; and she was invited to Granny's last reception."

It was thus, Archer reflected, that New York managed its transitions: conspiring to ignore them till they were well over, and then, in all good faith, imagining that they had taken place in a preceding age. There was always a traitor in the citadel; and after he (or generally she) had surrendered the keys, what was the use of pretending that it was impregnable? Once people had tasted of Mrs. Struthers's easy Sunday hospitality they were not likely to sit at home remembering that her champagne was transmuted Shoe-Polish.

"I know, dear, I know," Mrs. Archer sighed. "Such things have to be, I suppose, as long as *amusement* is what people go out for;

but I've never quite forgiven your cousin Madame Olenska for being the first person to countenance Mrs. Struthers."

A sudden blush rose to young Mrs. Archer's face; it surprised her husband as much as the other guests about the table. "Oh, *Ellen*—" she murmured, much in the same accusing and yet deprecating tone in which her parents might have said: "Oh, *the Blenkers*—."

It was the note which the family had taken to sounding on the mention of the Countess Olenska's name, since she had surprised and inconvenienced them by remaining obdurate to her husband's advances; but on May's lips it gave food for thought, and Archer looked at her with the sense of strangeness that sometimes came over him when she was most in the tone of her environment.

His mother, with less than her usual sensitiveness to atmosphere, still insisted: "I've always thought that people like the Countess Olenska, who have lived in aristocratic societies, ought to help us to keep up our social distinctions, instead of ignoring them."

May's blush remained permanently vivid: it seemed to have a significance beyond that implied by the recognition of Madame Olenska's social bad faith.

"I've no doubt we all seem alike to foreigners," said Miss Jackson tartly.

"I don't think Ellen cares for society; but nobody knows exactly what she does care for," May continued, as if she had been groping for something noncommittal.

"Ah, well—" Mrs. Archer sighed again.

Everybody knew that the Countess Olenska was no longer in the good graces of her family. Even her devoted champion, old Mrs. Manson Mingott, had been unable to defend her refusal to return to her husband. The Mingotts had not proclaimed their disapproval aloud: their sense of solidarity was too strong. They had simply, as Mrs. Welland said, "let poor Ellen find her own level"—and that, mortifyingly and incomprehensibly, was in the dim depths where the Blenkers prevailed, and "people who wrote" celebrated their untidy rites. It was incredible, but it was a fact, that Ellen, in spite of all her opportunities and her privileges, had become simply "Bohemian." The fact enforced the contention that she had made a fatal mistake in not returning to Count Olenski. After all, a young woman's place was under her husband's roof, especially when she had left it in circumstances that ... well ... if one had cared to look into them ...

"Madame Olenska is a great favourite with the gentlemen," said Miss Sophy, with her air of wishing to put forth something conciliatory when she knew that she was planting a dart.

"Ah, that's the danger that a young woman like Madame Olenska is always exposed to," Mrs. Archer mournfully agreed; and the ladies, on this conclusion, gathered up their trains to seek the carcel globes of the drawing-room, while Archer and Mr. Sillerton Jackson withdrew to the Gothic library.

Once established before the grate, and consoling himself for the inadequacy of the dinner by the perfection of his cigar, Mr. Jackson became portentous and communicable.

"If the Beaufort smash comes," he announced, "there are going to be disclosures."

Archer raised his head quickly: he could never hear the name without the sharp vision of Beaufort's heavy figure, opulently furred and shod, advancing through the snow at Skuytercliff.

"There's bound to be," Mr. Jackson continued, "the nastiest kind of a cleaning up. He hasn't spent all his money on Regina."

"Oh, well—that's discounted, isn't it? My belief is he'll pull out yet," said the young man, wanting to change the subject.

"Perhaps—perhaps. I know he was to see some of the influential people today. Of course," Mr. Jackson reluctantly conceded, "it's to be hoped they can tide him over—this time anyhow. I shouldn't like to think of poor Regina's spending the rest of her life in some shabby foreign watering-place for bankrupts."

Archer said nothing. It seemed to him so natural—however tragic—that money ill-gotten should be cruelly expiated, that his mind, hardly lingering over Mrs. Beaufort's doom, wandered back to closer questions. What was the meaning of May's blush when the Countess Olenska had been mentioned?

Four months had passed since the midsummer day that he and Madame Olenska had spent together; and since then he had not seen her. He knew that she had returned to Washington, to the little house which she and Medora Manson had taken there: he had written to her once—a few words, asking when they were to meet again—and she had even more briefly replied: "Not yet."

Since then there had been no farther communication between them, and he had built up within himself a kind of sanctuary in which she throned among his secret thoughts and longings. Little by little it became the scene of his real life, of his only rational activities; thither he brought the books he read, the ideas and feelings which nourished him, his judgments and his visions. Outside it, in the scene of his actual life, he moved with a growing sense of unreality and insufficiency, blundering against familiar prejudices and traditional points of view as an absent-minded man goes on bumping into the furniture of his own room. Absent—that was what he was: so absent from everything most densely real and near to those about him that it sometimes startled him to find they still imagined he was there.

He became aware that Mr. Jackson was clearing his throat preparatory to farther revelations.

"I don't know, of course, how far your wife's family are aware of what people say about—well, about Madame Olenska's refusal to accept her husband's latest offer."

Archer was silent, and Mr. Jackson obliquely continued: "It's a pity—it's certainly a pity—that she refused it."

"A pity? In God's name, why?"

Mr. Jackson looked down his leg to the unwrinkled sock that joined it to a glossy pump.

"Well—to put it on the lowest ground—what's she going to live on now?"

"Now—?"

"If Beaufort—"

Archer sprang up, his fist banging down on the black walnut-edge of the writing-table. The wells of the brass double-inkstand danced in their sockets.

"What the devil do you mean, sir?"

Mr. Jackson, shifting himself slightly in his chair, turned a tranquil gaze on the young man's burning face.

"Well—I have it on pretty good authority—in fact, on old Catherine's herself—that the family reduced Countess Olenska's allowance considerably when she definitely refused to go back to her husband; and as, by this refusal, she also forfeits the money settled on her when she married—which Olenski was ready to make over to her if she returned—why, what the devil do *you* mean, my dear boy, by asking me what *I* mean?" Mr. Jackson good-humouredly retorted.

Archer moved toward the mantelpiece and bent over to knock his ashes into the grate.

"I don't know anything of Madame Olenska's private affairs; but I don't need to, to be certain that what you insinuate—"

"Oh, *I* don't: it's Lefferts, for one," Mr. Jackson interposed.

"Lefferts—who made love to her and got snubbed for it!" Archer broke out contemptuously.

"Ah—*did* he?" snapped the other, as if this were exactly the fact he had been laying a trap for. He still sat sideways from the fire, so that his hard old gaze held Archer's face as if in a spring of steel.

"Well, well: it's a pity she didn't go back before Beaufort's cropper," he repeated. "If she goes *now*, and if he fails, it will only confirm the general impression: which isn't by any means peculiar to Lefferts, by the way."

"Oh, she won't go back now: less than ever!" Archer had no sooner said it than he had once more the feeling that it was exactly what Mr. Jackson had been waiting for.

The old gentleman considered him attentively. "That's your opinion, eh? Well, no doubt you know. But everybody will tell you that the few pennies Medora Manson has left are all in Beaufort's hands; and how the two women are to keep their heads above water unless he does, I can't imagine. Of course, Madame Olenska may still soften old Catherine, who's been the most inexorably opposed to her staying; and old Catherine could make her any allowance she chooses. But we all know that she hates parting with good money; and the rest of the family have no particular interest in keeping Madame Olenska here."

Archer was burning with unavailing wrath: he was exactly in the state when a man is sure to do something stupid, knowing all the while that he is doing it.

He saw that Mr. Jackson had been instantly struck by the fact that Madame Olenska's differences with her grandmother and her other relations were not known to him, and that the old gentleman had drawn his own conclusions as to the reasons for Archer's exclusion from the family councils. This fact warned Archer to go warily; but the insinuations about Beaufort made him reckless. He was mindful, however, if not of his own danger, at least of the fact that Mr. Jackson was under his mother's roof, and consequently his guest. Old New York scrupulously observed the etiquette of hospitality, and no discussion with a guest was ever allowed to degenerate into a disagreement.

"Shall we go up and join my mother?" he suggested curtly, as Mr. Jackson's last cone of ashes dropped into the brass ash-tray at his elbow.

On the drive homeward May remained oddly silent; through the darkness, he still felt her enveloped in her menacing blush. What its menace meant he could not guess: but he was sufficiently warned by the fact that Madame Olenska's name had evoked it.

They went upstairs, and he turned into the library. She usually followed him; but he heard her passing down the passage to her bedroom.

"May!" he called out impatiently; and she came back, with a slight glance of surprise at his tone.

"This lamp is smoking again; I should think the servants might see that it's kept properly trimmed," he grumbled nervously.

"I'm so sorry: it shan't happen again," she answered, in the firm bright tone she had learned from her mother; and it exasperated Archer to feel that she was already beginning to humour him like a younger Mr. Welland. She bent over to lower the wick, and as the light struck up on her white shoulders and the clear curves of her face he thought: "How young she is! For what endless years this life will have to go on!"

He felt, with a kind of horror, his own strong youth and the bounding blood in his veins. "Look here," he said suddenly, "I may have to go to Washington for a few days—soon; next week perhaps."

Her hand remained on the key of the lamp as she turned to him slowly. The heat from its flame had brought back a glow to her face, but it paled as she looked up.

"On business?" she asked, in a tone which implied that there could be no other conceivable reason, and that she had put the question automatically, as if merely to finish his own sentence.

"On business, naturally. There's a patent case coming up before the Supreme Court—" He gave the name of the inventor, and went on furnishing details with all Lawrence Lefferts's practised glibness, while she listened attentively, saying at intervals: "Yes, I see."

"The change will do you good," she said simply, when he had finished; "and you must be sure to go and see Ellen," she added, looking him straight in the eyes with her cloudless smile, and speaking in the tone she might have employed in urging him not to neglect some irksome family duty.

It was the only word that passed between them on the subject; but in the code in which they had both been trained it meant: "Of course you understand that I know all that people have been saying about Ellen, and heartily sympathise with my family in their effort to get her to return to her husband. I also know that, for some reason you have not chosen to tell me, you have advised her against this course, which all the older men of the family, as well as our grandmother, agree in approving; and that it is owing to your encouragement that Ellen defies us all, and exposes herself to the kind of criticism of which Mr. Sillerton Jackson probably gave you, this evening, the hint that has made you so irritable.... Hints have indeed not been wanting; but since you appear unwilling to take them from others, I offer you this one myself, in the only form in which well-bred people of our kind can communicate unpleasant things to each other: by letting you understand that I know you mean to see Ellen when you are in Washington, and are perhaps going there expressly for that purpose; and that, since you are sure to see her, I wish you to do so with my full and explicit approval—and to take the opportunity of letting her know what the course of conduct you have encouraged her in is likely to lead to."

Her hand was still on the key of the lamp when the last word of this mute message reached him. She turned the wick down, lifted off the globe, and breathed on the sulky flame.

"They smell less if one blows them out," she explained, with her bright housekeeping air. On the threshold she turned and paused for his kiss.

XXVII

WALL STREET, the next day, had more reassuring reports of Beaufort's situation. They were not definite, but they were hopeful. It was generally understood that he could call on powerful influences in case of emergency, and that he had done so with success; and that evening, when Mrs. Beaufort appeared at the Opera wearing her old smile and a new emerald necklace, society drew a breath of relief.

New York was inexorable in its condemnation of business irregularities. So far there had been no exception to its tacit rule that those who broke the law of probity must pay; and every one was aware that even Beaufort and Beaufort's wife would be offered up unflinchingly to this principle. But to be obliged to offer them up would be not only painful but inconvenient. The disappearance of the Beauforts would leave a considerable void in their compact little circle; and those who were too ignorant or too careless to shudder at the moral catastrophe bewailed in advance the loss of the best ball-room in New York.

Archer had definitely made up his mind to go to Washington. He was waiting only for the opening of the law-suit of which he had spoken to May, so that its date might coincide with that of his visit; but on the following Tuesday he learned from Mr. Letterblair that the case might be postponed for several weeks. Nevertheless, he went home that afternoon determined in any event to leave the next evening. The chances were that May, who knew nothing of his professional life, and had never shown any interest in it, would not learn of the postponement, should it take place, nor remember the names of the litigants if they were mentioned before her; and at any rate he could no longer put off seeing Madame Olenska. There were too many things that he must say to her.

On the Wednesday morning, when he reached his office, Mr. Letterblair met him with a troubled face. Beaufort, after all, had not managed to "tide over"; but by setting afloat the rumour that he had done so he had reassured his depositors, and heavy payments had poured into the bank till the previous evening, when disturbing reports again began to predominate. In consequence, a run on the bank had begun, and its doors were likely to close before the day was over. The ugliest things were being said of Beaufort's dastardly manœuvre, and his failure promised to be one of the most discreditable in the history of Wall Street.

The extent of the calamity left Mr. Letterblair white and incapacitated. "I've seen bad things in my time; but nothing as bad as this. Everybody we know will be hit, one way or another. And what will be done about Mrs. Beaufort? What *can* be done about her? I pity Mrs. Manson Mingott as much as anybody: coming at her age, there's no knowing what effect this affair may have on her. She always believed in Beaufort—she made a friend of him! And there's the whole Dallas connection: poor Mrs. Beaufort is related to every one of you. Her only chance would be to leave her husband—yet how can any one tell her so? Her duty is at his side; and luckily she seems always to have been blind to his private weaknesses."

There was a knock, and Mr. Letterblair turned his head sharply. "What is it? I can't be disturbed."

A clerk brought in a letter for Archer and withdrew. Recognising his wife's hand, the young man opened the envelope and read: "Won't you please come up town as early as you can? Granny had a slight stroke last night. In some mysterious way she found out before any one else this awful news about the bank. Uncle Lovell is away shooting, and the idea of the disgrace has made poor Papa so nervous that he has a temperature and can't leave his room. Mamma needs you dreadfully, and I do hope you can get away at once and go straight to Granny's."

Archer handed the note to his senior partner, and a few minutes later was crawling northward in a crowded horse-car, which he exchanged at Fourteenth Street for one of the high staggering omnibuses of the Fifth Avenue line.[1] It was after twelve o'clock when this laborious vehicle dropped him at old Catherine's. The sitting-room window on the ground floor, where she usually throned, was tenanted by the inadequate figure of her daughter, Mrs. Welland, who signed a haggard welcome as she caught sight of Archer; and at the door he was met by May.

---

[1] *horse-car*: a tram-car drawn by a horse or horses along tracks; *omnibuses*: four-wheeled passenger vehicles with seats along the sides, entrance, rear, and occasionally roof, that traveled along fixed routes.

The hall wore the unnatural appearance peculiar to well-kept houses suddenly invaded by illness: wraps and furs lay in heaps on the chairs, a doctor's bag and overcoat were on the table, and beside them letters and cards had already piled up unheeded.

May looked pale but smiling: Dr. Bencomb, who had just come for the second time, took a more hopeful view, and Mrs. Mingott's dauntless determination to live and get well was already having an effect on her family. May led Archer into the old lady's sitting-room, where the sliding doors opening into the bedroom had been drawn shut, and the heavy yellow damask portières dropped over them; and here Mrs. Welland communicated to him in horri-fied undertones the details of the catastrophe. It appeared that the evening before something dreadful and mysterious had happened. At about eight o'clock, just after Mrs. Mingott had finished the game of solitaire that she always played after dinner, the door-bell had rung, and a lady so thickly veiled that the servants did not immediately recognise her had asked to be received.

The butler, hearing a familiar voice, had thrown open the sitting-room door, announcing: "Mrs. Julius Beaufort"—and had then closed it again on the two ladies. They must have been together, he thought, about an hour. When Mrs. Mingott's bell rang Mrs. Beaufort had already slipped away unseen, and the old lady, white and vast and terrible, sat alone in her great chair, and signed to the butler to help her into her room. She seemed, at that time, though obviously distressed, in complete control of her body and brain. The mulatto maid put her to bed, brought her a cup of tea as usual, laid everything straight in the room, and went away; but at three in the morning the bell rang again, and the two servants, hastening in at this unwonted summons (for old Catherine usually slept like a baby), had found their mistress sitting up against her pillows with a crooked smile on her face and one little hand hanging limp from its huge arm.

The stroke had clearly been a slight one, for she was able to artic-ulate and to make her wishes known; and soon after the doctor's first visit she had begun to regain control of her facial muscles. But the alarm had been great; and proportionately great was the indig-nation when it was gathered from Mrs. Mingott's fragmentary phrases that Regina Beaufort had come to ask her—incredible effrontery!—to back up her husband, see them through—not to "desert" them, as she called it—in fact to induce the whole family to cover and condone their monstrous dishonour.

"I said to her: 'Honour's always been honour, and honesty honesty, in Manson Mingott's house, and will be till I'm carried out of it feet first,'" the old woman had stammered into her daughter's ear, in the thick voice of the partly paralysed. "And when she said: 'But my name, Auntie—my name's Regina Dallas,' I said: 'It was Beaufort when he covered you with jewels, and it's got to stay Beaufort now that he's covered you with shame.'"

So much, with tears and gasps of horror, Mrs. Welland imparted, blanched and demolished by the unwonted obligation of having at last to fix her eyes on the unpleasant and the discreditable. "If only I could keep it from your father-in-law: he always says: 'Augusta, for pity's sake, don't destroy my last illusions'—and how am I to prevent his knowing these horrors?" the poor lady wailed.

"After all, Mamma, he won't have *seen* them," her daughter suggested; and Mrs. Welland sighed: "Ah, no; thank heaven he's safe in bed. And Dr. Bencomb has promised to keep him there till poor Mamma is better, and Regina has been got away somewhere."

Archer had seated himself near the window and was gazing out blankly at the deserted thoroughfare. It was evident that he had been summoned rather for the moral support of the stricken ladies than because of any specific aid that he could render. Mr. Lovell Mingott had been telegraphed for, and messages were being despatched by hand to the members of the family living in New York; and meanwhile there was nothing to do but to discuss in hushed tones the consequences of Beaufort's dishonour and of his wife's unjustifiable action.

Mrs. Lovell Mingott, who had been in another room writing notes, presently reappeared, and added her voice to the discussion. In *their* day, the elder ladies agreed, the wife of a man who had done anything disgraceful in business had only one idea: to efface herself, to disappear with him. "There was the case of poor Grandmamma Spicer; your great-grandmother, May. Of course," Mrs. Welland hastened to add, "your great-grandfather's money difficulties were private—losses at cards, or signing a note for somebody—I never quite knew, because Mamma would never speak of it. But she was brought up in the country because her mother had to leave New York after the disgrace, whatever it was: they lived up the Hudson alone, winter and summer, till Mamma was sixteen. It would never have occurred to Grandmamma Spicer to ask the family to 'countenance' her, as I understand Regina calls it; though a private disgrace is nothing compared to the scandal of ruining hundreds of innocent people."

"Yes, it would be more becoming in Regina to hide her own countenance than to talk about other people's," Mrs. Lovell Mingott agreed. "I understand that the emerald necklace she wore at the Opera last Friday had been sent on approval from Ball and Black's in the afternoon.[1] I wonder if they'll ever get it back?"

Archer listened unmoved to the relentless chorus. The idea of absolute financial probity as the first law of a gentleman's code was too deeply ingrained in him for sentimental considerations to weaken it. An adventurer like Lemuel Struthers might build up the millions of his Shoe Polish on any number of shady dealings; but unblemished honesty was the *noblesse oblige* of old financial New York. Nor did Mrs. Beaufort's fate greatly move Archer. He felt, no doubt, more sorry for her than her indignant relatives; but it seemed to him that the tie between husband and wife, even if breakable in prosperity, should be indissoluble in misfortune. As Mr. Letterblair had said, a wife's place was at her husband's side when he was in trouble; but society's place was not at his side, and Mrs. Beaufort's cool assumption that it was seemed almost to make her his accomplice. The mere idea of a woman's appealing to her family to screen her husband's business dishonour was inadmissible, since it was the one thing that the Family, as an institution, could not do.

The mulatto maid called Mrs. Lovell Mingott into the hall, and the latter came back in a moment with a frowning brow.

"She wants me to telegraph for Ellen Olenska. I had written to Ellen, of course, and to Medora; but now it seems that's not enough. I'm to telegraph to her immediately, and to tell her that she's to come alone."

The announcement was received in silence. Mrs. Welland

---

[1] *Ball and Black*: the oldest firm of jewelers in the United States (now Black, Starr and Frost).

sighed resignedly, and May rose from her seat and went to gather up some newspapers that had been scattered on the floor.

"I suppose it must be done," Mrs. Lovell Mingott continued, as if hoping to be contradicted; and May turned back toward the middle of the room.

"Of course it must be done," she said. "Granny knows what she wants, and we must carry out all her wishes. Shall I write the telegram for you, Auntie? If it goes at once Ellen can probably catch tomorrow morning's train." She pronounced the syllables of the name with a peculiar clearness, as if she had tapped on two silver bells.

"Well, it can't go at once. Jasper and the pantry-boy are both out with notes and telegrams."

May turned to her husband with a smile. "But here's Newland, ready to do anything. Will you take the telegram, Newland? There'll be just time before luncheon."

Archer rose with a murmur of readiness, and she seated herself at old Catherine's rosewood "Bonheur du Jour,"[1] and wrote out the message in her large immature hand. When it was written she blotted it neatly and handed it to Archer.

"What a pity," she said, "that you and Ellen will cross each other on the way!—Newland," she added, turning to her mother and aunt, "is obliged to go to Washington about a patent law-suit that is coming up before the Supreme Court. I suppose Uncle Lovell will be back by tomorrow night, and with Granny improving so much it doesn't seem right to ask Newland to give up an important engagement for the firm—does it?"

She paused, as if for an answer, and Mrs. Welland hastily declared: "Oh, of course not, darling. Your Granny would be the last person to wish it." As Archer left the room with the telegram, he heard his mother-in-law add, presumably to Mrs. Lovell Mingott: "But why on earth she should make you telegraph for Ellen Olenska—" and May's clear voice rejoin: "Perhaps it's to urge on her again that after all her duty is with her husband."

The outer door closed on Archer and he walked hastily away toward the telegraph office.

---

1   *Bonheur du Jour:* a small writing table.

XXVIII

"Ol—ol—howjer spell it, anyhow?" asked the tart young lady to whom Archer had pushed his wife's telegram across the brass ledge of the Western Union office.

"Olenska—O-len-ska," he repeated, drawing back the message in order to print out the foreign syllables above May's rambling script.

"It's an unlikely name for a New York telegraph office; at least in this quarter," an unexpected voice observed; and turning around Archer saw Lawrence Lefferts at his elbow, pulling an imperturbable moustache and affecting not to glance at the message.

"Hallo, Newland: thought I'd catch you here. I've just heard of old Mrs. Mingott's stroke; and as I was on my way to the house I saw you turning down this street and nipped after you. I suppose you've come from there?"

Archer nodded, and pushed his telegram under the lattice.

"Very bad, eh?" Lefferts continued. "Wiring to the family, I suppose. I gather it *is* bad, if you're including Countess Olenska."

Archer's lips stiffened; he felt a savage impulse to dash his fist into the long vain handsome face at his side.

"Why?" he questioned.

Lefferts, who was known to shrink from discussion, raised his eye-brows with an ironic grimace that warned the other of the watching damsel behind the lattice. Nothing could be worse "form," the look reminded Archer, than any display of temper in a public place.

Archer had never been more indifferent to the requirements of form; but his impulse to do Lawrence Lefferts a physical injury was only momentary. The idea of bandying Ellen Olenska's name with him at such a time, and on whatsoever provocation, was unthinkable. He paid for his telegram, and the two young men went out together into the street. There Archer, having regained his self-control, went on: "Mrs. Mingott is much better: the doctor feels no anxiety whatever"; and Lefferts, with profuse expressions of relief, asked him if he had heard that there were beastly bad rumours again about Beaufort....

That afternoon the announcement of the Beaufort failure was in all the papers. It overshadowed the report of Mrs. Manson Mingott's stroke, and only the few who had heard of the mysterious connection between the two events thought of ascribing old Catherine's illness to anything but the accumulation of flesh and years.

The whole of New York was darkened by the tale of Beaufort's dishonour. There had never, as Mr. Letterblair said, been a worse case in his memory, nor, for that matter, in the memory of the far-off Letterblair who had given his name to the firm. The bank had continued to take in money for a whole day after its failure was inevitable; and as many of its clients belonged to one or another of the ruling clans, Beaufort's duplicity seemed doubly cynical. If Mrs. Beaufort had not taken the tone that such misfortunes (the word was her own) were "the test of friendship," compassion for her might have tempered the general indignation against her husband. As it was—and especially after the object of her nocturnal visit to Mrs. Manson Mingott had become known—her cynicism was held to exceed his; and she had not the excuse—nor her detractors the satisfaction—of pleading that she was "a foreigner." It was some comfort (to those whose securities were not in jeopardy) to be able to remind themselves that Beaufort *was*; but, after all, if a Dallas of South Carolina took his view of the case, and glibly talked of his soon being "on his feet again," the argument lost its edge, and there was nothing to do but to accept this awful evidence of the indissolubility of marriage. Society must manage to get on without the Beauforts, and there was an end of it—except indeed for such hapless victims of the disaster as Medora Manson, the poor old Miss Lannings, and certain other misguided ladies of good family who, if only they had listened to Mr. Henry van der Luyden ...

"The best thing the Beauforts can do," said Mrs. Archer, summing it up as if she were pronouncing a diagnosis and prescribing a course of treatment, "is to go and live at Regina's little place in North Carolina. Beaufort has always kept a racing stable, and he had better breed trotting horses. I should say he had all the qualities of a successful horse-dealer." Every one agreed with her, but no one condescended to enquire what the Beauforts really meant to do.

The next day Mrs. Manson Mingott was much better: she

recovered her voice sufficiently to give orders that no one should mention the Beauforts to her again, and asked—when Dr. Bencomb appeared—what in the world her family meant by making such a fuss about her health.

"If people of my age *will* eat chicken-salad in the evening what are they to expect?" she enquired; and, the doctor having opportunely modified her dietary, the stroke was transformed into an attack of indigestion. But in spite of her firm tone old Catherine did not wholly recover her former attitude toward life. The growing remoteness of old age, though it had not diminished her curiosity about her neighbours, had blunted her never very lively compassion for their troubles; and she seemed to have no difficulty in putting the Beaufort disaster out of her mind. But for the first time she became absorbed in her own symptoms, and began to take a sentimental interest in certain members of her family to whom she had hitherto been contemptuously indifferent.

Mr. Welland, in particular, had the privilege of attracting her notice. Of her sons-in-law he was the one she had most consistently ignored; and all his wife's efforts to represent him as a man of forceful character and marked intellectual ability (if he had only "chosen") had been met with a derisive chuckle. But his eminence as a valetudinarian now made him an object of engrossing interest, and Mrs. Mingott issued an imperial summons to him to come and compare diets as soon as his temperature permitted; for old Catherine was now the first to recognise that one could not be too careful about temperatures.

Twenty-four hours after Madame Olenska's summons a telegram announced that she would arrive from Washington on the evening of the following day. At the Wellands', where the Newland Archers chanced to be lunching, the question as to who should meet her at Jersey City was immediately raised;[1] and the material difficulties amid which the Welland household struggled as if it had been a frontier outpost, lent animation to the debate. It was agreed that

---

[1] A major seaport, *Jersey City*, New Jersey, is located across the Hudson River from New York City. Several railroads, including the Pennsylvania Railroad, operated ferry routes from New York City to New Jersey with terminals in Jersey City.

Mrs. Welland could not possibly go to Jersey City because she was to accompany her husband to old Catherine's that afternoon, and the brougham could not be spared, since, if Mr. Welland were "upset" by seeing his mother-in-law for the first time after her attack, he might have to be taken home at a moment's notice. The Welland sons would of course be "down town," Mr. Lovell Mingott would be just hurrying back from his shooting, and the Mingott carriage engaged in meeting him; and one could not ask May, at the close of a winter afternoon, to go alone across the ferry to Jersey City, even in her own carriage. Nevertheless, it might appear inhospitable—and contrary to old Catherine's express wishes—if Madame Olenska were allowed to arrive without any of the family being at the station to receive her. It was just like Ellen, Mrs. Welland's tired voice implied, to place the family in such a dilemma. "It's always one thing after another," the poor lady grieved, in one of her rare revolts against fate; "the only thing that makes me think Mamma must be less well than Dr. Bencomb will admit is this morbid desire to have Ellen come at once, however inconvenient it is to meet her."

The words had been thoughtless, as the utterances of impatience often are; and Mr. Welland was upon them with a pounce.

"Augusta," he said, turning pale and laying down his fork, "have you any other reason for thinking that Bencomb is less to be relied on than he was? Have you noticed that he has been less conscientious than usual in following up my case or your mother's?"

It was Mrs. Welland's turn to grow pale as the endless consequences of her blunder unrolled themselves before her; but she managed to laugh, and take a second helping of scalloped oysters, before she said, struggling back into her old armour of cheerfulness: "My dear, how could you imagine such a thing? I only meant that, after the decided stand Mamma took about its being Ellen's duty to go back to her husband, it seems strange that she should be seized with this sudden whim to see her, when there are half a dozen other grandchildren that she might have asked for. But we must never forget that Mamma, in spite of her wonderful vitality, is a very old woman."

Mr. Welland's brow remained clouded, and it was evident that his perturbed imagination had fastened at once on this last remark. "Yes: your mother's a very old woman; and for all we know Bencomb may not be as successful with very old people. As you say, my dear, it's always one thing after another; and in another ten or fifteen years I suppose I shall have the pleasing duty of looking about for a new doctor. It's always better to make such a change before it's absolutely necessary." And having arrived at this Spartan decision Mr. Welland firmly took up his fork.

"But all the while," Mrs. Welland began again, as she rose from the luncheon-table, and led the way into the wilderness of purple satin and malachite known as the back drawing-room, "I don't see how Ellen's to be got here tomorrow evening; and I do like to have things settled for at least twenty-four hours ahead."

Archer turned from the fascinated contemplation of a small painting representing two Cardinals carousing, in an octagonal ebony frame set with medallions of onyx.

"Shall I fetch her?" he proposed. "I can easily get away from the office in time to meet the brougham at the ferry, if May will send it there." His heart was beating excitedly as he spoke.

Mrs. Welland heaved a sigh of gratitude, and May, who had moved away to the window, turned to shed on him a beam of approval. "So you see, Mamma, everything *will* be settled twenty-four hours in advance," she said, stooping over to kiss her mother's troubled forehead.

May's brougham awaited her at the door, and she was to drive Archer to Union Square, where he could pick up a Broadway car to carry him to the office. As she settled herself in her corner she said: "I didn't want to worry Mamma by raising fresh obstacles; but how can you meet Ellen tomorrow, and bring her back to New York, when you're going to Washington?"

"Oh, I'm not going," Archer answered.

"Not going? Why, what's happened?" Her voice was as clear as a bell, and full of wifely solicitude.

"The case is off—postponed."

"Postponed? How odd! I saw a note this morning from Mr. Letterblair to Mamma saying that he was going to Washington tomorrow for the big patent case that he was to argue before the Supreme Court. You said it was a patent case, didn't you?"

"Well—that's it: the whole office can't go. Letterblair decided to go this morning."

"Then it's *not* postponed?" she continued, with an insistence so unlike her that he felt the blood rising to his face, as if he were blushing for her unwonted lapse from all the traditional delicacies.

"No: but my going is," he answered, cursing the unnecessary explanations that he had given when he had announced his intention of going to Washington, and wondering where he had read that clever liars give details, but that the cleverest do not. It did not hurt him half as much to tell May an untruth as to see her trying to pretend that she had not detected him.

"I'm not going till later on: luckily for the convenience of your family," he continued, taking base refuge in sarcasm. As he spoke he felt that she was looking at him, and he turned his eyes to hers in order not to appear to be avoiding them. Their glances met for a second, and perhaps let them into each other's meanings more deeply than either cared to go.

"Yes; it *is* awfully convenient," May brightly agreed, "that you should be able to meet Ellen after all; you saw how much Mamma appreciated your offering to do it."

"Oh, I'm delighted to do it." The carriage stopped, and as he jumped out she leaned to him and laid her hand on his. "Goodbye, dearest," she said, her eyes so blue that he wondered afterward if they had shone on him through tears.

He turned away and hurried across Union Square, repeating to himself, in a sort of inward chant: "It's all of two hours from Jersey City to old Catherine's. It's all of two hours—and it may be more."

XXIX

HIS wife's dark blue brougham (with the wedding varnish still on it) met Archer at the ferry, and conveyed him luxuriously to the Pennsylvania terminus in Jersey City.[1]

It was a sombre snowy afternoon, and the gas-lamps were lit in

---

[1] The Pennsylvania Railroad, formed in 1846, since 1871 operated a harbour terminus in Jersey City for travelers from New York City.

the big reverberating station. As he paced the platform, waiting for the Washington express, he remembered that there were people who thought there would one day be a tunnel under the Hudson through which the trains of the Pennsylvania railway would run straight into New York. They were of the brotherhood of visionaries who likewise predicted the building of ships that would cross the Atlantic in five days, the invention of a flying machine, lighting by electricity, telephonic communication without wires, and other Arabian Night marvels.[1]

"I don't care which of their visions comes true," Archer mused, "as long as the tunnel isn't built yet." In his senseless school-boy happiness he pictured Madame Olenska's descent from the train, his discovery of her a long way off, among the throngs of meaningless faces, her clinging to his arm as he guided her to the carriage, their slow approach to the wharf among slipping horses, laden carts, vociferating teamsters, and then the startling quiet of the ferry-boat, where they would sit side by side under the snow, in the motionless carriage, while the earth seemed to glide away under them, rolling to the other side of the sun. It was incredible, the number of things he had to say to her, and in what eloquent order they were forming themselves on his lips ...

The clanging and groaning of the train came nearer, and it staggered slowly into the station like a prey-laden monster into its lair. Archer pushed forward, elbowing through the crowd, and staring blindly into window after window of the high-hung

---

[1] *tunnel under the Hudson*: in 1874, Colonel Dewitt C. Haskin unsuccessfully attempted to build a tunnel under the Hudson River from Hoboken, New Jersey to lower Manhattan. Adding more tunnels to the original plan, William Gibbs McAdoo took over the project in 1902 and opened the tunnels in 1908 and 1909. *Cross the Atlantic in five days*: by the early 1880s, Cunard's steamers were making seven day trans-Atlantic crossings, soon to decrease to five day crossings in the 1890s. *Flying machine*: Orville and Wilbur Wright made their first biplane flight in December 1903. The first international aviation races were held in New York in 1907. *Lighting by electricity*: New York City was lit by gas lights for most of the nineteenth century; electric arc lamps were introduced in December 1880. Thomas Edison invented the incandescent lamp in 1879, and by 1882, the Edison Electric Illuminating Station had opened its first power station for incandescent lighting. *Arabian Night marvels*: after *The Arabian Nights Entertainments,* or *The Thousand and One Nights,* a collection of widely translated Arabic stories told by Scheherazade, who resists the fate of a king's earlier wives by keeping his attention with marvellous tales.

carriages. And then, suddenly, he saw Madame Olenska's pale and surprised face close at hand, and had again the mortified sensation of having forgotten what she looked like.

They reached each other, their hands met, and he drew her arm through his. "This way—I have the carriage," he said.

After that it all happened as he had dreamed. He helped her into the brougham with her bags, and had afterward the vague recollection of having properly reassured her about her grandmother and given her a summary of the Beaufort situation (he was struck by the softness of her: "Poor Regina!"). Meanwhile the carriage had worked its way out of the coil about the station, and they were crawling down the slippery incline to the wharf, menaced by swaying coal-carts, bewildered horses, dishevelled express-wagons, and an empty hearse—ah, that hearse! She shut her eyes as it passed, and clutched at Archer's hand.

"If only it doesn't mean—poor Granny!"

"Oh, no, no—she's much better—she's all right, really. There—we've passed it!" he exclaimed, as if that made all the difference. Her hand remained in his, and as the carriage lurched across the gang-plank onto the ferry he bent over, unbuttoned her tight brown glove, and kissed her palm as if he had kissed a relic. She disengaged herself with a faint smile, and he said: "You didn't expect me today?"

"Oh, no."

"I meant to go to Washington to see you. I'd made all my arrangements—I very nearly crossed you in the train."

"Oh—" she exclaimed, as if terrified by the narrowness of their escape.

"Do you know—I hardly remembered you?"

"Hardly remembered me?"

"I mean: how shall I explain? I—it's always so. *Each time you happen to me all over again.*"

"Oh, yes: I know! I know!"

"Does it—do I too: to you?" he insisted.

She nodded, looking out of the window.

"Ellen—Ellen—Ellen!"

She made no answer, and he sat in silence, watching her profile grow indistinct against the snow-streaked dusk beyond the window. What had she been doing in all those four long months, he wondered? How little they knew of each other, after all! The precious moments were slipping away, but he had forgotten everything that he had meant to say to her and could only helplessly brood on the mystery of their remoteness and their proximity, which seemed to be symbolised by the fact of their sitting so close to each other, and yet being unable to see each other's faces.

"What a pretty carriage! Is it May's?" she asked, suddenly turning her face from the window.

"Yes."

"It was May who sent you to fetch me, then? How kind of her!"

He made no answer for a moment; then he said explosively: "Your husband's secretary came to see me the day after we met in Boston."

In his brief letter to her he had made no allusion to M. Rivière's visit, and his intention had been to bury the incident in his bosom. But her reminder that they were in his wife's carriage provoked him to an impulse of retaliation. He would see if she liked his reference to Rivière any better than he liked hers to May! As on certain other occasions when he had expected to shake her out of her usual composure, she betrayed no sign of surprise: and at once he concluded: "He writes to her, then."

"M. Rivière went to see you?"

"Yes: didn't you know?"

"No," she answered simply.

"And you're not surprised?"

She hesitated. "Why should I be? He told me in Boston that he knew you; that he'd met you in England I think."

"Ellen—I must ask you one thing."

"Yes."

"I wanted to ask it after I saw him, but I couldn't put it in a letter. It was Rivière who helped you to get away—when you left your husband?"

His heart was beating suffocatingly. Would she meet this question with the same composure?

"Yes: I owe him a great debt," she answered, without the least tremor in her quiet voice.

Her tone was so natural, so almost indifferent, that Archer's turmoil subsided. Once more she had managed, by her sheer simplicity, to make him feel stupidly conventional just when he thought he was flinging convention to the winds.

"I think you're the most honest woman I ever met!" he exclaimed.

"Oh, no—but probably one of the least fussy," she answered, a smile in her voice.

"Call it what you like: you look at things as they are."

"Ah—I've had to. I've had to look at the Gorgon."[1]

"Well—it hasn't blinded you! You've seen that she's just an old bogey like all the others."

"She doesn't blind one; but she dries up one's tears."

The answer checked the pleading on Archer's lips: it seemed to come from depths of experience beyond his reach. The slow advance of the ferry-boat had ceased, and her bows bumped against the piles of the slip with a violence that made the brougham stagger, and flung Archer and Madame Olenska against each other. The young man, trembling, felt the pressure of her shoulder, and passed his arm about her.

"If you're not blind, then, you must see that this can't last."

"What can't?"

"Our being together—and not together."

"No. You ought not to have come today," she said in an altered voice; and suddenly she turned, flung her arms about him and pressed her lips to his. At the same moment the carriage began to move, and a gas-lamp at the head of the slip flashed its light into the window. She drew away, and they sat silent and motionless while the brougham struggled through the congestion of carriages about the ferry-landing. As they gained the street Archer began to speak hurriedly.

"Don't be afraid of me: you needn't squeeze yourself back into your corner like that. A stolen kiss isn't what I want. Look: I'm not even trying to touch the sleeve of your jacket. Don't suppose that I don't understand your reasons for not wanting to let this feeling

---

[1]   The *Gorgon*, or Medusa, from classical mythology; a woman with snakes for hair and huge wings, whose glare could turn people to stone.

between us dwindle into an ordinary hole-and-corner love-affair. I couldn't have spoken like this yesterday, because when we've been apart, and I'm looking forward to seeing you, every thought is burnt up in a great flame. But then you come; and you're so much more than I remembered, and what I want of you is so much more than an hour or two every now and then, with wastes of thirsty waiting between, that I can sit perfectly still beside you, like this, with that other vision in my mind, just quietly trusting to it to come true."

For a moment she made no reply; then she asked, hardly above a whisper: "What do you mean by trusting to it to come true?"

"Why—you know it will, don't you?"

"Your vision of you and me together?" She burst into a sudden hard laugh. "You choose your place well to put it to me!"

"Do you mean because we're in my wife's brougham? Shall we get out and walk, then? I don't suppose you mind a little snow?"

She laughed again, more gently. "No; I shan't get out and walk, because my business is to get to Granny's as quickly as I can. And you'll sit beside me, and we'll look, not at visions, but at realities."

"I don't know what you mean by realities. The only reality to me is this."

She met the words with a long silence, during which the carriage rolled down an obscure side-street and then turned into the searching illumination of Fifth Avenue.

"Is it your idea, then, that I should live with you as your mistress—since I can't be your wife?" she asked.

The crudeness of the question startled him: the word was one that women of his class fought shy of, even when their talk flitted closest about the topic. He noticed that Madame Olenska pronounced it as if it had a recognised place in her vocabulary, and he wondered if it had been used familiarly in her presence in the horrible life she had fled from. Her question pulled him up with a jerk, and he floundered.

"I want—I want somehow to get away with you into a world where words like that—categories like that—won't exist. Where we shall be simply two human beings who love each other, who are the whole of life to each other; and nothing else on earth will matter."

She drew a deep sigh that ended in another laugh. "Oh, my dear—where is that country? Have you ever been there?" she asked; and as he remained sullenly dumb she went on: "I know so many who've tried to find it; and, believe me, they all got out by mistake at wayside stations: at places like Boulogne, or Pisa, or Monte Carlo—and it wasn't at all different from the old world they'd left, but only rather smaller and dingier and more promiscuous."

He had never heard her speak in such a tone, and he remembered the phrase she had used a little while before.

"Yes, the Gorgon *has* dried your tears," he said.

"Well, she opened my eyes too; it's a delusion to say that she blinds people. What she does is just the contrary—she fastens their eyelids open, so that they're never again in the blessed darkness. Isn't there a Chinese torture like that? There ought to be. Ah, believe me, it's a miserable little country!"

The carriage had crossed Forty-second Street: May's sturdy brougham-horse was carrying them northward as if he had been a Kentucky trotter. Archer choked with the sense of wasted minutes and vain words.

"Then what, exactly, is your plan for us?" he asked.

"For *us*? But there's no *us* in that sense! We're near each other only if we stay far from each other. Then we can be ourselves. Otherwise we're only Newland Archer, the husband of Ellen Olenska's cousin, and Ellen Olenska, the cousin of Newland Archer's wife, trying to be happy behind the backs of the people who trust them."

"Ah, I'm beyond that," he groaned.

"No, you're not! You've never been beyond. And *I* have," she said, in a strange voice, "and I know what it looks like there."

He sat silent, dazed with inarticulate pain. Then he groped in the darkness of the carriage for the little bell that signalled orders to the coachman. He remembered that May rang twice when she wished to stop. He pressed the bell, and the carriage drew up beside the curbstone.

"Why are we stopping? This is not Granny's," Madame Olenska exclaimed.

"No: I shall get out here," he stammered, opening the door and jumping to the pavement. By the light of a street-lamp he saw her startled face, and the instinctive motion she made to detain him. He closed the door, and leaned for a moment in the window.

"You're right: I ought not to have come today," he said, lowering his voice so that the coachman should not hear. She bent forward, and seemed about to speak; but he had already called out the order to drive on, and the carriage rolled away while he stood on the corner. The snow was over, and a tingling wind had sprung up, that lashed his face as he stood gazing. Suddenly he felt something stiff and cold on his lashes, and perceived that he had been crying, and that the wind had frozen his tears.

He thrust his hands in his pockets, and walked at a sharp pace down Fifth Avenue to his own house.

XXX

THAT evening when Archer came down before dinner he found the drawing-room empty.

He and May were dining alone, all the family engagements having been postponed since Mrs. Manson Mingott's illness; and as May was the more punctual of the two he was surprised that she had not preceded him. He knew that she was at home, for while he dressed he had heard her moving about in her room; and he wondered what had delayed her.

He had fallen into the way of dwelling on such conjectures as a means of tying his thoughts fast to reality. Sometimes he felt as if he had found the clue to his father-in-law's absorption in trifles; perhaps even Mr. Welland, long ago, had had escapes and visions, and had conjured up all the hosts of domesticity to defend himself against them.

When May appeared he thought she looked tired. She had put on the low-necked and tightly-laced dinner-dress which the Mingott ceremonial exacted on the most informal occasions, and had built her fair hair into its usual accumulated coils; and her face, in contrast, was wan and almost faded. But she shone on him with her usual tenderness, and her eyes had kept the blue dazzle of the day before.

"What became of you, dear?" she asked. "I was waiting at

Granny's, and Ellen came alone, and said she had dropped you on the way because you had to rush off on business. There's nothing wrong?"

"Only some letters I'd forgotten, and wanted to get off before dinner."

"Ah—" she said; and a moment afterward: "I'm sorry you didn't come to Granny's—unless the letters were urgent."

"They were," he rejoined, surprised at her insistence. "Besides, I don't see why I should have gone to your grandmother's. I didn't know you were there."

She turned and moved to the looking-glass above the mantelpiece. As she stood there, lifting her long arm to fasten a puff that had slipped from its place in her intricate hair, Archer was struck by something languid and inelastic in her attitude, and wondered if the deadly monotony of their lives had laid its weight on her also. Then he remembered that, as he had left the house that morning, she had called over the stairs that she would meet him at her grandmother's so that they might drive home together. He had called back a cheery "Yes!" and then, absorbed in other visions, had forgotten his promise. Now he was smitten with compunction, yet irritated that so trifling an omission should be stored up against him after nearly two years of marriage. He was weary of living in a perpetual tepid honeymoon, without the temperature of passion yet with all its exactions. If May had spoken out her grievances (he suspected her of many) he might have laughed them away; but she was trained to conceal imaginary wounds under a Spartan smile.[1]

To disguise his own annoyance he asked how her grandmother was, and she answered that Mrs. Mingott was still improving, but had been rather disturbed by the last news about the Beauforts.

"What news?"

"It seems they're going to stay in New York. I believe he's going into an insurance business, or something. They're looking about for a small house."

---

[1] *a Spartan smile*: after Sparta, the ancient Greek city-state noted for its harsh militarism, and hence for the discipline, physical endurance, and stoicism of its citizens.

The preposterousness of the case was beyond discussion, and they went in to dinner. During dinner their talk moved in its usual limited circle; but Archer noticed that his wife made no allusion to Madame Olenska, nor to old Catherine's reception of her. He was thankful for the fact, yet felt it to be vaguely ominous.

They went up to the library for coffee, and Archer lit a cigar and took down a volume of Michelet.[1] He had taken to history in the evenings since May had shown a tendency to ask him to read aloud whenever she saw him with a volume of poetry: not that he disliked the sound of his own voice, but because he could always foresee her comments on what he read. In the days of their engagement she had simply (as he now perceived) echoed what he told her; but since he had ceased to provide her with opinions she had begun to hazard her own, with results destructive to his enjoyment of the works commented on.

Seeing that he had chosen history she fetched her work-basket, drew up an arm-chair to the green-shaded student lamp, and uncovered a cushion she was embroidering for his sofa. She was not a clever needle-woman; her large capable hands were made for riding, rowing and open-air activities; but since other wives embroidered cushions for their husbands she did not wish to omit this last link in her devotion.

She was so placed that Archer, by merely raising his eyes, could see her bent above her work-frame, her ruffled elbow-sleeves slipping back from her firm round arms, the betrothal sapphire shining on her left hand above her broad gold wedding-ring, and the right hand slowly and laboriously stabbing the canvas. As she sat thus, the lamplight full on her clear brow, he said to himself with a secret dismay that he would always know the thoughts behind it, that never, in all the years to come, would she surprise him by an unexpected mood, by a new idea, a weakness, a cruelty or an emotion. She had spent her poetry and romance on their short courting: the function was exhausted because the need was

---

[1] Jules *Michelet* (1798–1874), French historian and Romantic nationalist, author of the *Histoire de France* (1833–1844 and 1847–1853). Director of the National Archives of France, Michelet conceived of France as a person and insisted on the organic unity and identity of the nation.

past. Now she was simply ripening into a copy of her mother, and mysteriously, by the very process, trying to turn him into a Mr. Welland. He laid down his book and stood up impatiently; and at once she raised her head.

"What's the matter?"

"The room is stifling: I want a little air."

He had insisted that the library curtains should draw backward and forward on a rod, so that they might be closed in the evening, instead of remaining nailed to a gilt cornice, and immovably looped up over layers of lace, as in the drawing-room; and he pulled them back and pushed up the sash, leaning out into the icy night. The mere fact of not looking at May, seated beside his table, under his lamp, the fact of seeing other houses, roofs, chimneys, of getting the sense of other lives outside his own, other cities beyond New York, and a whole world beyond his world, cleared his brain and made it easier to breathe.

After he had leaned out into the darkness for a few minutes he heard her say: "Newland! Do shut the window. You'll catch your death."

He pulled the sash down and turned back. "Catch my death!" he echoed; and he felt like adding: "But I've caught it already. I *am* dead—I've been dead for months and months."

And suddenly the play of the word flashed up a wild suggestion. What if it were *she* who was dead! If she were going to die—to die soon—and leave him free! The sensation of standing there, in that warm familiar room, and looking at her, and wishing her dead, was so strange, so fascinating and overmastering, that its enormity did not immediately strike him. He simply felt that chance had given him a new possibility to which his sick soul might cling. Yes, May might die—people did: young people, healthy people like herself: she might die, and set him suddenly free.

She glanced up, and he saw by her widening eyes that there must be something strange in his own.

"Newland! Are you ill?"

He shook his head and turned toward his arm-chair. She bent over her work-frame, and as he passed he laid his hand on her hair. "Poor May!" he said.

"Poor? Why poor?" she echoed with a strained laugh.

"Because I shall never be able to open a window without worrying you," he rejoined, laughing also.

For a moment she was silent; then she said very low, her head bowed over her work: "I shall never worry if you're happy."

"Ah, my dear; and I shall never be happy unless I can open the windows!"

"In *this* weather?" she remonstrated; and with a sigh he buried his head in his book.

Six or seven days passed. Archer heard nothing from Madame Olenska, and became aware that her name would not be mentioned in his presence by any member of the family. He did not try to see her; to do so while she was at old Catherine's guarded bedside would have been almost impossible. In the uncertainty of the situation he let himself drift, conscious, somewhere below the surface of his thoughts, of a resolve which had come to him when he had leaned out from his library window into the icy night. The strength of that resolve made it easy to wait and make no sign.

Then one day May told him that Mrs. Manson Mingott had asked to see him. There was nothing surprising in the request, for the old lady was steadily recovering, and she had always openly declared that she preferred Archer to any of her other grandsons-in-law. May gave the message with evident pleasure: she was proud of old Catherine's appreciation of her husband.

There was a moment's pause, and then Archer felt it incumbent on him to say: "All right. Shall we go together this afternoon?"

His wife's face brightened, but she instantly answered; "Oh, you'd much better go alone. It bores Granny to see the same people too often."

Archer's heart was beating violently when he rang old Mrs. Mingott's bell. He had wanted above all things to go alone, for he felt sure the visit would give him the chance of saying a word in private to the Countess Olenska. He had determined to wait till the chance presented itself naturally; and here it was, and here he was on the doorstep. Behind the door, behind the curtains of the yellow damask room next to the hall, she was surely awaiting him; in another moment he should see her, and be able to speak to her before she led him to the sick-room.

He wanted only to put one question: after that his course would be clear. What he wished to ask was simply the date of her return to Washington; and that question she could hardly refuse to answer.

But in the yellow sitting-room it was the mulatto maid who waited. Her white teeth shining like a keyboard, she pushed back the sliding doors and ushered him into old Catherine's presence.

The old woman sat in a vast throne-like arm-chair near her bed. Beside her was a mahogany stand bearing a cast bronze lamp with an engraved globe, over which a green paper shade had been balanced. There was not a book or a newspaper in reach, nor any evidence of feminine employment: conversation had always been Mrs. Mingott's sole pursuit, and she would have scorned to feign an interest in fancywork.

Archer saw no trace of the slight distortion left by her stroke. She merely looked paler, with darker shadows in the folds and recesses of her obesity; and, in the fluted mob-cap tied by a starched bow between her first two chins, and the muslin kerchief crossed over her billowing purple dressing-gown, she seemed like some shrewd and kindly ancestress of her own who might have yielded too freely to the pleasures of the table.

She held out one of the little hands that nestled in a hollow of her huge lap like pet animals, and called to the maid: "Don't let in any one else. If my daughters call, say I'm asleep."

The maid disappeared, and the old lady turned to her grandson.

"My dear, am I perfectly hideous?" she asked gaily, launching out one hand in search of the folds of muslin on her inaccessible bosom. "My daughters tell me it doesn't matter at my age—as if hideousness didn't matter all the more the harder it gets to conceal!"

"My dear, you're handsomer than ever!" Archer rejoined in the same tone; and she threw back her head and laughed.

"Ah, but not as handsome as Ellen!" she jerked out, twinkling at him maliciously; and before he could answer she added: "Was she so awfully handsome the day you drove her up from the ferry?"

He laughed, and she continued: "Was it because you told her so that she had to put you out on the way? In my youth young men didn't desert pretty women unless they were made to!" She gave another chuckle, and interrupted it to say almost querulously: "It's a pity she didn't marry you; I always told her so. It would have spared me all this worry. But who ever thought of sparing their grandmother worry?"

Archer wondered if her illness had blurred her faculties; but suddenly she broke out: "Well, it's settled, anyhow: she's going to stay with me, whatever the rest of the family say! She hadn't been here five minutes before I'd have gone down on my knees to keep her—if only, for the last twenty years, I'd been able to see where the floor was!"

Archer listened in silence, and she went on: "They'd talked me over, as no doubt you know: persuaded me, Lovell, and Letterblair, and Augusta Welland, and all the rest of them, that I must hold out and cut off her allowance, till she was made to see that it was her duty to go back to Olenski. They thought they'd convinced me when the secretary, or whatever he was, came out with the last proposals: handsome proposals I confess they were. After all, marriage is marriage, and money's money—both useful things in their way ... and I didn't know what to answer—" She broke off and drew a long breath, as if speaking had become an effort. "But the minute I laid eyes on her, I said: 'You sweet bird, you! Shut you up in that cage again? Never!' And now it's settled that she's to stay here and nurse her Granny as long as there's a Granny to nurse. It's not a gay prospect, but she doesn't mind; and of course I've told Letterblair that she's to be given her proper allowance."

The young man heard her with veins aglow; but in his confusion of mind he hardly knew whether her news brought joy or pain. He had so definitely decided on the course he meant to pursue that for the moment he could not readjust his thoughts. But gradually there stole over him the delicious sense of difficulties deferred and opportunities miraculously provided. If Ellen had consented to come and live with her grandmother it must surely be because she had recognised the impossibility of giving him up. This was her answer to his final appeal of the other day: if she would not take the extreme step he had urged, she had at last yielded to half-measures. He sank back into the thought with the involuntary relief of a man who has been ready to risk everything, and suddenly tastes the dangerous sweetness of security.

"She couldn't have gone back—it was impossible!" he exclaimed.

"Ah, my dear, I always knew you were on her side; and that's why I sent for you today, and why I said to your pretty wife, when she proposed to come with you: 'No, my dear, I'm pining to see Newland, and I don't want anybody to share our transports.' For you see, my dear—" she drew her head back as far as its tethering chins permitted, and looked him full in the eyes—" you see, we shall have a fight yet. The family don't want her here, and they'll say it's because I've been ill, because I'm a weak old woman, that she's persuaded me. I'm not well enough yet to fight them one by one, and you've got to do it for me."

"I?" he stammered.

"You. Why not?" she jerked back at him, her round eyes suddenly as sharp as pen-knives. Her hand fluttered from its chair-arm and lit on his with a clutch of little pale nails like bird-claws. "Why not?" she searchingly repeated.

Archer, under the exposure of her gaze, had recovered his self-possession.

"Oh, I don't count—I'm too insignificant."

"Well, you're Letterblair's partner, ain't you? You've got to get at them through Letterblair. Unless you've got a reason," she insisted.

"Oh, my dear, I back you to hold your own against them all without my help; but you shall have it if you need it," he reassured her.

"Then we're safe!" she sighed; and smiling on him with all her ancient cunning she added, as she settled her head among the cushions: "I always knew you'd back us up, because they never quote you when they talk about its being her duty to go home."

He winced a little at her terrifying perspicacity, and longed to ask: "And May—do they quote her?" But he judged it safer to turn the question.

"And Madame Olenska? When am I to see her?" he said.

The old lady chuckled, crumpled her lids, and went through the pantomime of archness. "Not today. One at a time, please. Madame Olenska's gone out."

He flushed with disappointment, and she went on: "She's gone out, my child: gone in my carriage to see Regina Beaufort."

She paused for this announcement to produce its effect. "That's what she's reduced me to already. The day after she got here she put on her best bonnet, and told me, as cool as a cucumber, that she was going to call on Regina Beaufort. 'I don't know her; who is she?' says I. 'She's your grand-niece, and a most unhappy woman,' she says. 'She's the wife of a scoundrel,' I answered. 'Well,' she says, 'and so am I, and yet all my family want me to go back to him.' Well, that floored me, and I let her go; and finally one day she said it was raining too hard to go out on foot, and she wanted me to lend her my carriage. 'What for?' I asked her; and she said: 'To go and see cousin Regina'—*cousin*! Now, my dear, I looked out of the window, and saw it wasn't raining a drop; but I understood her, and I let her have the carriage ... After all, Regina's a brave woman, and so is she; and I've always liked courage above everything."

Archer bent down and pressed his lips on the little hand that still lay on his.

"Eh—eh—eh! Whose hand did you think you were kissing, young man—your wife's, I hope?" the old lady snapped out with her mocking cackle; and as he rose to go she called out after him: "Give her her Granny's love; but you'd better not say anything about our talk."

XXXI

ARCHER had been stunned by old Catherine's news. It was only natural that Madame Olenska should have hastened from Washington in response to her grandmother's summons; but that she should have decided to remain under her roof—especially now that Mrs. Mingott had almost regained her health—was less easy to explain.

Archer was sure that Madame Olenska's decision had not been influenced by the change in her financial situation. He knew the exact figure of the small income which her husband had allowed her at their separation. Without the addition of her grandmother's allowance it was hardly enough to live on, in any sense known to the Mingott vocabulary; and now that Medora Manson, who shared her life, had been ruined, such a pittance would barely keep the two women clothed and fed. Yet Archer was convinced that Madame Olenska had not accepted her grandmother's offer from interested motives.

She had the heedless generosity and the spasmodic extravagance of persons used to large fortunes, and indifferent to money; but she could go without many things which her relations considered indispensable, and Mrs. Lovell Mingott and Mrs. Welland had often been heard to deplore that any one who had enjoyed the cosmopolitan luxuries of Count Olenski's establishments should care so little about "how things were done." Moreover, as Archer knew, several months had passed since her allowance had been cut off; yet in the interval she had made no effort to regain her grandmother's favour. Therefore if she had changed her course it must be for a different reason.

He did not have far to seek for that reason. On the way from the ferry she had told him that he and she must remain apart; but she had said it with her head on his breast. He knew that there was no calculated coquetry in her words; she was fighting her fate as he had fought his, and clinging desperately to her resolve that they should not break faith with the people who trusted them. But during the ten days which had elapsed since her return to New York she had perhaps guessed from his silence, and from the fact of his making no attempt to see her, that he was meditating a decisive step, a step from which there was no turning back. At the thought, a sudden fear of her own weakness might have seized her, and she might have felt that, after all, it was better to accept the compromise usual in such cases, and follow the line of least resistance.

An hour earlier, when he had rung Mrs. Mingott's bell, Archer had fancied that his path was clear before him. He had meant to have a word alone with Madame Olenska, and failing that, to learn from her grandmother on what day, and by which train, she was returning to Washington. In that train he intended to join her, and travel with her to Washington, or as much farther as she was willing to go. His own fancy inclined to Japan. At any rate she would understand at once that, wherever she went, he was going. He meant to leave a note for May that should cut off any other alternative.

He had fancied himself not only nerved for this plunge but eager to take it; yet his first feeling on hearing that the course of events was changed had been one of relief. Now, however, as he walked home from Mrs. Mingott's, he was conscious of a growing distaste for what lay before him. There was nothing unknown or unfamiliar in the path he was presumably to tread; but when he had trodden it before it was as a free man, who was accountable to no one for his actions, and could lend himself with an amused detachment to the game of precautions and prevarications, concealments and compliances, that the part required. This procedure was called "protecting a woman's honour"; and the best fiction, combined with the after-dinner talk of his elders, had long since initiated him into every detail of its code.

Now he saw the matter in a new light, and his part in it seemed singularly diminished. It was, in fact, that which, with a secret fatuity, he had watched Mrs. Thorley Rushworth play toward a fond and unperceiving husband: a smiling, bantering, humouring, watchful and incessant lie. A lie by day, a lie by night, a lie in every touch and every look; a lie in every caress and every quarrel; a lie in every word and in every silence.

It was easier, and less dastardly on the whole, for a wife to play such a part toward her husband. A woman's standard of truthfulness was tacitly held to be lower: she was the subject creature, and versed in the arts of the enslaved. Then she could always plead moods and nerves, and the right not to be held too strictly to account; and even in the most strait-laced societies the laugh was always against the husband.

But in Archer's little world no one laughed at a wife deceived, and a certain measure of contempt was attached to men who continued their philandering after marriage. In the rotation of crops there was a recognised season for wild oats; but they were not to be sown more than once.

Archer had always shared this view: in his heart he thought Lefferts despicable. But to love Ellen Olenska was not to become a man like Lefferts: for the first time Archer found himself face to face with the dread argument of the individual case. Ellen Olenska was like no other woman, he was like no other man: their situation, therefore, resembled no one else's, and they were answerable to no tribunal but that of their own judgment.

Yes, but in ten minutes more he would be mounting his own doorstep; and there were May, and habit, and honour, and all the old decencies that he and his people had always believed in ...

At his corner he hesitated, and then walked on down Fifth Avenue.

Ahead of him, in the winter night, loomed a big unlit house. As he drew near he thought how often he had seen it blazing with lights, its steps awninged and carpeted, and carriages waiting in double line to draw up at the curbstone. It was in the conservatory that stretched its dead-black bulk down the side street that he had taken his first kiss from May; it was under the myriad candles of the ball-room that he had seen her appear, tall and silver-shining as a young Diana.

Now the house was as dark as the grave, except for a faint flare of gas in the basement, and a light in one upstairs room where the blind had not been lowered. As Archer reached the corner he saw that the carriage standing at the door was Mrs. Manson Mingott's. What an opportunity for Sillerton Jackson, if he should chance to pass! Archer had been greatly moved by old Catherine's account of Madame Olenska's attitude toward Mrs. Beaufort; it made the righteous reprobation of New York seem like a passing by on the other side. But he knew well enough what construction the clubs and drawing-rooms would put on Ellen Olenska's visits to her cousin.

He paused and looked up at the lighted window. No doubt the two women were sitting together in that room: Beaufort had probably sought consolation elsewhere. There were even rumours that he had left New York with Fanny Ring; but Mrs. Beaufort's attitude made the report seem improbable.

Archer had the nocturnal perspective of Fifth Avenue almost to himself. At that hour most people were indoors, dressing for dinner; and he was secretly glad that Ellen's exit was likely to be unobserved. As the thought passed through his mind the door opened, and she came out. Behind her was a faint light, such as might have been carried down the stairs to show her the way. She turned to say a word to some one; then the door closed, and she came down the steps.

"Ellen," he said in a low voice, as she reached the pavement.

She stopped with a slight start, and just then he saw two young men of fashionable cut approaching. There was a familiar air about their overcoats and the way their smart silk mufflers were folded over their white ties; and he wondered how youths of their quality happened to be dining out so early. Then he remembered that the Reggie Chiverses, whose house was a few doors above, were taking a large party that evening to see Adelaide Neilson in Romeo and Juliet,[1] and guessed that the two were of the number. They passed under a lamp, and he recognised Lawrence Lefferts and a young Chivers.

A mean desire not to have Madame Olenska seen at the Beauforts' door vanished as he felt the penetrating warmth of her hand.

"I shall see you now—we shall be together," he broke out, hardly knowing what he said.

"Ah," she answered, "Granny has told you?"

While he watched her he was aware that Lefferts and Chivers, on reaching the farther side of the street corner, had discreetly struck away across Fifth Avenue. It was the kind of masculine solidarity that he himself often practised; now he sickened at their connivance. Did she really imagine that he and she could live like this? And if not, what else did she imagine?

"Tomorrow I must see you—somewhere where we can be alone," he said, in a voice that sounded almost angry to his own ears.

She wavered, and moved toward the carriage.

"But I shall be at Granny's—for the present that is," she added, as if conscious that her change of plans required some explanation.

"Somewhere where we can be alone," he insisted.

She gave a faint laugh that grated on him.

"In New York? But there are no churches ... no monuments."

"There's the Art Museum—in the Park,"[2] he explained, as she looked puzzled. "At half-past two. I shall be at the door ... "

---

1   *Adelaide Neilson*, or Elizabeth Ann Brown (1848-1880), English actress who successfully toured the United States, famous for her portrayal of such Shakespearean roles as Juliet, Viola, and Rosalind.

2   *the Art Museum in the Park*: an anachronism caught by early readers. The Metropolitan Museum's first residence, after being incorporated in 1870 by members of the Union League Club, was in the building of the Allen Dodworth's Dancing Academy on Fifth Avenue, between Fifty-Third and Fifty-Fourth Streets. In 1873, the museum moved to Douglas Mansion on West Fourteenth Street until 1879. The original red-brick structure designed by Calvert Vaux and Jacob Wrey Mould opened in 1880 in Central Park on Fifth Avenue between Eightieth and Eighty-Fourth Street. A new south wing opened in 1888, and a north wing in 1894.

She turned away without answering and got quickly into the carriage. As it drove off she leaned forward, and he thought she waved her hand in the obscurity. He stared after her in a turmoil of contradictory feelings. It seemed to him that he had been speaking not to the woman he loved but to another, a woman he was indebted to for pleasures already wearied of: it was hateful to find himself the prisoner of this hackneyed vocabulary.

"She'll come!" he said to himself, almost contemptuously.

Avoiding the popular "Wolfe collection," whose anecdotic canvases filled one of the main galleries of the queer wilderness of cast-iron and encaustic tiles known as the Metropolitan Museum, they had wandered down a passage to the room where the "Cesnola antiquities" mouldered in unvisited loneliness.[1]

They had this melancholy retreat to themselves, and seated on the divan enclosing the central steam-radiator, they were staring silently at the glass cabinets mounted in ebonised wood which contained the recovered fragments of Ilium.[2]

"It's odd," Madame Olenska said, "I never came here before."

"Ah, well—. Some day, I suppose, it will be a great Museum."

"Yes," she assented absently.

She stood up and wandered across the room. Archer, remaining seated, watched the light movements of her figure, so girlish even under its heavy furs, the cleverly planted heron wing in her fur cap, and the way a dark curl lay like a flattened vine spiral on each cheek above the ear. His mind, as always when they first

---

[1]   *Wolfe collection*: after Catherine Lorillard Wolfe (1828–1887), American art collector and philanthropist. She collected 143 pictures from the French Salon which included such artists as Bouguereau and Cabanel. On her death in 1887, Wolfe made a gift of her collection to the Metropolitan Museum along with an endowment of $200,000 to preserve and increase her collection. *Cesnola antiquities*: after Luigi Palma di Cesnola (1832–1904), American Civil War veteran, archaeologist, and museum director. Born in Italy, Cesnola came to New York in 1860, and after serving in the Union Army, went to Cyprus for eleven years as the United States Consul where he gathered a huge collection of antiquities. The Metropolitan Museum purchased two large lots of his collection in 1872 and 1876, and Cesnola acted as the first paid Director of the Museum from 1879–1901.

[2]   *recovered fragments of Ilium*: excavations of the ancient Greek city of Troy began in 1870.

met, was wholly absorbed in the delicious details that made her herself and no other. Presently he rose and approached the case before which she stood. Its glass shelves were crowded with small broken objects—hardly recognisable domestic utensils, ornaments and personal trifles—made of glass, of clay, of discoloured bronze and other time-blurred substances.

"It seems cruel," she said, "that after a while nothing matters ... any more than these little things, that used to be necessary and important to forgotten people, and now have to be guessed at under a magnifying glass and labelled: 'Use unknown.'"

"Yes; but meanwhile—"

"Ah, meanwhile—"

As she stood there, in her long sealskin coat, her hands thrust in a small round muff, her veil drawn down like a transparent mask to the tip of her nose, and the bunch of violets he had brought her stirring with her quickly-taken breath, it seemed incredible that this pure harmony of line and colour should ever suffer the stupid law of change.

"Meanwhile everything matters—that concerns you," he said.

She looked at him thoughtfully, and turned back to the divan. He sat down beside her and waited; but suddenly he heard a step echoing far off down the empty rooms, and felt the pressure of the minutes.

"What is it you wanted to tell me?" she asked, as if she had received the same warning.

"What I wanted to tell you?" he rejoined. "Why, that I believe you came to New York because you were afraid."

"Afraid?"

"Of my coming to Washington."

She looked down at her muff, and he saw her hands stir in it uneasily.

"Well—?"

"Well—yes," she said.

"You *were* afraid? You knew—?"

"Yes: I knew ..."

"Well, then?" he insisted.

"Well, then: this is better, isn't it?" she returned with a long questioning sigh.

"Better—?"

"We shall hurt others less. Isn't it, after all, what you always wanted?"

"To have you here, you mean—in reach and yet out of reach? To meet you in this way, on the sly? It's the very reverse of what I want. I told you the other day what I wanted."

She hesitated. "And you still think this—worse?"

"A thousand times!" He paused. "It would be easy to lie to you; but the truth is I think it detestable."

"Oh, so do I!" she cried with a deep breath of relief.

He sprang up impatiently. "Well, then—it's my turn to ask: what is it, in God's name, that you think better?"

She hung her head and continued to clasp and unclasp her hands in her muff. The step drew nearer, and a guardian in a braided cap walked listlessly through the room like a ghost stalking through a necropolis. They fixed their eyes simultaneously on the case opposite them, and when the official figure had vanished down a vista of mummies and sarcophagi Archer spoke again.

"What do you think better?"

Instead of answering she murmured: "I promised Granny to stay with her because it seemed to me that here I should be safer."

"From me?"

She bent her head slightly, without looking at him.

"Safer from loving me?"

Her profile did not stir, but he saw a tear overflow on her lashes and hang in a mesh of her veil.

"Safer from doing irreparable harm. Don't let us be like all the others!" she protested.

"What others? I don't profess to be different from my kind. I'm consumed by the same wants and the same longings."

She glanced at him with a kind of terror, and he saw a faint colour steal into her cheeks.

"Shall I—once come to you; and then go home?" she suddenly hazarded in a low clear voice.

The blood rushed to the young man's forehead. "Dearest!" he said, without moving. It seemed as if he held his heart in his hands, like a full cup that the least motion might overbrim.

Then her last phrase struck his ear and his face clouded. "Go home? What do you mean by going home?"

"Home to my husband."

"And you expect me to say yes to that?"

She raised her troubled eyes to his. "What else is there? I can't stay here and lie to the people who've been good to me."

"But that's the very reason why I ask you to come away!"

"And destroy their lives, when they've helped me to remake mine?"

Archer sprang to his feet and stood looking down on her in inarticulate despair. It would have been easy to say: "Yes, come; come once." He knew the power she would put in his hands if she consented; there would be no difficulty then in persuading her not to go back to her husband.

But something silenced the word on his lips. A sort of passionate honesty in her made it inconceivable that he should try to draw her into that familiar trap. "If I were to let her come," he said to himself, "I should have to let her go again." And that was not to be imagined.

But he saw the shadow of the lashes on her wet cheek, and wavered.

"After all," he began again, "we have lives of our own....There's no use attempting the impossible. You're so unprejudiced about some things, so used, as you say, to looking at the Gorgon, that I don't know why you're afraid to face our case, and see it as it really is—unless you think the sacrifice is not worth making."

She stood up also, her lips tightening under a rapid frown.

"Call it that, then—I must go," she said, drawing her little watch from her bosom.

She turned away, and he followed and caught her by the wrist. "Well, then: come to me once," he said, his head turning suddenly at the thought of losing her; and for a second or two they looked at each other almost like enemies.

"When?" he insisted. "Tomorrow?"

She hesitated. "The day after."

"Dearest—!" he said again.

She had disengaged her wrist; but for a moment they continued to hold each other's eyes, and he saw that her face, which had grown very pale, was flooded with a deep inner radiance. His heart beat with awe: he felt that he had never before beheld love visible.

"Oh, I shall be late—good-bye. No, don't come any farther than this," she cried, walking hurriedly away down the long room, as if the reflected radiance in his eyes had frightened her. When she reached the door she turned for a moment to wave a quick farewell.

Archer walked home alone. Darkness was falling when he let himself into his house, and he looked about at the familiar objects in the hall as if he viewed them from the other side of the grave.

The parlour-maid, hearing his step, ran up the stairs to light the gas on the upper landing.

"Is Mrs. Archer in?"

"No, sir; Mrs. Archer went out in the carriage after luncheon, and hasn't come back."

With a sense of relief he entered the library and flung himself down in his armchair. The parlour-maid followed, bringing the student lamp and shaking some coals onto the dying fire. When she left he continued to sit motionless, his elbows on his knees, his chin on his clasped hands, his eyes fixed on the red grate.

He sat there without conscious thoughts, without sense of the lapse of time, in a deep and grave amazement that seemed to suspend life rather than quicken it. "This was what had to be, then ... this was what had to be," he kept repeating to himself, as if he hung in the clutch of doom. What he had dreamed of had been so different that there was a mortal chill in his rapture.

The door opened and May came in.

"I'm dreadfully late—you weren't worried, were you?" she asked, laying her hand on his shoulder with one of her rare caresses.

He looked up astonished. "Is it late?"

"After seven. I believe you've been asleep!" She laughed, and drawing out her hat pins tossed her velvet hat on the sofa. She looked paler than usual, but sparkling with an unwonted animation.

"I went to see Granny, and just as I was going away Ellen came in from a walk; so I stayed and had a long talk with her. It was ages since we'd had a real talk...." She had dropped into her usual armchair, facing his, and was running her fingers through her rumpled hair. He fancied she expected him to speak.

"A really good talk," she went on, smiling with what seemed to Archer an unnatural vividness. "She was so dear—just like the old Ellen. I'm afraid I haven't been fair to her lately. I've sometimes thought—"

Archer stood up and leaned against the mantelpiece, out of the radius of the lamp.

"Yes, you've thought—?" he echoed as she paused.

"Well, perhaps I haven't judged her fairly. She's so different— at least on the surface. She takes up such odd people—she seems to like to make herself conspicuous. I suppose it's the life she's led in that fast European society; no doubt we seem dreadfully dull to her. But I don't want to judge her unfairly."

She paused again, a little breathless with the unwonted length of her speech, and sat with her lips slightly parted and a deep blush on her cheeks.

Archer, as he looked at her, was reminded of the glow which had suffused her face in the Mission Garden at St. Augustine. He became aware of the same obscure effort in her, the same reaching out toward something beyond the usual range of her vision.

"She hates Ellen," he thought, "and she's trying to overcome the feeling, and to get me to help her to overcome it."

The thought moved him, and for a moment he was on the point of breaking the silence between them, and throwing himself on her mercy.

"You understand, don't you," she went on, "why the family have sometimes been annoyed? We all did what we could for her at first; but she never seemed to understand. And now this idea of going to see Mrs. Beaufort, of going there in Granny's carriage! I'm afraid she's quite alienated the van der Luydens ... "

"Ah," said Archer with an impatient laugh. The open door had closed between them again.

"It's time to dress; we're dining out, aren't we?" he asked, moving from the fire.

She rose also, but lingered near the hearth. As he walked past her she moved forward impulsively, as though to detain him: their eyes met, and he saw that hers were of the same swimming blue as when he had left her to drive to Jersey City.

She flung her arms about his neck and pressed her cheek to his.

"You haven't kissed me today," she said in a whisper; and he felt her tremble in his arms.

XXXII

"AT the Court of the Tuileries," said Mr. Sillerton Jackson with his reminiscent smile, "such things were pretty openly tolerated."

The scene was the van der Luydens' black walnut dining-room in Madison Avenue, and the time the evening after Newland Archer's visit to the Museum of Art. Mr. and Mrs. van der Luyden had come to town for a few days from Skuytercliff, whither they had precipitately fled at the announcement of Beaufort's failure. It had been represented to them that the disarray into which society had been thrown by this deplorable affair made their presence in town more necessary than ever. It was one of the occasions when, as Mrs. Archer put it, they "owed it to society" to show themselves at the Opera, and even to open their own doors.

"It will never do, my dear Louisa, to let people like Mrs. Lemuel Struthers think they can step into Regina's shoes. It is just at such times that new people push in and get a footing. It was owing to the epidemic of chicken-pox in New York the winter Mrs. Struthers first appeared that the married men slipped away to her house while their wives were in the nursery. You and dear Henry, Louisa, must stand in the breach as you always have."

Mr. and Mrs. van der Luyden could not remain deaf to such a call, and reluctantly but heroically they had come to town, unmuffled the house, and sent out invitations for two dinners and an evening reception.

On this particular evening they had invited Sillerton Jackson, Mrs. Archer and Newland and his wife to go with them to the Opera, where Faust was being sung for the first time that winter. Nothing was done without ceremony under the van der Luyden roof, and though there were but four guests the repast had begun at seven punctually, so that the proper sequence of courses might be served without haste before the gentlemen settled down to their cigars.

Archer had not seen his wife since the evening before. He had left early for the office, where he had plunged into an accumulation of unimportant business. In the afternoon one of the senior partners had made an unexpected call on his time; and he had reached home so late that May had preceded him to the van der Luydens', and sent back the carriage.

Now, across the Skuytercliff carnations and the massive plate, she struck him as pale and languid; but her eyes shone, and she talked with exaggerated animation.

The subject which had called forth Mr. Sillerton Jackson's favourite allusion had been brought up (Archer fancied not without intention) by their hostess. The Beaufort failure, or rather the Beaufort attitude since the failure, was still a fruitful theme for the drawing-room moralist; and after it had been thoroughly examined and condemned Mrs. van der Luyden had turned her scrupulous eyes on May Archer.

"Is it possible, dear, that what I hear is true? I was told your grandmother Mingott's carriage was seen standing at Mrs. Beaufort's door." It was noticeable that she no longer called the offending lady by her Christian name.

May's colour rose, and Mrs. Archer put in hastily: "If it was, I'm convinced it was there without Mrs. Mingott's knowledge."

"Ah, you think—?" Mrs. van der Luyden paused, sighed, and glanced at her husband.

"I'm afraid," Mr. van der Luyden said, "that Madame Olenska's kind heart may have led her into the imprudence of calling on Mrs. Beaufort."

"Or her taste for peculiar people," put in Mrs. Archer in a dry tone, while her eyes dwelt innocently on her son's.

"I'm sorry to think it of Madame Olenska," said Mrs. van der Luyden; and Mrs. Archer murmured: "Ah, my dear—and after you'd had her twice at Skuytercliff!"

It was at this point that Mr. Jackson seized the chance to place his favourite allusion.

"At the Tuileries," he repeated, seeing the eyes of the company expectantly turned on him, "the standard was excessively lax in some respects; and if you'd asked where Morny's money came from—![1] Or who paid the debts of some of the Court beauties..."

"I hope, dear Sillerton," said Mrs. Archer, "you are not suggesting that we should adopt such standards?"

"I never suggest," returned Mr. Jackson imperturbably. "But Madame Olenska's foreign bringing-up may make her less particular—"

"Ah," the two elder ladies sighed.

"Still, to have kept her grandmother's carriage at a defaulter's door!" Mr. van der Luyden protested; and Archer guessed that he was remembering, and resenting, the hampers of carnations he had sent to the little house in Twenty-third Street.

"Of course I've always said that she looks at things quite differently," Mrs. Archer summed up.

A flush rose to May's forehead. She looked across the table at her husband, and said precipitately: "I'm sure Ellen meant it kindly."

"Imprudent people are often kind," said Mrs. Archer, as if the fact were scarcely an extenuation; and Mrs. van der Luyden murmured: "If only she had consulted some one—"

"Ah, that she never did!" Mrs. Archer rejoined.

At this point Mr. van der Luyden glanced at his wife, who bent her head slightly in the direction of Mrs. Archer; and the glimmering trains of the three ladies swept out of the door while the gentlemen settled down to their cigars. Mr. van der Luyden supplied short ones on Opera nights; but they were so good that they made his guests deplore his inexorable punctuality.

Archer, after the first act, had detached himself from the party and made his way to the back of the club box. From there he watched, over various Chivers, Mingott and Rushworth shoulders, the same scene that he had looked at, two years previously, on the night of his first meeting with Ellen Olenska. He had

---

[1] *Morny's money*: refers to Charles Auguste Louis Joseph Morny (1811–1865), who played an important role in the coup d'état that established his half brother, Louis Napoleon, as Emperor Napoleon III. He made a fortune by speculating in and manufacturing beet sugar; he became the Minister of the Interior after Louis Napoleon's coup and was made a duke in 1862.

half-expected her to appear again in old Mrs. Mingott's box, but it remained empty; and he sat motionless, his eyes fastened on it, till suddenly Madame Nilsson's pure soprano broke out into *"M'ama, non m'ama ..."*

Archer turned to the stage, where, in the familiar setting of giant roses and pen-wiper pansies, the same large blonde victim was succumbing to the same small brown seducer.

From the stage his eyes wandered to the point of the horseshoe where May sat between two older ladies, just as, on that former evening, she had sat between Mrs. Lovell Mingott and her newly-arrived "foreign" cousin. As on that evening, she was all in white; and Archer, who had not noticed what she wore, recognised the blue-white satin and old lace of her wedding dress.

It was the custom, in old New York, for brides to appear in this costly garment during the first year or two of marriage: his mother, he knew, kept hers in tissue paper in the hope that Janey might some day wear it, though poor Janey was reaching the age when pearl grey poplin and no bridesmaids would be thought more "appropriate."

It struck Archer that May, since their return from Europe, had seldom worn her bridal satin, and the surprise of seeing her in it made him compare her appearance with that of the young girl he had watched with such blissful anticipations two years earlier.

Though May's outline was slightly heavier, as her goddess-like build had foretold, her athletic erectness of carriage, and the girlish transparency of her expression, remained unchanged: but for the slight languor that Archer had lately noticed in her she would have been the exact image of the girl playing with the bouquet of lilies-of-the-valley on her betrothal evening. The fact seemed an additional appeal to his pity: such innocence was as moving as the trustful clasp of a child. Then he remembered the passionate generosity latent under that incurious calm. He recalled her glance of understanding when he had urged that their engagement should be announced at the Beaufort ball; he heard the voice in which she had said, in the Mission garden: "I couldn't have my happiness made out of a wrong—a wrong to some one else;" and an uncontrollable longing seized him to tell her the truth, to throw himself on her generosity, and ask for the freedom he had once refused.

Newland Archer was a quiet and self-controlled young man. Conformity to the discipline of a small society had become almost his second nature. It was deeply distasteful to him to do anything melodramatic and conspicuous, anything Mr. van der Luyden would have deprecated and the club box condemned as bad form. But he had become suddenly unconscious of the club box, of Mr. van der Luyden, of all that had so long enclosed him in the warm shelter of habit. He walked along the semi-circular passage at the back of the house, and opened the door of Mrs. van der Luyden's box as if it had been a gate into the unknown.

"*M'ama!*" thrilled out the triumphant Marguerite; and the occupants of the box looked up in surprise at Archer's entrance. He had already broken one of the rules of his world, which forbade the entering of a box during a solo.

Slipping between Mr. van der Luyden and Sillerton Jackson, he leaned over his wife.

"I've got a beastly headache; don't tell any one, but come home, won't you?" he whispered.

May gave him a glance of comprehension, and he saw her whisper to his mother, who nodded sympathetically; then she murmured an excuse to Mrs. van der Luyden, and rose from her seat just as Marguerite fell into Faust's arms. Archer, while he helped her on with her Opera cloak, noticed the exchange of a significant smile between the older ladies.

As they drove away May laid her hand shyly on his. "I'm so sorry you don't feel well. I'm afraid they've been over-working you again at the office."

"No—it's not that: do you mind if I open the window?" he returned confusedly, letting down the pane on his side. He sat staring out into the street, feeling his wife beside him as a silent watchful interrogation, and keeping his eyes steadily fixed on the passing houses. At their door she caught her skirt in the step of the carriage, and fell against him.

"Did you hurt yourself?" he asked, steadying her with his arm.

"No; but my poor dress—see how I've torn it!" she exclaimed. She bent to gather up a mud-stained breadth, and followed him up the steps into the hall. The servants had not expected them so early, and there was only a glimmer of gas on the upper landing.

Archer mounted the stairs, turned up the light, and put a match to the brackets on each side of the library mantelpiece. The curtains were drawn, and the warm friendly aspect of the room smote him like that of a familiar face met during an unavowable errand.

He noticed that his wife was very pale, and asked if he should get her some brandy.

"Oh, no," she exclaimed with a momentary flush, as she took off her cloak. "But hadn't you better go to bed at once?" she added, as he opened a silver box on the table and took out a cigarette.

Archer threw down the cigarette and walked to his usual place by the fire.

"No; my head is not as bad as that." He paused. "And there's something I want to say; something important—that I must tell you at once."

She had dropped into an armchair, and raised her head as he spoke. "Yes, dear?" she rejoined, so gently that he wondered at the lack of wonder with which she received this preamble.

"May—" he began, standing a few feet from her chair, and looking over at her as if the slight distance between them were an unbridgeable abyss. The sound of his voice echoed uncannily through the homelike hush, and he repeated: "There is something I've got to tell you ... about myself... "

She sat silent, without a movement or a tremor of her lashes. She was still extremely pale, but her face had a curious tranquillity of expression that seemed drawn from some secret inner source.

Archer checked the conventional phrases of self-accusal that were crowding to his lips. He was determined to put the case baldly, without vain recrimination or excuse.

"Madame Olenska—" he said; but at the name his wife raised her hand as if to silence him. As she did so the gas-light struck on the gold of her wedding-ring.

"Oh, why should we talk about Ellen tonight?" she asked, with a slight pout of impatience.

"Because I ought to have spoken before."

Her face remained calm. "Is it really worth while, dear? I know I've been unfair to her at times—perhaps we all have. You've understood her, no doubt, better than we did: you've always been kind to her. But what does it matter, now it's all over?"

Archer looked at her blankly. Could it be possible that the sense of unreality in which he felt himself imprisoned had communicated itself to his wife?

"All over—what do you mean?" he asked in an indistinct stammer.

May still looked at him with transparent eyes. "Why—since she's going back to Europe so soon; since Granny approves and understands, and has arranged to make her independent of her husband—"

She broke off, and Archer, grasping the corner of the mantelpiece in one convulsed hand, and steadying himself against it, made a vain effort to extend the same control to his reeling thoughts.

"I supposed," he heard his wife's even voice go on, "that you had been kept at the office this evening about the business arrangements. It was settled this morning, I believe." She lowered her eyes under his unseeing stare, and another fugitive flush passed over her face.

He understood that his own eyes must be unbearable, and turning away, rested his elbows on the mantel-shelf and covered his face. Something drummed and clanged furiously in his ears; he could not tell if it were the blood in his veins, or the tick of the clock on the mantel.

May sat without moving or speaking while the clock slowly measured out five minutes. A lump of coal fell forward in the grate, and hearing her rise to push it back, Archer at length turned and faced her.

"It's impossible," he exclaimed.

"Impossible—?"

"How do you know—what you've just told me?"

"I saw Ellen yesterday—I told you I'd seen her at Granny's."

"It wasn't then that she told you?"

"No; I had a note from her this afternoon.—Do you want to see it?"

He could not find his voice, and she went out of the room, and came back almost immediately.

"I thought you knew," she said simply.

She laid a sheet of paper on the table, and Archer put out his hand and took it up. The letter contained only a few lines.

"May dear, I have at last made Granny understand that my visit to her could be no more than a visit; and she has been as kind and generous as ever. She sees now that if I return to Europe I must live by myself, or rather with poor Aunt Medora, who is coming with me. I am hurrying back to Washington to pack up, and we sail next week. You must be very good to Granny when I'm gone—as good as you've always been to me. Ellen.

"If any of my friends wish to urge me to change my mind, please tell them it would be utterly useless."

Archer read the letter over two or three times; then he flung it down and burst out laughing.

The sound of his laugh startled him. It recalled Janey's midnight fright when she had caught him rocking with incomprehensible mirth over May's telegram announcing that the date of their marriage had been advanced.

"Why did she write this?" he asked, checking his laugh with a supreme effort.

May met the question with her unshaken candour. "I suppose because we talked things over yesterday—"

"What things?"

"I told her I was afraid I hadn't been fair to her—hadn't always understood how hard it must have been for her here, alone among so many people who were relations and yet strangers; who felt the right to criticise, and yet didn't always know the circumstances." She paused. "I knew you'd been the one friend she could always count on; and I wanted her to know that you and I were the same—in all our feelings."

She hesitated, as if waiting for him to speak, and then added slowly: "She understood my wishing to tell her this. I think she understands everything."

She went up to Archer, and taking one of his cold hands pressed it quickly against her cheek.

"My head aches too; good-night, dear," she said, and turned to the door, her torn and muddy wedding-dress dragging after her across the room.

XXXIII

IT was, as Mrs. Archer smilingly said to Mrs. Welland, a great event for a young couple to give their first big dinner.

The Newland Archers, since they had set up their household, had received a good deal of company in an informal way. Archer was fond of having three or four friends to dine, and May welcomed them with the beaming readiness of which her mother had set her the example in conjugal affairs. Her husband questioned whether, if left to herself, she would ever have asked any one to the house; but he had long given up trying to disengage her real self from the shape into which tradition and training had moulded her. It was expected that well-off young couples in New York should do a good deal of informal entertaining, and a Welland married to an Archer was doubly pledged to the tradition.

But a big dinner, with a hired *chef* and two borrowed footmen, with Roman punch, roses from Henderson's, and *menus* on gilt-edged cards, was a different affair, and not to be lightly undertaken. As Mrs. Archer remarked, the Roman punch made all the difference; not in itself but by its manifold implications— since it signified either canvas-backs or terrapin, two soups, a hot and a cold sweet, full *décolletage* with short sleeves, and guests of a proportionate importance.

It was always an interesting occasion when a young pair launched their first invitations in the third person, and their summons was seldom refused even by the seasoned and sought-after. Still, it was admittedly a triumph that the van der Luydens, at May's request, should have stayed over in order to be present at her farewell dinner for the Countess Olenska.

The two mothers-in-law sat in May's drawing-room on the afternoon of the great day, Mrs. Archer writing out the *menus* on Tiffany's thickest gilt-edged bristol,[1] while Mrs. Welland superintended the placing of the palms and standard lamps.

Archer, arriving late from his office, found them still there. Mrs. Archer had turned her attention to the name-cards for the table, and Mrs. Welland was considering the effect of bringing

---

[1] *Tiffany's*: famous jewelry firm since 1841, it initially sold stationary.

forward the large gilt sofa, so that another "corner" might be created between the piano and the window.

May, they told him, was in the dining-room inspecting the mound of Jacqueminot roses and maidenhair in the centre of the long table, and the placing of the Maillard bonbons in openwork silver baskets between the candelabra. On the piano stood a large basket of orchids which Mr. van der Luyden had had sent from Skuytercliff. Everything was, in short, as it should be on the approach of so considerable an event.

Mrs. Archer ran thoughtfully over the list, checking off each name with her sharp gold pen.

"Henry van der Luyden—Louisa—the Lovell Mingotts—the Reggie Chiverses—Lawrence Lefferts and Gertrude—(yes, I suppose May was right to have them)—the Selfridge Merrys, Sillerton Jackson, Van Newland and his wife. (How time passes! It seems only yesterday that he was your best man, Newland)—and Countess Olenska—yes, I think that's all...."

Mrs. Welland surveyed her son-in-law affectionately. "No one can say, Newland, that you and May are not giving Ellen a handsome send-off."

"Ah, well," said Mrs. Archer, "I understand May's wanting her cousin to tell people abroad that we're not quite barbarians."

"I'm sure Ellen will appreciate it. She was to arrive this morning, I believe. It will make a most charming last impression. The evening before sailing is usually so dreary," Mrs. Welland cheerfully continued.

Archer turned toward the door, and his mother-in-law called to him: "Do go in and have a peep at the table. And don't let May tire herself too much." But he affected not to hear, and sprang up the stairs to his library. The room looked at him like an alien countenance composed into a polite grimace; and he perceived that it had been ruthlessly "tidied," and prepared, by a judicious distribution of ash-trays and cedar-wood boxes, for the gentlemen to smoke in.

"Ah, well," he thought, "it's not for long—" and he went on to his dressing-room.

Ten days had passed since Madame Olenska's departure from New York. During those ten days Archer had had no sign from her but that conveyed by the return of a key wrapped in tissue paper, and sent to his office in a sealed envelope addressed in her hand. This retort to his last appeal might have been interpreted as a classic move in a familiar game; but the young man chose to give it a different meaning. She was still fighting against her fate; but she was going to Europe, and she was not returning to her husband. Nothing, therefore, was to prevent his following her; and once he had taken the irrevocable step, and had proved to her that it was irrevocable, he believed she would not send him away.

This confidence in the future had steadied him to play his part in the present. It had kept him from writing to her, or betraying, by any sign or act, his misery and mortification. It seemed to him that in the deadly silent game between them the trumps were still in his hands; and he waited.

There had been, nevertheless, moments sufficiently difficult to pass; as when Mr. Letterblair, the day after Madame Olenska's departure, had sent for him to go over the details of the trust which Mrs. Manson Mingott wished to create for her grand-daughter. For a couple of hours Archer had examined the terms of the deed with his senior, all the while obscurely feeling that if he had been consulted it was for some reason other than the obvious one of his cousinship; and that the close of the conference would reveal it.

"Well, the lady can't deny that it's a handsome arrangement," Mr. Letterblair had summed up, after mumbling over a summary of the settlement. "In fact I'm bound to say she's been treated pretty handsomely all round."

"All round?" Archer echoed with a touch of derision. "Do you refer to her husband's proposal to give her back her own money?"

Mr. Letterblair's bushy eyebrows went up a fraction of an inch. "My dear sir, the law's the law; and your wife's cousin was married under the French law. It's to be presumed she knew what that meant."

"Even if she did, what happened subsequently—." But Archer paused. Mr. Letterblair had laid his pen-handle against his big corrugated nose, and was looking down it with the expression assumed by virtuous elderly gentlemen when they wish their youngers to understand that virtue is not synonymous with ignorance.

"My dear sir, I've no wish to extenuate the Count's transgressions; but—but on the other side ... I wouldn't put my hand in the fire ... well, that there hadn't been tit for tat ... with the young champion...." Mr. Letterblair unlocked a drawer and pushed a folded paper toward Archer. "This report, the result of discreet enquiries ... " And then, as Archer made no effort to glance at the paper or to repudiate the suggestion, the lawyer somewhat flatly continued: "I don't say it's conclusive, you observe; far from it. But straws show ... and on the whole it's eminently satisfactory for all parties that this dignified solution has been reached."

"Oh, eminently," Archer assented, pushing back the paper.

A day or two later, on responding to a summons from Mrs. Manson Mingott, his soul had been more deeply tried.

He had found the old lady depressed and querulous.

"You know she's deserted me?" she began at once; and without waiting for his reply: "Oh, don't ask me why! She gave so many reasons that I've forgotten them all. My private belief is that she couldn't face the boredom. At any rate that's what Augusta and my daughters-in-law think. And I don't know that I altogether blame her. Olenski's a finished scoundrel; but life with him must have been a good deal gayer than it is in Fifth Avenue. Not that the family would admit that: they think Fifth Avenue is Heaven with the rue de la Paix[1] thrown in. And poor Ellen, of course, has no idea of going back to her husband. She held out as firmly as ever against that. So she's to settle down in Paris with that fool Medora..... Well, Paris is Paris; and you can keep a carriage there on next to nothing. But she was as gay as a bird, and I shall miss her." Two tears, the parched tears of the old, rolled down her puffy cheeks and vanished in the abysses of her bosom.

"All I ask is," she concluded, "that they shouldn't bother me any more. I must really be allowed to digest my gruel...." And she twinkled a little wistfully at Archer.

It was that evening, on his return home, that May announced her intention of giving a farewell dinner to her cousin. Madame Olenska's name had not been pronounced between them since

---

[1]   rue de la Paix: posh street in Paris famous for its jewellers.

the night of her flight to Washington; and Archer looked at his wife with surprise.

"A dinner—why?" he interrogated.

Her colour rose. "But you like Ellen—I thought you'd be pleased."

"It's awfully nice—your putting it in that way. But I really don't see—"

"I mean to do it, Newland," she said, quietly rising and going to her desk. "Here are the invitations all written. Mother helped me—she agrees that we ought to." She paused, embarrassed and yet smiling, and Archer suddenly saw before him the embodied image of the Family.

"Oh, all right," he said, staring with unseeing eyes at the list of guests that she had put in his hand.

When he entered the drawing-room before dinner May was stooping over the fire and trying to coax the logs to burn in their unaccustomed setting of immaculate tiles.

The tall lamps were all lit, and Mr. van der Luyden's orchids had been conspicuously disposed in various receptacles of modern porcelain and knobby silver. Mrs. Newland Archer's drawing-room was generally thought a great success. A gilt bamboo *jardinière*, in which the primulas and cinerarias were punctually renewed, blocked the access to the bay window (where the old-fashioned would have preferred a bronze reduction of the Venus of Milo);[1] the sofas and arm-chairs of pale brocade were cleverly grouped about little plush tables densely covered with silver toys, porcelain animals and efflorescent photograph frames; and tall rosy-shaded lamps shot up like tropical flowers among the palms.

"I don't think Ellen has ever seen this room lighted up," said May, rising flushed from her struggle, and sending about her a glance of pardonable pride. The brass tongs which she had propped against the side of the chimney fell with a crash that drowned her husband's answer; and before he could restore them Mr. and Mrs. van der Luyden were announced.

---

[1]   *Venus of Milo*: marble statue of Aphrodite with missing arms found on the Greek island of Melos or Milos in 1820. Now in the Louvre.

The other guests quickly followed, for it was known that the van der Luydens liked to dine punctually. The room was nearly full, and Archer was engaged in showing to Mrs. Selfridge Merry a small highly-varnished Verbeckhoven "Study of Sheep," [1] which Mr. Welland had given May for Christmas, when he found Madame Olenska at his side.

She was excessively pale, and her pallor made her dark hair seem denser and heavier than ever. Perhaps that, or the fact that she had wound several rows of amber beads about her neck, reminded him suddenly of the little Ellen Mingott he had danced with at children's parties, when Medora Manson had first brought her to New York.

The amber beads were trying to her complexion, or her dress was perhaps unbecoming: her face looked lustreless and almost ugly, and he had never loved it as he did at that minute. Their hands met, and he thought he heard her say: "Yes, we're sailing tomorrow on the Russia—"; then there was an unmeaning noise of opening doors, and after an interval May's voice: "Newland! Dinner's been announced. Won't you please take Ellen in?"

Madame Olenska put her hand on his arm, and he noticed that the hand was ungloved, and remembered how he had kept his eyes fixed on it the evening that he had sat with her in the little Twenty-third Street drawing-room. All the beauty that had forsaken her face seemed to have taken refuge in the long pale fingers and faintly dimpled knuckles on his sleeve, and he said to himself: "If it were only to see her hand again I should have to follow her—."

It was only at an entertainment ostensibly offered to a "foreign visitor" that Mrs. van der Luyden could suffer the diminution of being placed on her host's left. The fact of Madame Olenska's "foreignness" could hardly have been more adroitly emphasised than by this farewell tribute; and Mrs. van der Luyden accepted her displacement with an affability which left no doubt as to her approval. There were certain things that had to be done, and if done at all, done handsomely and thoroughly; and one of these, in the old New York code, was the tribal rally around a kinswoman

---

[1]   *Study of Sheep*: unidentified painting by Eugène *Verboeckhoven* (1798–1881), Belgian painter and print maker who produced popular pictures of cattle and donkeys.

about to be eliminated from the tribe. There was nothing on earth that the Wellands and Mingotts would not have done to proclaim their unalterable affection for the Countess Olenska now that her passage for Europe was engaged; and Archer, at the head of his table, sat marvelling at the silent untiring activity with which her popularity had been retrieved, grievances against her silenced, her past countenanced, and her present irradiated by the family approval. Mrs. van der Luyden shone on her with the dim benevolence which was her nearest approach to cordiality, and Mr. van der Luyden, from his seat at May's right, cast down the table glances plainly intended to justify all the carnations he had sent from Skuytercliff.

Archer, who seemed to be assisting at the scene in a state of odd imponderability, as if he floated somewhere between chandelier and ceiling, wondered at nothing so much as his own share in the proceedings. As his glance travelled from one placid well-fed face to another he saw all the harmless-looking people engaged upon May's canvas-backs as a band of dumb conspirators, and himself and the pale woman on his right as the centre of their conspiracy. And then it came over him, in a vast flash made up of many broken gleams, that to all of them he and Madame Olenska were lovers, lovers in the extreme sense peculiar to "foreign" vocabularies. He guessed himself to have been, for months, the centre of countless silently observing eyes and patiently listening ears, he understood that, by means as yet unknown to him, the separation between himself and the partner of his guilt had been achieved, and that now the whole tribe had rallied about his wife on the tacit assumption that nobody knew anything, or had ever imagined anything, and that the occasion of the entertainment was simply May Archer's natural desire to take an affectionate leave of her friend and cousin.

It was the old New York way of taking life "without effusion of blood": the way of people who dreaded scandal more than disease, who placed decency above courage, and who considered that nothing was more ill-bred than "scenes," except the behaviour of those who gave rise to them.

As these thoughts succeeded each other in his mind Archer felt like a prisoner in the centre of an armed camp. He looked about the table, and guessed at the inexorableness of his captors from the tone in which, over the asparagus from Florida, they were dealing with Beaufort and his wife. "It's to show me," he thought, "what would happen to *me*—" and a deathly sense of the superiority of implication and analogy over direct action, and of silence over rash words, closed in on him like the doors of the family vault.

He laughed, and met Mrs. van der Luyden's startled eyes.

"You think it laughable?" she said with a pinched smile. "Of course poor Regina's idea of remaining in New York has its ridiculous side, I suppose;" and Archer muttered: "Of course."

At this point, he became conscious that Madame Olenska's other neighbour had been engaged for some time with the lady on his right. At the same moment he saw that May, serenely enthroned between Mr. van der Luyden and Mr. Selfridge Merry, had cast a quick glance down the table. It was evident that the host and the lady on his right could not sit through the whole meal in silence. He turned to Madame Olenska, and her pale smile met him. "Oh, do let's see it through," it seemed to say.

"Did you find the journey tiring?" he asked in a voice that surprised him by its naturalness; and she answered that, on the contrary, she had seldom travelled with fewer discomforts.

"Except, you know, the dreadful heat in the train," she added; and he remarked that she would not suffer from that particular hardship in the country she was going to.

"I never," he declared with intensity, "was more nearly frozen than once, in April, in the train between Calais and Paris."

She said she did not wonder, but remarked that, after all, one could always carry an extra rug, and that every form of travel had its hardships; to which he abruptly returned that he thought them all of no account compared with the blessedness of getting away. She changed colour, and he added, his voice suddenly rising in pitch: "I mean to do a lot of travelling myself before long." A tremor crossed her face, and leaning over to Reggie Chivers, he cried out: "I say, Reggie, what do you say to a trip round the world: now, next month, I mean? I'm game if you are—" at which Mrs. Reggie piped up that she could not think of letting Reggie go till after the Martha Washington Ball she was getting up for the Blind Asylum in Easter week; and her husband placidly observed that by that time he would have to be practising for the International Polo match.

But Mr. Selfridge Merry had caught the phrase "round the world," and having once circled the globe in his steam-yacht, he seized the opportunity to send down the table several striking items concerning the shallowness of the Mediterranean ports. Though, after all, he added, it didn't matter; for when you'd seen Athens and Smyrna and Constantinople, what else was there? And Mrs. Merry said she could never be too grateful to Dr. Bencomb for having made them promise not to go to Naples on account of the fever.

"But you must have three weeks to do India properly," her husband conceded, anxious to have it understood that he was no frivolous globe-trotter.

And at this point the ladies went up to the drawing-room.

In the library, in spite of weightier presences, Lawrence Lefferts predominated.

The talk, as usual, had veered around to the Beauforts, and even Mr. van der Luyden and Mr. Selfridge Merry, installed in the honorary arm-chairs tacitly reserved for them, paused to listen to the younger man's philippic.

Never had Lefferts so abounded in the sentiments that adorn Christian manhood and exalt the sanctity of the home. Indignation lent him a scathing eloquence, and it was clear that if others had followed his example, and acted as he talked, society would never have been weak enough to receive a foreign upstart like Beaufort—no, sir, not even if he'd married a van der Luyden or a Lanning instead of a Dallas. And what chance would there have been, Lefferts wrathfully questioned, of his marrying into such a family as the Dallases, if he had not already wormed his way into certain houses, as people like Mrs. Lemuel Struthers had managed to worm theirs in his wake? If society chose to open its doors to vulgar women the harm was not great, though the gain was doubtful; but once it got in the way of tolerating men of obscure origin and tainted wealth the end was total disintegration—and at no distant date.

"If things go on at this pace," Lefferts thundered, looking like a young prophet dressed by Poole,[1] and who had not yet been stoned, "we shall see our children fighting for invitations to swindlers' houses, and marrying Beaufort's bastards."

"Oh, I say—draw it mild!" Reggie Chivers and young Newland protested, while Mr. Selfridge Merry looked genuinely alarmed, and an expression of pain and disgust settled on Mr. van der Luyden's sensitive face.

"Has he got any?" cried Mr. Sillerton Jackson, pricking up his ears; and while Lefferts tried to turn the question with a laugh, the old gentleman twittered into Archer's ear: "Queer, those fellows who are always wanting to set things right. The people who have the worst cooks are always telling you they're poisoned when they dine out. But I hear there are pressing reasons for our friend Lawrence's diatribe:—type-writer this time, I understand...."

The talk swept past Archer like some senseless river running and running because it did not know enough to stop. He saw, on the faces about him, expressions of interest, amusement and even mirth. He listened to the younger men's laughter, and to the praise of the Archer Madeira, which Mr. van der Luyden and Mr. Merry were thoughtfully celebrating. Through it all he was dimly aware of a general attitude of friendliness toward himself, as if the guard of the prisoner he felt himself to be were trying to soften his captivity; and the perception increased his passionate determination to be free.

In the drawing-room, where they presently joined the ladies, he met May's triumphant eyes, and read in them the conviction that everything had "gone off" beautifully. She rose from Madame Olenska's side, and immediately Mrs. van der Luyden beckoned the latter to a seat on the gilt sofa where she throned. Mrs. Selfridge Merry bore across the room to join them, and it became clear to Archer that here also a conspiracy of rehabilitation and obliteration was going on. The silent organisation which held his little world together was determined to put itself on record as never for a moment having questioned the propriety of Madame Olenska's conduct, or the completeness of Archer's

---

[1] *dressed by Poole*: Henry Poole, considered the first of the great Savile Row tailors of London.

domestic felicity. All these amiable and inexorable persons were resolutely engaged in pretending to each other that they had never heard of, suspected, or even conceived possible, the least hint to the contrary; and from this tissue of elaborate mutual dissimulation Archer once more disengaged the fact that New York believed him to be Madame Olenska's lover. He caught the glitter of victory in his wife's eyes, and for the first time understood that she shared the belief. The discovery roused a laughter of inner devils that reverberated through all his efforts to discuss the Martha Washington ball with Mrs. Reggie Chivers and little Mrs. Newland; and so the evening swept on, running and running like a senseless river that did not know how to stop.

At length he saw that Madame Olenska had risen and was saying good-bye. He understood that in a moment she would be gone, and tried to remember what he had said to her at dinner; but he could not recall a single word they had exchanged.

She went up to May, the rest of the company making a circle about her as she advanced. The two young women clasped hands; then May bent forward and kissed her cousin.

"Certainly our hostess is much the handsomer of the two," Archer heard Reggie Chivers say in an undertone to young Mrs. Newland; and he remembered Beaufort's coarse sneer at May's ineffectual beauty.

A moment later he was in the hall, putting Madame Olenska's cloak about her shoulders.

Through all his confusion of mind he had held fast to the resolve to say nothing that might startle or disturb her. Convinced that no power could now turn him from his purpose he had found strength to let events shape themselves as they would. But as he followed Madame Olenska into the hall he thought with a sudden hunger of being for a moment alone with her at the door of her carriage.

"Is your carriage here?" he asked; and at that moment Mrs. van der Luyden, who was being majestically inserted into her sables, said gently: "We are driving dear Ellen home."

Archer's heart gave a jerk, and Madame Olenska, clasping her cloak and fan with one hand, held out the other to him. "Good-bye," she said.

"Good-bye—but I shall see you soon in Paris," he answered aloud—it seemed to him that he had shouted it.

"Oh," she murmured, "if you and May could come—!"

Mr. van der Luyden advanced to give her his arm, and Archer turned to Mrs. van der Luyden. For a moment, in the billowy darkness inside the big landau, he caught the dim oval of a face, eyes shining steadily—and she was gone.

As he went up the steps he crossed Lawrence Lefferts coming down with his wife. Lefferts caught his host by the sleeve, drawing back to let Gertrude pass.

"I say, old chap: do you mind just letting it be understood that I'm dining with you at the club tomorrow night? Thanks so much, you old brick! Good-night."

"It *did* go off beautifully, didn't it?" May questioned from the threshold of the library.

Archer roused himself with a start. As soon as the last carriage had driven away, he had come up to the library and shut himself in, with the hope that his wife, who still lingered below, would go straight to her room. But there she stood, pale and drawn, yet radiating the factitious energy of one who has passed beyond fatigue.

"May I come and talk it over?" she asked.

"Of course, if you like. But you must be awfully sleepy—"

"No, I'm not sleepy. I should like to sit with you a little."

"Very well," he said, pushing her chair near the fire.

She sat down and he resumed his seat; but neither spoke for a long time. At length Archer began abruptly: "Since you're not tired, and want to talk, there's something I must tell you. I tried to the other night—."

She looked at him quickly. "Yes, dear. Something about yourself?"

"About myself. You say you're not tired: well, I am. Horribly tired ... "

In an instant she was all tender anxiety. "Oh, I've seen it coming on, Newland! You've been so wickedly overworked—"

"Perhaps it's that. Anyhow, I want to make a break—"

"A break? To give up the law?"

"To go away, at any rate—at once. On a long trip, ever so far off—away from everything—"

He paused, conscious that he had failed in his attempt to speak with the indifference of a man who longs for a change, and is yet too weary to welcome it. Do what he would, the chord of eagerness vibrated. "Away from everything—" he repeated.

"Ever so far? Where, for instance?" she asked.

"Oh, I don't know. India—or Japan."

She stood up, and as he sat with bent head, his chin propped on his hands, he felt her warmly and fragrantly hovering over him.

"As far as that? But I'm afraid you can't, dear ... " she said in an unsteady voice. "Not unless you'll take me with you." And then, as he was silent, she went on, in tones so clear and evenly-pitched that each separate syllable tapped like a little hammer on his brain: "That is, if the doctors will let me go ... but I'm afraid they won't. For you see, Newland, I've been sure since this morning of something I've been so longing and hoping for—"

He looked up at her with a sick stare, and she sank down, all dew and roses, and hid her face against his knee.

"Oh, my dear," he said, holding her to him while his cold hand stroked her hair.

There was a long pause, which the inner devils filled with strident laughter; then May freed herself from his arms and stood up.

"You didn't guess—?"

"Yes—I; no. That is, of course I hoped—"

They looked at each other for an instant and again fell silent; then, turning his eyes from hers, he asked abruptly: "Have you told any one else?"

"Only Mamma and your mother." She paused, and then added hurriedly, the blood flushing up to her forehead: "That is—and Ellen. You know I told you we'd had a long talk one afternoon—and how dear she was to me."

"Ah—" said Archer, his heart stopping.

He felt that his wife was watching him intently. "Did you *mind* my telling her first, Newland?"

"Mind? Why should I?" He made a last effort to collect himself. "But that was a fortnight ago, wasn't it? I thought you said you weren't sure till today."

Her colour burned deeper, but she held his gaze. "No; I wasn't sure then—but I told her I was. And you see I was right!" she exclaimed, her blue eyes wet with victory.

XXXIV

NEWLAND ARCHER sat at the writing-table in his library in East Thirty-ninth Street.

He had just got back from a big official reception for the inauguration of the new galleries at the Metropolitan Museum,[1] and the spectacle of those great spaces crowded with the spoils of the ages, where the throng of fashion circulated through a series of scientifically catalogued treasures, had suddenly pressed on a rusted spring of memory.

"Why, this used to be one of the old Cesnola rooms," he heard some one say; and instantly everything about him vanished, and he was sitting alone on a hard leather divan against a radiator, while a slight figure in a long sealskin cloak moved away down the meagrely-fitted vista of the old Museum.

The vision had roused a host of other associations, and he sat looking with new eyes at the library which, for over thirty years, had been the scene of his solitary musings and of all the family confabulations.

It was the room in which most of the real things of his life had happened. There his wife, nearly twenty-six years ago, had broken to him, with a blushing circumlocution that would have caused the young women of the new generation to smile, the news that she was to have a child; and there their eldest boy, Dallas, too delicate to be taken to church in midwinter, had been christened by their old friend the Bishop of New York, the ample magnificent irreplaceable Bishop, so long the pride and ornament of his

---

[1] *new galleries ... Museum*: Completed in 1902 and covering the original building in a facade of limestone, the Fifth Avenue wing was designed by Richard Morris Hunt, the most fashionable architect of his time. After Luigi Cesnola's death in 1904, J.P. Morgan was elected President of the museum; he commissioned the firm of McKim, Mead and White to design a new wing (completed in 1909), running parallel to and behind the Fifth Avenue wing, to house the Hoentschel collection of 18th century decorative arts.

diocese.[1] There Dallas had first staggered across the floor shouting "Dad," while May and the nurse laughed behind the door; there their second child, Mary (who was so like her mother), had announced her engagement to the dullest and most reliable of Reggie Chivers's many sons; and there Archer had kissed her through her wedding veil before they went down to the motor which was to carry them to Grace Church—for in a world where all else had reeled on its foundations the "Grace Church wedding" remained an unchanged institution.

It was in the library that he and May had always discussed the future of the children: the studies of Dallas and his young brother Bill, Mary's incurable indifference to "accomplishments," and passion for sport and philanthropy, and the vague leanings toward "art" which had finally landed the restless and curious Dallas in the office of a rising New York architect.

The young men nowadays were emancipating themselves from the law and business and taking up all sorts of new things. If they were not absorbed in state politics or municipal reform, the chances were that they were going in for Central American archæology, for architecture or landscape-engineering; taking a keen and learned interest in the pre-revolutionary buildings of their own country, studying and adapting Georgian types, and protesting at the meaningless use of the word "Colonial." Nobody nowadays had "Colonial" houses except the millionaire grocers of the suburbs.

But above all—sometimes Archer put it above all—it was in that library that the Governor of New York,[2] coming down from Albany one evening to dine and spend the night, had turned to his host, and said, banging his clenched fist on the table and gnashing his eye-glasses: "Hang the professional politician! You're the kind of man the country wants, Archer. If the stable's ever to be cleaned out, men like you have got to lend a hand in the cleaning."

---

[1] *irreplaceable Bishop*: probably Horatio Potter, the Bishop of New York from 1854 to 1887.

[2] *Governor of New York*: Theodore Roosevelt (1858-1919) was elected governor of New York in 1898 and ran as William McKinley's vice-presidential candidate in 1900. He became President of the United States after McKinley was assassinated in 1901. He was a distant cousin of Wharton's by marriage, and a good friend.

"Men like you—" how Archer had glowed at the phrase! How eagerly he had risen up at the call! It was an echo of Ned Winsett's old appeal to roll his sleeves up and get down into the muck; but spoken by a man who set the example of the gesture, and whose summons to follow him was irresistible.

Archer, as he looked back, was not sure that men like himself *were* what his country needed, at least in the active service to which Theodore Roosevelt had pointed; in fact, there was reason to think it did not, for after a year in the State Assembly he had not been re-elected, and had dropped back thankfully into obscure if useful municipal work, and from that again to the writing of occasional articles in one of the reforming weeklies that were trying to shake the country out of its apathy. It was little enough to look back on; but when he remembered to what the young men of his generation and his set had looked forward— the narrow groove of money-making, sport and society to which their vision had been limited—even his small contribution to the new state of things seemed to count, as each brick counts in a well-built wall. He had done little in public life; he would always be by nature a contemplative and a dilettante; but he had had high things to contemplate, great things to delight in; and one great man's friendship to be his strength and pride.

He had been, in short, what people were beginning to call "a good citizen." In New York, for many years past, every new movement, philanthropic, municipal or artistic, had taken account of his opinion and wanted his name. People said: "Ask Archer" when there was a question of starting the first school for crippled children, reorganising the Museum of Art, founding the Grolier Club, inaugurating the new Library, or getting up a new society of chamber music.[1] His days were full, and they were filled decently. He supposed it was all a man ought to ask.

Something he knew he had missed: the flower of life. But he thought of it now as a thing so unattainable and improbable that

---

[1]   *Grolier Club*: after Jean Grolier, a sixteenth-century French bibliophile. The Grolier club was formed in 1884 by nine city leaders interested in book and print collecting. *The new Library*: the New York Public Library was formed in 1895 after merging the Tilden Trust with the Astor and Lennox libraries. The vast building on Fifth Avenue and Forty-second Street would not be completed and opened to the public until 1911.

to have repined would have been like despairing because one had not drawn the first prize in a lottery. There were a hundred million tickets in *his* lottery, and there was only one prize; the chances had been too decidedly against him. When he thought of Ellen Olenska it was abstractly, serenely, as one might think of some imaginary beloved in a book or a picture: she had become the composite vision of all that he had missed. That vision, faint and tenuous as it was, had kept him from thinking of other women. He had been what was called a faithful husband; and when May had suddenly died—carried off by the infectious pneumonia through which she had nursed their youngest child—he had honestly mourned her. Their long years together had shown him that it did not so much matter if marriage was a dull duty, as long as it kept the dignity of a duty: lapsing from that, it became a mere battle of ugly appetites. Looking about him, he honoured his own past, and mourned for it. After all, there was good in the old ways.

His eyes, making the round of the room—done over by Dallas with English mezzotints, Chippendale cabinets, bits of chosen blue-and-white and pleasantly shaded electric lamps—came back to the old Eastlake writing-table that he had never been willing to banish, and to his first photograph of May, which still kept its place beside his inkstand.

There she was, tall, round-bosomed and willowy, in her starched muslin and flapping Leghorn, as he had seen her under the orange-trees in the Mission garden. And as he had seen her that day, so she had remained; never quite at the same height, yet never far below it: generous, faithful, unwearied; but so lacking in imagination, so incapable of growth, that the world of her youth had fallen into pieces and rebuilt itself without her ever being conscious of the change. This hard bright blindness had kept her immediate horizon apparently unaltered. Her incapacity to recognise change made her children conceal their views from her as Archer concealed his; there had been, from the first, a joint pretence of sameness, a kind of innocent family hypocrisy, in which father and children had unconsciously collaborated. And she had died thinking the world a good place, full of loving and harmonious households like her own, and resigned to leave it because she was convinced that, whatever happened, Newland would continue to inculcate in Dallas the same principles and prejudices which had shaped his parents' lives, and that Dallas in turn (when Newland followed her) would transmit the sacred trust to little Bill. And of Mary she was sure as of her own self. So, having snatched little Bill from the grave, and given her life in the effort, she went contentedly to her place in the Archer vault in St. Mark's,[1] where Mrs. Archer already lay safe from the terrifying "trend" which her daughter-in-law had never even become aware of.

Opposite May's portrait stood one of her daughter. Mary Chivers was as tall and fair as her mother, but large-waisted, flat-chested and slightly slouching, as the altered fashion required. Mary Chivers's mighty feats of athleticism could not have been performed with the twenty-inch waist that May Archer's azure sash so easily spanned. And the difference seemed symbolic; the mother's life had been as closely girt as her figure. Mary, who was no less conventional, and no more intelligent, yet led a larger life and held more tolerant views. There was good in the new order too.

The telephone clicked, and Archer, turning from the photographs, unhooked the transmitter at his elbow. How far they were from the days when the legs of the brass-buttoned messenger boy had been New York's only means of quick communication!

"Chicago wants you."

Ah—it must be a long-distance from Dallas, who had been sent to Chicago by his firm to talk over the plan of the Lake-side palace they were to build for a young millionaire with ideas. The firm always sent Dallas on such errands.

"Hallo, Dad—yes: Dallas. I say—how do you feel about sailing on Wednesday? Mauretania:[2] Yes, next Wednesday as ever is. Our client wants me to look at some Italian gardens before we settle anything, and has asked me to nip over on the next boat. I've got to be back on the first of June—" the voice broke into a joyful

---

[1] *St. Mark's* Church in the Bowery, at East Tenth St. and Second Avenue, is the second oldest church in the city.

[2] Launched on 20 September 1906 by Cunard, the *Mauretania* took its maiden voyage in 1907, leaving Liverpool on 16 November 1907 and arriving in New York on 22 November 1907. In 1909, the ship made its fastest crossing at 4 days, 10 hours, and 51 minutes. The *Mauretania* held the record for the fastest transatlantic crossing for nearly two decades.

conscious laugh—"so we must look alive. I say, Dad, I want your help: do come."

Dallas seemed to be speaking in the room: the voice was as near by and natural as if he had been lounging in his favourite armchair by the fire. The fact would not ordinarily have surprised Archer, for long-distance telephoning had become as much a matter of course as electric lighting and five-day Atlantic voyages. But the laugh did startle him; it still seemed wonderful that across all those miles and miles of country—forest, river, mountain, prairie, roaring cities and busy indifferent millions—Dallas's laugh should be able to say: "Of course, whatever happens, I must get back on the first, because Fanny Beaufort and I are to be married on the fifth."

The voice began again: "Think it over? No, sir: not a minute. You've got to say yes now. Why not, I'd like to know? If you can allege a single reason—No; I knew it. Then it's a go, eh? Because I count on you to ring up the Cunard office first thing tomorrow; and you'd better book a return on a boat from Marseilles. I say, Dad; it'll be our last time together, in this kind of way—. Oh, good! I knew you would."

Chicago rang off, and Archer rose and began to pace up and down the room.

It would be their last time together in this kind of way: the boy was right. They would have lots of other "times" after Dallas's marriage, his father was sure; for the two were born comrades, and Fanny Beaufort, whatever one might think of her, did not seem likely to interfere with their intimacy. On the contrary, from what he had seen of her, he thought she would be naturally included in it. Still, change was change, and differences were differences, and much as he felt himself drawn toward his future daughter-in-law, it was tempting to seize this last chance of being alone with his boy.

There was no reason why he should not seize it, except the profound one that he had lost the habit of travel. May had disliked to move except for valid reasons, such as taking the children to the sea or in the mountains: she could imagine no other motive for leaving the house in Thirty-ninth Street or their comfortable quarters at the Wellands' in Newport. After Dallas had taken his degree she had thought it her duty to travel for six months; and the whole family had made the old-fashioned tour through England, Switzerland and Italy. Their time being limited (no one knew why) they had omitted France. Archer remembered Dallas's wrath at being asked to contemplate Mont Blanc instead of Rheims and Chartres. But Mary and Bill wanted mountain-climbing, and had already yawned their way in Dallas's wake through the English cathedrals; and May, always fair to her children, had insisted on holding the balance evenly between their athletic and artistic proclivities. She had indeed proposed that her husband should go to Paris for a fortnight, and join them on the Italian lakes after they had "done" Switzerland; but Archer had declined. "We'll stick together," he said; and May's face had brightened at his setting such a good example to Dallas.

Since her death, nearly two years before, there had been no reason for his continuing in the same routine. His children had urged him to travel: Mary Chivers had felt sure it would do him good to go abroad and "see the galleries." The very mysteriousness of such a cure made her the more confident of its efficacy. But Archer had found himself held fast by habit, by memories, by a sudden startled shrinking from new things.

Now, as he reviewed his past, he saw into what a deep rut he had sunk. The worst of doing one's duty was that it apparently unfitted one for doing anything else. At least that was the view that the men of his generation had taken. The trenchant divisions between right and wrong, honest and dishonest, respectable and the reverse, had left so little scope for the unforeseen. There are moments when a man's imagination, so easily subdued to what it lives in, suddenly rises above its daily level, and surveys the long windings of destiny. Archer hung there and wondered....

What was left of the little world he had grown up in, and whose standards had bent and bound him? He remembered a sneering prophecy of poor Lawrence Lefferts's, uttered years ago in that very room: "If things go on at this rate, our children will be marrying Beaufort's bastards."

It was just what Archer's eldest son, the pride of his life, was doing; and nobody wondered or reproved. Even the boy's Aunt Janey, who still looked so exactly as she used to in her elderly youth, had taken her mother's emeralds and seed-pearls out of their pink cotton-wool, and carried them with her own twitching hands to the future bride; and Fanny Beaufort, instead of looking disappointed at not receiving a "set" from a Paris jeweller, had exclaimed at their old-fashioned beauty, and declared that when she wore them she should feel like an Isabey miniature.

Fanny Beaufort, who had appeared in New York at eighteen, after the death of her parents, had won its heart much as Madame Olenska had won it thirty years earlier; only instead of being distrustful and afraid of her, society took her joyfully for granted. She was pretty, amusing and accomplished: what more did any one want? Nobody was narrow-minded enough to rake up against her the half-forgotten facts of her father's past and her own origin. Only the older people remembered so obscure an incident in the business life of New York as Beaufort's failure, or the fact that after his wife's death he had been quietly married to the notorious Fanny Ring, and had left the country with his new wife, and a little girl who inherited her beauty. He was subsequently heard of in Constantinople, then in Russia; and a dozen years later American travellers were handsomely entertained by him in Buenos Ayres, where he represented a large insurance agency. He and his wife died there in the odour of prosperity; and one day their orphaned daughter had appeared in New York in charge of May Archer's sister-in-law, Mrs. Jack Welland, whose husband had been appointed the girl's guardian. The fact threw her into almost cousinly relationship with Newland Archer's children, and nobody was surprised when Dallas's engagement was announced.

Nothing could more clearly give the measure of the distance that the world had travelled. People nowadays were too busy— busy with reforms and "movements," with fads and fetishes and frivolities—to bother much about their neighbours. And of what account was anybody's past, in the huge kaleidoscope where all the social atoms spun around on the same plane?

Newland Archer, looking out of his hotel window at the stately gaiety of the Paris streets, felt his heart beating with the confusion and eagerness of youth.

It was long since it had thus plunged and reared under his

widening waistcoat, leaving him, the next minute, with an empty breast and hot temples. He wondered if it was thus that his son's conducted itself in the presence of Miss Fanny Beaufort—and decided that it was not. "It functions as actively, no doubt, but the rhythm is different," he reflected, recalling the cool composure with which the young man had announced his engagement, and taken for granted that his family would approve.

"The difference is that these young people take it for granted that they're going to get whatever they want, and that we almost always took it for granted that we shouldn't. Only, I wonder— the thing one's so certain of in advance: can it ever make one's heart beat as wildly?"

It was the day after their arrival in Paris, and the spring sunshine held Archer in his open window, above the wide silvery prospect of the Place Vendôme. One of the things he had stipulated—almost the only one—when he had agreed to come abroad with Dallas, was that, in Paris, he shouldn't be made to go to one of the new-fangled "palaces."

"Oh, all right—of course," Dallas good-naturedly agreed. "I'll take you to some jolly old-fashioned place—the Bristol say—" leaving his father speechless at hearing that the century-long home of kings and emperors was now spoken of as an old-fashioned inn,[1] where one went for its quaint inconveniences and lingering local colour.

Archer had pictured often enough, in the first impatient years, the scene of his return to Paris; then the personal vision had faded, and he had simply tried to see the city as the setting of Madame Olenska's life. Sitting alone at night in his library, after the household had gone to bed, he had evoked the radiant outbreak of spring down the avenues of horse-chestnuts, the flowers and statues in the public gardens, the whiff of lilacs from the flower-carts, the majestic roll of the river under the great bridges, and the life of art and study and pleasure that filled each mighty artery to bursting. Now the spectacle was before him in its glory, and as he looked out on it he felt shy, old-fashioned,

---

[1]   *Bristol*: originally the residence of Madame de Pompadour, Hôtel Le Bristol is one of the most luxurious and expensive hotels in Paris.

inadequate: a mere grey speck of a man compared with the ruthless magnificent fellow he had dreamed of being....

Dallas's hand came down cheerily on his shoulder. "Hullo, father: this is something like, isn't it?" They stood for a while looking out in silence, and then the young man continued: "By the way, I've got a message for you: the Countess Olenska expects us both at half-past five."

He said it lightly, carelessly, as he might have imparted any casual item of information, such as the hour at which their train was to leave for Florence the next evening. Archer looked at him, and thought he saw in his gay young eyes a gleam of his great-grandmother Mingott's malice.

"Oh, didn't I tell you?" Dallas pursued. "Fanny made me swear to do three things while I was in Paris: get her the score of the last Debussy songs, go to the Grand-Guignol and see Madame Olenska.[1] You know she was awfully good to Fanny when Mr. Beaufort sent her over from Buenos Ayres to the Assomption. Fanny hadn't any friends in Paris, and Madame Olenska used to be kind to her and trot her about on holidays. I believe she was a great friend of the first Mrs. Beaufort's. And she's our cousin, of course. So I rang her up this morning, before I went out, and told her you and I were here for two days and wanted to see her."

Archer continued to stare at him. "You told her I was here?"

"Of course—why not?" Dallas's eye brows went up whimsically. Then, getting no answer, he slipped his arm through his father's with a confidential pressure.

"I say, father: what was she like?"

Archer felt his colour rise under his son's unabashed gaze. "Come, own up: you and she were great pals, weren't you? Wasn't she most awfully lovely?"

"Lovely? I don't know. She was different."

"Ah—there you have it! That's what it always comes to, doesn't it? When she comes, *she's different*—and one doesn't know why. It's exactly what I feel about Fanny."

---

[1] *Debussy songs*: modern music by Claude *Debussy* (1862-1918), French composer, creator of such innovative pieces as *Clair de Lune* (1890) and *Prélude à L'Après-midi d'un Faune* (1894). The Théâtre du *Grand Guignol* was founded in 1895 by Oscar Méténier to showcase naturalistic drama.

His father drew back a step, releasing his arm. "About Fanny? But, my dear fellow—I should hope so! Only I don't see—"

"Dash it, Dad, don't be prehistoric! Wasn't she—once—your Fanny?"

Dallas belonged body and soul to the new generation. He was the first-born of Newland and May Archer, yet it had never been possible to inculcate in him even the rudiments of reserve. "What's the use of making mysteries? It only makes people want to nose 'em out," he always objected when enjoined to discretion. But Archer, meeting his eyes, saw the filial light under their banter.

"My Fanny—?"

"Well, the woman you'd have chucked everything for: only you didn't," continued his surprising son.

"I didn't," echoed Archer with a kind of solemnity.

"No: you date, you see, dear old boy. But mother said—"

"Your mother?"

"Yes: the day before she died. It was when she sent for me alone—you remember? She said she knew we were safe with you, and always would be, because once, when she asked you to, you'd given up the thing you most wanted."

Archer received this strange communication in silence. His eyes remained unseeingly fixed on the thronged sunlit square below the window. At length he said in a low voice: "She never asked me."

"No. I forgot. You never did ask each other anything, did you? And you never told each other anything. You just sat and watched each other, and guessed at what was going on underneath. A deaf-and-dumb asylum, in fact! Well, I back your generation for knowing more about each other's private thoughts than we ever have time to find out about our own.—I say, Dad," Dallas broke off, "you're not angry with me? If you are, let's make it up and go and lunch at Henri's. I've got to rush out to Versailles afterward."[1]

Archer did not accompany his son to Versailles. He preferred to spend the afternoon in solitary roamings through Paris. He had

---

[1] *Versailles*: a royal residence for over 100 years, this vast palace outside Paris was turned into a museum by Louis Phillipe in 1837.

to deal all at once with the packed regrets and stifled memories of an inarticulate lifetime.

After a little while he did not regret Dallas's indiscretion. It seemed to take an iron band from his heart to know that, after all, some one had guessed and pitied.... And that it should have been his wife moved him indescribably. Dallas, for all his affectionate insight, would not have understood that. To the boy, no doubt, the episode was only a pathetic instance of vain frustration, of wasted forces. But was it really no more? For a long time Archer sat on a bench in the Champs Elysées and wondered, while the stream of life rolled by....

A few streets away, a few hours away, Ellen Olenska waited. She had never gone back to her husband, and when he had died, some years before, she had made no change in her way of living. There was nothing now to keep her and Archer apart—and that afternoon he was to see her.

He got up and walked across the Place de la Concorde and the Tuileries gardens to the Louvre.[1] She had once told him that she often went there, and he had a fancy to spend the intervening time in a place where he could think of her as perhaps having lately been. For an hour or more he wandered from gallery to gallery through the dazzle of afternoon light, and one by one the pictures burst on him in their half-forgotten splendour, filling his soul with the long echoes of beauty. After all, his life had been too starved....

Suddenly, before an effulgent Titian,[2] he found himself saying: "But I'm only fifty-seven—" and then he turned away. For such summer dreams it was too late; but surely not for a quiet harvest of friendship, of comradeship, in the blessed hush of her nearness.

He went back to the hotel, where he and Dallas were to meet; and together they walked again across the Place de la Concorde and over the bridge that leads to the Chamber of Deputies.[3]

---

1 The *Place de la Concorde* is situated between the Tuileries Gardens and the Champs-Elysées; also known as the Place de la Révolution because it was the site of numerous executions during the French Revolution. *The Louvre*: centuries old palace turned into a museum by Napoleon Bonaparte.

2 A painting by *Titian*, or Tiziano Vicellio (1485–1576), Venetian painter famous for his large mythological and religious paintings, frescoes, and portraits.

3 The *Chamber of Deputies*, or the Palais Bourbon, is located across the Seine from the Place de la Concorde. Once a private mansion, the government converted the building to legislative use in 1827.

Dallas, unconscious of what was going on in his father's mind, was talking excitedly and abundantly of Versailles. He had had but one previous glimpse of it, during a holiday trip in which he had tried to pack all the sights he had been deprived of when he had had to go with the family to Switzerland; and tumultuous enthusiasm and cock-sure criticism tripped each other up on his lips.

As Archer listened, his sense of inadequacy and inexpressiveness increased. The boy was not insensitive, he knew; but he had the facility and self-confidence that came of looking at fate not as a master but as an equal. "That's it: they feel equal to things—they know their way about," he mused, thinking of his son as the spokesman of the new generation which had swept away all the old landmarks, and with them the sign-posts and the danger-signals.

Suddenly Dallas stopped short, grasping his father's arm. "Oh, by Jove," he exclaimed.

They had come out into the great tree-planted space before the Invalides.[1] The dome of Mansart floated ethereally above the budding trees and the long grey front of the building: drawing up into itself all the rays of afternoon light, it hung there like the visible symbol of the race's glory.

Archer knew that Madame Olenska lived in a square near one of the avenues radiating from the Invalides; and he had pictured the quarter as quiet and almost obscure, forgetting the central splendour that lit it up. Now, by some queer process of association, that golden light became for him the pervading illumination in which she lived. For nearly thirty years, her life—of which he knew so strangely little—had been spent in this rich atmosphere that he already felt to be too dense and yet too stimulating for his lungs. He thought of the theatres she must have been to, the pictures she must have looked at, the sober and splendid old houses she must have frequented, the people she must have talked with, the incessant stir of ideas, curiosities, images and associations thrown out by an intensely social race in

---

[1]   Built in 1671–76 as a home for disabled veterans, the Hôtel des *Invalides* also includes L'Eglise du Dôme which was added to the chapel of Saint-Louis by Jules Hardouin-Mansart beginning in 1677. The chapel has housed the body of Napoleon Bonaparte since 1840.

a setting of immemorial manners; and suddenly he remembered the young Frenchman who had once said to him: "Ah, good conversation—there is nothing like it, is there?"

Archer had not seen M. Rivière, or heard of him, for nearly thirty years; and that fact gave the measure of his ignorance of Madame Olenska's existence. More than half a lifetime divided them, and she had spent the long interval among people he did not know, in a society he but faintly guessed at, in conditions he would never wholly understand. During that time he had been living with his youthful memory of her; but she had doubtless had other and more tangible companionship. Perhaps she too had kept her memory of him as something apart; but if she had, it must have been like a relic in a small dim chapel, where there was not time to pray every day....

They had crossed the Place des Invalides, and were walking down one of the thoroughfares flanking the building. It was a quiet quarter, after all, in spite of its splendour and its history; and the fact gave one an idea of the riches Paris had to draw on, since such scenes as this were left to the few and the indifferent.

The day was fading into a soft sun-shot haze, pricked here and there by a yellow electric light, and passers were rare in the little square into which they had turned. Dallas stopped again, and looked up.

"It must be here," he said, slipping his arm through his father's with a movement from which Archer's shyness did not shrink; and they stood together looking up at the house.

It was a modern building, without distinctive character, but many-windowed, and pleasantly balconied up its wide cream-coloured front. On one of the upper balconies, which hung well above the rounded tops of the horse-chestnuts in the square, the awnings were still lowered, as though the sun had just left it.

"I wonder which floor—?" Dallas conjectured; and moving toward the *porte-cochère* he put his head into the porter's lodge, and came back to say: "The fifth. It must be the one with the awnings."

Archer remained motionless, gazing at the upper windows as if the end of their pilgrimage had been attained.

"I say, you know, it's nearly six," his son at length reminded him.

The father glanced away at an empty bench under the trees.

"I believe I'll sit there a moment," he said.

"Why—aren't you well?" his son exclaimed.

"Oh, perfectly. But I should like you, please, to go up without me."

Dallas paused before him, visibly bewildered. "But, I say, Dad: do you mean you won't come up at all?"

"I don't know," said Archer slowly.

"If you don't she won't understand."

"Go, my boy; perhaps I shall follow you."

Dallas gave him a long look through the twilight.

"But what on earth shall I say?"

"My dear fellow, don't you always know what to say?" his father rejoined with a smile.

"Very well. I shall say you're old-fashioned, and prefer walking up the five flights because you don't like lifts."

His father smiled again. "Say I'm old-fashioned: that's enough."

Dallas looked at him again, and then, with an incredulous gesture, passed out of sight under the vaulted doorway.

Archer sat down on the bench and continued to gaze at the awninged balcony. He calculated the time it would take his son to be carried up in the lift to the fifth floor, to ring the bell, and be admitted to the hall, and then ushered into the drawing-room. He pictured Dallas entering that room with his quick assured step and his delightful smile, and wondered if the people were right who said that his boy "took after him."

Then he tried to see the persons already in the room—for probably at that sociable hour there would be more than one—and among them a dark lady, pale and dark, who would look up quickly, half rise, and hold out a long thin hand with three rings on it…. He thought she would be sitting in a sofa-corner near the fire, with azaleas banked behind her on a table.

"It's more real to me here than if I went up," he suddenly heard himself say; and the fear lest that last shadow of reality should lose its edge kept him rooted to his seat as the minutes succeeded each other.

He sat for a long time on the bench in the thickening dusk, his eyes never turning from the balcony. At length a light shone through the windows, and a moment later a man-servant came out on the balcony, drew up the awnings, and closed the shutters.

At that, as if it had been the signal he waited for, Newland Archer got up slowly and walked back alone to his hotel.

Appendix A: Wharton's Outlines

[Wharton wrote at least three plot outlines for her novel which reveal intentions that underwent revision in the course of writing the novel. These outlines remain among her papers deposited with the Beinecke Rare Book and Manuscript Library at Yale University. What are generally agreed to be the first and third of these outlines are on separate sheets of paper; the second is in a notebook Wharton titled "Subjects and Notes, 1918-1923."]

1. "1st plan"

Lawrence sees Countess X in the Wellands box. Horrified. The Ctess (Ellen) had married a Polish nobleman living in Paris & Nice. Reports of his debaucheries had come home; but it was also said that *she* had become "fast," & "talked about." Vague rumours were current & some embarrassment was felt when she came home, saying simply that she had left her husband & obtained a divorce. Still, her behaviour was so discreet & retiring, & she seemed so genuinely glad to be at home, in a purer atmosphere, that every one became very friendly after the first recoil, & she was used as an Awful Warning to young girls with an inclination to "marry foreigners." ✕

Gradually Archer falls in love with her & sees that life with May Welland, or any other young woman who has not had Ellen's initiation, would be unutterably dull. It is very painful for him to break his engagement, but he finally has the courage to do so. Though he does not tell May why he no longer cares for her.

She gives him up magnanimously ~~but when she finds that Ellen is the cause she is very bitter, & reproaches Ellen for Ellen too is very much distressed but still~~ because she has been taught that "ladies do not make scenes," & she continues to pretend that she does not suspect Ellen of being her rival, till the latter's engagement is announced. Even then May is heroically generous, & is among the first to bring her good wishes to her cousin.

Archer, his struggle over, is sublimely, supremely happy. He urges Ellen to marry him at once. She shocks him deeply by proposing that they should first "go off for a few weeks" so that he can be sure he is not making a mistake. He reproaches her for thinking that he "feels about her in that way," & she begins to feel ashamed of having made the suggestion, & to ~~dread the~~ say to herself that the "European corruption" has tainted her soul. To efface this impression from her own mind & his, she consents to a hasty marriage; but then, when they come back from their honeymoon, & she realizes that for the next 30 or 40 years they are going to live in Madison Ave in winter & on the Hudson in the Spring & autumn, with a few weeks of Europe or Newport every summer, her whole soul recoils, & she knows at once that she has eaten of the Pomegranate Seed & can never never live without it.

She flies to Europe, & Archer consents to a separation. He realizes dimly that there is no use in struggling with her. He arranges his own life as best he can, & occasionally goes to Europe, & usually calls on his wife, & is asked to dine with her. She is very poor, & very lonely, but she has a real life.

He grows more & more absorbed in business, more & more subdued to "New York." He returns to live with his mother & sister. May Welland marries some one else & nothing ever happens to him again.

[Source: Edith Wharton Collection, Yale Collection of American Literature, Beinecke Rare Book and Manuscript Library.]

2. [Entry in Wharton's notebook, "Subjects and Notes," pages 37, 39]

[The entry appears to have been revised, perhaps in light of a later outline or even in light of the developing manuscript. The original entry title, Old New York, is crossed out in black ink, over which is written "The Age of Innocence." In a different ink from either title is written the phrase "(Begun 1919)"; below this is written "Finished 1920," underlined. Under the original title are the dates and general time frame for the novel: "(1875-80.) Length of action about 18 months." Then a list of characters follows.]

~~Langdon~~ Newland Archer
May Welland
Comtesse Olenska
(~~Clementine~~ Ellen)   Book I. New York

~~Clementine~~ Ellen Olenska (cousin of May) has married young. Lived in Paris, Nice, ~~Étrétat~~ Rome, glimpses of London.... Husband charming gambler, drug-taker & debauché. Spends all her money, & marriage goes to smash. ~~He~~ She comes back to America longing for virtue, innocence & "Old New York."

Archer is engaged to May Welland. He falls in love with ~~Clementine~~ Ellen, ~~She~~ but resists & marries May. (Conventional impossibility of a man's breaking his engagement in those days. ~~Clementine~~ Ellen enthusiastically converted to all that is "province," honour, decency, &c.... applauds his resolution.) ~~& finally goes back to her husband~~

~~In a two or three years she reappears~~

He goes on a wedding trip with May, comes back & settles down to married life in N.Y. ~~Clementine~~ Ellen still there—but less enthusiastic about New York. He sees a great deal of her. May is going to have a baby. At last he & ~~Clementine~~ Ellen ~~have~~ fly together (contrast between bridal night with May & *this* one). Archer is fascinated & yet terrified. ~~He~~ They ~~go to Europe~~ go to the South together—some little place in Florida.

Arrange somehow that all this is done *very secretly*. No one knows they are together. Both get tired—she of the idea of living in America, he of the idea of a scandal & a dislocation of his life.

He cannot live without Newport & respectability, nor she without Europe & emotions.

They return to N.Y. separately, & the last scene is a dinner which the happy May (who has had a boy) insists on giving to her cousin *Mme* Olenska before the latter sails.

... *End*

[Source: Edith Wharton Collection, Yale Collection of American Literature, Beinecke Rare Book and Manuscript Library.]

3. [The final outline?]

Old New York. (The scene is laid in 1875.)

Langdon Archer, a young man of very good "Old New York," is engaged to May Welland, a charming young girl of the same set, with whom he is deeply in love.

Her cousin, Clementine Welland, whose parents had lived in

Paris & ~~"gone to the"~~ been popular at the court of Louis Napoleon, & in fashionable French society, has been married very young to Count Olenska, a ~~a very rich~~ Polish nobleman of great family. She has led a brilliant cosmopolitan life in Paris, London, Florence & Nice, but her husband's extravagance & dissipation have obliged her to leave him, & she returns to N.Y. at 28, disillusioned & unhappy, & thirsting (as she imagines) for "the simple life," as represented by the quiet respectable "Old New York" of the seventies. Scenes at the Old Academy of Music, the "Assembly" balls, Christine Nilsson, Capoul, etc.—Clementine Olenska & Langdon Archer meet & fall madly in love with each other.

He is almost carried off his feet; but in "Old New York" a girl is almost disgraced if her fiancé jilts her, & Archer dares not break with May. Mme Olenska applauds his resolution, & with an aching heart he marries May, & they go on their tame colourless & eminently respectable wedding trip.

When they return they settle down in New York & begin to lead the life wh. is to go on till the grave. Clementine is there too, beginning to be bored with New York & virtue & renunciation & thirsting for the freedom & variety of her European existence.

She falls into Archer's arms, & they go off secretly & meet in Florida where they spend a few mad weeks. But Mme Olenska cannot divorce as she & her husband are Roman Catholics.

Gradually Archer realizes that he cannot break with society & live as an outcast with ~~an "immor~~ another man's wife. Mme Olenska, on her side, is weary of their sentimental tête à tête & his scruples, & they finally go back, & ~~end~~ the story ends by Mme Olenska's returning to Europe.

Before she goes, May (who is going to have a baby & who suspects nothing) insists on giving A her cousin a farewell dinner, at which all of Old New York is present.

[Source: Edith Wharton Collection, Yale Collection of American Literature, Beinecke Rare Book and Manuscript Library.]

Appendix B: Wharton's Correspondence *About* The Age of Innocence

[The correspondence between Wharton and her editor at Appleton, Rutger B. Jewett, reveals among other things some of the pressures under which Wharton worked—word count requirements and deadlines, as well as her publisher's demand for a certain kind of product signalled by the name "Edith Wharton." The selections below also record Wharton's response to the anachronisms early readers were complaining about, which included a never acted-upon proposal to write a preface that would clarify her artistic aims in writing an "historic" novel. Finally, letters to her sister-in-law and to the younger novelist Sinclair Lewis reveal among other things Wharton's excitement about an impending Broadway dramatization of her novel, her finicky sense of the past, and her delight at being recognized as a writer of contemporary importance by a modern writer whose star was on the rise.]

1. From Rutger B. Jewett to Edith Wharton (excerpt), November 18, 1919.

Congratulations upon this opening section of "The Age of Innocence." You have caught the flavor of Old New York in the days when it possessed some social cohesion, and have pictured a by gone period when it was not a series of disconnected villages. You can readily check up the points to which you refer, and if you find any anachronisms send forward your corrections. If possible, I will have the errors checked up before they appear in the magazine. In any case they will be in time for the book. We shall issue the novel just as soon as the magazine serial terminates and the book market is open. The existing contract which was made between you and us for a novel of the "House of Mirth" type will stand for "The Age of Innocence."

[Source: Edith Wharton Collection, Yale Collection of American Literature, Beinecke Rare Book and Manuscript Library.]

2. From Edith Wharton to Rutger B. Jewett (excerpt), January 5, 1920.

I am sending you by hand by tomorrow's steamer another 25,000 words of "The Age of Innocence," and also the final revision of Book I. Two or three details important for the holding together of the story have been inserted in this revision and I have written my sister-in-law that you will be kind enough to send it to her at once so that she can make the necessary changes in the proofs. They are all slight but nevertheless important.

I was very much surprised to hear from my sister-in-law the other day that when she called at the Pictorial Review Office for proofs the lady representing Mr. Vance told her that the book was evidently to be a long one and that the editor would evidently have to cut out some passages.

As you know, it was stipulated that the novel furnished to the Pictorial Review should not be less than 100,000 words long. I see no reason to expect that it will exceed this length and it may even fall short by 3 or 4,000 words. In any case as I am prepared to keep my part of the agreement I shall expect the Magazine to do the same and not to tamper with the text of my novel.

I have done really a super-human piece of work in writing, within a year, the best part of two long novels, entirely different in subject and treatment, simply to suit the convenience of the Editor of the Pictorial, and I cannot consent to have my work treated as if it were prose-by-the-yard.

[Source: *The Letters of Edith Wharton*, eds. R. W.B. Lewis and Nancy Lewis (New York: Macmillan, 1988), 428.]

3. From Rutger B. Jewett to Edith Wharton (excerpt), August 16, 1920.

My previous letter has explained to you that we put on all speed possible when we received your manuscript, and rushed the galley proofs off to you without any delay. We are expecting to issue the book in October unless printers' strikes and other Bolshevik demonstrations prevent. It is of the greatest importance that we have the full autumn season to market the book. We prepared dummies six months ago and have had our men showing advance samples all over the country. The orders are coming in well. We are most hopeful.

Personally I am delighted with the story. It is a valuable contribution—a picture of old New York which has been thrown into the discard. I do not know of anyone else who could have created the picture.

How you would detest New York life to-day! If it seemed petty and narrow before, it would now seem blatant and chaotic, without rhyme or reason.

[Source: Edith Wharton Collection, Yale Collection of American Literature, Beinecke Rare Book and Manuscript Library.]

4. From Rutger B. Jewett to Edith Wharton (excerpt), October 21, 1920.

Under separate cover I have sent you Professor Phelps' review of "The Age of Innocence." ...You will see that Phelps challenges one or two statements in your story. Please give me a reply for the points he has raised. Our French Encyclopaedia states that de Maupassant published his first work in 1880. "Middlemarch" appeared in 1872.

[Source: Edith Wharton Collection, Yale Collection of American Literature, Beinecke Rare Book and Manuscript Library.]

5. From Edith Wharton to Rutger B. Jewett (excerpt), November 5, 1920.

With regard to Maupassant, Mr. Phelps is of course quite right. Such inaccuracies annoy me very much, but you know under what high pressure the book was written and revised. I asked a clever young librarian in Paris to verify all my dates in French fiction, but evidently this one was overlooked. Personally, I do not attach much importance to questions of exact dates in a novel of this kind, as the main thing is to render the atmosphere, and Maupassant was in the atmosphere of young men of Archer's generation. Still, it is always the kind of mistake that people pick up, and as I hope that there will soon be a second printing of the book, I suggest replacing Maupassant's name by that of [left blank].

[Source: Edith Wharton Collection, Yale Collection of American Literature, Beinecke Rare Book and Manuscript Library.]

6. From Rutger B. Jewett to Edith Wharton (excerpt), November 13, 1920.

Words fail me when I think of this confusion in wedding and funeral ceremonials. The ministers are beginning to discover the mistake. They are quaint birds and know the difference between wedding and funeral fees. I am mortified that I accepted your churchmanship so trustingly, especially as there are only two events which ever lure me inside church portals, namely, a funeral or a wedding. Therefore even my feeble memory should have sounded a warning bell. I suppose, however, I was so appalled with the fate of May Welland and Newland Archer when they started for the church altar that I would have accepted sections of the temple ceremonial from Aida.[1] I am not cynical enough to insinuate that perhaps for Archer you selected the correct service after all.

[Source: Edith Wharton Collection, Yale Collection of American Literature, Beinecke Rare Book and Manuscript Library.]

7. From Edith Wharton to Rutger B. Jewett (excerpt), December 22, 1920.

I am dreadfully distressed about the unfortunate quotation of the marriage service; but as you know I had no time for revision, and cannot hold myself to blame for such accidents. Mr. Fraser's letter is most amusing; thank you for sending it.

I have discovered some more misprints, and in the hope that the success of the book will make more editions necessary I shall send a new list in a day or two.

[Source: Edith Wharton Collection, Yale Collection of American Literature, Beinecke Rare Book and Manuscript Library.]

8. From Rutger B. Jewett to Edith Wharton, January 20, 1921.

We have substituted your reference to Daudet in place of de Maupassant. The marriage and burial services have been straightened

---

[1]   *the temple ceremonial from Aida*: a reference to Act I of Giuseppe Verdi's opera *Aida* (1871) in which Egyptian priests consecrate Radamès' sword in preparation for the ensuing battle with Ethiopia.

out. This error has added greatly to my daily correspondence!

[Source: Edith Wharton Collection, Yale Collection of American Literature, Beinecke Rare Book and Manuscript Library.]

9. From Edith Wharton to Rutger B. Jewett (excerpt), February 7, 1921.

In view of the continued success of the book, and of the foolish letters which your [*sic*] are receiving, I am almost inclined to write a short preface for the next edition, explaining:

1. That owing to the printing strikes the proofs reached me so late that I was obliged to revise them in great haste.
2. That what I was trying to do, and what I believe every novelist who write [*sic*] an "historic" novel should do, was to evoke the intellectual, moral, and artistic atmosphere not of one year but of ten years: that is to say my allusions range from, say, 1875 to 1885. Any narrower field of evocation must necessarily reduce the novel to a piece of archaeological pedantry instead of a living image of the times.

I have never written a preface to one of my novels, or publicly discussed my methods of work, but I am perfectly willing to do this if you think it advisable?
The anxious critic who thinks that the phrase "gnashing his eyeglasses" is a misprint, can never have known Mr. Roosevelt, or watched him in the course of a heated argument.

[Source: Edith Wharton Collection, Yale Collection of American Literature, Beinecke Rare Book and Manuscript Library.]

10. From Edith Wharton to Mary Cadwalader Jones (excerpt), February 17, 1921.[1]

Your letter announcing the signature of the contract with Shubert

---

[1] Wharton is responding here to news that *The Age of Innocence* had been sold to the Shubert organization for adaptation on Broadway. Zoë *Akins* was initially to write the stage version, but she ultimately did not.

has just come, & I must give you an immediate hug.—Did ever any lucky author have such a business-manager before, I wonder? As you know, I had no hopes of anything of the kind coming my way; & your news was a real surprise.

I am particularly pleased that Miss Akins intends to dramatize the book. I hope you will tell her so; & also that she will send me "Déclassée" if it has been published.

I am very anxious about the staging & dressing. I could do every stick of furniture & every rag of clothing myself, for every detail of that far-off scene was indelibly stamped on my infant brain. I am so much afraid that the young actors will be "Summit Collar" athletes, with stern jaws & shaven lips, instead of gentlemen. Of course they ought all to have moustaches, & not tooth brush ones, but curved & slightly twisted at the ends. They should wear dark grey frock-coats & tall hats, & always buttonhole-violets by day, a gardenia in evening dress. White waistcoats with their evening clothes, & pumps, *I think*. But you will remember all this as well as I do.—As for their "façons" & their language, since you say that Miss Akins knows European society, please tell her that a N.Y. drawing-room of my childhood was far more like a London one—a du Maurier[1] one of old-fashioned gentlefolk—than anything that modern N.Y. can give her. Above all, beg her to avoid slang & Americanisms, & tell her that English was then the language spoken by American ladies & gentlemen—since she is too young, I'm sure, to have known those happy days herself. Few people nowadays know that many of the young men of our day (in N.Y.) were educated in English Universities, & that English tutors & governesses were frequent & that no *girl* went to a school! If she does not know this—& does not (equally) keep away from that grotesque stage invention of "Southern chivalry"—she will never get the right atmosphere.

How thrilling if Doris Keane should do Ellen! How I wish I had seen her act. Have you any idea when they mean to bring it out? ...

Thanks for the revised copy of "The Age." I have written to Jewett suggesting that I should write a preface for the next edition, explaining under what difficulties the book was written, as regards revising & proof-correcting, & also stating my theory as to the writing of "historical" novels, & the small importance of anachronisms.

---

[1]   *a du Maurier one*: after George *du Maurier* (1834-1896), novelist, illustrator, and contributor to *Punch* for over 30 years; author of *Trilby* (1894).

[Source: *The Letters of Edith Wharton*, eds. R.W.B. Lewis and Nancy Lewis (New York: Macmillan, 1988), 439-440.]

11. From Edith Wharton to Sinclair Lewis (excerpt), August 6, 1921.

Your letter touched me very deeply; & I should have told you so sooner if it hadn't gone to America (where I have not been since the war), & then travelled back to me here.

What you say is so kind, so generous & so unexpected, that I don't know where to begin to answer. It is the first sign I have ever had—literally—that "les jeunes"[1] at home had ever read a word of me. I had long since resigned myself to the idea that I was regarded by you all as the—say the Mrs. Humphry Ward[2] of the Western Hemisphere; though at times I wondered why. Your book & Susan Lenox (unexpurgated) have been the only things out of America that have made me cease to despair of the republic—of letters; so you can imagine what a pleasure it is to know that you have read *me*, & cared, & understood....

As for the Columbia Prize, the kind Appletons have smothered me in newspaper commentary; & when I discovered that I was being rewarded—by one of our leading Universities—for uplifting American morals, I confess I *did* despair.—Hope returns to me, however, with your letter, & with the enclosed article, just received.— Some sort of standard *is* emerging from the welter of cant & sentimentality, & if two or three of us are gathered together, I believe we can still save fiction in America.

[Source: *The Letters of Edith Wharton*, eds. R.W.B. Lewis and Nancy Lewis (New York: Macmillan, 1988), 445.]

---

[1] "*les jeunes*": French for "the young people."

[2] *Mrs. Humphrey Ward*: Mary Augusta Ward (1851-1920), British novelist, philanthropist, and author of twenty-five novels including *Robert Elsmere* (1888). Though Wharton was on good terms with her, she is associated here with an outmoded Victorian culture.

Appendix C: Contemporary Reviews

[The reviews re-printed below represent a cross section of initial opinion about the novel chosen not only for their typical or idiosyncratic insights into the novel, but for the views of the author and her work that they reflected, shaped, and circulated. Of considerable interest are opinions penned by figures who would have a significant impact on American literary history. Thus the young Edmund Wilson's very positive review is especially remarkable in light of the stature he would attain as one of the premier critics representing a generation receptive to modernist experimentation and political change (he would temper his enthusiasm for Wharton in later years). So is Gilbert Seldes's astute review in the *Dial*, a little magazine devoted to innovation in the literary arts: Seldes would be instrumental in publishing T.S. Eliot's *The Waste Land* in its pages in the near future. Vernon Parrington's ultimately negative assessment of Wharton's art is founded on the progressivist premises that would inform his briefly influential *Main Currents in American Thought* (1927-1930): namely, that a genuinely democratic (and superior) literature is that which represents panoramically the lives and struggles of ordinary, working Americans. The reviews selected below reveal that Parrington's view of Wharton as out of touch with contemporary American life was atypical. The best contemporary reviews saw her portrait of an older America as an oblique reflection on the American present; and collectively they testify to the very high esteem in which Wharton's satirical and formally nuanced art was held by serious readers.]

1. Edmund Wilson, "Edith Wharton," 1921.

Has Mrs. Wharton ever been given her rightful place as the foremost of living American novelists and one of the foremost living novelists of the world? I have seen very little intelligent criticism of her by American and none by English critics. The best discussion of her novels I have ever read was written by a Frenchman,—M. Régis Michaud, in his *Réalistes et Mystiques Anglo-Saxons*. In America she is commonly regarded as a sort of super-Robert W. Chambers, preoccupied exclusively with the lives of very smart and very rich people,—though *Ethan Frome* and *Summer* and *Bunner Sisters* are there to prove that she is interested in people of all sorts and though the four of her major novels which do deal with the rich cover entirely different areas of society.

But really she is the only one of our novelists whose work, for intensity and finish, stands comparison with the best fiction of England and France. She is the only one who combines thorough knowledge of a section of the national life with a brilliant and polished style and an expert mastery of form. Has Thomas Hardy ever done anything better than *Ethan Frome* or Anatole France any satire that was truer to France than *The Custom of the Country* is to America?

The hardness and insistence on material things that people object to in her novels are the hardness and materialism of New York and New England themselves. What could be more like New York than Mrs. Wharton's novels about it? Like New York, they are full of glitter and exasperated nerves, luxurious and unlovely appointments and unpicturesque sordidness. Was Thackeray more of London or Balzac of Paris? She has been accused of being snobbish; but in regard to money and social distinction, no one could be less snobbish. She is really a bitter intellectual snob toward both money and society. Her novels about New York are written with a corrosive scorn which sees the soul and intelligence of men ground down and finally destroyed by the weight of material possessions and the pressure of money-getting.

And in her most recently published novel, *The Age of Innocence*, she has delivered an even more drastic judgment than she has ever done before. It is true that *The Age of Innocence* has not the intensity of her earlier work and that its style is feebler and less sharp; one suspects that her mastery of English has begun to disintegrate a little through her long residence in France. But as an intrepid examination of American manners and morals she has, I think, never equalled it. *The Custom of the Country* and *The House of Mirth* attack the *nouveau riche* America a little from the point of view of Washington Square,—from the point of view of the older class who had at least some education and taste. But *The Age of Innocence* attacks the tradition of the people of education and taste from the point of view of the artist and the citizen of the world.

In this severest of American novels, Mrs. Wharton makes no respectable assumptions; she begins by accepting no conventions. The old tradition, with its provincialism and prudery and hollowness, with its abject slavery to custom and its lack of intellectual curiosity, is exhibited as no less cruel than the grosser world which supplanted it: in it every brave passion is smothered, every impulse toward beauty extinguished; the potentially superior man is strangled in an all-embracing mesh of idiotic conventions. There is nothing but respectability,—the fear of not being respectable.

And *The Age of Innocence* is not merely a picture of a world which is obsolete: we are all of us living to a great extent in the air of that inherited tradition. By showing it in its pure state, when nothing else had broken in on it, Mrs. Wharton is able to make it so monstrous that the most conventional of readers cannot help but shudder at it. But it is really, in its cruder form, our master and our tyrant still. Newland Archer, the extraordinary man who always does the ordinary thing, is still an American figure: the universities are full of him; he hears echoes from strange lands of freedom and romance and for a moment one catches in his eyes the reflected splendour of their light; then he marries some stupid woman, decides to make a great deal of money and lives and dies as a supporter of our commercial civilization. Mrs. Wharton should have written at the end of her novel: *De te, fabula!*[1]

[Source: "Things I Consider Underrated: Three Little Essays in Constructive Criticism," *Vanity Fair* 16 (March 1921), 38.]

2. Vernon L. Parrington, "Our Literary Aristocrat," 1921.

The note of distinction is as natural to Edith Wharton as it is rare in our present day literature. She belongs to the "quality," and the grand manner is hers by right of birth. She is as finished as a Sheraton sideboard, and, with her poise, grace, high standards, and perfect breeding, she suggests as inevitably old wine and slender decanters. The severe ethical code which Puritanism has bequeathed to her, and the keen intellect which has made her a critical analyst, increase her native distinction; and the irony that plays lambently over her commentary, adds piquancy to her art. She belongs to an earlier age, before a strident generation had come to deny the excellence of standards. No situation which she has conceived in her novels is so ironical as the situation in which she herself is placed;

---

[1] *De te, fabula!*: Latin for "the story is about you!".

shaken out of an unquestioned acceptance of the aristocratic world to which she belongs, she turns her keen analysis upon her environment, and satirizes what in her heart she loves most.

The Age of Innocence is perfect Whartonian. It is historical satire done with immaculate art, but though she laughs at the deification of "form" by the van der Luydens of Skuytercliff, and the tyranny of their rigid social taboos, she loves them too well to suffer them to be forgotten by a careless generation. She has painted them at full length, to hang upon our walls, where they lend historical dignity to the background of the present and utter a silent reproof to our scrambling vulgarities. New York society of the eighteen seventies, with its little clan of first families that gently simmers in its own dullness—it would be inelegant to say stews—provides a theme that exactly suits Mrs. Wharton's talent. She delights in the make-believe of the clan, in "the Pharisaic voice of a society wholly absorbed in barricading itself against the unpleasant," and she half regrets an age whose innocence "seals the mind against imagination and the heart against experience." She herself, of course, will not defend herself against reality by a decorous denial, but she likes too well many things in that world to be harsh or angry with it. Against this background of the clan she projects three figures who come perilously near to realizing a quite vulgar situation. Between May Welland, physically magnificent but mentally equipped with no more than the clan negations, and Ellen Olenska, a clan member who has freed herself from its provincialisms by a European experience that ends in separation from her Polish husband, and whose "disgrace" rocks New York society till the clan rallies to her defense, stands Newland Archer, a third member of the clan, who has played with books and ideas without liberating his mind, who is shocked into naturalness by the more vital Ellen, endeavours to break the ties of clan convention, but is held fast and ends his rebellion in a mood of ironic abnegation. There are no scenes, no vulgar jealousies or accusations, nothing to offend the finest sensibility. A few frank phrases sound almost startling in their context of reticent pretense, but they do not really startle. The book unwinds slowly, somewhat meagrely, with much analysis and little vivacity of conversation. In an environment of dull and selfish respectability, how could there be vivacity; with no ideas, no spontaneity, no intellectual sincerity, it is idle to expect vivacity. The formal routine and hinting gossip wrap themselves like a boa constrictor about the characters and squeeze the naturalness out of them. Nevertheless the story never lags and is never dull. The skill with which dulness is made interesting is a triumph of art.

But when one has said that the craftsmanship is a very great success, why not go further and add that it doesn't make the slightest difference whether one reads the book or not, unless one is a literary epicure who lives for the savor of things. What do the van der Luydens matter to us; or what did they or their kind matter a generation ago? Why waste such skill upon such insignificant material? There were vibrant realities in the New York of the seventies, Commodore Vanderbilt, for example, or even Jay Gould or Jim Fiske.[1] If Mrs. Wharton had only chose to throw such figures upon her canvas, brutal, cynical, dominating, what a document of American history—but the suggestion is foolish. Mrs. Wharton could not do it. Her distinction is her limitation. She loathes the world of Jim Fiske too much to understand it. She is too well bred to be a snob, but she escapes it only by sheer intelligence. The background of her mind, the furniture of her habits, are packed with potential snobbery, and it is only by scrupulous care that it is held in leash. She is unconsciously shut in behind plate glass, where butlers serve formal dinners, and white shoulders go up at the mere suggestion of everyday gingham. She belongs in spite of herself to the caste which she satirizes, and she cannot make herself at home in households where the mother washes the dishes and the father tends the furnace. If she had lived less easily, if she had been forced to skimp and save and plan, she would have been a greater and richer artist, more significant because more native, more continental. But unfortunately her doors open only to the smart set; the windows from which she surveys life open only to the east, to London, Paris, Rome. She is one of our cosmopolitans, flitting lightly about and at ease with all who bear titles. And this the stay-at-home American secretly resents. What are titles to him, and for that matter, what are the vulgar rich of New York? Let the newspapers exploit them, for that becomes their vulgarity. But for Mrs. Wharton to spend her talents upon rich nobodies is no less than sheer waste.

---

[1] *Commodore* Cornelius *Vanderbilt* (1794-1877), American railroad tycoon, who became the president of the New York Central Railroad in 1867, later consolidated three other railroads into a more efficient system, and built Grand Central Depot in 1871. *Jay Gould* (1836-1892) and *Jim Fiske* (1834-1872), American financiers and speculators, fought Vanderbilt for control of the Erie Railroad in the 1860s and won. Gould and Fiske's names have come to represent the rapacious capitalism and the political corruption of the Gilded Age.

Since we are quarreling with Mrs. Wharton let us go through with it and suggest another irritation that arises from less creditable, but quite human sources. She unconsciously irritates because she reveals so unobtrusively how much she knows and how perfect is her breeding. She pricks one's complacency with such devastating certainty; reveals so cruelly one's plebeian limitations. Her readers are always on pins and needles not to appear out of her class. It is impossible to be easy and slouchy in presence of her poise, and it is hard on us not to let down occasionally. We cannot always be mentally on the alert. It was inevitable, to fall back upon an illustration, that her dilettante hero should have gone in for Eastlake furniture, as Mrs. Wharton assures us that he did. But the easy way in which she assumes that the reader will understand her casual reference to Sir Charles's endeavour to revive a "sincere" furniture, puts one scrambling to recall that Eastlakeism was the polite counterpart, in the seventies, of the robust rebellions of William Morris against a dowdy Victorianism.[1] If Mrs. Wharton had only let slip the fact that she once wrote a book on household decoration, and "got up" on the Eastlake movement, it would have reassured us, and made us feel that she is a common mortal like the rest of us who have to "get up" on things. Which criticism, of course, arises from mere petulancy and self-conceit.

With her ripe culture, her clear and clean intelligence, her classical spirit, her severe standards and austere ethics, Mrs. Wharton is our outstanding literary aristocrat. She has done notable things, but she has paid a great price in aloofness from her own America. There is more hope for our literature in the honest crudities of the younger naturalists, than in her classic irony; they at least are trying to understand America as it is. "You'll never amount to anything, any of you, till you roll up your sleeves and get right down into the muck," commented the one plebeian in the book to Newland Archer, who "mentally shrugged his shoulders and turned the conversations to books." Mrs. Wharton too often mentally shrugs her shoulders over America. That she should ever roll up her sleeves and get down into the muck is unthinkable.

[Source: *Pacific Review* 2 (June 1921), 157-160.]

---

[1]   On *Eastlake* furniture and *Sir Charles* Eastlake, see Chapter IX of Wharton's text, p. 112, note 1; on *William Morris*, see Chapter XII, p. 137, note 2.

3. Henry Seidel Canby, "Our America" (excerpt), 1920.

The only objection I have ever heard urged against Mrs. Wharton's fine art of narrative is that it is narrow—an art of dress suit and sophistication. And this book is the answer. For, of course, her art is narrow—like Jane Austen's, like Sheridan's, like Pope's, like Maupassant's, like that of all writers who prefer to study human nature in its most articulate instead of its best or its broadest manifestations.[1] It is narrow because it is focussed, but this does not mean that it is small. The story of "The Age of Innocence" could be set in a far broader background. It is the circumstances of the New York society which Mrs. Wharton knows so well that give it a piquancy, a reality that "epics" lack. They are like the accidents of voice, eye, gesture which determine individuality. But her subject is America.

This treating of large themes by highly personal symbols makes possible Mrs. Wharton's admirable perfection of technique. Hers is the technique of sculpture rather than the technique of architecture. It permits the fine play of a humor that has an eye of irony in it, but is more human than irony. It makes possible an approach to perfection....

Her art is restrained, focussed upon those points where America, in its normality and in its eccentricity, has become articulate. Therefore it is sharp and convincing.

Who is the central figure in this story of the leaven of intellectual and emotional unrest, working in a society that has perfected its code and intends to live by it? Is it Newland Archer, who bears the uncomfortable ferment within him? Is it his wife, the lovely May, whose clear blue eyes will see only innocence? Is it the Countess Olenska, the American who has seen reality and suffered by it, and sacrifices her love for Newland in order to preserve his innocence? It is none of these, but rather the "family," moral according to its lights, provincial, narrow—but intensely determined that its world shall appear upright, faithful, courageous, in despite of facts and regardless of how poor

---

[1]   *Jane Austen* (1775-1817), British novelist, author of *Pride and Prejudice* (1813) and *Emma* (1816). Richard Brinsley *Sheridan* (1751-1816), Irish-born playwright, most famous for *The School for Scandal* (1777). Alexander *Pope* (1688-1744), British poet and satirist, author of *The Rape of the Lock* (1712 and 1714) and *An Essay on Man* (1733-34).

reality must be tortured into conformity. And the "family" is just the bourgeois Puritanism of nineteenth century America.

Was May right when, with the might of innocence, she forced Newland to give up life for mere living? Was the Countess right when in spite of her love for him she aided and abetted her, making him live up to the self-restraint that belonged to his code? The story does not answer, being concerned with the qualities of the "family," not with didacticism.

It says that the insistent innocence of America had its rewards as well as its penalties. It says, in so far as it states any conclusion definitely, that the new and less trammelled generation must answer whether it was the discipline of the parents that saved it from anarchy, or the suppressions of its parents that made it rebellious. And the answer is not yet.

A fine novel, beautifully written, "big" in the best sense, which has nothing to do with size, a credit to American literature—for if its author is cosmopolitan, her novel, as much as "Ethan Frome," is a fruit of the soil.

[Source: *New York Evening Post*, 6 November, 1920, "Literary Review," 3.]

4. C. V. D. [Carl Van Doren], "An Elder America" (excerpt), 1920.

We can no more do without some notion or other of an age more golden than our own than we can do without bread. There must be, we assure ourselves, a more delectable day yet to come, or there must have been one once. The evidence of prophecy, however, is stronger than that of history, which, somehow, fails to find the perfect age. Mrs. Wharton has never ranged herself with the prophets, contented, apparently, with being the most intellectual of our novelists and surveying with level, satirical eyes the very visible world. By "The Age of Innocence" she means the seventies in New York during the past century; and the innocence she finds there is "the innocence that seals the mind against imagination and the heart against experience." To the hotter attacks which angrier critics have recently been making upon that age she does not lend herself. Her language is cool and suave. And yet the effect of her picture is an unsparing accusation of that genteel decade when the van der Luydens of Skuytercliff were the ultimate arbiters of "form" in Manhattan, and "form" was occupation and religion for the little aristocracy which still held its tight fortress in the shaggy city so soon about to overwhelm it. The imminence of the rising tide is never quite indicated. How could it be, when the characters of the action themselves do not see it, bound up as they are with walking their wintry paths and hugging their iron taboos? Newland Archer suspects a change, but that is because he is a victim of the tribal order which sentences him to a life without passion, without expression, without satisfaction. The Countess Olenska suspects it, but she too is a victim, too fine for the rougher give-and-take of her husband's careless European society and yet not conventional enough for the dull routine which in her native New York covers the fineness to which also she is native. The peculiar tragedy of their sacrifice is that it is for the sake of a person, Archer's wife, who is virtuous because she is incapable of any deep perturbation, and willing to suit herself to the least decorum of their world because she is incapable of understanding that there is anywhere anything larger or freer. The unimaginative not only miss the flower of life themselves but they shut others from it as well.

Mrs. Wharton's structure and methods show no influence of the impressionism now broadening the channel of fiction; she does not avoid one or two touches of the florid in her impassioned scenes; she rounds out her story with a reminiscent chapter which forces in the note of elegy where it only partially belongs. But "The Age of Innocence" is a masterly achievement. In lonely contrast to almost all the novelists who write about fashionable New York, she knows her world. In lonely contrast to the many who write about what they know without understanding it or interpreting it, she brings a superbly critical disposition to arrange her knowledge in significant forms. These characters who move with such precision and veracity through the ritual of a frozen caste are here as real as their actual lives would ever have let them be. They are stiff with ceremonial garments and heavy with the weight of imagined responsibilities. Mrs. Wharton's triumph is that she has described these rites and surfaces and burdens as familiarly as if she loved them and as lucidly as if she hated them.

[Source: *The Nation* III (3 November 1920), 510.]

5. William Lyon Phelps, "As Mrs. Wharton Sees Us" (excerpt), 1920.

The style of "The Age of Innocence" is filled with the "silver correspondences" spoken of by Henry James; and the book would be a solid satisfaction, as it is an exquisite delight, had the writer only possessed the homeliness, the rugged simplicity that is lost under the enamel of finished sophistication....

Yet I am in no mood to complain. Edith Wharton is a writer who brings glory on the name America, and this is her best book....

Here is a novel whose basis is a story. It begins on a night at the opera. The characters are introduced naturally—every action and every conversation advance the plot. The style is a thing of beauty from first page to last. One dwells with pleasure on the "exquisite moments" of passion and tragedy, and on the "silver correspondences" that rise from the style like the moon on a cloudless night.

New York society and customs in the seventies are described with an accuracy that is almost uncanny; to read these pages is to live again. The absolute imprisonment in which her characters stagnate, their artificial and false standards, the desperate monotony of trivial routine, the slow petrifaction of generous ardours, the paralysis of emotion, the accumulation of ice around the heart, the total loss of life in upholstered existence—are depicted with a high excellence that never falters. And in the last few pages the younger generation comes in like fresh air. Mrs. Wharton is all for the new and against the old; here, at all events, her sympathies are warm....

The two young women of the story are contrasted in a manner that is the essence of drama without being in the least artificial. The radiantly beautiful young wife might have had her way without a shadow on it, were it not for the appearance of the Countess Olenska, who is, what the other women are not, a personality. Newland Archer, between these two women, and loved by both, is not at all to be envied. The love scenes between him and Ellen are wonderful in their terrible, inarticulate passion; it is curious how much more real they are than the unrestrained detailed descriptions thought by so many writers to be "realism." Here is where Mrs. Wharton resembles Joseph Conrad[1] and Henry James, for the love

---

[1] *Joseph Conrad* (1857-1924), Polish-born English novelist, author of *Lord Jim* (1900) and *Nostromo* (1904).

scenes in this book are full worthy of those two men of genius. So little is said, so little is done, yet one feels the infinite passion in the finite hearts that burn. I wonder what old Browning would have thought of this frustration; for the story is not altogether unlike "The Statue and the Bust."[1]

I do not believe I shall ever forget three scenes between Archer and Ellen—the "outing" at Boston, the night carriage drive from the ferry in New York, and the interview in the corner of the Museum of Art, with its setting of relics. These are scenes of passion that Conrad, or Henry James, yes, that Turgenev[2] might have written.

I wonder if the horrible moment when Newland Archer, looking at his incomparably lovely and devoted young wife, suddenly has the diabolical wish that she were dead, is a reminiscence of Mrs. Wharton's early studies of Sudermann.[3]...

The harmony of Mrs. Wharton's management of English sentences is so seldom marred that I wish she would change this phrase, the only discord I found in the book: "varied by an occasional dance at the primitive inn when a man-of-war came in."

And is not Guy de Maupassant out of place in the early seventies? ... I suppose Mrs. Wharton knows her Maupassant thoroughly; but unless I am quite at fault, it was not in the early seventies, but in the early eighties, that his tales began to appear.

But these are flecks. The appearance of such a book as "The Age of Innocence" by an American is a matter for public rejoicing. It is one of the best novels of the twentieth century and looks like a permanent addition to literature.

[Source: *The New York Times Book Review and Magazine*, Sect. 3 (17 October 1920), 1, 11.]

---

1 *The Statue and the Bust*: poem by Robert Browning about the frustrated love between the Grand Duke of Florence, Ferdinand de Medici, and his lover, locked inside a palace by her jealous husband. The Duke commissions a statue to eternally watch his lover's window, while Browning imagines the imprisoned lover commissioning a bust of herself to watch the statue.

2 Ivan Sergievich *Turgenev* (1818–1883), Russian novelist, author of *Fathers and Sons* (1862) and *Virgin Soil* (1877).

3 Hermann *Sudermann* (1857–1928), German novelist and playwright, author of *Magda* (1892) and *Die Ehre* (1880). Wharton translated Sudermann's *Es Lebe das Leben* (*The Joy of Living*) in 1902 as a favour to an actress friend who had the rights to the play.

6. *Times Literary Supplement* reviewer, "The Age of Innocence" (excerpt), 1920.

Mrs. Wharton's new book, her first "full-length" novel for some years, is perhaps a sign of the times. When the war broke in upon the settled, accepted "present day" of the novelists, it was easy to foresee the predicament in which they would find themselves before long. Since 1914 there has been no present day, in the old sense. Now we must know from the start whether we are dealing with the world before or during or since the war, and the action must be precisely timed; any and every novel, in other words, is bound to be now "historic." And since it is a hazardous venture to set about treating very recent times historically—it needs a great deal of information or a great deal of assurance to move upon that *cineri doloso*[1]—it was probable that a writer like Mrs. Wharton, critical of the impressions of life, should hesitate to use the crude new material of 1920, while it is still daily shifting and cracking before our eyes. And so she goes back—back to the old world, and far enough into it to make the action of her story openly historic; she goes as far back as the early seventies, in fact, and to that New York of the early seventies which is now so much more remote, as it happens, than even our own past of that day, over here. Changes of the same general kind we too have seen, no doubt, but nothing to compare in extent with the change that has turned New York, socially speaking, from a trim and substantial old family mansion to a resounding, glittering, promiscuous monster hotel.

[Source: *Times Literary Supplement* [England], 25 November 1920, 775.]

7. Gilbert Seldes, "The Last Stand" (excerpt), 1921.

[Review of The Age of Innocence alongside John Galsworthy's In Chancery.]

What concerns me most is not the separate value of these novels in themselves. They impress me rather gallantly as the last stand of the old order of novelists. When Mrs. Wharton and Mr. Galsworthy betrayed their talents (or, let us say, had an off year) they did not utilize their weakness by experimenting in fiction. (They actually wrote very bad

---

[1] *cineri doloso*: Latin for "sad ash."

magazine stories in part, and did war work of various sorts.) If one has written novels rather finely in one tradition it is probably perilous to try another. There was the documentary fashion—it is almost *the* manner of the younger English novelists and is becoming our own—the manner of say Romain Rolland and Compton Mackenzie; or that of May Sinclair's Romantic, of Winifred Bryher's Development; of Dorothy Richardson; or James Joyce.[1] The art of the novel is going through its *Sturm und Drang*;[2] it will never be as it has been and one is tempted to impatience with those who practise it in the least exciting of its forms. Unfairly tempted, because their form—especially Mrs. Wharton's adaptation of it—has not only its place, but a definite freshness and validity.

It is, in brief, the novel as written by Henry James—the novel which is *composed*, with a definite centre of interest, a defined progression in scenes, a planned incidence of stress: it is the novel in which everything that has bearing *must* be put in and everything else *must* be left out. It is, I suppose, the art-novel. If you find, as I do, that that is the method which gives the highest degree of satisfaction, which gives the sense of life at its most vivid and the sense of beauty at its most profound, you will be glad that its enormous difficulties have not deterred Mrs. Wharton from clinging to it, and you will rejoice in the felicities which the method allows her. No doubt, the novel of the immediate future will not be cast in this mould. No doubt that writers of far less delicacy than Mr. Galsworthy will attempt it and, in a way, belittle it. I am inclined to think that it will remain—not as a dead formula, but as a living, a classic, form. For I have never heard it assailed except on the ground

---

[1]   *Romain Rolland* (1866-1944), prolific French novelist, author of *Jean-Christophe* (1904-1912), for which he won the Nobel Prize in Literature in 1915. Sir Edward Montague *Compton Mackenzie* (1883-1972), British novelist and journalist, author of *Sinister Street* (1913). *May Sinclair* (1863-1946), British novelist who was an early proponent of both the stream of consciousness and the psychological novel, author of *The Three Sisters* (1914) and *Mary Oliver* (1919). *Winifred* Ellerman, otherwise known as Bryher (1894-1983), British novelist, author of *Development* (1919). *Dorothy Richardson* (1873-1957), British novelist and journalist, author of *Pilgrimage*, a collection of thirteen autobiographical novels (1915-1938) written in a stream of consciousness style. *James Joyce* (1882-1941), Irish novelist, author of such major modernist texts as *A Portrait of the Artist as a Young Man* (1916) and *Ulysses* (1922), the latter of which recreates in intricate detail and various styles one day in the life of two men in Dublin.

[2]   *Sturm und Drang*: German for "storm and stress."

that it is not realistic, not true to life, not in keeping with the spirit of our time. And that objection, I am afraid, will have to be overruled as irrelevant.

[Source: *The Dial* 70 (March 1921), 340–342.]

Appendix D: From "A Little Girl's New York"

[Wharton wrote her last autobiographical piece "A Little Girl's New York" near the end of her life; it was published in 1938 shortly after her death. Along with the unpublished manuscript "Life and I," it reveals the powerful hold Wharton's early girlhood in New York City continued to have on her imagination, even after she had re-visited it so extensively in *The Age of Innocence* and *A Backward Glance*. She justified her return to the scene of her girlhood only a few years after the latter work appeared, by insisting hyperbolically that, given the social and political convulsions of the mid-1930s, "the change between the customs of my youth and the world of even ten years ago [is] a mere crack in the ground compared with the chasm now dividing that world from the present one."]

Those were the days—à propos of Fifth Avenue—when my mother used to say: "Society is completely changed nowadays. When I was first married we knew everyone who kept a carriage."

And this tempts me to another digression, sending me forward to my seventeenth year, when there suddenly appeared in Fifth Avenue a very small canary-yellow brougham with dark trimmings, drawn by a big high-stepping bay and driven by a coachman who matched the brougham in size and the high-stepper in style. In this discreet yet brilliant equipage one just caught a glimpse of a lady whom I faintly remember as dark-haired, quietly dressed, and enchantingly pale, with a hat-brim lined with cherry color, which shed a lovely glow on her cheeks. It was an apparition surpassing in elegance and mystery any that Fifth Avenue had ever seen; but when our dark-blue brougham encountered the yellow one, and I cried: "Oh, Mamma, look—what a smart carriage! Do you know the lady?" I was hurriedly drawn back with the stern order not to stare at strange people and to remember that whenever our carriage passed the yellow one I was to turn my head away and look out of the other window.

For the lady in the canary-colored carriage was New York's first fashionable hetaera.[1] Her name and history were known in all the

---

[1]   *hetaera*: Greek for "female companion or paramour."

clubs, and the name of her proud proprietor was no secret in New York drawing-rooms. I may add that, being an obedient daughter, I always thereafter *did* look out of the other window when the forbidden brougham passed; but that one and only glimpse of the loveliness within it peopled my imagination with images of enchantment from Broceliande and Shalott (we were all deep in the "Idylls of the King"), and from the Cornwall of Yseult.[1] She was, in short, sweet unsuspecting creature, my first doorway to romance, destined to become for me successively Guinevere and Francesca da Rimini, Beatrix Esmond and the *Dame aux Camélias*.[2] And in the impoverished emotional atmosphere of old New York such a glimpse was like the marriage of palm trees in the desert.

I have often sighed, in looking back at my childhood, to think how pitiful a provision was made for the life of the imagination behind those uniform brownstone façades, and then have concluded that since, for reasons which escape us, the creative mind thrives best on a reduced diet, I probably had the fare best suited to me. But this is not to say that the average well-to-do New Yorker of my child-hood was not starved for a sight of the high gods. Beauty, passion, and danger were automatically excluded from his life (for the men were almost as starved as the women); and the average human being deprived of air from the heights is likely to produce other lives equally starved, which was what happened in old New York, where the tepid sameness of the moral atmosphere resulted in a prolonged immaturity of mind.

But we must return to the brownstone houses, and penetrate from the vestibule (painted in Pompeian red, and frescoed with a

---

[1] In Arthurian legend, the forest of *Broceliande* in Brittany is the place where Vivien enchanted Merlin; *Shalott*, home of the Lady of Shalott in Alfred, Lord Tennyson's poem by that name and later *The Idylls of the King*, the isolated lady who lives on an island until she gazes directly at Sir Lancelot and dies. *Cornwall of Iseult*: alludes to the medieval story of the ill-starred lovers Tristam and Isolde (Iseult).

[2] *Guinevere*: the wife of King Arthur and the lover of Launcelot, whose story is recounted in Tennyson's *Idylls of the King*; *Francesca da Rimini*, sentenced to death for her adulterous love affair with Paolo, her husband's brother, who, in the fifth canto of Dante's *Inferno*, tells Dante that she was influenced by the story of Launcelot and Guinevere; *Beatrix Esmond*, the wilful daughter of Viscount Castlewood in William Makepeace Thackeray's 1852 novel, *The History of Henry Esmond, Esquire*; *La Dame aux Camélias*, heroine of Alexandre Dumas fils's 1848 novel of the same name, a Parisienne courtier who enjoys a brief but doomed love affair with Armand Duval.

frieze of stencilled lotus-leaves, taken from Owen Jones's *Grammar of Ornament*)[1] into the carefully guarded interior. What would the New Yorker of the present day say to those interiors, and the lives lived in them? Both would be equally unintelligible to any New Yorker under fifty.

Beyond the vestibule (in the average house) was a narrow drawing-room. Its tall windows were hung with three layers of curtains: sash-curtains through which no eye from the street could possibly penetrate, and next to these draperies of lace or embroidered tulle, richly beruffled, and looped back under the velvet or damask hangings which were drawn in the evening. This window garniture always seemed to me to symbolize the super-imposed layers of under-garments worn by the ladies of the period—and even, alas, by the little girls. They were in fact almost purely a symbol, for in many windows even the inner "sash-curtains" were looped back far enough to give the secluded dwellers a narrow glimpse of the street; but no self-respecting mistress of a house (a brownstone house) could dispense with this triple display of window-lingerie, and among the many things I did which pained and scandalized my Bostonian mother-in-law, she was not least shocked by the banishment from our house in the country of all the thicknesses of muslin which should have intervened between ourselves and the robins on the lawn.

The brownstone drawing-room was likely to be furnished with monumental pieces of modern Dutch marquetry, among which there was almost always a cabinet with glazed doors for the display of "bric-à-brac." Oh, that bric-à-brac! Our mothers, who prided themselves on the contents of these cabinets, really knew about only two artistic productions—old lace and old painted fans. With regard to these the eighteenth-century tradition was still alive, and in nearly every family there were yards and yards of precious old lace and old fans of ivory, chicken-skin, or pale tortoise-shell, exquisitely carved and painted. But as to the other arts a universal ignorance prevailed, and the treasures displayed in the wealthiest houses were no better than those of the average brownstone-dweller.

My mother had a collection of old lace which was famous

---

[1] *The Grammar of Ornament* (1856), a resource book for designers featuring a review of ornamental motifs from the ancient world to the Renaissance, by *Owen Jones* (1809–1874), British architect and designer, superintendent of works at the Great Exhibition of 1851.

among her friends, and a few fragments of it still remain to me, piously pinned up in the indigo-blue paper supposed (I have never known why) to be necessary to the preservation of fine lace. But the yards are few, alas; for true to my conviction that what was made to be used should be used, and not locked up, I have outlived many and many a yard of noble *point de Milan*, of stately Venetian point, of shadowy Mechlin, and exquisitely flowered *point de Paris*, not to speak of the delicate Valenciennes which ruffled the tiny handkerchiefs and incrusted and edged the elaborate *lingerie* of my youth. Nor do I regret having worn out what was meant to be worn out. I know few sadder sights than Museum collections of these Arachne-webs[1] that were designed to borrow life and color from the nearness of young flesh and blood. Museums are cemeteries, as unavoidable, no doubt, as the other kind, but just as unrelated to the living beauty of what we have loved.

I have said that the little brown houses, marching up Fifth Avenue like disciplined schoolgirls, now and then gave way to a more important façade, sometimes of their own chocolate hue, but with occasional pleasing alternatives in brick. Many successive Fifth Avenues have since been erected on the site of the one I first knew, and it is hard to remember that none of the "new" millionaire houses which, ten or fifteen years later, were to invade that restless thoroughfare (and all of which long ago joined the earlier layers of ruins) had been dreamed of by the boldest innovator. Even the old families, who were subsequently to join the newcomers in transforming Fifth Avenue into a street of would-be palaces, were still content with plain wide-fronted houses, mostly built in the 'forties or 'fifties. In those simple days one could count on one's two hands the New York houses with ballrooms: to the best of my recollection, only the Goelets, Astors, Butler Duncans, Belmonts, Schermerhorns, and Mason Joneses possessed these frivolous appendages; though a few years later, by the time I made my first curtsy at the "Assemblies," several rich couples, the Mortons, Waterburys, Coleman Draytons, and Francklyns among them, had added ballrooms to their smart establishments.

In the smaller houses a heavy linen called "crash," laid on the

---

[1] *Arachne-webs*: after Arachne, who in classical mythology challenged Athena to a weaving contest and was changed into a spider for her presumption.

floors of two adjoining drawing-rooms, and gilt chairs hired from "old Brown" (the Grace Church sexton, who so oddly combined ecclesiastical and worldly duties) created temporary ballrooms for small dances; but the big balls of the season (from January to Lent) were held at Delmonico's, then, if I am not mistaken, at the corner of Twenty-eighth Street and Fifth Avenue.

The Assemblies were the most important of these big balls—if the word "big" as now understood could be applied to any social event in our old New York! There were, I think, three Assemblies in the winter, presided over by a committee of ladies who delegated three of their number to receive the guests at the ballroom door. The evening always opened with a quadrille, in which the ladies of the committee and others designated by them took part; and there followed other square dances, waltzes and polkas, which went on until the announcement of supper. A succulent repast of canvasback ducks, terrapin, foie-gras, and the best champagnes was served at small tables below stairs, in what was then New York's only fashionable restaurant; after which we re-ascended to the ballroom (in a shaky little lift) to begin the complicated maneuvers of the cotillion.

The "Thursday Evening Dances," much smaller and more exclusive, were managed by a committee of the younger married women—and how many young and pretty ones there were in our little society! I cannot, oddly enough, remember where these dances were held—and who is left, I wonder, to refresh my memory? There was no Sherry's restaurant as yet, and no Waldorf-Astoria, or any kind of modern hotel with a suite for entertaining; yet I am fairly sure we did not meet at "Del's" for the "Thursday Evenings."

At all dances, large or small, a custom prevailed which caused untold misery to the less popular girls. This was the barbarous rule that if a young man asked a girl for a dance or, between dances, for a turn about the ballroom, he was obliged to keep her on his arm until another candidate replaced him; with the natural result that "to him (or rather *her*) that hath shall be given," and the wily young men risked themselves only in the vicinity of young women already provided with attendant swains. To remedy this embarrassing situation the more tactful girls always requested their partners, between dances, to bring them back to their mothers or "chaperons," a somnolent row of stout ladies in velvet and ostrich feathers enthroned on a row of settees against the ballroom walls.

The custom persisted for some years, and spoilt the enjoyment of many a "nice" girl not attractive enough to be perpetually surrounded by young men, and too proud to wish to chain at her side a dancer who might have risked captivity out of kindness of heart. I do not know when the fashion changed, and the young men were set free, for we went back to Europe when I was nineteen, and I had only brief glimpses of New York until I returned to it as a married woman.

The most conspicuous architectural break in the brownstone procession occurred where its march ended, at the awkwardly shaped entrance to the Central Park. Two of my father's cousins, Mrs. Mason Jones and Mrs. Colford Jones, bought up the last two blocks on the east side of Fifth Avenue, facing the so-called "Plaza" at the Park gates, and built thereon their houses and their children's houses; a bold move which surprised and scandalized society. Fifty-seventh Street was then a desert, and ball-goers anxiously wondered whether even the ubiquitous "Brown coupés" destined to carry home belated dancers would risk themselves so far a-field. But old Mrs. Mason Jones and her submissive cousin laughed at such apprehensions, and presently there rose before our astonished eyes a block of pale-greenish limestone houses (almost uglier than the brownstone ones) for the Colford Jones cousins, adjoining which our audacious Aunt Mary, who had known life at the Court of the Tuileries, erected her own white marble residence and a row of smaller dwellings of the same marble to lodge her progeny. The "Jones blocks" were so revolutionary that I doubt whether any subsequent architectural upheavals along that historic thoroughfare have produced a greater impression. In our little provincial town (without electricity, telephones, taxis, or cab-stands) it had seemed inconceivable that houses or habits should ever change; whereas by the time the new millionaires arrived with their palaces in their pockets Fifth Avenue had become cosmopolitan, and was prepared for anything.

[Source: Edith Wharton, "A Little Girl's New York," *Harper's Monthly Magazine* 176 (March 1938), 356-360.]

Appendix E: Wharton and Others on the Status of Women

[Wharton's relation to "feminism" remains a vexed issue. The following writings—by Theodore Roosevelt, Carrie Chapman Catt, Emma Goldman and Wharton herself—are meant to give the reader some sense of the parameters of American feminism when Wharton wrote *The Age of Innocence*. Wharton certainly would have been aware of the views of her friend, the popular ex-president Roosevelt, who thought women's suffrage compatible with the maintenance of separate spheres for men and women and the idealization of motherhood. She must likewise have known of Catt, president of the National American Woman Suffrage Association, who expressed the arguments of those mainstream feminists whose struggles helped win in 1919 a constitutional amendment guaranteeing women the right to vote. Though Wharton hardly thought of herself as a feminist and was largely indifferent to the issue of women's suffrage, she clearly represents the institution of marriage in a critical light in her novel, a critical light that uncannily resembles that cast by far more radical thinkers such as Goldman, the anarchist from New York's Lower East Side, who was deported from the United States in 1919. Wharton's own writings on women's social position from this period are ambiguous and embedded in larger cross-cultural studies. In comparing American women to French women in terms favorable to the latter, she seems to reject the language of abstract rights for a vision of social cooperation and mutual regard rooted in custom and national pride. But when recounting her visit to a Moroccan harem, she registers with barely restrained disgust and condescension the plight of women whose subjection to patriarchal law and custom seems unredeemable outside the terms of a Western enlightenment project of emancipation.]

1. Theodore Roosevelt, "Women's Rights; and the Duties of Both Men and Women" (excerpt), 1912.

The causes which brought about so much of dreadful failure and wrongdoing to alloy the benefits and advances which followed on the French Revolution were symbolized and foreshadowed in the action of the first revolutionary national legislature. The body passed with wild applause resolutions declaring that the people were to have all imaginable rights, and then voted down a resolution setting forth that the same people had grave and onerous duties. Much, indeed, has America owed to the fact that her two greatest men, Washington and Lincoln, though they did not neglect rights, were even more concerned with duties.

 I believe in woman's rights. I believe even more earnestly in the performance of duty by both men and women; for unless the average man and the average woman live lives of duty, not only our democracy but civilization itself will perish. I heartily believe in the equality of rights as between man and woman, but also in full and emphatic recognition of the fact that normally there cannot be identity of function. Indeed, there must normally be complete dissimilarity of function between them, and the effort to ignore this patent fact is silly. I believe in woman's suffrage wherever the women want it. Where they do not want it, the suffrage should not be forced upon them. I think that it would be well to let the women themselves, and only the women, vote at some special election as to whether they do or do not wish the vote as a permanent possession. In other words, this is peculiarly a case for the referendum to those most directly affected—that is, the women themselves. I believe such a referendum was held in Massachusetts, in which a majority of the women who voted, voted in favor of the ballot. But they included only about five per cent of the women who were entitled to vote, and where the vote is so light, those not voting should be held to have voted no. This was in 1895. It would be well to try the experiment again in the more doubtful States like Massachusetts or New York. I should be entirely content to abide the decision, either way; for, though I do not think that the damage prophesied from women's voting would come, or has come where it has been tried, I also think that very much less effect would be produced, one way or the other, than the enthusiasts believe. In other words, I do not regard the movement as anything like as important as either its extreme friends or extreme opponents think....

Perhaps one reason why so many men who believe as emphatically as I do in woman's full equality with man take little interest in the suffrage movement is to be found in the very unfortunate actions of certain leaders in that movement, who seem desirous of associating it with disorderly conduct in public and with thoroughly degrading and vicious assaults upon the morality and the duty of women within and without marriage.

★   ★   ★

The advocates of woman suffrage, unless they utterly and mischievously lose their perspective, will necessarily remember that the highest type of the woman of the future must be essentially identical with the highest type of the woman of the present and of the past—the wife and mother who performs the most important of all social duties with wisdom, courage, and efficiency. She is the woman who is, and always has been, and always will be the most useful and important of all the citizens of the State. No other work, done by any other woman, or by any man, is, or ever will be, as vital as hers to the well-being of society. No other work is, or ever will be, as difficult or as important. There are of course individual cases where the unmarried man or unmarried woman renders great service, just as in every efficient army there are certain men who do not carry arms and who yet render indispensable service. But exactly as in the last analysis the efficiency of the army depends primarily upon the efficiency of the average man who bears arms, so in society as a whole in the last analysis the welfare of the commonwealth rests fundamentally upon the high character of the average family—that is, upon the way in which the average father and the average mother do their duty to one another and to their children. The highest type of such family is already, in the present, of just the kind that it should be in the future. It is a partnership in which the partners are on a full equality of right, and have in common the strongest sense of duty, but in which the duties and the functions are on many points necessarily different. There should be the same level of love, of consideration, of respect and forbearance, to which each partner is bound to attain in his or her treatment of the other. Each should ever think of the rights of the other, and each should ever think of what is even more important than the rights—that is, of his or her own duties.

I believe in the movement for woman suffrage, and believe that it will ultimately succeed and will justify itself. But I regard it as of far less consequence than many another movement for the betterment of present-day conditions as affecting both men and women.... No woman will ever be developed who will stand above the highest and finest of the wives and mothers of today and of the yesterdays. The exercise of the suffrage can never be the most important of women's rights and women's duties. The vital need for women, as for men, is to war against vice, and frivolity, and cold selfishness, and timid shrinking from necessary risk and effort.

[Source: *The Outlook* 100 (3 February, 1912), 262-266.]

2. Carrie Chapman Catt, "Why the Federal Amendment?" (excerpt), 1917.

Woman suffrage is coming—no intelligent person in the United States or in the world will deny that fact. The most an intelligent opponent expects to accomplish is to postpone its establishment as long as possible. When it comes and how it will come are still open questions. Woman Suffrage by Federal Amendment is supported by seven main reasons. These main reasons are evaded or avoided; they are not answered.

1. Keeping Pace With Other Countries Demands It.

Suffrage for men and suffrage for women in other lands, with few and minor exceptions, has been granted by parliamentary act and not by referenda. By such enactment the women of Australia were granted full suffrage in Federal elections by the Federal Parliament (1902), and each state or province granted full suffrage in all other elections by act of their Provincial Parliaments. By such enactment the Isle of Man, New Zealand, Finland, Norway, Iceland and Denmark gave equal suffrage in all elections to women. By such process the Parliaments of Manitoba, Saskatchewan and Alberta gave full provincial suffrage to their women in 1916. British Columbia referred the question to the voters in 1916, but the Provincial Parliament had already extended all suffrage rights except the parliamentary vote, and both political parties lent their aid in the referendum which consequently gave a majority in every precinct on the home vote and a majority of the soldier vote was returned from Europe later. By parliamentary act all other Canadian Provinces, the Provinces of South Africa, the countries of Sweden and Great Britain have extended far more voting privileges than any woman citizen of the United States east of the Missouri River (except those of Illinois) has received.... The suffragists of France reported just before the war broke out that the French Parliament was pledged to extend universal municipal suffrage to women. Men and women of high repute say the full suffrage is certain to be extended by the British Parliament to the women of England, Scotland, Ireland and Wales soon after the close of the war and already these women have all suffrage rights except the vote for Parliamentary members. These facts are strange since it was the United States which first established general suffrage for men upon the two principles that "taxation without representation is tyranny" and that governments to be just should "derive their consent from the governed." The unanswerable logic of these two principles is responsible for the extension of suffrage to men and women the world over. In the United States, however, women are still taxed without "representation" and still live under a government to which they have given no "consent." *It is obviously unfair to subject women of this country—which boasts that it is the leader in the movement toward universal suffrage—to a longer, harder, more difficult process than has been imposed by other nations upon men or women.* American constitutions of the nation and the states have closed the door to the simple processes by which men and women of other countries have been enfranchised. An amendment to our Federal Constitution is the nearest approach to them. To deny the benefits of this method to the women of this country is to put upon them a *penalty for being Americans.*

2. Equal Rights Demand It.

Men of this country have been enfranchised by various extensions of the voting privilege but IN NO SINGLE INSTANCE were they compelled to appeal to an electorate containing groups of recently naturalized and even unnaturalized foreigners, Indians, Negroes, large numbers of illiterates, ne'er-do-wells, and drunken loafers. The Jews, denied the vote in all our colonies, and the Catholics, denied the vote in most of them, received their franchise through the revolutionary constitutions which removed all religious qualifications for the vote in a manner consistent with the self-respect of all....

The next extensions of the vote to men were made to certain tribes of Indians by act of Congress; and to the Negro by amendment to the Federal Constitution.

At least three-fourths of the present electors secured their votes through direct naturalization or that of their forefathers. Congress determines conditions of citizenship and state constitutions fix qualifications of voters. The suffrage has been "thrust upon him" without effort or even request on his part. National and State constitutions not only close to women the comparatively easy processes by which the vote was extended to men and women of other countries but also those processes by which the vote was secured to men of our own land. The simplest method now possible is by amendment of the Federal Constitution. To deny the privilege of that method to women is a discrimination against them so unjust and insufferable that no fair-minded man North or South, East or West, can logically share in the denial.

3. Relief from Unjust Constitutional Obstructions Demands It.

The constitutions of many states have provided for amendments by such difficult processes that they either have never been amended or have not been amended when the subject is in the least controversial. Their provisions not infrequently are utilized by opponents of a cause to delay action for years....

There are state constitutions so impossible of amendment that women of those states can only secure enfranchisement through Federal action and fair play demands the submission of a Federal constitutional amendment.

4. Protection from Inadequate Election Laws Demands It.

The election laws of all states make inadequate provision for safeguarding the vote on constitutional amendments. Since election laws do not protect suffrage referenda, suffragists justly demand the method prescribed by our national constitution to appeal their case from male voters at large to the higher court of Congress and the Legislatures.

5. Equal Status of Men and Women Voters Demand It.

Until the adoption of the Fourteenth Amendment the National Constitution did not discriminate against women but in Section 2 of that amendment provision was made whereby a penalty may be directed against any state which denies the right to vote to its *male inhabitants* possessed of the necessary qualifications as prescribed by nation and state. If the entire 48 states should severally enfranchise women their political status would still be inferior to that of men, since no provision for national protection in their right to vote would exist.

The women of eleven states are said to vote on equal terms with men. As a matter of fact they do not, since they not only lose their vote whenever they change their residence to any one of the 37 other states (except Illinois, where they lose only a portion of their privileges), but they enjoy no national protection in their right to vote. Women justly demand "Equal Rights for All and Special Privileges for None." ...

6. National Significance of Question Demands It.

Woman suffrage in every other country is a National question. With eleven American states and nearly half the territory of the civilized world already won; with the statement of the press still unchallenged that women voters were "the balance of power" which decided the last presidential election, the movement has reached a position of national significance in the United States. Any policy which seeks to shift responsibility or to procrastinate action, is, to use the mildest phraseology, unworthy of the Congress in whose charge the making of American political history reposes.

7. Treatment of Question Demands Intelligence.

The handicaps of a popular vote upon a question of human liberty which must be described in technical language will be clear to all who think. It is probable that at least a fourth of the voters in West Virginia, one of the recent suffrage campaign states, could not define the following words intelligently: constitution, amendment, franchise, suffrage, majority, plurality. It is probable they would succeed even less well at an attempt to give an account of the Declaration of Independence, the Revolution, Taxation without Representation, the will of the majority, popular government. Such men might make a fairly intelligent choice of men for local offices because their minds are trained to deal with persons and concrete things. They could decide between Mr. Wilson and Mr. Hughes with some discrimination, but would have slight if any knowledge of the platform upon which either stood. A referendum in many of our states, means to defer woman suffrage until the most ignorant, most narrow-minded, most un-American, are ready for it. The removal of the question to the higher court of the Congress and the Legislatures of the several states means that it will be established when the intelligent, Americanized, progressive people of the country are ready for it.

[Source: Carrie Chapman Catt, ed., *Woman Suffrage by Federal Constitutional Amendment* (New York: National Woman Suffrage Publishing Co., 1917), 1-11.]

3. Emma Goldman, "Marriage and Love," 1911.

The popular notion about marriage and love is that they are synonymous, that they spring from the same motives, and cover the same human needs. Like most popular notions this also rests not on actual facts, but on superstition.

Marriage and love have nothing in common; they are as far apart as the poles; are, in fact, antagonistic to each other. No doubt some marriages have been the result of love. Not, however, because love could assert itself only in marriage; much rather is it because few people can completely outgrow a convention. There are today large numbers of men and women to whom marriage is naught but a farce, but who submit to it for the sake of public opinion. At any rate, while it is true that some marriages are based on love, and while it is equally true that in some cases love continues in married life, I maintain that it does so regardless of marriage, and not because of it.

On the other hand, it is utterly false that love results from marriage. On rare occasions one does hear of a miraculous case of a married couple falling in love after marriage, but on close examination it will be found that it is a mere adjustment to the inevitable. Certainly the growing-used to each other is far away from the spontaneity, the intensity, and beauty of love, without which the intimacy of marriage must prove degrading to both the woman and the man.

Marriage is primarily an economic arrangement, an insurance pact. It differs from the ordinary life insurance agreement only in that it is more binding, more exacting. Its returns are insignificantly small compared with the investments. In taking out an insurance policy one pays for it in dollars and cents, always at liberty to discontinue payments. If, however, woman's premium is her husband, she pays for it with her name, her privacy, her self-respect, her very life, "until death doth part." Moreover, the marriage insurance condemns her to life-long dependency, to parasitism, to complete uselessness, individual as well as social. Man, too, pays his toll, but as his sphere is wider, marriage does not limit him as much as woman. He feels his chains more in an economic sense.

Thus Dante's motto over Inferno applies with equal force to marriage: "Ye who enter here leave all hope behind."

That marriage is a failure none but the very stupid will deny. One has but to glance over the statistics of divorce to realize how bitter a failure marriage really is. Nor will the stereotyped Philistine argument that the laxity of divorce laws and the growing looseness of woman account for the fact that: first, every twelfth marriage ends in divorce; second, that since 1870 divorces have increased from 28 to 73 for every hundred thousand population; third, that adultery, since 1867, as ground for divorce, has increased 270.8 per cent.; fourth, that desertion increased 369.8 per cent.

Added to these startling figures is a vast amount of material, dramatic and literary, further elucidating this subject. Robert Herrick, in *Together*; Pinero, in *Mid-Channel*; Eugene Walter, in *Paid in Full*,[1] and scores of other writers are discussing the barrenness, the monotony, the sordidness, the inadequacy of marriage as a factor for harmony and understanding. The thoughtful social student will not content himself with the popular superficial excuse for this phenomenon. He will have to dig deeper into the very life of the sexes to know why marriage proves so disastrous.

Edward Carpenter[2] says that behind every marriage stands the

---

[1]   *Robert Herrick* (1868–1938), American novelist, whose novel *Together* (1908) candidly deals with the problems of married life; Sir Arthur Wing *Pinero* (1855–1934), British playwright, author of social problem plays such as *Mid-Channel* (1909), which deals with a couple's marital boredom and resulting infidelity; *Eugene Walter* (1874–1941), American-born playwright, whose melodrama, *Paid in Full* (1908), depicts a wife who leaves her degenerate husband after bailing him out of jail.

[2]   *Edward Carpenter* (1844–1929), British poet and social reformer, author of *Love's Coming of Age* (1896) and *The Intermediate Sex* (1908). Carpenter lectured and wrote on several controversial topics, most notably women's rights and homosexuality.

life-long environment of the two sexes; an environment so different from each other that man and woman must remain strangers. Separated by an insurmountable wall of superstition, custom, and habit, marriage has not the potentiality of developing knowledge of, and respect for, each other, without which every union is doomed to failure.

Henrik Ibsen, the hater of all social shams, was probably the first to realize this great truth. Nora leaves her husband, not—as the stupid critic would have it—because she is tired of her responsibilities or feels the need of woman's rights, but because she has come to know that for eight years she had lived with a stranger and borne him children.[1] Can there be anything more humiliating, more degrading than a life-long proximity between two strangers? No need for the woman to know anything of the man, save his income. As to the knowledge of the woman—what is there to know except that she has a pleasing appearance? We have not yet outgrown the theologic myth that woman has no soul, that she is a mere appendix to man, made out of his rib just for the convenience of the gentleman who was so strong that he was afraid of his own shadow.

Perchance the poor quality of the material whence woman comes is responsible for her inferiority. At any rate, woman has no soul—what is there to know about her? Besides, the less soul a woman has the greater her asset as a wife, the more readily will she absorb herself in her husband. It is this slavish acquiescence to man's superiority that has kept the marriage institution seemingly intact for so long a period. Now that woman is coming into her own, now that she is actually growing aware of herself as being outside of the master's grace, the sacred institution of marriage is gradually being undermined, and no amount of sentimental lamentation can stay it.

From infancy, almost, the average girl is told that marriage is her ultimate goal; therefore her training and education must be directed towards that end. Like the mute beast fattened for slaughter, she is prepared for that. Yet, strange to say, she is allowed to know much less about her function as wife and mother than the ordinary artisan of his trade. It is indecent and filthy for a respectable girl to know

---

[1] *Henrik Ibsen* (1828–1906), Norwegian playwright most famous in the English speaking world for his controversial plays *A Doll's House* (1879) and *Ghosts* (1881). In the former play, *Nora* Helmer forges a banknote to help her husband, but she cannot forgive his lack of support once she is exposed. She leaves her husband after realizing she is only an amusing plaything to him.

anything of the marital relation. Oh, for the inconsistency of respectability, that needs the marriage vow to turn something which is filthy into the purest and most sacred arrangement that none dare question or criticize. Yet that is exactly the attitude of the average upholder of marriage. The prospective wife and mother is kept in complete ignorance of her only asset in the competitive field—sex. Thus she enters into life-long relations with a man only to find herself shocked, repelled, outraged beyond measure by the most natural and healthy instinct, sex. It is safe to say that a large percentage of the unhappiness, misery, distress, and physical suffering of matrimony is due to the criminal ignorance in sex matters that is being extolled as a great virtue. Nor is it at all an exaggeration when I say that more than one home has been broken up because of this deplorable fact.

If, however, woman is free and big enough to learn the mystery of sex without the sanction of State or Church, she will stand condemned as utterly unfit to become the wife of a "good" man, his goodness consisting of an empty brain and plenty of money. Can there be anything more outrageous than the idea that a healthy, grown woman, full of life and passion, must deny nature's demand, must subdue her most intense craving, undermine her health and break her spirit, must stunt her vision, abstain from the depth and glory of sex experience until a "good" man comes along to take her unto himself as a wife? That is precisely what marriage means. How can such an arrangement end except in failure? This is one, though not the least important, factor of marriage, which differentiates it from love.

Ours is a practical age. The time when Romeo and Juliet risked the wrath of their fathers for love, when Gretchen exposed herself to the gossip of her neighbors for love,[1] is no more. If, on rare occasions, young people allow themselves the luxury of romance, they are taken in care by the elders, drilled and pounded until they become "sensible."

The moral lesson instilled in the girl is not whether the man has aroused her love, but rather is it, "How much?" The important and only God of practical American life: Can the man make a living? can he support a wife? That is the only thing that justifies marriage. Gradually this saturates every thought of the girl; her dreams are not

---

[1]   *Gretchen:* also known as Margaret, the young woman seduced by Faust in Goethe's *Faust* (see Chapter I, p. 60, note 2).

of moonlight and kisses, of laughter and tears; she dreams of shopping tours and bargain counters. This soul poverty and sordidness are the elements inherent in the marriage institution. The State and Church approve of no other ideal, simply because it is the one that necessitates the State and Church control of men and women.

Doubtless there are people who continue to consider love above dollars and cents. Particularly this is true of that class whom economic necessity has forced to become self-supporting. The tremendous change in woman's position, wrought by that mighty factor, is indeed phenomenal when we reflect that it is but a short time since she has entered the industrial arena. Six million women wage workers; six million women, who have the equal right with men to be exploited, to be robbed, to go on strike; aye, to starve even. Anything more, my lord? Yes, six million wage workers in every walk of life, from the highest brain work to the mines and railroad tracks; yes, even detectives and policemen. Surely the emancipation is complete.

Yet with all that, but a very small number of the vast army of women wage workers look upon work as a permanent issue, in the same light as does man. No matter how decrepit the latter, he has been taught to be independent, self-supporting. Oh, I know that no one is really independent in our economic treadmill; still, the poorest specimen of a man hates to be a parasite; to be known as such, at any rate.

The woman considers her position as worker transitory, to be thrown aside for the first bidder. That is why it is infinitely harder to organize women than men. "Why should I join a union? I am going to get married, to have a home." Has she not been taught from infancy to look upon that as her ultimate calling? She learns soon enough that the home, though not so large a prison as the factory, has more solid doors and bars. It has a keeper so faithful that naught can escape him. The most tragic part, however, is that the home no longer frees her from wage slavery; it only increases her task.

According to the latest statistics submitted before a Committee "on labor and wages, and congestion of population," ten per cent. of the wage workers in New York City alone are married, yet they must continue to work at the most poorly paid labor in the world. Add to this horrible aspect the drudgery of housework, and what remains of the protection and glory of the home? As a matter of fact, even the middle-class girl in marriage can not speak of her home, since it is the man who creates her sphere. It is not important whether the husband is a brute or a darling. What I wish to prove is that marriage guarantees woman a home only by the grace of her husband. There she moves about in *his* home, year after year, until her aspect of life and human affairs becomes as flat, narrow, and drab as her surroundings. Small wonder if she becomes a nag, petty, quarrelsome, gossipy, unbearable, thus driving the man from the house. She could not go, if she wanted to; there is no place to go. Besides, a short period of married life, of complete surrender of all faculties, absolutely incapacitates the average woman for the outside world. She becomes reckless in appearance, clumsy in her movements, dependent in her decisions, cowardly in her judgment, a weight and a bore, which most men grow to hate and despise. Wonderfully inspiring atmosphere for the bearing of life, is it not?

But the child, how is it to be protected, if not for marriage? After all, is not that the most important consideration? The sham, the hypocrisy of it! Marriage protecting the child, yet thousands of children destitute and homeless. Marriage protecting the child, yet orphan asylums and reformatories overcrowded, the Society for the Prevention of Cruelty to Children keeping busy in rescuing the little victims from "loving" parents, to place them under more loving care, the Gerry Society. Oh, the mockery of it!

Marriage may have the power to bring the horse to water, but has it ever made him drink? The law will place the father under arrest, and put him in convict's clothes; but has that ever stilled the hunger of the child? If the parent has no work, or if he hides his identity, what does marriage do then? It invokes the law to bring the man to "justice," to put him safely behind closed doors; his labor, however, goes not to the child, but to the State. The child receives but a blighted memory of his father's stripes.

As to the protection of the woman,—therein lies the curse of marriage. Not that it really protects her, but the very idea is so revolting, such an outrage and insult on life, so degrading to human dignity, as to forever condemn this parasitic institution.

It is like that other paternal arrangement—capitalism. It robs man of his birthright, stunts his growth, poisons his body, keeps him in ignorance, in poverty, and dependence, and then institutes charities that thrive on the last vestige of man's self-respect.

The institution of marriage makes a parasite of woman, an absolute dependent. It incapacitates her for life's struggle, annihilates her social consciousness, paralyzes her imagination, and then imposes its gracious protection, which is in reality a snare, a travesty on human character.

If motherhood is the highest fulfillment of woman's nature, what other protection does it need, save love and freedom? Marriage but defiles, outrages, and corrupts her fulfillment. Does it not say to woman, Only when you follow me shall you bring forth life? Does it not condemn her to the block, does it not degrade and shame her if she refuses to buy her right to motherhood by selling herself? Does not marriage only sanction motherhood, even though conceived in hatred, in compulsion? Yet, if motherhood be of free choice, of love, of ecstasy, of defiant passion, does it not place a crown of thorns upon an innocent head and carve in letters of blood the hideous epithet, Bastard? Were marriage to contain all the virtues claimed for it, its crimes against motherhood would exclude it forever from the realm of love.

Love, the strongest and deepest element in all life, the harbinger of hope, of joy, of ecstasy; love, the defier of all laws, of all conventions; love, the freest, the most powerful moulder of human destiny; how can such an all-compelling force be synonymous with that poor little State and Church-begotten weed, marriage?

Free love? As if love is anything but free! Man has bought brains, but all the millions in the world have failed to buy love. Man has subdued bodies, but all the power on earth has been unable to subdue love. Man has conquered whole nations, but all his armies could not conquer love. Man has chained and fettered the spirit, but he has been utterly helpless before love. High on a throne, with all the splendor and pomp his gold can command, man is yet poor and desolate, if love passes him by. And if it stays, the poorest hovel is radiant with warmth, with life and color. Thus love has the magic power to make of a beggar a king. Yes, love is free; it can dwell in no other atmosphere. In freedom it gives itself unreservedly, abundantly, completely. All the laws on the statutes, all the courts in the universe, cannot tear it from the soil, once love has taken root. If, however, the soil is sterile, how can marriage make it bear fruit? It is like the last desperate struggle of fleeting life against death.

Love needs no protection; it is its own protection. So long as love begets life no child is deserted, or hungry, or famished for the want of affection. I know this to be true. I know women who became mothers in freedom by the men they loved. Few children in wedlock enjoy the care, the protection, the devotion free motherhood is capable of bestowing.

The defenders of authority dread the advent of a free motherhood, lest it will rob them of their prey. Who would fight wars? Who would create wealth? Who would make the policeman, the jailer, if woman were to refuse the indiscriminate breeding of children? The race, the race! shouts the king, the president, the capitalist, the priest. The race must be preserved, though woman be degraded to a mere machine,— and the marriage institution is our only safety valve against the pernicious sex awakening of woman. But in vain these frantic efforts to maintain a state of bondage. In vain, too, the edicts of the Church, the mad attacks of rulers, in vain even the arm of the law. Woman no longer wants to be a party to the production of a race of sickly, feeble, decrepit, wretched human beings, who have neither the strength nor moral courage to throw off the yoke of poverty and slavery. Instead she desires fewer and better children, begotten and reared in love and through free choice; not by compulsion, as marriage imposes. Our pseudo-moralists have yet to learn the deep sense of responsibility toward the child, that love in freedom has awakened in the breast of woman. Rather would she forego forever the glory of motherhood than bring forth life in an atmosphere that breathes only destruction and death. And if she does become a mother, it is to give to the child the deepest and best her being can yield. To grow with the child is her motto; she knows that in that manner alone can she help build true manhood and womanhood.

Ibsen must have had a vision of a free mother, when, with a master stroke, he portrayed Mrs. Alving. She was the ideal mother because she had outgrown marriage and all its horrors, because she had broken her chains, and set her spirit free to soar until it returned a personality, regenerated and strong. Alas, it was too late to rescue her life's joy, her Oswald; but not too late to realize that love in freedom is the only condition of a beautiful life.[1] Those who, like Mrs. Alving, have paid with blood and tears for their spiritual awakening, repudiate marriage as an imposition, a shallow, empty mockery. They know, whether love last but one brief span of time or for eternity, it is the only creative, inspiring, elevating basis for a new race, a new world.

In our present pygmy state love is indeed a stranger to most people. Misunderstood and shunned, it rarely takes root; or if it does, it soon

---

[1] *Mrs. Alving*: the candid and rebellious heroine of Henrik *Ibsen*'s most controversial play, *Ghosts* (1881), who learns that her son, *Oswald*, is suffering from congenital syphilis resulting from his father's debauched lifestyle.

withers and dies. Its delicate fiber can not endure the stress and strain of the daily grind. Its soul is too complex to adjust itself to the slimy woof of our social fabric. It weeps and moans and suffers with those who have need of it, yet lack the capacity to rise to love's summit.

Some day, some day men and women will rise, they will reach the mountain peak, they will meet big and strong and free, ready to receive, to partake, and to bask in the golden rays of love. What fancy, what imagination, what poetic genius can foresee even approximately the potentialities of such a force in the life of men and women. If the world is ever to give birth to true companionship and oneness, not marriage, but love will be the parent.

[Source: *Anarchism and Other Essays* (New York: Mother Earth, 1911), 233-245.]

4. Edith Wharton, "The New Frenchwoman," 1919.

There is no new Frenchwoman; but the real Frenchwoman is new to America, and it may be of interest to American women to learn something of what she is really like.

In saying that the real Frenchwoman is new to America I do not intend to draw the old familiar contrast between the so-called "real Frenchwoman" and the Frenchwoman of fiction and the stage. Americans have been told a good many thousand times in the last four years that the real Frenchwoman is totally different from the person depicted under that name by French novelists and dramatists; but in truth every literature, in its main lines, reflects the chief characteristics of the people for whom, and about whom, it is written and none more so than French literature, the freest and frankest of all.

The statement that the real Frenchwoman is new to America simply means that America has never before taken the trouble to look at her and try to understand her. She has always been there, waiting to be understood, and a little tired, perhaps, of being either caricatured or idealised. It would be easy enough to palm her off as a "new" Frenchwoman because the war has caused her to live a new life and do unfamiliar jobs; but one need only look at the illustrated papers to see what she looks like as a tram-conductor, a taxi-driver or a munition-maker. It is certain, even now, that all these new experiences are going to modify her character, and to enlarge her view of life; but that is not the point with which these papers are concerned. The first thing for the American woman to do is to learn to know the Frenchwoman as she has always been; to try to find out what she is, and why she is what she is. After that it will be easy to see why the war has developed in her certain qualities rather than others, and what its after-effects on her are likely to be.

First of all, she is, in nearly all respects, as different as possible from the average American woman. That proposition is fairly evident, though not always easy to explain. Is it because she dresses better, or knows more about cooking, or is more "coquettish," or more "feminine," or more excitable, or more emotional, or more immoral? All these reasons have been often suggested, but none of them seems to furnish a complete answer. Millions of American women are, to the best of their ability (which is not small), coquettish, feminine, emotional, and all the rest of it; a good many dress as well as Frenchwomen; some even know a little about cooking—and the real reason is quite different, and not nearly as flattering to our national vanity. It is simply that, like the men of her race, the Frenchwoman is *grown up*.

Compared with the women of France the average American woman is still in the kindergarten. The world she lives in is exactly like the most improved and advanced and scientifically equipped Montessori-method baby-school. At first sight it may seem preposterous to compare the American woman's independent and resonant activities—her "boards" and clubs and sororities, her public investigation of everything under the heavens from "the social evil" to baking-powder, and from "physical culture" to the newest esoteric religion—to compare such free and busy and seemingly influential lives with the artless exercises of an infant class. But what is the fundamental principle of the Montessori system? It is the development of the child's individuality, unrestricted by the traditional nursery discipline: a Montessori school is a baby world where, shut up together in the most improved hygienic surroundings, a number of infants noisily develop their individuality.

The reason why American women are not really "grown up" in comparison with the women of the most highly civilised countries—such as France—is that all their semblance of freedom, activity and authority bears not much more likeness to real living than the exercises of the Montessori infant. Real living, in any but the most elementary sense of the word, is a deep and complex and slowly developed thing, the outcome of an old and rich social experience. It cannot be "got up" like gymnastics, or a proficiency in foreign languages; it has its roots in the fundamental things, and above all in close and constant and interesting and important relations between men and women.

It is because American women are each other's only audience, and to a great extent each other's only companions, that they seem, compared to women who play an intellectual and social part in the lives of men, like children in a baby-school. They are "developing their individuality," but developing it in the void, without the checks, the stimulus, and the discipline that comes of contact with the stronger masculine individuality. And it is not only because the man is the stronger and the closer to reality that his influence is necessary to develop woman to real womanhood; it is because the two sexes complete each other mentally as well as physiologically that no modern civilisation has been really rich or deep, or stimulating to other civilisations, which has not been based on the recognised interaction of influences between men and women.

There are several ways in which the Frenchwoman's relations with men may be called more important than those of her American sister. In the first place, in the commercial class, the Frenchwoman is always her husband's business partner. The lives of the French bourgeois couple are based on the primary necessity of getting enough money to live on, and of giving their children educational and material advantages. In small businesses the woman is always her husband's bookkeeper or clerk, or both; above all, she is his business adviser. France, as you know, is held up to all other countries as a model of thrift, of wise and prudent saving and spending. No other country in the world has such immense financial vitality, such powers of recuperation from national calamity. After the Franco-Prussian war of 1870, when France, beaten to earth, her armies lost, half her territory occupied, and with all Europe holding aloof, and not a single ally to defend her interests—when France was called on by her conquerors to pay an indemnity of five thousand million francs in order to free her territory of the enemy, she raised the sum, and paid it off, *eighteen months sooner than the date agreed upon*: to the rage and disappointment of Germany, and the amazement and admiration of the rest of the world.

Every economist knows that if France was able to make that incredible effort it was because, all over the country, millions of Frenchwomen, labourers' wives, farmers' wives, small shopkeepers' wives, wives of big manufacturers and commission-merchants and bankers, were to all intents and purposes their husbands' business-partners, and had had a direct interest in saving and investing the millions and millions piled up to pay France's ransom in her day of need. At every stage in French history, in war, in politics, in literature, in art and in religion, women have played a splendid and a decisive part; but none more splendid or more decisive than the obscure part played by the millions of wives and mothers whose thrift and prudence silently built up her salvation in 1872.

When it is said that the Frenchwoman of the middle class is her husband's business partner the statement must not be taken in too literal a sense. The French wife has less legal independence than the American or English wife, and is subject to a good many legal disqualifications from which women have freed themselves in other countries. That is the technical situation; but what is the practical fact? That the Frenchwoman has gone straight through these theoretical restrictions to the heart of reality, and become her husband's associate, because, for her children's sake if not for her own, her heart is in his job, and because he has long since learned that the best business partner a man can have is one who has the same interests at stake as himself.

It is not only because she saves him a salesman's salary, or a bookkeeper's salary, or both, that the French tradesman associates his wife with his business; it is because he has the sense to see that no hired assistant will have so keen a perception of his interests, that none will receive his customers so pleasantly, and that none will so patiently and willingly work over hours when it is necessary to do so. There is no drudgery in this kind of partnership, because it is voluntary, and because each partner is stimulated by exactly the same aspirations. And it is this practical, personal and daily participation in her husband's job that makes the Frenchwoman more grown up than others. She has a more interesting and more living life, and therefore she develops more quickly.

It may be objected that money-making is not the most interesting thing in life, and that the "higher ideals" seem to have little place in this conception of feminine efficiency. The answer to such a criticism is to be found by considering once more the difference between the French and the American views as to the main object of money-making—a point to which any study of the two races inevitably leads one back.

Americans are too prone to consider moneymaking as interesting in itself: they regard the fact that a man has made money as something intrinsically meritorious. But moneymaking is interesting only in proportion as its object is interesting. If a man piles up millions in order to pile them up, having already all he needs to live humanly and decently, his occupation is neither interesting in itself, nor conducive to any sort of real social development in the money-maker or in those about him. No life is more sterile than one into which nothing enters to balance such an output of energy. To see how different is the French view of the object of money-making one must put one's self in the place of the average French household. For the immense majority of the French it is a far more modest ambition, and consists simply in the effort to earn one's living and put by enough for sickness, old age, and a good start in life for the children.

This conception of "business" may seem a tame one to Americans; but its advantages are worth considering. In the first place, it has the immense superiority of leaving time for living, time for men and women both. The average French business man at the end of his life may not have made as much money as the American; but meanwhile he has had, every day, something the American has not had: Time. Time, in the middle of the day, to sit down to an excellent luncheon, to eat it quietly with his family, and to read his paper afterward; time to go off on Sundays and holidays on long pleasant country rambles; time, almost any day, to feel fresh and free enough for an evening at the theatre, after a dinner as good and leisurely as his luncheon. And there is one thing certain: the great mass of men and women grow up and reach real maturity only through their contact with the material realities of living, with business, with industry, with all the great bread-winning activities; but the growth and the maturing take place *in the intervals between these activities*: and in lives where there are no such intervals there will be no real growth.

That is why the "slow" French business methods so irritating to the American business man produce, in the long run, results which he is often the first to marvel at and admire. Every intelligent American who has seen something of France and French life has had a first moment of bewilderment on trying to explain the seeming contradiction between the slow, fumbling, timid French business methods and the rounded completeness of French civilisation. How is it that a country which seems to have almost everything to learn in the way of "up-to-date" business has almost everything to teach, not only in the way of art and literature, and all the graces of life, but also in the way of municipal order, state administration, agriculture, forestry, engineering, and the whole harmonious running of the vast national machine? The answer is the last the American business man is likely to think of until he has had time to study France somewhat closely: it is that France is what she is because every Frenchman and every Frenchwoman takes time to live, and has an extraordinarily clear and sound sense of what constitutes *real living*.

We are too ready to estimate business successes by their individual results: a point of view revealed in our national awe of large fortunes. That is an immature and even childish way of estimating success. In terms of civilisation it is the total and ultimate result of a nation's business effort that matters, not the fact of Mr. Smith's being able to build a marble villa in place of his wooden cottage. If the collective life which results from our individual moneymaking is not richer, more interesting and more stimulating than that of countries where the individual effort is less intense, then it looks as if there were something wrong about our method.

This parenthesis may seem to have wandered rather far from the Frenchwoman who heads the chapter; but in reality she is at its very heart. For if Frenchmen care too much about other things to care as much as we do about making money, the chief reason is largely because their relations with women are more interesting. The Frenchwoman rules French life, and she rules it under a triple crown, as a business woman, as a mother, and above all as an artist. To explain the sense in which the last word is used it is necessary to go back to the contention that the greatness of France lies in her sense of the beauty and importance of living. As life is an art in France, so woman is an artist. She does not teach man, but she inspires him. As the Frenchwoman of the bread-winning class influences her husband, and inspires in him a respect for her judgment and her wishes, so the Frenchwoman of the rich and educated class is admired and held in regard for other qualities. But in this class of society her influence naturally extends much farther. The more civilised a society is, the wider is the range of each woman's influence over men, and of each man's influence over women. Intelligent and cultivated people of either sex will never limit themselves to communing with their own households. Men and women equally, when they have the range of interests that real cultivation gives, need the stimulus of different points of view, the refreshment of new ideas as well as of new faces. The long hypocrisy which Puritan England handed on to America concerning the danger of frank and free social relations between men and women has done more than anything else to retard real civilisation in America.

Real civilisation means an education that extends to the whole of life, in contradistinction to that of school or college: it means an education that forms speech, forms manners, forms taste, forms ideals, and above all forms judgment. This is the kind of civilisation of which France has always been the foremost model: it is because she possesses its secret that she has led the world so long not only in art and taste and elegance, but in ideas and in ideals. For it must never be forgotten that if the fashion of our note-paper and the cut of our dresses come from France, so do the conceptions of liberty and justice on which our republican institutions are based. No nation can have grown-up ideas till it has a ruling caste of grown-up men and women; and it is possible to have a ruling caste of grown-up men and women only in a civilisation where the power of each sex is balanced by that of the other.

It may seem strange to draw precisely this comparison between France, the country of all the old sex-conventions, and America, which is supposedly the country of the greatest sex-freedom; and the American reader may ask: "But where is there so much freedom of intercourse between men and women as in America?" The misconception arises from the confusion between two words, and two states of being that are fundamentally different. In America there is complete freedom of intercourse between boys and girls, but not between men and women; and there is a general notion that, in essentials, a girl and a woman are the same thing. It is true, in essentials, that a boy and a man are very much the same thing; but a girl and a woman—a married woman—are totally different beings. Marriage, union with a man, completes and transforms a woman's character, her point of view, her sense of the relative importance of things, far more thoroughly than a boy's nature is changed by the same experience. A girl is only a sketch; a married woman is the finished picture. And it is only the married woman who counts as a social factor.

Now it is precisely at the moment when her experience is rounded by marriage, motherhood, and the responsibilities, cares and interests of her own household, that the average American woman is, so to speak, "withdrawn from circulation." It is true that this does not apply to the small minority of wealthy and fashionable women who lead an artificial cosmopolitan life, and therefore represent no particular national tendency. It is not to them that the country looks for the development of its social civilisation, but to the average woman who is sufficiently free from bread-winning cares to act as an incentive to other women and as an influence upon men. In America this woman, in the immense majority of cases, has roamed through life in absolute freedom of communion with young men until the day when the rounding-out of her own experience by marriage puts her in a position to become a social influence; and from that day she is cut off from men's society in all but the most formal and intermittent ways. On her wedding-day she ceases, in any open, frank and recognised manner, to be an influence in the lives of the men of the community to which she belongs.

In France, the case is just the contrary. France, hitherto, has kept young girls under restrictions at which Americans have often smiled, and which have certainly, in some respects, been a bar to their growth. The doing away of these restrictions will be one of the few benefits of the war: the French young girl, even in the most exclusive and most tradition-loving society, will never again be the prisoner she has been in the past. But this is relatively unimportant, for the French have always recognised that, as a social factor, a woman does not count till she is married; and in the well-to-do classes girls marry extremely young, and the married woman has always had extraordinary social freedom. The famous French "Salon," the best school of talk and of ideas that the modern world has known, was based on the belief that the most stimulating conversation in the world is that between intelligent men and women who see each other often enough to be on terms of frank and easy friendship. The great wave of intellectual and social liberation that preceded the French revolution and prepared the way, not for its horrors but for its benefits, originated in the drawing-rooms of French wives and mothers, who received every day the most thoughtful and the most brilliant men of the time, who shared their talk, and often directed it. Think what an asset to the mental life of any country such a group of women forms! And in France they were not then, and they are not now, limited to the small class of the wealthy and fashionable. In France, as soon as a woman has a personality, social circumstances permit her to make it felt. What does it matter if she had spent her girlhood in seclusion, provided she is free to emerge from it at the moment when she is fitted to become a real factor in social life?

It may, of course, be asked at this point, how the French freedom of intercourse between married men and women affects domestic life, and the happiness of a woman's husband and children. It is hard to say what kind of census could be devised to ascertain the relative percentage of happy marriages in the countries where different social systems prevail. Until such a census can be taken, it is, at any rate, rash to assert that the French system is less favourable to domestic happiness than the Anglo-Saxon. At any rate, it acts as a greater incentive to the husband, since it rests with him to keep his wife's admiration and affection by making himself so agreeable to her, and by taking so much trouble to appear at an advantage in the presence of her men friends, that no rival shall supplant him. It would not occur to any Frenchman of the cultivated class to object to his wife's friendship with other men, and the mere fact that he has the influence of other men to compete with is likely to conduce to considerate treatment of his wife, and courteous relations in the household.

It must also be remembered that a man who comes home to a wife who has been talking with intelligent men will probably find her companionship more stimulating than if she has spent all her time with other women. No matter how intelligent women are individually, they tend, collectively, to narrow down their interests, and take a feminine, or even a female, rather than a broadly human view of things. The woman whose mind is attuned to men's minds has a much larger view of the world, and attaches much less importance to trifles, because men, being usually brought by circumstances into closer contact with reality, insensibly communicate their breadth of view to women. A "man's woman" is never fussy and seldom spiteful, because she breathes too free an air, and is having too good a time.

If, then, being "grown up" consists in having a larger and more liberal experience of life, in being less concerned with trifles, and less afraid of strong feelings, passions and risks, then the French woman is distinctly more grown up than her American sister; and she is so because she plays a much larger and more interesting part in men's lives.

It may, of course, also be asked whether the fact of playing this part—which implies all the dangers implied by taking the open seas instead of staying in port—whether such a fact is conducive to the eventual welfare of woman and of society. Well—the answer to-day is: *France!* Look at her as she has stood before the world for the last four years and a half, uncomplaining, undiscouraged, undaunted, holding up the banner of liberty: liberty of speech, liberty of thought, liberty of conscience, all the liberties that we of the western world have been taught to revere as the only things worth living for—look at her, as the world has beheld her since August, 1914, fearless, tearless, indestructible, in face of the most ruthless and formidable enemy the world has ever known, determined to fight on to the end for the principles she has always lived for. Such she is today; such are the millions of men who have spent their best years in her trenches, and the millions of brave, uncomplaining, self-denying mothers and wives and sisters who sent them forth smiling, who waited for them patiently and courageously, or who are mourning them silently and unflinchingly, and not one of whom, at the end of the most awful struggle in history, is ever heard to say that the cost has been too great or the trial too bitter to be borne.

No one who has seen Frenchwomen since the war can doubt that their great influence on French life, French thought, French imagination and French sensibility, is one of the strongest elements in the attitude that France holds before the world to-day.

[Source: *French Ways and Their Meaning* (New York: D. Appleton & Co, 1919), 98-121.]

5. Edith Wharton, "In Fez,"[1] 1920.

What thoughts, what speculations, one wonders, go on under the narrow veiled brows of the little creatures destined to the high honour of marriage or concubinage in Moroccan palaces?

Some are brought down from mountains and cedar forests, from the free life of the tents where the nomad women go unveiled. Others come from harems in the turreted cities beyond the Atlas, where blue palm-groves beat all night against the stars and date-caravans journey across the desert from Timbuctoo. Some, born and bred in an airy palace among pomegranate gardens and white terraces, pass thence to one of the feudal fortresses near the snows, where for half the year the great chiefs of the south live in their clan, among fighting men and falconers and packs of *sloughis*.[2] And still others grow up in a stifling Mellah,[3] trip unveiled on its blue terraces overlooking the gardens of the great, and, seen one day at sunset by a fat vizier or his pale young master, are acquired for a handsome sum and

---

[1] Wharton visited Morocco in September 1917 with Walter Berry. This selection from *In Morocco* recounts her visit to a harem.

[2] *sloughis*: Arabic for "hounds."

[3] *Mellah*: the Jewish ghetto of Fez that adjoins the royal palace.

transferred to the painted sepulchre of the harem. Worst of all must be the fate of those who go from tents and cedar forests, or from some sea blown garden above Rabat, into one of the houses of Old Fez. They are well-nigh impenetrable, these palaces of Elbali: the Fazi dignitaries do not welcome the visits of strange women. On the rare occasions when they are received, a member of the family (one of the sons, or a brother-in-law who has "studied in Algeria") usually acts as interpreter; and perhaps it is as well that no one from the outer world should come to remind these listless creatures that somewhere the gulls dance on the Atlantic and the wind murmurs through olive yards and clatters the metallic fronds of palm groves.

We had been invited, one day, to visit the harem of one of the chief dignitaries of the Makhzen at Fez,[1] and these thoughts came to me as I sat among the pale women in their mouldering prison. The descent through the steep tunnelled streets gave one the sense of being lowered into the shaft of a mine. At each step the strip of sky grew narrower, and was more often obscured by the low vaulted passages into which we plunged. The noises of the Bazaar had died out, and only the sound of fountains behind garden walls and the clatter of our mules' hoofs on the stones went with us. Then fountains and gardens ceased also, the towering masonry closed in, and we entered an almost subterranean labyrinth which sun and air never reach. At length our mules turned into a *cul-de-sac* blocked by a high building. On the right was another building, one of those blind mysterious house-fronts of Fez that seem like a fragment of its ancient fortifications. Clients and servants lounged on the stone benches built into the wall; it was evidently the house of an important person. A charming youth with intelligent eyes waited on the threshold to receive us: he was one of the sons of the house, the one who had "studied in Algeria" and knew how to talk to visitors. We followed him into a small arcaded *patio* hemmed in by the high walls of the house. On the right was the usual long room with archways giving on the court. Our host, a patriarchal personage, draped in fat as in a toga, came toward us, a mountain of majestic muslins, his eyes sparkling in a swarthy silver-bearded face. He seated us on divans and lowered his voluminous person to a heap of cushions on the

---

[1] *Makhzen at Fez*: Dar el-Makhzen is a seventeenth-century Sultan's palace in Fez, famous for its bright brass doors.

step leading into the court; and the son who had studied in Algeria instructed a negress to prepare the tea.

Across the *patio* was another arcade closely hung with unbleached cotton. From behind it came the sound of chatter, and now and then a bare brown child in a scant shirt would escape, and be hurriedly pulled back with soft explosions of laughter, while a black woman came out to readjust the curtains.

There were three of these negresses, splendid bronze creatures, wearing white djellabahs over bright-coloured caftans, striped scarves knotted about their large hips, and gauze turbans on their crinkled hair. Their wrists clinked with heavy silver bracelets, and big circular earrings danced in their purple ear-lobes. A languor lay on all the other inmates of the household, on the servants and hangers-on squatting in the shade under the arcade, on our monumental host and his smiling son; but the three negresses, vibrating with activity, rushed continually from the curtained chamber to the kitchen, and from the kitchen to the master's reception-room, bearing on their pinky-blue palms trays of Britannia metal with tall glasses and fresh bunches of mint, shouting orders to dozing menials, and calling to each other from opposite ends of the court; and finally the stoutest of the three, disappearing from view, reappeared suddenly on a pale green balcony overhead, where, profiled against a square of blue sky, she leaned over in a Veronese attitude[1] and screamed down to the others like an excited parrot.

In spite of their febrile activity and tropical bird-shrieks, we waited in vain for tea; and after a while our host suggested to his son that I might like to visit the ladies of the household. As I had expected, the young man led me across the *patio*, lifted the cotton hanging and introduced me into an apartment exactly like the one we had just left. Divans covered with striped mattress-ticking stood against the white walls, and on them sat seven or eight passive-looking women over whom a number of pale children scrambled.

The eldest of the group, and evidently the mistress of the house, was an Algerian lady, probably of about fifty, with a sad and delicately-modelled face; the others were daughters, daughters-in-law and concubines. The latter word evokes to occidental ears images of

---

[1] *Veronese attitude*: after the work of *Veronese* (1528–1588), Italian painter and master of the Venetian school, whose early work frequently featured a "worm's-eye view" and figures in contorted poses.

sensual seduction which the Moroccan harem seldom realizes. All the ladies of this dignified official household wore the same look of somewhat melancholy respectability. In their stuffy curtained apartment they were like cellar-grown flowers, pale, heavy, fuller but frailer than the garden sort. Their dresses, rich but sober, the veils and diadems put on in honour of my visit, had a dignified dowdiness in odd contrast to the frivolity of the Imperial harem. But what chiefly struck me was the apathy of the younger women. I asked them if they had a garden, and they shook their heads wistfully, saying that there were no gardens in Old Fez. The roof was therefore their only escape: a roof overlooking acres and acres of other roofs, and closed in by the naked fortified mountains which stand about Fez like prison-walls.

After a brief exchange of compliments silence fell. Conversing through interpreters is a benumbing process, and there are few points of contact between the open-air occidental mind and beings imprisoned in a conception of sexual and domestic life based on slave-service and incessant espionage. These languid women on their muslin cushions toil not, neither do they spin. The Moroccan lady knows little of cooking, needlework or any household arts. When her child is ill she can only hang it with amulets and wail over it; the great lady of the Fazi palace is as ignorant of hygiene as the peasant-woman of the *bled*.[1] And all these colourless eventless lives depend on the favour of one fat tyrannical man, bloated with good living and authority, himself almost as inert and sedentary as his women, and accustomed to impose his whims on them ever since he ran about the same *patio* as a little short-smocked boy.

The redeeming point in this stagnant domesticity is the tenderness of the parents for their children, and western writers have laid so much stress on this that one would suppose children could be loved only by inert and ignorant parents. It is in fact charming to see the heavy eyes of the Moroccan father light up when a brown grass-hopper baby jumps on his knee, and the unfeigned tenderness with which the childless women of the harem caress the babies of their happier rivals. But the sentimentalist moved by this display of family feeling would do well to consider the lives of these much-petted children. Ignorance, unhealthiness and a precocious sexual initiation prevail in all classes. Education consists in learning by heart endless passages of the Koran, and amusement in assisting at spectacles that would be unintelligible

---

[1] *bled*: Arabic for rural area, countryside.

to western children, but that the pleasantries of the harem make perfectly comprehensible to Moroccan infancy. At eight or nine the little girls are married, at twelve the son of the house is "given his first negress"; and thereafter, in the rich and leisured class, both sexes live till old age in an atmosphere of sensuality without seduction.

The young son of the house led me back across the court, where the negresses were still shrieking and scurrying, and passing to and fro like a stage-procession with the vain paraphernalia of a tea that never came. Our host still smiled from his cushions, resigned to Oriental delays. To distract the impatient westerners, a servant unhooked from the wall the cage of a gently-cooing dove. It was brought to us, still cooing, and looked at me with the same resigned and vacant eyes as the ladies I had just left. As it was being restored to its hook the slaves lolling about the entrance scattered respectfully at the approach of a handsome man of about thirty, with delicate features and a black beard. Crossing the court, he stooped to kiss the shoulder of our host, who introduced him as his eldest son, the husband of one or two of the little pale wives with whom I had been exchanging platitudes.

From the increasing agitation of the negresses it became evident that the ceremony of tea-making had been postponed till his arrival. A metal tray bearing a Britannia samovar and tea-pot was placed on the tiles of the court, and squatting beside it the newcomer gravely proceeded to infuse the mint. Suddenly the cotton hangings fluttered again, and a tiny child in the scantest of smocks rushed out and scampered across the court. Our venerable host, stretching out rapturous arms, caught the fugitive to his bosom, where the little boy lay like a squirrel, watching us with great sidelong eyes. He was the last-born of the patriarch, and the youngest brother of the majestic bearded gentleman engaged in tea-making. While he was still in his father's arms two more sons appeared: charming almond-eyed schoolboys returning from their Koran-class, escorted by their slaves. All the sons greeted each other affectionately, and caressed with almost feminine tenderness the dancing baby so lately added to their ranks; and finally, to crown this scene of domestic intimacy, the three negresses, their gigantic effort at last accomplished, passed about glasses of steaming mint and trays of gazelles' horns and white sugar-cakes.

[Source: *In Morocco* (New York: Scribner's, 1920), 187-196.]

Appendix F: Ethnographic Discourse, Victorian to Modern

[Wharton read widely in anthropology and other nascent social sciences, and she clearly drew on some of this reading for her depiction of the "tribe" of old New York in *The Age of Innocence*. She was also writing at a moment when anthropology was at a crossroads, with its foundational evolutionary paradigm giving way to (while residually co-existing with) a more culturally relativistic model for understanding human societies. Members of the "tribe" she depicts, such as Newland Archer, are themselves reading "Books of Primitive Man," little imagining that they themselves might come to be regarded as ethnographic specimen within a couple of generations. The selections below are meant to help trace for readers the shift from Victorian ethnography, with its theoretical assumption that "primitive" peoples are less highly evolved versions of "civilized" peoples and thus a key to understanding humanity in general, to modernist ethnography, more shaped by field work, which challenges the assumption of a unified and uniform human history and raises the possibility that no human perspective is free from cultural determination. *The Age of Innocence* registers this shift, though whether or not Wharton held precise and systematic ideas about the relative values of human cultures and about human evolution is likely to remain a matter of some speculation. Evolutionary anthropology is represented here by selections from Edward Tylor, James McLennan, Edward Westermarck, and Sir James Frazer, most of whose major works Wharton owned and read (there is no hard evidence that she read McLennan, though he gives one of the more noteworthy accounts of the bridal captivity ceremony, something Newland Archer seems to have been reading about). The evolutionary paradigm was fundamentally challenged as early as 1896 by the American anthropologist Franz Boas, whose work Wharton does not seem to have been familiar with. It is possible that she was familiar with the work of his student, Elsie Clews Parsons, with whose pioneering writings of the 1910s Wharton's novel was compared by an early reviewer. A brief selection from Parsons' work, along with a fragment from Boas's popular disciple Ruth

Benedict written nearly a decade after Wharton's novel, will help define an anthropological perspective that Wharton's novel itself was articulating, whatever contradictory intentions Wharton might have had. Finally, a brief passage from the British anthropologist Bronislaw Malinowski is included that insists on a new methodology in anthropology (involving field work and a functionalist understanding of data) that Wharton's own work arguably anticipates. Though Malinowski's major work appeared after Wharton's novel was written, she would later read it with enthusiasm.]

1. Edward B. Tylor, from *Primitive Culture*, 1871.

a. [Definition of "culture"]

Culture or Civilization, taken in its wide ethnographic sense, is that complex whole which includes knowledge, belief, art, morals, law, custom, and any other capabilities and habits acquired by man as a member of society. The condition of culture among the various societies of mankind, insofar as it is capable of being investigated on general principles, is a subject apt for the study of laws of human thought and action. On the one hand, the uniformity which so largely pervades civilization may be ascribed, in great measure, to the uniform action of uniform causes: while on the other hand its various grades may be regarded as stages of development or evolution, each the outcome of previous history, and about to do its proper part in shaping the history of the future.

b. ["Survivals"]

Among evidence aiding us to trace the course which the civilization of the world has actually followed, is that great class of facts to denote which I have found it convenient to introduce the term 'survivals.' These are processes, customs, opinions, and so forth, which have been carried on by force of habit into a new state of society different from that in which they had their original home, and they thus remain as proofs and examples of an older condition of culture out of which a newer has been evolved. Thus, I know an old Somersetshire woman whose hand-loom dates from the time before the introduction of the 'flying shuttle,' which new-fangled appliance she has never even learnt to use, and I have seen her throw her shuttle from hand to hand in true classic fashion; this old woman is not a century behind her times, but she is a case of survival. Such examples often lead us back to the habits of hundreds and even thousands of years ago. The ordeal of the Key and Bible, still in use, is a survival; the Midsummer bonfire is a survival; the Breton peasants 'All Souls' supper for the spirits of the dead is a survival. The simple keeping up of ancient habits is only part of the transition from old into new and changing times. The serious business of ancient society may be seen to sink into the sport of later generations, and its serious belief to linger on in nursery folk-lore, while superseded habits of old-world life may be modified into new-world forms still powerful for good and evil. Sometimes old thoughts and practices will burst out afresh, to the amazement of a world that thought them long since dead or dying; here survival passes into revival, as has lately happened in so remarkable a way in the history of modern spiritualism, a subject full of instruction from the ethnographer's point of view. The study of the principles of survival has, indeed, no small practical importance, for most of what we call superstition is included within survival, and in this way lies open to the attack of its deadliest enemy, a reasonable explanation. Insignificant, moreover, as multitudes of the facts of survival are in themselves, their study is so effective for tracing the course of the historical development through which alone it is possible to understand their meaning, that it becomes a vital part of ethnographic research to gain the clearest possible insight into their nature. This importance must justify the detail here devoted to an examination of survival, on the evidence of such games, popular sayings, customs, superstitions, and the like, as may serve well to bring into view the manner of its operation.

Progress, degradation, survival, revival, modification, are all modes of the connexion that binds together the complex network of civilization. It needs but a glance into the trivial details of our own daily life to set us thinking how far we are really its originators, and how far but the transmitters and modifiers of the results of long past ages.

c. ["The evolutionary thesis"]

The thesis which I venture to sustain, within limits, is simply this, that the savage state in some measure represents an early condition of mankind, out of which the higher culture has gradually been developed or evolved, by processes still in regular operation as of old, the result showing that, on the whole, progress has far prevailed over relapse.

On this proposition, the main tendency of human society during its long term of existence has been to pass from a savage to a civilized state. Now all must admit a great part of this assertion to be not only truth, but truism. Referred to direct history, a great section of it proves to belong not to the domain of speculation, but to that of positive knowledge. It is mere matter of chronicle that modern civilization is a development of mediaeval civilization, which again is a development from civilization of the order represented in Greece, Assyria, or Egypt. Thus the highest culture being clearly traced back to what may be called the middle culture, the question which remains is whether this middle culture may be traced back to the lower culture, that is, to savagery. To affirm this, is merely to assert that the same kind of development in culture which has gone on inside our range of knowledge has also gone on outside it, its course of proceeding being unaffected by our having or not having reporters present. If any one holds that human thought and action were worked out in primaeval times according to laws essentially other than those of the modern world, it is for him to prove by valid evidence this anomalous state of things, otherwise the doctrine of permanent principle will hold good, as in astronomy or geology. That the tendency of culture has been similar throughout the existence of human society, and that we may fairly judge from its known historic course what its prehistoric course may have been, is a theory clearly entitled to precedence as a fundamental principle of ethnographic research.

[Source: *Primitive Culture: Researches Into the Development of Mythology, Philosophy, Religion, Language, Art, and Custom*, 7th ed. (New York: Brentano's, 1924), I; 16–17; 32–33. First published in 1871.]

2. John F. McLennan, from *Primitive Marriage*, 1865.

a. "The Form of Capture in Marriage Ceremonies" (excerpt)

The symbol of capture occurs whenever, after a contract of marriage, it is necessary for the constitution of the relation of husband and wife that the bridegroom or his friends should go through the form of feigning to steal the bride, or carry her off from her friends by superior force. The marriage is agreed upon by bargain, and the theft or abduction follows as a concerted matter of form, to make valid the marriage. The test, then, of the presence of the symbol in any case is, that the capture is concerted, and is preceded by a contract of marriage....

So far of the nature of the symbol. We proceed to examine the instances of its occurrence. That the form was observed in the marriages of the Dorians, and was, equally with betrothal, requisite as a preliminary to marriage, rests chiefly on the authority of Herodotus and Plutarch.... [Plutarch states] that the Spartan bridegroom always carried off the bride by feigned violence. He says, indeed, *by violence*; but at the same time he shews that the seizure was made by friendly concert between the parties. These passages must be held sufficiently to prove that the custom existed at Sparta. It is equally certain that it was observed at Rome.... The bridegroom and his friends—the time agreed upon having arrived—invaded the house of the bride, and carried off the lady with feigned force from the lap of her mother, or of her nearest female relation if the mother were dead or absent. The seizure is vividly described by Apuleius in the story of the Captive Damsel, in which he is understood to have had the plebeian form of marriage in view. The lady, narrating how she had been carried off, says that her mother having dressed her becomingly in nuptial apparel, was loading her with kisses, and looking forward to a future line of descendants, when on a sudden a band of robbers, armed like gladiators, rushed in with glittering swords, made straight for her chamber in a compact column, and, without any struggle or resistance whatever on the part of the servants, tore her away half dead with fear from the bosom of her trembling mother. The custom is said still to prevail to a great extent among the Hindus.

b. "The Origin of the Form of Capture" (excerpt)

It may be easily conceived how, among exogamous tribes, out of respect to immemorial usage, when friendly relations came to be established between tribes and families, and their members intermarried by purchase instead of capture, the form of invasion and capture should become an essential ceremony at weddings. It was unheard of from the remotest times that a woman became a man's wife except through being made his captive, forced or stolen away from her friends by him or for him. Surely something shall be wanting if there is not at least the appearance of a capture! So the Roman youths rush in with drawn swords, and feign to enact a tragedy; so the Kalmuck girl rides, as if for life, from her lord and master by prearrangement!

[Source: *Primitive Marriage: An Inquiry into the Origin of the Form of Capture in Marriage Ceremonies* (1865; rpt: Chicago: University of Chicago Press, 1970), 12–14, 25.]

3. Sir James George Frazer, "Taboo" (excerpt), 1888.

Taboo (also written "Tabu" and "Tapu") is the name given to a system of religious prohibitions which attained its fullest development in Polynesia (from Hawaii to New Zealand), but of which under different names traces may be discovered in most parts of the world.

★   ★   ★

The original character of the taboo must be looked for not in its civil but in its religious element. It was not the creation of a legislator but the gradual outgrowth of animistic beliefs, to which the ambition and avarice of chiefs and priests afterwards gave an artificial extension. But in serving the cause of avarice and ambition it subserved the progress of civilization, by fostering conceptions of the rights of property and the sanctity of the marriage tie—conceptions which in time grew strong enough to stand by themselves and to fling away the crutch of superstition which in earlier days had been their sole support. For we shall scarcely err in believing that even in advanced societies the moral sentiments, in so far as they are merely sentiments and are not based on an induction from experience, derive much of their force from an original system of taboo. Thus on the taboo were grafted the golden fruits of law and morality, while the parent stem dwindled slowly into the sour crabs and empty husks of popular superstition on which the swine of modern society are still content to feed.

[Source: *Garnered Sheaves: Essays, Addresses, and Reviews* (Freeport: Books for Libraries Press, 1931), 80, 86–87; first published in *Encyclopedia Britannica*, 9th edition, volume 23 (1888), 15–18.)]

4. Sir James George Frazer, "Our Debt to the Savage" (excerpt), 1911.

We stand upon the foundation reared by the generations that have gone before, and we can but dimly realise the painful and prolonged efforts which it has cost humanity to struggle up to the point, no very exalted one after all, which we have reached. Our gratitude is due to the nameless and forgotten toilers, whose patient thought and active exertions have largely made us what we are. The amount of new knowledge which one age, certainly which one man, can add to the common store is small, and it argues stupidity or dishonesty, besides ingratitude, to ignore the heap while vaunting the few grains which it may have been our privilege to add to it. There is indeed little danger at present of undervaluing the contributions which modern times and even classical antiquity have made to the general advancement of our race. But when we pass these limits, the case is different. Contempt and ridicule and abhorrence and denunciation are too often the only recognition vouchsafed to the savage and his ways. Yet of the benefactors whom we are bound thankfully to commemorate, many, perhaps most, were savages. For when all is said and done our resemblances to the savage are still far more numerous than our differences from him; and what we have in common with him, and deliberately retain as true and useful, we owe to our savage forefathers who slowly acquired by experience and transmitted to us by inheritance those seemingly fundamental ideas which we are apt to regard as original and intuitive. We are like heirs to a fortune which has been handed down for so many ages that the memory of those who built it up is lost, and its possessors for the time being regard it as having been an original and unalterable possession of their race since the beginning of the world. But reflection and enquiry should satisfy us that to our predecessors we are indebted for much of what we thought most our own, and that their errors were not wilful extravagances or the ravings of insanity, but simply hypotheses, justifiable as such at the time when they were propounded, but which a fuller experience has proved to be inadequate. It is only by the successive testing of hypotheses and rejection of the false that truth is at last elicited. After all, what we call truth is only the hypothesis which is found to work best. Therefore in reviewing the opinions and practices of ruder ages and races we shall do well to look with leniency upon their errors as inevitable slips made in the search for truth, and to give them the benefit of that indulgence which we ourselves may one day stand in need of: *cum excusatione itaque veteres audiendi sunt.*[1]

[Source: *The Golden Bough: A Study in Magic and Religion*, 3rd ed. (London: Macmillan, 1911), Vol. 3, 420–422.]

5. Edward Westermarck, from *The History of Human Marriage*, 1903.

["Tendency of endogamous peoples to die out"]

According to v. Martius, who is a great authority on Brazilian ethnography, it is a well-established fact, observed everywhere, that the smaller and more isolated of the Indian communities, scarcely any members of which marry members of other communities, are much more liable to every kind of deterioration than the larger groups. "It is probable," Mr. Bates, another most capable judge, remarks with reference to the savage tribes on the Upper Amazons, "that the strange inflexibility of the Indian organization, both bodily and mental, is owing to the isolation in which each small tribe has lived, and to the narrow round of life and thought, and close intermarriages for countless generations, which are the necessary results. Their fecundity is of a low degree, for it is very rare to find an Indian family having so many as four children, and we have seen how great is their liability to sickness and death on removal from place to place." Touching the Isánna Indians, Mr. Wallace asserts that they are said not to be nearly so numerous, nor to increase so rapidly, as the Uaupés; which may perhaps be owing to their marrying with relations, while the latter prefer strangers. And v. Tschudi supposes that the low fecundity of the Botocudos is caused by their endogamous habits; for when their women marry out of their own horde, especially with whites or negroes, they are generally very fertile.

The Caledonian Indians of the Isthmus of Darien, according to Mr. Gisborne, are bound never to cross the breed with foreigners; hence intermarriage is very constant, and, as he remarks, the race degenerates. The Pueblos in New Mexico, too, are said to deteriorate because of their constant intermarriage in the same village. As regards

---

[1] *cum … sunt*: Latin for "We must listen to the elderly with forbearance."

the Hottentots, Barrow remarks, "The impolitic custom of hoarding together in families, and of not marrying out of their own kraals, has no doubt tended to enervate this race of men, and reduced them to their present degenerated condition, which is that of a languid, listless, phlegmatic people, in whom the prolific powers of nature seem to be almost exhausted." Few of the women have more than two or three children, and many of them are barren. But this is not the case when a Hottentot woman is connected with a white man. "The fruit of such an alliance," says Barrow, "is not only in general numerous, but they are beings of a very different nature from the Hottentot."

[Source: *The History of Human Marriage*, 3rd ed. (London: Macmillan, 1903), 346–348.]

6. Edward Westermarck, from *The Origin and Development of the Moral Ideas*, 1906.

a. ["Custom and morality"]

We have seen that a custom, in the strict sense of the word, is not merely the habit of a certain circle of men, but at the same time involves a moral rule. There is a close connection between these two characteristics of custom: its habitualness and its obligatoriness. Whatever be the foundation for a certain practice, and however trivial it may be, the unreflecting mind has a tendency to disapprove of any deviation from it for the simple reason that such a deviation is unusual. As Abraham Tucker observes, "it is a constant argument among the common people, that a thing must be done, and ought to be done, because it always has been done." Children show respect for the customary, and so do savages. "If you ask a Kaffir why he does so and so, he will answer–'How can I tell? It has always been done by our forefathers'." The only reason which the Eskimo can give for some of their present customs, to which they adhere from fear of ill report among their people, is that "the old Innuits did so, and therefore they must." In the behaviour of the Aleut, who "is bashful if caught doing anything unusual among his people," and in the average European's dread of appearing singular, we recognise the influence of the same force of habit.

On the other hand, it should be remembered that not every public habit is a custom, involving an obligation; certain practices, though very general in a society, may be even reprobated by almost every one of its members. The habits of a people must therefore be handled with discretion by the student of moral ideas. Yet when he has not reason to conclude as to some special habit that it is held obligatory, he may, probably always, be sure that it is either allowed, or, in spite of all assurances of its wickedness, that the disapproval of it is not generally very deep or genuine. In a community where lying is a prevailing vice, truthfulness cannot be regarded as a very sacred duty; and where sexual immorality is widely spread, the public condemnation of it always smacks of hypocrisy. Men's standard of morality is not independent of their practice. The conscience of a community follows the same rule as the conscience of an individual. "Commit a sin twice," says the Talmud, "and you will think it perfectly allowable." Hence for the study of the inmost convictions of a nation, its "bad habits" form a valuable complement to its professed opinions.

The dictates of custom being dictates of morality, it is obvious that the study of moral ideas will, to a large extent, be a study of customs. But at the same time it should be borne in mind that custom never covers the whole field of morality, and that the uncovered space grows larger in proportion as the moral consciousness develops. Being a rule of duty, custom may only indirectly be an expression of moral approval, by claiming, in certain cases, that goodness should be rewarded. But even when demanding praise, custom is not always a reliable exponent of merit; it includes politeness, and politeness is a great deceiver. Custom may compel us to praise a man for form's sake, when he deserves no praise, and to thank him when he deserves no thanks. Moreover, custom regulates external conduct only. It tolerates all kinds of volitions and opinions if not openly expressed. It does not condemn the heretical mind, but the heretical act. It demands that under certain circumstances certain actions shall be either performed or omitted, and, provided that this demand is fulfilled, it takes no notice of the motive of the agent or omitter. Again, in case the course of conduct prescribed by custom is not observed, the mental facts connected with the transgression, if regarded at all, are dealt with in a rough and ready manner, according to general rules which hardly admit of individualisation. Yet the incongruity between custom and morality which ensues from these circumstances is on the whole more apparent than real. It is rather an incongruity between different moral standards. The unreflecting moral consciousness, like custom, cares comparatively little for the internal aspect of conduct. It does not ask whether a man goes to church on Sunday from a religious motive or from fear of public opinion; it does not ask whether he stays at home from love of ease or from dissent of belief and avoidance of hypocrisy. It is ready to blame as soon as the dictate of custom is disobeyed. The rule of custom is the rule of duty at early stages of development. Only progress in culture lessens its sway.

Finally, the moral ideas which are expressed in the customs of a certain circle of men are not necessarily shared by every one of its members. This may, in the present connection, be considered a matter of slight importance by him who regards morality as "objectively" realised in the customs of a people, and who denies the individual the right to a private conscience. But from the subjective point of view which I am vindicating, individual conviction has a claim to equal consideration with public opinion, nay frequently, to higher respect, representing as it does in many cases a higher morality, a moral standard more purified by reflection and impartiality. At the lower stages of civilisation, however, where a man is led by his feelings more than by his thoughts, such a differentiation of moral ideas hardly occurs. The opinions of the many are the opinions of all, and the customs of a society are recognised as rules of duty by all its members.

In primitive society custom stands for law, and even where social organisation has made some progress it may still remain the sole rule of conduct. The authority of a chief does not necessarily involve a power to make laws. Even kings who are described as autocrats may be as much tied by custom as is any of their subjects.

b. "The Subjection of Wives" (excerpts)

Among the lower races, as a rule, a woman is always more or less in a state of dependence. When she is emancipated by marriage from the power of her father, she generally passes into the power of her husband. But the authority which the latter possesses over his wife varies extremely among different peoples.

Frequently the wife is said to be the property or slave of her husband. In Fiji "the women are kept in great subjection…. Like other property, wives may be sold at pleasure, and the usual price is a musket." "The Carib woman is always in bondage to her male relations. To her father, brother, or husband she is ever a slave, and seldom has any power in the disposal of herself." Many North American Indians are said to treat their wives much as they treat their dogs. Among the Shoshones "the man is the sole proprietor of his wives and daughters, and can barter them away, or dispose of them in any manner he may think proper." Among the East African Wanika a woman "is a toy, a tool, a slave in the very worst sense; indeed she is treated as though she were a mere brute." Many other statements to a similar effect are met with in ethnographical literature.

Yet it seems that even in cases where the husband's power over his wife is described as absolute custom has not left her entirely destitute of rights. Of the Australian aborigines in general it is said that "the husband is the absolute owner of his wife (or wives)"; of the natives of Central Australia, that "each father of a family rules absolutely over his own circle"; of certain tribes in West Australia, that the state of slavery in which the women are kept is truly deplorable, and that the mere presence of their husbands makes them tremble. But we have reason to believe that there is some exaggeration in these statements, and that they certainly do not hold good of the whole Australian race. We have noticed above that custom does not really allow the Australian husband full liberty to kill his wife. For punishing or divorcing her he must sometimes have the consent of the tribe. There are even cases in which a wife whose husband has been unfaithful to her may complain of his conduct to the elders of the tribe, and he may have to suffer for it....

Other instances may be added to show that the so-called absolute authority of husbands over their wives is not to be taken too literally.

★ ★ ★

It is obvious that this strict division of labour is apt to mislead the travelling stranger. He sees the women hard at work, and the men idly looking on; and it escapes him that the latter will have to be busy in their turn, within their own sphere of action. What is largely due to the force of custom is taken to be sheer tyranny on the part of the men; and the wife is pronounced to be an abject slave of her husband, destitute of all rights. And yet the strong differentiation of work, however burdensome it may be to the wife, is itself a source of rights, giving her authority within the circle which is exclusively her own. Among the Banaka and Bapuka the wife, though said to be her husband's property and slave, is nevertheless an autocrat in her own house, strong enough to bid defiance to her lord and master. Among the North American Indians, Schoolcraft observes, "the lodge itself, with all its arrangements, is the precinct of the rule and government of the wife....The husband has no voice in this matter." Many other statements to a similar effect will be quoted below.

[Source: *The Origin and Development of the Moral Ideas* (London: Macmillan, 1906),Vol. I, 159–162; 628–630, 637.]

7. Franz Boas, "The Limitations of the Comparative Method of Anthropology" (excerpt), 1896.

The comparative studies of which I am speaking here attempt to explain customs and ideas of remarkable similarity which are found here and there. But they pursue also the more ambitious scheme of discovering the laws and the history of the evolution of human society. The fact that many fundamental features of culture are universal, or at least occur in many isolated places, interpreted by the assumption that the same features must always have developed from the same causes, leads to the conclusion that there is one grand system according to which mankind has developed everywhere; that all occurring variations are no more than minor details in this grand uniform evolution. It is clear that this theory has for its logical basis the assumption that the same phenomena are always due to the same causes. To give an instance: We find many types of structure of family. It can be proved that paternal families have often developed from maternal ones. Therefore, it is said, all paternal families have developed from maternal ones. If we do not make the assumption that the same phenomena have everywhere developed from the same causes, then we may just as well conclude that paternal families have in some cases arisen from maternal institutions, in other cases in other ways. To give another example: Many conceptions of the future life have evidently developed from dreams and hallucinations. Consequently, it is said, all notions of this character have had the same origin. This is also true only if no other causes could possibly lead to the same ideas.

We have seen that the facts do not favor the assumption of which we are speaking at all; that they much rather point in the opposite direction. Therefore we must also consider all the ingenious attempts at constructions of a grand system of the evolution of society as of very doubtful value, unless at the same time proof is given that the same phenomena could not develop by any other method. Until this is done, the presumption is always in favor of a variety of courses which historical growth may have taken.

It will be well to restate at this place one of the principal aims of anthropological research. We agreed that certain laws exist which govern the growth of human culture, and it is our endeavor to discover these laws. The object of our investigation is to find the *processes* by which certain stages of culture have developed. The customs and beliefs themselves are not the ultimate objects of research. We desire to learn the reasons why such customs and beliefs exist—in other words, we wish to discover the history of their development. The method which is at present most frequently applied in investigations of this character compares the variations under which the customs or beliefs occur and endeavors to find the common psychological cause that underlies them all. I have stated that this method is open to a very fundamental objection.

We have another method, which in many respects is much safer. A detailed study of customs in their bearings to the total culture of the tribe practicing them, and in connection with an investigation of their geographical distribution among neighboring tribes, afford us almost always a means of determining with considerable accuracy the historical causes that led to the formation of the customs in question and to the psychological processes that were at work in their development. The results of inquiries conducted by this method may be three-fold. They may reveal the environmental conditions which have created or modified cultural elements; they may clear up psychological factors which are at work in shaping the culture; or they may bring before our eyes the effects that historical connections have had upon the growth of the culture.

We have in this method a means of reconstructing the history of the growth of ideas with much greater accuracy than the generalizations of the comparative method will permit. The latter must always proceed from a hypothetical mode of development, the probability of which may be weighed more or less accurately by means of observed data. But so far I have not yet seen any extended attempt to prove the correctness of a theory by testing it at the hand of developments with whose histories we are familiar. This method of starting with a hypothesis is infinitely inferior to the one in which by truly inductive processes the actual history of definite phenomena is derived. The latter is no other than the much ridiculed historical method. Its way of proceeding is, of course, no longer that of former times when slight similarities of culture were considered proofs of relationships, but it duly recognizes the results obtained by comparative studies. Its application is based, first of all, on a well-defined, small geographical territory, and its comparisons are not extended beyond the limits of the cultural area that forms the basis of the study. Only when definite results have been obtained in regard to this area is it permissible to extend the horizon beyond its limits, but the greatest care must be taken not to proceed too hastily in this, as else the fundamental proposition which I formulated before might be overlooked, viz: that when we find an analogy of single traits of culture among distant peoples the presumption is not that there has been a common historical source, but that they have arisen independently. Therefore the investigation must always demand continuity of distribution as one of the essential conditions for proving historical connection, and the assumption of lost connecting links must be applied most sparingly. This clear distinction between the new and the old historical methods is still often overlooked by the passionate defenders of the comparative method. They do not appreciate the difference between the indiscriminate use of similarities of culture for proving historical connection and the careful and slow detailed study of local phenomena.

[Source: *Science* 4 (18 December, 1896), 904–906.]

8. Elsie Clews Parsons, from *Fear and Conventionality*, 1914.

Customs once generally questioned are apt to change or decay, in other words, conventionalities are naturally short-lived. We might almost define them as customs in decomposition, more or less conscious of their own decay. In fact, many of the conventionalities we are to consider are fast disappearing. For some of my readers therefore a certain amount of detailed description seemed necessary. For their sake I hope to be forgiven if to the more conventionally minded I seem at times too expository or too explicit.

"Why in view of their imminent disappearance bestow so much attention upon them?" I may be asked. "Why not take their decease for granted and pass on?" It is a query implying too great a doubt of the value of ethnology in general, or let us say of science, to be met here. But to the reader of ethnological bias may I say that I trust this study will be a contribution, however humble, to his understanding of society.

Fear of change is a part of the state of fear man has ever lived in but out of which he has begun to escape. Civilization might be defined indeed as the steps in his escape. What he now calls conventionality is that part of his system of protection against change he has begun to examine and, his fear lessening, even to forego.

[Source: *Fear and Conventionality* (New York: G.P. Putnam's, 1914), xxxvi–xxxvii.]

9. Bronislaw Malinowski, from *Argonauts of the Western Pacific*, 1922.

"Subject, Method and Scope" (excerpt)

As always happens when scientific interest turns towards and begins to labour on a field so far only prospected by the curiosity of amateurs, Ethnology has introduced law and order into what seemed chaotic and freakish. It has transformed for us the sensational, wild and unaccountable world of "savages" into a number of well ordered communities, governed by law, behaving and thinking according to consistent principles. The word "savage," whatever association it might have had originally, connotes ideas of boundless liberty, of irregularity, of something extremely and extraordinarily quaint. In popular thinking, we imagine that the natives live on the bosom of Nature, more or less as they can and like, the prey of irregular, phantasmagoric beliefs and apprehensions. Modern science, on the contrary, shows that their social institutions have a very definite organisation, that they are governed by authority, law, and order in their public and personal relations, while the latter are, besides, under the control of extremely complex ties of kinship and clanship. Indeed, we see them entangled in a mesh of duties, functions and privileges which correspond to an elaborate tribal, communal and kinship organisation .... Their beliefs and practices do not by any means lack consistency of a certain type, and their knowledge of the outer world is sufficient to guide them in many of their strenuous enterprises and activities. Their artistic productions again lack neither meaning nor beauty.

It is a very far cry from the famous answer given long ago by a representative authority who, asked, what are the manners and customs of the natives, answered, "Customs none, manners beastly," to the position of the modern Ethnographer! This latter, with his tables of kinship terms, genealogies, maps, plans and diagrams, proves the existence of an extensive and big organisation, shows the constitution of the tribe, of the clan, of the family; and he gives us a picture of the natives subjected to a strict code of behaviour and good manners, to which in comparison the life at the Court of Versailles or Escurial was free and easy.

Thus the first and basic ideal of ethnographic field-work is to give a clear and firm outline of the social constitution, and disentangle the laws and regularities of all cultural phenomena from the irrelevances. The firm skeleton of the tribal life has to be first ascertained. This ideal imposes in the first place the fundamental obligation of giving a complete survey of the phenomena, and not of picking out the sensational, the singular, still less the funny and quaint. The time when we could tolerate accounts presenting us the native as a distorted, childish caricature of a human being are gone. This picture is false, and like many other falsehoods, it has been killed by Science. The field Ethnographer has seriously and soberly to cover the full extent of the phenomena in each aspect of tribal culture studied, making no difference between what is commonplace, or drab, or ordinary, and what strikes him as astonishing and out-of-the-way. At the same time, the whole area of tribal culture *in all its aspects* has to be gone over in research. The consistency, the law and order which obtain within each aspect make also for joining them into one coherent whole.

[Source: *Argonauts of the Western Pacific: An Account of Native Enterprise and Adventure in the Archipelagoes of Melanesian New Guinea* (London: Routledge & Kegan Paul, 1922), 9–11.]

10. Ruth Benedict, "The Science of Custom" (excerpt), 1934.

Anthropology was by definition impossible as long as these distinctions between ourselves and the primitive, ourselves and the barbarian, ourselves and the pagan, held sway over people's minds. It was necessary first to arrive at that degree of sophistication where we no longer set our own belief over against our neighbour's superstition. It was necessary to recognize that those institutions which are based on the same premises, let us say the supernatural, must be considered together, our own among the rest.

★ ★ ★

The study of different cultures has another important bearing upon present-day thought and behaviour. Modern existence has thrown many civilizations into closer contact, and at the moment the overwhelming response to this situation is nationalism and racial snobbery. There has never been a time when civilization stood more in need of individuals who are genuinely culture-conscious, who can see objectively the socially conditioned behavior of other peoples without fear and recrimination.

Contempt for the alien is not the only possible solution of our present contact of races and nationalities. It is not even a scientifically founded solution. Traditional Anglo-Saxon intolerance is a local and temporal culture-trait like any other. Even people as nearly of the same blood and culture as the Spanish have not had it, and race prejudice in the Spanish-settled countries is a thoroughly different thing from that in countries dominated by England and the United States. In this country it is obviously not an intolerance directed against the mixture of blood of biologically far-separated races, for upon occasion excitement mounts as high against the Irish Catholic in Boston, or the Italian in New England mill towns, as against the Oriental in California. It is the old distinction between the in-group and the out-group, and if we carry on the primitive traditions in this matter, we have far less excuse than savage tribes. We have travelled, we pride ourselves on our sophistication. But we have failed to understand the relativity of cultural habits, and we remain debarred from much profit and enjoyment in our human relations with peoples of different standards, and untrustworthy in our dealings with them.

[Source: *Patterns of Culture* (Boston: Houghton Mifflin, 1934), 3–4, 10–11.]

Appendix G: Wharton on Modernity and Tradition

[Wharton's war experience compelled her to think about the very foundations of what she thought of as civilization, that is, the civilization of modern Europe that the United States was the natural heir to and, as a dynamic new nation in its own right, destined to re-make in its own image. While Wharton proclaimed herself "unafraid of change" at the outset of her 1934 autobiography, she was acutely aware of the destructive aspects of that change integral to that transnational phenomenon we call modernity. That destructiveness is figured most poignantly in Wharton's war-time writings in the battered, abandoned villages of France Wharton visited; it is figured on a larger scale in her preoccupation with vanishing provincial or "tribal" orders such as the one she re-creates in *The Age of Innocence*. Still, the following excerpts from her war-time and immediate post-war writing about American, French, and Moroccan culture demonstrate that Wharton unsentimentally accepted as inevitable the uprooting of local cultures and the transformations wrought by Western imperialism, technology and capitalism. In appealing to the power of tradition and the importance of continuity, she sought to anchor such transformations to a sense of history and place. She sought to reconcile tradition and modernity, in effect, which in practice meant idealizing an imperial nation-state like France—which she upheld as a model to the United States—for the extent to which its reverence for tradition enabled it to risk embracing the new without losing its cultural identity.]

1. Notebook entry, c. 1918–1923.

I want the idols broken, but I want them broken by people who understand why they were made....

[Source: "Subjects and Notes, 1918–23," Edith Wharton Collection, Yale Collection of American Literature, Beinecke Rare Book and Manuscript Library.]

2. From *A Backward Glance*, 1934.

The readers (and I should doubtless have been among them) who twenty years ago would have smiled at the idea that time could transform a group of *bourgeois* colonials and their republican descendants into a sort of social aristocracy, are now better able to measure the formative value of nearly three hundred years of social observance: the concerted living up to long-established standards of honour and conduct, of education and manners. The value of duration is slowly asserting itself against the welter of change, and sociologists without a drop of American blood in them have been the first to recognize what the traditions of three centuries have contributed to the moral wealth of our country. Even negatively, these traditions have acquired, with the passing of time, an unsuspected value. When I was young it used to seem to me that the group in which I grew up was like an empty vessel into which no new wine would ever again be poured. Now I see that one of its uses lay in preserving a few drops of an old vintage too rare to be savoured by a youthful palate; and I should like to atone for my unappreciativeness by trying to revive that faint fragrance.

If any one had suggested to me, before 1914, to write my reminiscences, I should have answered that my life had been too uneventful to be worth recording. Indeed, I had never even thought of recording it for my own amusement, and the fact that until 1918 I never kept even the briefest of diaries has greatly hampered this tardy reconstruction. Not until the successive upheavals which culminated in the catastrophe of 1914 had "cut all likeness from the name" of my old New York, did I begin to see its pathetic picturesqueness. The first change came in the 'eighties, with the earliest detachment of big money-makers from the West, soon to be followed by the lords of Pittsburgh. But their infiltration did not greatly affect old manners and customs, since the dearest ambition of the newcomers was to assimilate existing traditions. Social life, with us as in the rest of the world, went on with hardly perceptible changes till the war abruptly tore down the old frame-work, and what had seemed unalterable rules of conduct became of a sudden observances as quaintly arbitrary as the domestic rites of the Pharaohs. Between the point of view of my Huguenot great-great-grandfather, who came from the French Palatinate to participate in the founding of New Rochelle, and my own father, who died in 1882, there were fewer differences than between my father and the post-war generation of Americans. That I was born into a world in which telephones, motors, electric light, central heating (except by hot-air furnaces), X-rays, cinemas, radium, aeroplanes and wireless telegraphy were not only unknown but still mostly unforeseen, may seem the most striking difference between then and now; but the really vital change is that, in my youth, the Americans of the original States, who in moments of crisis still shaped the national point of view, were the heirs of an old tradition of European culture which the country has now totally rejected. This rejection (which Mr. Walter Lippmann[1] regards as the chief cause of the country's present moral impoverishment) has opened a gulf between those days and these. The compact world of my youth has receded into a past from which it can only be dug up in bits by the assiduous relic-hunter; and its smallest fragments begin to be worth collecting and putting together before the last of those who knew the live structure are swept away with it.

My little-girl life, safe, guarded, monotonous, was cradled in the only world about which, according to Goethe, it is impossible to write poetry. The small society into which I was born was "good" in the most prosaic sense of the term, and its only interest, for the generality of readers, lies in the fact of its sudden and total extinction, and for the imaginative few in the recognition of the moral treasures that went with it. Let me try to call it back....

[Source: Edith Wharton, *A Backward Glance* (New York: D. Appleton-Century Co., 1934), 5–7.]

3. From *Fighting France: From Dunkerque to Belfort*, 1915.

The country between Marne and Meuse is one of the regions on which German fury spent itself most bestially during the abominable September days. Half way between Châlons and Sainte Menehould we came on the first evidence of the invasion: the lamentable ruins of the village of Auve. These pleasant villages of the Aisne, with their one long street, their half-timbered houses and

---

[1] *Walter Lippman* (1889–1974), American journalist, one of the founders of *The New Republic*, author of several books on liberalism including *Drift and Mastery* (1914) and *The Political Scene* (1919).

high-roofed granaries with espaliered gable-ends, are all much of one pattern, and one can easily picture what Auve must have been as it looked out, in the blue September weather, above the ripening pears of its gardens to the crops in the valley and the large landscape beyond. Now it is a mere waste of rubble and cinders, not one threshold distinguishable from another. We saw many other ruined villages after Auve, but this was the first, and perhaps for that reason one had there, most hauntingly, the vision of all the separate terrors, anguishes, uprootings and rendings apart involved in the destruction of the obscurest of human communities. The photographs on the walls, the twigs of withered box above the crucifixes, the old wedding-dresses in brass-clamped trunks, the bundles of letters laboriously written and as painfully deciphered, all the thousand and one bits of the past that give meaning and continuity to the present—of all that accumulated warmth nothing was left but a brick-heap and some twisted stove-pipes!

[Source: Edith Wharton, *Fighting France: From Dunkerque to Belfort* (New York: Scribner's, 1915), 57–58.]

4. From *French Ways and Their Meaning*, 1919.

["A new people"]

We are a new people, a pioneer people, a people destined by fate to break up new continents and experiment in new social conditions; and therefore it may be useful to see what part is played in the life of a nation by some of the very qualities we have had the least time to acquire.

["Reverence and irreverence"]

Reverence and irreverence are both needed to help the world along, and each is most needed where the other most naturally abounds.

In this respect France and America are in the same case. America, because of her origin, tends to irreverence, impatience, to all sorts of rash and contemptuous short-cuts; France, for the same reason, to routine, precedent, tradition, the beaten path. Therefore it ought to help each nation to apply to herself the corrective of the other's example; and America can profit more by seeking to find out why

France is reverent, and what she reveres, than by trying to inoculate her with a flippant disregard of her own past.

★ ★ ★

There is nothing like a Revolution for making a people conservative; that is one of the reasons why, for instance, our Constitution, the child of Revolution, is the most conservative in history. But, in other respects, why should we Americans be conservative? To begin with, there is not much as yet for us to "conserve" except a few root-principles of conduct, social and political; and see how they spring up and dominate every other interest in each national crisis!

In France it is different. The French have nearly two thousand years of history and art and industry and social and political life to "conserve"; that is another of the reasons why their intense intellectual curiosity, their perpetual desire for the new thing, is counteracted by clinging to rules and precedents that have often become meaningless.

Reverence is the life-belt of those whose home is on a raft, and Americans have not pored over the map of France for the last four years without discovering that she may fairly be called a raft. But geographical necessity is far from being the only justification of reverence. It is not chiefly because the new methods of warfare lay America open to the same menace as continental Europe that it is good for us to consider the meaning of this ancient principle of civilised societies.

We are growing up at last; and it is only in maturity that a man glances back along the past, and sees the use of the constraints that irritated his impatient youth. So with races and nations; and America has reached the very moment in her development when she may best understand what has kept older races and riper civilisations sound.

Reverence is one of these preserving elements, and it is worth while studying it in its action in French life. If geographical necessity is the fundamental cause, another, almost as deep-seated, is to be found in the instinct of every people to value and preserve what they themselves have created and made beautiful.

★ ★ ★

America is already showing this instinct [of reverence] in her eagerness to beautify her towns, and to preserve her few pre-Revolutionary
buildings—that small fragment of her mighty European heritage.

["The sense of continuity"]

Only children think that one can make a garden with flowers broken
from the plant; only inexperience imagines that novelty is always
synonymous with improvement. To go on behaving as if one
believed these things and to foster their belief in others, is to encourage the intellectual laziness which rapid material prosperity is too apt
to develop. It is to imprison one's self in a perpetual immaturity. The
French express, perhaps unconsciously, their sense of the weight of
their own long moral experience by their universal comment on the
American fellows-in-arms whose fine qualities they so fully recognise: "*Ce sont des enfants*—they are mere children!" is what they
always say of the young Americans: say it tenderly, almost anxiously,
like people passionately attached to youth and to the young, but also
with a little surprise at the narrow surface of perception which most
of these young minds offer to the varied spectacle of the universe.

A new race, working out its own destiny in new conditions,
cannot hope for the moral and intellectual maturity of a race seated
at the cross-roads of the old civilisations. But America has, in part at
least, a claim on the great general inheritance of Western culture. She
inherits France through England, and Rome and the Mediterranean
culture, through France. These are indirect and remote sources of
enrichment; but she has directly, in her possession and in her keeping, the magnificent, the matchless inheritance of English speech and
English letters.

Had she had a more mature sense of the value of tradition and
the strength of continuity she would have kept a more reverent hold
upon this treasure, and the culture won from it would have been an
hundredfold greater. She would have preserved the language instead
of debasing and impoverishing it; she would have learned the
historic meaning of its words instead of wasting her time inventing
short-cuts in spelling them; she would jealously have upheld the
standards of its literature instead of lowering them to meet an
increased "circulation."

In all this, France has a lesson to teach and a warning to give. It was
our English forbears who taught us to flout tradition and break away

from their own great inheritance; France may teach us that, side by side with the qualities of enterprise and innovation that English blood has put in us, we should cultivate the sense of continuity, that "sense of the past" which enriches the present and binds us up with the world's great stabilising traditions of art and poetry and knowledge.

[Source: Edith Wharton, *French Ways and Their Meaning* (New York: D. Appleton & Co., 1919), 18–19, 31–32, 34–37, 95–97.]

5. From *In Morocco*, 1920.

"Preface" (excerpt)

The next best thing to a Djinn's carpet, a military motor, was at my disposal every morning, but war conditions imposed restrictions, and the wish to use the minimum of petrol often stood in the way of the second visit which alone makes it possible to carry away a definite and detached impression.

These drawbacks were more than offset by the advantage of making my quick trip at a moment unique in the history of the country; the brief moment of transition between its virtually complete subjection to European authority, and the fast approaching hour when it is thrown open to all the banalities and promiscuities of modern travel.

Morocco is too curious, too beautiful, too rich in landscape and architecture, and above all too much of a novelty, not to attract one of the main streams of spring travel as soon as Mediterranean passenger traffic is resumed. Now that the war is over, only a few months' work on roads and railways divide it from the great torrent of "tourism"; and once that deluge is let loose, no eye will ever again see Moulay Idriss and Fez and Marrakech as I saw them.

In spite of the incessant efforts of the present French administration to preserve the old monuments of Morocco from injury, and her native arts and industries from the corruption of European bad taste, the impression of mystery and remoteness which the country now produces must inevitably vanish with the approach of the "Circular Ticket." Within a few years far more will be known of the past of Morocco, but that past will be far less visible to the traveller than it is to-day. Excavations will reveal fresh traces of Roman and Phenician occupation; the remote affinities between Copts and

Berbers, between Bagdad and Fez, between Byzantine art and the architecture of the Souss, will be explored and elucidated; but, while these successive discoveries are being made, the strange survival of mediaeval life, of a life contemporary with the crusaders, with Saladin, even with the great days of the Caliphate of Bagdad, which now greets the astonished traveller, will gradually disappear, till at last even the mysterious autocthones of the Atlas will have folded their tents and silently stolen away.

["the mausoleum of Marrakech"]

It is not only the novelty of its plan that makes the Saadian mausoleum singular among the Moroccan monuments. The details of its ornament are of the most intricate refinement: it seems as though the last graces of the expiring Merinid art had been gathered up into this rare blossom. And the slant of sunlight on lustrous columns, the depths of fretted gold, the dusky ivory of the walls and the pure white of the cenotaphs, so classic in spareness of ornament and simplicity of design—this subtle harmony of form and color gives to the dim rich chapel an air of dream-like unreality.

And how can it seem other than a dream? Who can have conceived, in the heart of a savage Saharan camp, the serenity and balance of this hidden place? And how came such fragile loveliness to survive, preserving, behind a screen of tumbling walls, of nettles and offal and dead beasts, every curve of its traceries and every cell of its honey-combing?

Such questions inevitably bring one back to the central riddle of the mysterious North African civilization: the perpetual flux and the immovable stability, the barbarous customs and sensuous refinements, the absence of artistic originality and the gift for regrouping borrowed motives, the patient and exquisite workmanship and the immediate neglect and degradation of the thing once made.

Revering the dead and camping on their graves, elaborating exquisite monuments only to abandon and defile them, venerating scholarship and wisdom and living in ignorance and grossness, these gifted races, perpetually struggling to reach some higher level of culture from which they have always been swept down by a fresh wave of barbarism, are still only a people in the making.

It may be that the political stability which France is helping them to acquire will at last give their higher qualities time for fruition; and when one looks at the mausoleum of Marrakech and the Medersas of Fez one feels that, were the experiment made on artistic grounds alone, it would yet be well worth making.

[Source: Edith Wharton, *In Morocco* (New York: Scribner's, 1920), vii–x, 156–158.]

Select Bibliography

1. Biography and Letters

Benstock, Shari. *No Gifts From Chance: A Biography of Edith Wharton.* New York: Scribner's, 1994.

Dwight, Eleanor. *Edith Wharton: An Extraordinary Life.* New York: Abrams, 1994.

Lewis, R.W.B. *Edith Wharton: A Biography.* New York: Harper & Row, 1975.

— and Nancy Lewis, eds. *The Letters of Edith Wharton.* New York: Macmillan, 1988.

Powers, Lyall H. *Henry James and Edith Wharton: Letters: 1900–1915.* New York: Scribner's, 1990.

Price, Alan. *The End of the Age of Innocence: Edith Wharton and the First World War.* New York: St. Martin's, 1996.

2. Bibliographies and Reference Guides

Garrison, Stephen. *Edith Wharton: A Descriptive Bibliography.* Pittsburgh: University of Pittsburgh Press, 1990.

Lauer, Kristin O. and Margaret P. Murray. *Edith Wharton: An Annotated Secondary Bibliography.* New York: Garland, 1990.

Springer, Marlene. *Edith Wharton and Kate Chopin: A Reference Guide.* Boston: G.K. Hall, 1976.

Wright, Sarah Bird. *Edith Wharton A to Z: The Essential Guide to the Life and Work.* New York: Facts on File, 1998.

3. Critical Studies and Collections

Ammons, Elizabeth. *Edith Wharton's Argument with America.* Athens: University of Georgia Press, 1980.

Bauer, Dale. *Edith Wharton's Brave New Politics.* Madison: University of Wisconsin Press, 1994.

Bell, Millicent, ed. *The Cambridge Companion to Edith Wharton.* New York: Cambridge, 1995.

Bell, Millicent. *Edith Wharton and Henry James: The Story of Their Friendship.* New York: Braziller, 1965.

Bentley, Nancy. *The Ethnography of Manners: Hawthorne*
New York: Cambridge University Press, 1995.

Colquitt, Clare, Susan Goodman and Candace Waid, e
Glance: New Essays on Edith Wharton. London
University Presses, 1999.

Dekker, George. *The American Historical Romance*. New York: (
University Press, 1987.

Erlich, Gloria. *The Sexual Education of Edith Wharton*. Berkeley
Angeles: University of California Press, 1992.

Fryer, Judith. *Felicitous Space: The Imaginative Structures of Edith W*
and Willa Cather. Chapel Hill: University of North Carolina
1986.

Gilbert, Sandra and Susan Gubar. *Sexchanges*. New Haven:
University Press, 1989.

Lindberg, Gary. *Edith Wharton and the Novel of Manners*. Charlottesvil
University of Virginia Press, 1975.

Nevius, Blake. *Edith Wharton: A Study of Her Fiction*. Berkeley and Lo:
Angeles: University of California Press, 1953.

Preston, Claire. *Edith Wharton's Social Register*. New York: St. Martin's,
2000.

Wagner-Martin, Linda. *"The Age of Innocence": A Novel of Ironic Nostalgia*.
New York: Twayne, 1996.

Wolff, Cynthia Griffin. *A Feast of Words: The Triumph of Edith Wharton*.
New York: Oxford University Press, 1977.

4. Articles in Journals and in Collections Cited Above

Ammons, Elizabeth. "Edith Wharton and Race," in Bell: 68–86.

Bentley, Nancy. "'Hunting for the Real': Wharton and the Science of
Manners," in Bell: 47–67.

Gargano, James W. "Tableaux of Renunciation: Edith Wharton's Use of
The Shaugraun in *The Age of Innocence*." *Studies in American Fiction*
15 (Spring 1987): 1–11.

Gibson, Mary Ellis. "Edith Wharton and the Ethnography of Old New
York," *Studies in the Novel* 13 (Spring 1985): 57–69.

Knights, Pamela. "Forms of Disembodiment: The Social Subject in *The
Age of Innocence*," in Bell: 20–46.

MacMaster, Anne. "Wharton, Race, and *The Age of Innocence*: Three
Historical Contexts," in Colquitt et al.: 188–205.

Nowlin, Michael. "'Where is that Country?':The Returning Masquerader in Edith Wharton's *The Age of Innocence.*" *Women's Studies: An Interdisciplinary Journal* 26 (1997): 285–314.

Pimple, Kenneth D. "Edith Wharton's 'Inscrutable Totem Terrors': Ethnography and *The Age of Innocence.*" *Southern Folklore* 51 (1994): 137–152.

Price, Alan. "The Composition of Edith Wharton's *The Age of Innocence.*" *Yale University Library Gazette* 55 (July 1980): 22–30.

Strout, Cushing. "Complementary Portraits: James's Lady and Wharton's *Age.*" *Hudson Review* 35 (1982): 405–415.

Trumpener, Katie and James M. Nyce. "The Recovered Fragments: Archeological and Anthropological Perspectives in Edith Wharton's *The Age of Innocence.*" In *Literary Anthropology*, ed. Fernando Poyatos. Philadelphia: John Benjamin, 1988.

Tuttleton, James W. "Edith Wharton: The Archaeological Motive." *Yale Review* 61 (1971–72): 562–574.

—. "The Feminist Takeover of Edith Wharton." *New Criterion* 7 (March 1989): 6–14.

—. "The President and the Lady: Edith Wharton and Theodore Roosevelt," *Bulletin of the New York Public Library* 69 (January 1965): 49–57.

Wagner-Martin, Linda. "A Note on Wharton's Use of *Faust.*" *Edith Wharton Newsletter* 3 (Spring 1986): 1, 8.

Wegener, Frederick. "'Rabid Imperialist': Edith Wharton and the Obligations of Empire in Modern American Fiction," *American Literature* 72 (December 2000): 783–812.